# For the Ones
# Who Liberate

R. Collins

Samsara Fleet | Book Four

## Books By Riley Collins

To learn more about Riley Collins, see an updated list of titles, and join his mailing list go to his webpage at www.rileycollins.info.

### Samsara Fleet Series

Book One: For the Ones Who Remain
Book Two: For the Ones Who Are Forgotten
Book Three: For the Ones Who Rebel
Book Four: For the Ones Who Liberate

This is a work of fiction. Unless otherwise indicated, all the names, characters, businesses, places, events, and incidents in this book are either the product of the author's imagination or used in a fictitious manner. Any resemblance to actual persons, living or dead, or actual events is purely coincidental.

Cover Art by: 17 Studio Book Design
Editing by: Lisa Binion
A special thank you to ⬚ Sal Spring

For Judy, Jacky, Bruce, Brian, Doug, and Andrew

# Chapter One

Lieutenant Colonel Nicole Bergeron shifted her feet and feigned a disinterested expression as she leaned against the battered wood fishing hut. She could feel the kinetic pistol pressing against her thigh, and it took every ounce of restraint for her to not rest a hand against it. That would be a dead giveaway.

"I said, what are you doing here?" A large patroller lifted his transparent visor and shoved his face within centimeters of Nicole's. She could smell alcohol and body odor above the stink of the fetid swamp around them.

"Oh. Oh, I am so sorry." She acted surprised, her voice an octave higher than normal. "I just didn't see you there."

The patroller's mouth curved upward in a predatory smile. "Maybe there's something I can *help* you with." He reached his arm around Nicole's waist and pulled her toward him.

"I appreciate that, but I'm waiting for someone," Nicole tried to push away, but the meaty arm didn't budge.

"That's okay. I'll be happy to help you find them," the man said, sounding as if he was talking to a precocious child. He pointed to a break in the yellow bushes surrounding the clearing they were in. "Just follow me."

"I can't," Nicole protested. She could feel the situation getting out of her control. She was there to contact the resistance. Shooting a local militia member could certainly scare them off.

The man continued to pull her in the direction of the edge of the clearing. Nicole glanced around. She knew the other members of the team were watching from the foliage around the clearing, but this was something she could handle herself.

"Stop!"

The steely tone in Nicole's voice stopped the man cold. He let go of her waist and turned around to face her, his hand darting toward the crude holster strapped to his threadbare pants.

"Who are you?" he asked, pulling his pistol out.

*You need help?* Staff Sergeant Ekon Kimathi asked through their neural net. Nicole's neural implant relayed the synthetic voice directly to her auditory nerves—the patroller couldn't hear a thing.

Neural implants were the key to Humanity's expansion into the galaxy. When someone reached adulthood, they had the small computer implanted into their brain. It directly interfaced with the neurological system and performed a variety of tasks—translation, communication, interfacing with computers, and much more. For Nicole, her implant was as much a part of her as her arms or legs—except even more essential.

*No,* Nicole replied as she seized the man's outstretched arm and dropped to the ground in a roll, sending him flying over her head.

Before the thug recovered, Nicole brought her full weight down on his knee with a booted foot. He shrieked in pain and she could hear cartilage snapping as she drove her foot home.

With a grunt, Nicole slammed her open hand into the man's throat, causing him to gasp and bring his hands up to his neck. His gurgling chokes and wide eyes reminded her of a fish out of water.

Nicole brought her sidearm out of its holster and pointed it at the man's head with one hand while making a shushing motion with her other. "Not a sound," she whispered.

The patroller's panicked noises subsided, and he stared at her with wide eyes full of fear as she adjusted the setting on her pistol and buried a tranquilizer dart into his neck.

Brigadier General Kal Norman watched from the periphery of the clearing as his executive officer easily disabled the local militia patroller. Although they called themselves patrollers, they were merely bandits. Thugs hired by the local warlord to shake residents out of money.

Kal was the commander of the Skulls, an elite group of soldiers that specialized in clandestine and highly complex missions. As the war dragged on, they'd gained an almost legendary status among Samsara Fleet. That notoriety had come at a cost though. If he closed his eyes, Kal could see the faces of the soldiers in his unit that had died in combat.

General Aamina Samaha, commander of Samsara Fleet, had ordered them to the watery planet of Wudexingqiu to meet with a local resistance group, the Silver Hand, to deliver needed weapons and gain any intel they could. Like every Human colony, Wudexingqiu had fallen under the control of the Nasi.

They had appeared in the galaxy a year earlier and destroyed Earth and the home worlds of several other species. With their enemies reeling, the Nasi had conquered their colonies, wiping out most of their fleets and demanding a regular tribute for their continued survival. On the Human ones, like Wudexingqiu, they created settlements called Footholds and established a permanent presence. On the other colonies, they kept a small garrison of soldiers and made a simple promise: if the citizens did not pay the tribute regularly, the Nasi would destroy the system.

On Wudexingqiu, the planetary government had folded when the Nasi arrived. Bands of small-time militias rose in its place as opportunistic criminals rushed to fill the power vacuum. The Nasi didn't care who ruled the planet as long as they kept in line and provided a regular tribute of resources.

It made situations like the one Kal was watching all too common. Unfortunately for the militia member, Nicole had been trained by some of the most elite soldiers in the galaxy.

*Someone get this scum out of here*, Nicole said over the net after she tranqed her assailant.

Private Karan Ramirez jumped out from the bushes on the opposite side of the clearing and dragged the unconscious man away.

*Nice work*, Kal said.

Nicole gave a quick thumbs-up in his direction and walked back to lean against the ramshackle fishing hut.

The planet was littered with small huts like that one. Water covered ninety-eight percent of Wudexingqiu's surface. The plants and animals that grew in the oceans were the local's only source of food. Cities stood on the little land there was and burrowed into the ground underneath or stretched onto the ocean floor beneath enormous domes.

The Skulls had landed in the marsh and walked through the small network of bridges and brackish water to make it to the rendezvous point. Now they needed to wait. There was no telling how long it might take for the Silver Hand to make contact.

"Don't move a muscle," whispered a voice in Kal's ear.

*I've been made,* Kal said over the net.

*We've all been made, sir,* Sergeant Kimathi, their Tac-I squad leader, said.

Tac-I's were the most elite soldiers in the entire fleet. Intended to be used for assaulting spacecraft or stations, the Skulls ended up doing a lot more. Before the Nasi had invaded, when there still was an Earth Defense Force, Tac-I soldiers had to undergo rigorous training before stepping foot on a ship. With the EDF gone, they were the soldiers that had proven themselves in battle rather than any training course.

Kal could see that Nicole had her hands raised and was looking into the bushes. He couldn't see who she was looking at; one of the large saltwater trees blocked his view.

"Don't worry," the voice hissed, "just tell me the password and we'll be a-okay."

"Madero," Kal said, providing the agreed upon password.

"Orange." It was the prearranged response. "Excellent job, Unc." Hal heard a sidearm being returned to its holster.

He turned around and came face to chest with the largest man he'd ever seen in his life. His enormous arms were larger than Kal's thighs. Tan eyes leapt out from his pale face, glowing in the bright light of the moons and stars above. His mouth was open in an enormous, almost goofy smile, the moonlight shining off his straight teeth.

"Never can be too safe, can ya?" The giant chuckled. "I'm Sue." He stuck out an enormous hand.

"Brigadier General Kal Norman," Kal replied as he shook the man's hand.

*Everyone okay?* Kal asked through the net.

*We're good,* Kimathi replied.

"Yup, we gotta be extra careful now," the large man said amicably. "The Nasi are ramping up their patrols in the area. Bastards hit one of our safe houses just yesterday. Killed everyone, thankfully."

The man noticed Kal's shocked expression.

"Better to die in the attack than be captured and tortured to death," he explained. "Saves us a lot of trouble too. At least we know no one gave up any secrets." He turned around and started walking through the brush. "Follow me."

Kal's feet sunk into the peat and decay of the swamp as Sue led him away from the clearing. The rest of the Skulls and several resistance fighters merged into a single-file line. The large broad-leafed trees stretched above them, and small patches of the night sky peered through the dense canopy. He could hear the whispers of creatures scurrying over the wrist-thick vines that stretched across the trees above their heads.

"Watch yourself, Unc," Sue cautioned with a turn of his head. "Half the plants here are poisonous to the touch. Also, got a few nasties runnin' round as well. Not a place to wander off the path. We lost more than a few recruits that way. Delicious though."

"The creatures or the recruits?" Ekon asked from behind Kal, eliciting a chuckle from a few of the Hand members.

Thinking of Sue's warning, Kal studied the swamp with a new respect. To him, the mix of green and yellow plants lining their narrow path seemed relatively harmless, but he wasn't willing to test his guide's words. He'd learned a long time ago that looks could be deceiving.

Sue led them to the edge of the swamp where the dense shrubs and trees ended abruptly at the ocean. Moonlight sparkled off the gentle swells of the water, and Kal could hear the laps of waves against the embankment created from the tangle of tree roots. He relished the salty smell of the ocean filling his nostrils, displacing the fetid stench of the swamp.

"Hope you don't mind getting wet," Sue said with an innocent laugh as he dropped from the bank with a splash.

Kal reluctantly followed the man into the frigid ocean; he wasn't the best swimmer. The water reached the midpoint of his thighs, causing him to suck in his breath with shock. He adjusted the sensory perception from his prosthetic feet and reduced the tingling cold sensation. The ability to regulate the pain in his feet was a silver lining to having had his feet blown off in a grenade attack several months back.

Sue strode confidently through the water, the sound of his movement drowned out the gentle lapping of the ocean swells against the embankment. By the time they'd walked several meters from land, the water reached the enormous man's waist and the top of Kal's chest.

11

"Follow me, Unc," Sue announced as he ducked down into the water.

Kal followed the gigantic man and dove into the water. He looked around as his goggle's night vision adjusted to compensate for the reduced light. Their walk over the ocean bottom had disturbed the fine silt floor and generated a hazy cloud that trailed from the shore. Fish darted around the legs of their party like kids running through a playground, creating bright trails of light in the water.

Sue dove into a metal-lined hatch that was flush with the ocean floor, his colossal frame barely fitting through the square opening. Kal followed him through and trailed the resistance fighter through the circular pipe dotted with faint lights. After a few meters, their path leveled off and then drew parallel to the ocean floor. Kal used the handholds on either side of the pipe to pull himself through as they glided along.

*How much farther?* The thought screamed across Kal's mind alongside an image of his dead body drifting inside the tunnel. His lungs burned, begging for air, as he willed himself to continue through the passageway.

Ahead, a soft light grew as Kal pulled himself along, wondering if he would make it. When he turned his head, the others were hard to make out but appeared to be following behind. Finally, the tunnel opened into a shallow open-top tank lit by bright lights fixed above the water's surface. Kal desperately stood up, his lungs screaming as he took a deep gasp of the stale air.

"You didn't use a breather, Unc?" Sue asked in surprise. He held up a small mask in his hand. "Impressive."

Kal looked around the tank. Sure enough, all the other members of his team had a breather around their mouth or in their hand.

*Why didn't anyone tell me to use a breather?* Kal asked.

*We thought you knew, sir,* replied Private First Class Bolin Ricci, one of the newest members of their squad. They had included him on the mission since he was a native of Wudexingqiu.

"Come on, General," Sue said as he climbed out of the tank.

Kal pulled himself onto the metal walkway that surrounded the tank and followed the Hand member through a small tunnel until they reached a set of closed doors.

"Okay, we have to wait here for a moment," Sue said. "Takes a bit for the lift to come."

"Where are we?" Ekon asked, an edge to his voice.

"It was a research station," one of the resistance fighters said, "built to study the Jellies."

Great Jellies were one of the largest species in the galaxy. The enormous invertebrates were estimated to weigh almost a million kilograms and were breathtaking to watch. They looked somewhat like the Jellyfish that were found on Earth— giant, almost transparent blobs—though they were completely unrelated species. They had hundreds of tentacles which they used to grab their prey and either rip it to shreds and eat or just eat completely whole. Although incredibly large, Jellies were also very rare. Kal had only seen them in the holos.

"Seems like everyone forgot about this place," Sue

added. "Cept the chief of course."

Their chief, Hadiza Taggart, had been an official in the Wudexingqiu government before the Nasi arrived. She'd created the Silver Hand after the government dissolved and led them to become the largest resistance faction on the planet. She was one of the few people who'd been more concerned with fighting the Nasi than grabbing power. Kal found the Nasi invasion had exposed a darkness in Humanity that had been hidden beneath the veneer of civilization created by the Unified Earth Government.

The doors leading out of the tank opened with a faint hiss, exposing a cylindrical chamber that turned out to be barely large enough to fit in all eight of them.

"Squeeze in. Squeeze in," Sue said. "We all gotta fit. You don't want to miss the dome."

"The dome?" Nicole asked as she shoved herself into the elevator chamber.

"You'll see, Unc" Sue winked. "It'll knock you outta your battle suit."

## Chapter Two

Nicole looked around at the members of the Silver Hand crammed into the elevator with her. They were a motley crew with gaunt faces, torn clothing, and an air of fatigue. However, she'd also noticed they had the same easy camaraderie as the Skulls, probably forged by countless missions.

She had thought they'd be just a group of backward swamp hicks, and they were to an extent, but they'd also gotten the jump on the Skulls. It wasn't an easy thing to do. She'd been waiting in the clearing after dispatching the militia thug when she'd felt the barrel of a pistol in her back and a voice whispering for her to not move a muscle.

Nicole felt the elevator start to move and realized the car was not only descending, but it was also moving them laterally, away from the shoreline. She took several deep swallows as she tried to clear the pressure in her ears. She couldn't swim well and didn't relish the thought of being underwater.

"We're here," said the giant Hand member, Sue, with a flourish.

Nicole followed the rest of the group out of the elevator. They'd arrived in a large circular room with several hallways leading from it. Several meters above their heads was an enormous glass dome at least thirty meters in diameter. Rainbow-colored lights danced and swam in the murky water above it, and consoles stood in clusters at regular intervals underneath. The Hand had clearly modified the consoles— exposed wires spilled out of open panels, viewscreens were crudely bolted onto the sides, and various devices had been hard-wired into adapter ports.

"Welcome to our little home," said a short woman standing a few paces in front of them. A broad smile filled her round face, and intricately braided long black hair trailed down her back past her waist. "I'm Chief Hadiza Taggart and you must be the Skulls. I have to say we're honored General Samaha sent you."

Nicole almost laughed at the expression on Kal's face.

"You've heard of us?" Kal asked, eyebrow raised.

"Yes, we have," Hadiza said. "The net is slowly returning, and we've started to get drops of information about events outside the system. Whenever we hear about a Nasi defeat, it seems your team is always involved."

The net, or probe network, was the network of automated probes that distributed information throughout the galaxy. Prior to the Nasi, it had connected every system with its probes automatically receiving and transmitting messages at each system before moving on to the next. The Nasi had destroyed much of it, sending a lot of the galaxy into darkness with no one knowing exactly what was happening on other planets. If it was being rebuilt, that was a good sign.

"Well, we're just doing our best with what we got," Sergeant Kimathi said. The young noncommissioned officer looked so full of himself that Nicole wanted to smack him.

"We've got a ship full of supplies," Nicole said. "We need to know where to put 'em."

"Why would they send you? Couldn't they have sent anyone?" asked Hadiza.

"Getting in and out of Wudexingqiu is almost impossible," Kal said. "We already lost a scout team trying."

"Sorry to hear that." The chief frowned. "The Nasi are increasing their patrols on the planet as well. They're cracking down hard too. Last week they destroyed an atoll in the western hemisphere. No warning, just destroyed it and everyone on it."

"It's because of the Jadid," Kal said. "The Nasi are desperate to tie up loose ends before their fleet is operational."

The Jadid were the descendants of Humanity, cast off into another universe hundreds of years earlier. When Humanity had overwhelmed Earth's resources, the governments of the time were desperate to find new planets to settle and raced to develop the fold drive. It allowed ships to instantly change positions in space through a wormhole, bypassing the limitations of the speed of light. They were able to develop an initial prototype, but it was temperamental and dangerous and couldn't be piloted using AIs. They had run countless experiments using ships filled with prisoners and citizens desperate to get out of their debts, trying to perfect the drive for use. Many of the tests resulted in nothing happening. Some resulted in the ship imploding, killing everyone on board. Some ships disappeared and never returned. Unbeknownst to the Humans on Earth, one ship had traveled to another universe rather than to another point in their own. The passengers struggled to survive in the strange and hostile environment for decades before ultimately thriving in their new world. The descendants of those original Human test subjects were the Jadid.

"The Jadid exist? So it's true?" Sue asked, his mouth wide.

"Yes, we've gone to their home planet, Altterra," Nicole replied. "The Nasi are just a group, a cult, within the Jadid. One of their leaders, or Ancients, named Esma Baykara created the Nasi. She's never forgotten being exiled from Earth."

"It was centuries ago," Sue protested.

"To us," Nicole replied. "But it actually happened to them. The Ancients were the ones who were forced into an experiment that destroyed their lives." One of the side effects of the Jadid's universe was that the aging process stopped at adulthood. It wasn't well-known, but she could see Humans one day begging to travel to Alterra.

"What? You agree with them?" Hadiza's eyes flashed.

"No, of course not," Nicole replied, her hand up. "But you've got to remember that to them, none of this is ancient history. It's in their lifetimes. I think Esma's unstable. But I've met the other Ancients, and I can tell you that what happened, happened to them."

"So you went to their home planet?" Hadiza asked, eyebrow arched.

Nicole nodded. "Yes. It was…strange. We met with the Ancients, and they've agreed to help us. Their fleet is under retrofit right now and should be ready soon. That's why the Nasi are desperate."

"Why do they need retrofit?" asked one of the Hand members.

"Why are the Nasi purple with superhuman strength?" asked Kimathi. "Their universe operates under different rules. Things don't work the same way there."

"I am so glad to hear the Jadid have joined us," Hadiza said, smiling. "We'd hoped, but we couldn't put our faith in rumors."

"There's still a long way to go," Kal said. "Even with the Jadid fleet on our side, we're outgunned. We're still standing though and now we have the strength to fight them head-to-head."

"Hopefully, you can see that what you're fighting for matters," Nicole added. "There is hope and there is an end to the Nasi rule."

"It'll be good to tell my people about this," Hadiza said. "I'd like to hear more though. Like I said, the nets only provide small drops of info. I haven't talked to anyone from the fleet in half a year."

"Private Ricci and I will take care of the supplies," Kimathi said.

"Come with me, Unc," Sue said, putting an enormous arm around Kimathi's shoulder. "I'll help you get back to your ship."

Chief Taggart nodded to the other members of the Hand standing around listening to the conversation, and they dispersed. As they melted away, Nicole heard a few murmured whispers of thanks.

"Impressive," Kal said, motioning at the glass dome above them.

"Yes," Hadiza admitted, "it's one of the more impressive

research facilities I've been in." She looked at the dome. "You're lucky we have a Jelly visiting us right now."

Nicole squinted, trying to make out anything in the murky water above them. Other than the small dancing lights, she couldn't see a thing. "I don't see anything," she admitted, "just those lights."

Hadiza smiled. "Those lights *are* the Jelly. It's sitting over us. This base is built next to a thermal vent. The Jellies love them. The lights are inside the creature. We don't know how their bodies make that glow, though it's not through any method we know of.

"I used to be the Minister of Education for the Wudexian Planetary Government," she said as she strolled through the control room with Nicole and Kal following. "When the Nasi attacked, I remembered this base. I'd supervised the administration of our marine research installations and knew it had been decommissioned a couple of years ago." She slid her arm along a console as she walked past. "Took a bit, but we were able to get everything running again."

The chief walked them around the room, pointing out how the Silver Hand had modified the older scientific equipment to work as a command center. Nicole knew little about electronics or computers but knew enough to be impressed that they had be able to make the base function.

After the quick tour, Hadiza led them to a set of metal stairs on the side of the circular command room. "The living quarters and supply storage are below," she said as she walked down. "It's not a lot of space, but it's enough. Like I said, the Nasi have been pressing us hard. The Hand has bases all over the planet, but this place is about as secure as you can get."

The stairs took them to the end of an aquamarine-colored hallway. Boxes and crates, stacked to the ceiling, lined the walls. There were small gaps to allow people striding through the hallway to use the doorways on either side. Nicole idly studied some crates, trying to see if she could tell what was inside.

"It's mostly raw nutrients," Hadiza said, noticing Nicole. "There's some medicine too. What we need are more weapons, armor, and ammunition."

"Well, our shipment should help with that," Nicole said. "We've got crates of high-powered kinetic rifles, personal shields, cloaking devices, and a bunch of other goodies."

Hadiza smiled. "Hope you wrapped it up all nice for us too." She continued to walk them through the floor, taking them into the bunk-lined living quarters, a mess hall, supply rooms, and even a small recreation area.

"How do you get the supplies in here?" Nicole asked.

"That's the best part," Hadiza replied with a gleeful smile. "Follow me." She took them through the storage area to a large rectangular room. As they entered, the viewscreen on the far wall turned on. It took Nicole a moment to realize it was displaying a live feed of the water outside the station. The water was so dark Nicole could barely make out the edges of a large sphere on the other side. Several cables and conduits extended from its bottom back toward the base and the ocean floor.

"That's how supplies get here," Hadiza said with a

flourish. "That is a suboceanic landing bay. We can pump it full of air to have it rise to the surface. The ship lands and we fill the bottom with liquid ballast to cause it to sink." She pretended to dust off her hands.

"Amazing. I've heard of them," Kal replied with obvious curiosity, "but never seen one in use."

"We can head back when your ship arrives," Hadiza said with a knowing smile. "Shouldn't be long." As she turned back toward the way they had entered, the viewscreen went blank, blending in with the rest of the wall.

Nicole and Kal followed the chief through the maze of crate-lined corridors and into a meeting room with a small circular table and four utilitarian chairs in the middle. Small aquatic creatures danced on the viewscreens around them. It took Nicole a moment to realize the video was a recording based on the streamers of light from the sun.

"While they're bringing your ship in to drop off the supplies, I was hoping you could tell me what's going on," Hadiza said as she sat down. "We're fighting our damnedest here. Is help coming? I mean, beyond a few crates of supplies?"

"With the Jadid fleet coming online, we'll make progress against the Nasi," Nicole began. "Perhaps—"

"No, not yet," Kal cut her off. "I'm not going to lie; you're still on your own. Samsara Fleet is doing its best, but we're fighting a war across hundreds of systems against the most advanced species we've ever seen."

"This planet is dying," Hadiza said. "Maybe not all at once. But irrevocably. The Nasi have continued to demand more from us—more food, fuel, machines, you name it."

"That's good," Kal replied. "It means they're getting desperate. The Nasi came into this universe and tried to hit us with a knockout punch." He mimicked a punching motion. "They failed and we are still here. The longer we hold out, the stronger we become."

"I don't know if I'd call our situation good." Hadiza frowned. "What about their capital ships?"

"They've already brought them over here," Nicole replied. "There's no more."

"But what about the ones they're building?"

Nicole closed her mouth. *They were building them?*

"Clearly, you haven't heard," Hadiza said as her frown deepened. "The Nasi have created terrestrial shipbuilding facilities."

"That shouldn't be possible," Kal said. "Capital ships are too large to leave a planet's atmosphere. They have to be built in space."

"I've seen a lot of things that shouldn't be possible," Nicole said. An image of the Sol System obliterated in a fireball popped into her mind.

"Not sure if it's possible or not," Hadiza said, "but they're doing it. They've got several facilities all around the planet. A few of my scouts have confirmed it."

"Maybe they're just building fighters or corvettes," Nicole suggested. She prayed the chief wasn't right.

"Nope." Hadiza shook her head. "We'll upload the intel we've got into your implants. Have your folks look at it."

"Okay, but I—"

"Your ship's arriving," Hadiza said. "Follow me."

Kal struggled to keep his mouth closed as he watched the metallic bubble slowly descend from the ocean's surface. Hadiza had ordered the base's exterior lights to be turned on so they could see the entire process more clearly. As the landing sphere drew closer, the cables and tubes connected to its bottom coiled along the ocean floor, producing a small cloud of fine sand. The sphere drew level with the room they were in, and a passageway extended to its surface and snapped against it with a small jolt. After a seal had been established, the water level in the passageway dropped. Finally, the doors on either end slid upward with a hiss, revealing their ship, the *Salamis*, dry and resting safely inside the landing dome.

"Amazing, huh?" Hadiza asked with a knowing smile.

Kal nodded. "Incredible."

"Well, that was a ride," Sergeant Kimathi announced as he sauntered through the bridge between the base and the landing sphere.

"Sergeant, what do you want us to do with the supplies?" asked Private Feh Nenge, another new member of the Skulls.

"Don't worry, Unc, we'll take care of it," said Sue, motioning to several Hand members nearby. They walked to the ship with cargo bots in tow and began stacking crates from the ship's interior onto them.

"What is this place?" Nenge asked uncertainly. Like Kal,

the kid was from Mariga—the only water they had on their planet was ice.

"It's a research station," Hadiza said. She launched into what Kal realized was a well-rehearsed overview of the base, the Hand, and their mission. It was the same speech she'd given to Kal and Nicole. She probably gave it to every visitor.

The chief led the four Skulls through the base, picking up where she'd left off when the *Salamis* had arrived. Her speech was a classic recruiting pitch, highlighting the Silver Hand's noble cause and their glorious victories against the Nasi. To hear Hadiza talk, you would have thought they were single-handedly winning the war. It was a far cry from her desperate message to Kal and Nicole earlier. They finally ended the tour standing beneath the impressive glass dome of the control room. The Jelly hadn't moved, its lights continuing to dance in the murky depths above them.

"How many bases does the Silver Hand have?" asked Nenge.

"I can't tell you that," Hadiza said with a small shake of her head. "What I *can* say is that despite the Nasi attacks, we've been growing. The base we're in is one of our smaller ones."

Hadiza paused for a moment, her eyes staring forward and mouth pursed, clearly receiving a message via her implant. "Sorry. Just got word that they've finished offloading your ship."

"Thanks," Kal said. "Looks—"

A high-pitched klaxon and the sudden blinking warning lights on the ceiling above them interrupted him.

"What happened?" Hadiza asked, turning to one of the

Hand members at a nearby console.

"Looks like perimeter alarm four was just triggered," the woman replied.

"Get it on-screen. Now," Hadiza ordered.

A large viewscreen on the wall blinked and a grainy security camera feed replaced the peaceful holo of Wudexian aquatic life. The feed was from the small chamber they had used to get out of the ocean on their way into the base. A group of battle-suited Nasi soldiers were leaping out of the water and approaching the entrance to the lift.

"We've got another problem," called out someone. "Several Nasi fighters are inbound."

"Dammit," Hadiza swore. "We need to clear out of here."

"Is there another way out?" Sergeant Kimathi asked as he scanned the room.

Hadiza nodded. "Yes, there are several, but we won't have time to get out before the Nasi arrive."

Kimathi looked at Kal with a raised eyebrow; the question was obvious. Kal gave a reluctant nod of his head; he hated the thought of fighting down here.

"We'll cover your exit," the sergeant said. "Get your people out."

*Tac-1,* Kimathi called out over their internal net, *get suited up and to my location now. We've got at least ten Nasi approaching the base.*

Hadiza shot them a look of gratitude. "Thank you. I'll have—"

"We've got another perimeter breach," someone called out.

Hadiza studied the nearby console's viewscreen. "Blow both entrances," she instructed. The chief looked at the Skulls. "They got several through, but that should help you. The base has a fail-safe. I'll set the timer for ten minutes, which should be plenty of time for us to evacuate. When you get to the suboceanic landing bay, you'll need to use the manual release on the control panel."

"Good luck," Kal said. "Now get out of here."

"Attention. This is Chief Taggart. We're under Nasi attack. All personnel evacuate immediately. You have ten minutes." The synthetic voice was completely emotionless since Hadiza used her implant to broadcast the message through the base's speakers.

Taggart looked Kal in the eyes. "Thank you, and good luck. Both of the entrances the Nasi are using exit into this room." She took a quick glance at the security feeds. "I'd say you've got thirty seconds until they arrive. They're almost through our security doors."

The other five members of the Tac-I squad rushed into the room, clad in their battle suits. The bulky gray suits were the only thing that allowed the Skulls to stand toe-to-toe with the Nasi during their missions. A battle suit was more than a piece of equipment, it was a work of art. One that operated as an extension of the wearer's body. It worked anywhere, provided a host of advanced weaponry, granted superhuman strength, and could even fly. Kal would have given almost anything to be inside one right now.

"Sergeant Chedjou," Kimathi said as he pointed to a section of the room's curved walls, "get your team arrayed there." He turned to his other squad leader. "Bhatt, your team over there. Standard displacement." He pointed to two entrances leading into the room. "Enemy is going to come from here and here. We need to buy enough time to let the Silver Hand escape."

"Sir," the sergeant turned toward Kal, "you want to head back to the ship? The Nasi are in battle suits."

"We're not going anywhere," Nicole interjected. She wasn't the paper-pushing attaché he'd first met.

"You heard her," Kal said. "Let's see what weapons they have on the lower level." The Skulls always carried their personal sidearms on them, but they wouldn't do much against a dozen or more of fully armored Nasi.

The four unarmored Humans ran down the stairs and began quickly searching through the crates lining the hallway. Kal tried to remember where he'd seen weapons and ammo but was drawing a blank.

"Found it!" Private Nenge cried out triumphantly.

The private stood over an open crate filled with half a dozen high-powered kinetic rifles. Their polished black metal stocks gleamed in the hallway's bright light. Without another word, all four of them grabbed rifles from the crate and hastily inspected them.

"There's ammo here," Nicole announced a few crates down. They each grabbed as many magazines as they could fit into their cargo pockets from the open crate in front of her.

*We've got contact!* Sergeant Koula Bhatt called out.

The staccato sounds of kinetic weapons fire, mixed with the hiss of plasma, clamored from above their heads.

"What about these?" asked Nenge, holding a grenade in her hand.

"Leave it," Kal ordered, "we're a kilometer under the water."

Sergeant Kimathi led them up the stairs, scanning in all directions as he furtively hurried up two steps at a time. As the leader of the Tac-I squad, he was in command when they were on the ground, and Kal let him call the shots. Although Kal was the commander of the Skulls, he knew that firefights like this weren't his area. As Sergeant First Class Asif Jones, Kimathi's predecessor, had said: Kal told them what to do and the squad leader figured out how they would do it.

Kal reached the top of the stairs to find plasma and kinetic fire streaking across the room. Several consoles, caught in the crossfire, were melted by the plasma or riddled with holes. An acrid cloud of smoke hung over the room, partially obscuring the lights from the Jelly sitting on the glass dome overhead.

Kal barely had time to react as a Nasi soldier landed next to him, stabbing forward with the mechanical arm which sprouted from the back of its suit. He jumped to the side and fell into the metal edge of a console, causing a stabbing pain in his ribs. The sinuous, black-suited creature stood over Kal and raised a boot to crush him.

The tip of a glistening metal blade burst from the creature's chest, grinding against the armored plate of the suit as it was pulled back out. The Nasi dropped to its knees and fell on its side with a metallic clunk, revealing a Tac-I soldier standing directly behind him. A meter-long blood-tinged serrated blade slowly retracted into their battle suit's forearm.

*So the blades work,* Sergeant Sandra Chedjou called out over the net.

As she spoke, a plasma bolt splashed against her suit's rear energy shield. Battle suits usually had enough power to handle only two or three direct hits from a plasma rifle; any more and the bolts would melt right through the armor. Chedjou crouched down and jumped sideways across the room, twisting her torso in midair to fire back at the Nasi.

Kal scrambled behind the console he'd fell against and leaned his head around the side. Two Nasi bodies were sprawled on the floor, not including the one Chedjou had just impaled. Thankfully, his implant reported that all the members of the Skulls were still alive. He checked the timer on his neural implant; only about three minutes were left until the Hand's fail-safe activated.

*We've got to get back to ship,* Kal said to Kimathi over their private link.

*Chedjou. Bhatt,* Kimathi called on the Skulls' general net. *Get your soldiers to the stairs. We're going to have to make a run for it.*

Kal was already close to the stairwell, so he leaned out from the console and laid down cover fire as the other Skulls moved in his direction. The Nasi fighters remained low to the ground and took cover behind the large consoles and equipment, preventing him from getting a clear line of sight to them. A few of his shots hit a Nasi leg or arm, but none of them pierced their suits' hard armor.

A small antipersonnel missile snaked across the room,

exploding against the wall above Kal's head and knocking him flat. Kal looked up to see the black scorch mark of the missile's impact only a meter from the glass dome.

*We've got to get out now*, Kal called out. If the Nasi battle suits were anything like the Human ones, they would be able to survive under water; the Nasi might take down the entire facility.

*Cover the unarmored personnel while we get down the stairs*, Ekon ordered.

Kal rolled sideways and backed down the stairs until the bottom half of his body was covered. He leaned his upper torso over the floor so he could fire into the room at foot level. Ekon and Nicole were not far behind. They backed down the stairs and then turned around to join Kal in sweeping the room for Nasi targets.

Private Nenge ran toward them, weapon held at chest level as she streaked across the room. Her eyes widened in shock as a plasma bolt hit her in the side, searing off a portion of her torso. The young woman dropped to the ground in a heap, not even able to cry out in pain before the life left her body.

Kal compartmentalized and put the nightmarish image of the woman's wide glassy eyes from his head. He knew he'd see them in his sleep, but for now, they had to escape.

*We're clear*, Ekon said. *Nenge's KIA. We're making our way to the ship.*

The three of them turned and ran down the stairs, taking them several at a time. As Kal landed at the bottom, an enormous explosion reverberated from the room upstairs.

*They're aiming at the dome*, Sergeant Chedjou said.

"Get to the ship," Kal yelled to Sergeant Kimathi and Nicole. They ran down the crate-strewn hallway, occasionally glancing back to check for any Nasi. As they turned into the storage area, Kal heard another explosion from above and felt a surge of air. He could hear the rush of the water filling the base.

An automated voice sounded from the speakers. "Attention, all personnel. The viewing dome has been compromised. Proceed to evacuation areas."

"Keep going," Kimathi called out. "The others are on their way."

The sounds of water rushing and gurgling came from above as it poured from the dome. The Nasi must have only damaged a portion of the dome. If they'd destroyed the entire thing, they'd already be dead from the pressure. There were only minutes until water flooded the entire base and less time than that before the base's fail-safe went off.

"We're right behind you," called out Sergeant Bhatt through her suit's external speaker as she turned the corner. The other four members of Skulls were right behind her and ran through the large portal into the storage area.

A sinuous tentacle darted from the hallway behind them and wrapped around Private Ricci's armored leg. The appendage was almost completely translucent except for a bundle of small wiry nerves running through its center. Ricci fell to the ground and tried to twist toward his attacker with his weapon. But the Jelly arm quickly coursed up his leg and wrapped around his suit's arms and torso before he could aim

32

his weapon.

*Help!* Ricci cried out.

Kal, along with the rest of the Skulls, fired on full auto at the Jelly. Their rounds pierced the animal's skin then stopped, frozen in place. The appendage pulled Ricci toward the door, undulating rhythmically as it absorbed hundreds of rounds from the Skulls. After a few seconds, it had completely enmeshed the young private; his suit was now a gray blur inside the coiled fist of the Jelly's tentacle.

"Closing emergency hatches." The synthetic voice blared from the speakers overhead.

A metal security gate slammed down and buried itself in the Jelly's tentacle. It instantly uncoiled, dumping Ricci on the storage bay floor, and writhed around desperately trying to free itself from the gate. Water poured from beneath the door, coursing along the storage area's floor and into the rooms beyond.

"Get him to the ship," Kal yelled as Bhatt picked Ricci up from the ground.

They ran through the storage rooms to the suboceanic landing pad and up the back cargo ramp of the *Salamis*. The scout corvette's engines let out a low whine as they spun at idle; the ship was ready to go.

Kimathi stopped at the entrance of the landing sphere and scrutinized the small control panel by the opening. After a few seconds, he slammed his fist down on a button and pulled the red lever next to it. The large door between the sphere and the base crashed down, sealing them inside. Metallic pings sounded from below them as wires and tubes detached from its base. The lights inside the sphere went out, and the interior was pitch black except for the glow coming from the few lights on the outside of the *Salamis*.

"Come on," Kal shouted to Kimathi, "get in the ship."

The sergeant sprinted at the ship and dove into the open cargo bay as the last wire holding them down snapped away. Kal almost fell as they shot upward toward the ocean's surface.

*We're all in. Close the bay,* Kal instructed to the pilots over the net.

"Get everyone ready for evasive maneuvers," he told Kimathi as the noncommissioned officer pulled himself up. "I'm heading to the cockpit." There would be Nasi fighters waiting for them when they reached the surface.

Kal ran through the ship's cargo bay, climbed the ladder to the second deck, and rushed into the cockpit. Lieutenant Hitesh Sampson and Chief Heather Ramos were in their seats waiting for the bubble to arrive on the ocean's surface. Kal sat down at the console behind the two pilots, quickly putting on his restraints.

"We've got at least ten Nasi fighters patrolling the area," Ramos said. "We'll need to get out of here fast."

"Just make sure the engines are ready," Sampson said. He pressed the intercom button. "Get ready back there. This take-off may be more than the ship's inertial dampeners can handle." He turned back to Chief Ramos. "Turn on the cloak."

"Cloak on," Ramos replied. The optical cloak hid the ship from Nasi sensors. Samsara Fleet's technicians still considered it experimental technology, meaning that it worked most—

but not all—of the time. The *Salamis* had started out as a standard scout corvette—sleek and fast—but the fleet's engineers had added a host of additional experimental features like the cloak, transforming it to the most advanced ship in Samsara Fleet. Many of the devices on the ship were like the cloak, cutting-edge but unreliable.

The metal dome around the ship slid open, revealing the sun rising directly in front of them, sending tendrils of green into the clouds on the horizon. Before the dome was fully open, an enormous spout of water erupted beneath them, catapulting the landing pad sideways. Kal braced against his console as he saw the ocean rushing toward them in the side viewscreen.

With a curse, Sampson immediately maxed out the ship's vertical thrusters, causing them to hurl laterally across the water, skipping across the swells like a stone thrown by a child. He slowly transitioned the ship's power to their main engines, adjusting their course to gain altitude. Kal let out a breath of relief as he saw the marshy islands where they'd met the Silver Hand glide beneath them.

"Looks like the cloak's working," Ramos said. Kal glanced at the tactical map by his console. The red icons of the Nasi fighters looked to be several kilometers away. They must not have seen the landing sphere pop out of the ocean.

"Good. Get us out of here and back to the fleet," Kal instructed.

"With pleasure, sir," Sampson said with a turn of his head. Kal felt himself pressed back in his seat as the ship exited the planet's atmosphere.

# Chapter Three

"Is terrestrial capital ship construction even possible?" General Aamina Samaha asked.

She looked at them through the viewscreen, her brow furrowed with concern. The general was sitting in her conference room aboard the Tounous carrier, *Gedorhan's Return*. The viewscreens behind her made it appear as if she was talking from a snow-covered peak with fertile green valleys stretching out below her. Nicole had learned that Samaha had always deeply appreciated nature.

"Seems like it, ma'am," Nicole replied.

She was sitting at the desk in the stateroom she shared with Kal aboard the Human carrier, *Ofira*. As a general officer, Kal had been assigned one of the nicest staterooms on the ship. From what Nicole gathered, letting her stay with him wasn't totally in regs, but no one really cared. The layout was simple: a bunk, seating area, and desk filled the small chamber. A door led to their private shower and biological recycler. Normally, they had the viewscreens on the wall of the room set to the live video feed from the external cameras of the ship. Combined with the sleek wood highlights around the room, it made her feel like she was on the civilian luxury ships she'd seen in the holos.

After escaping Wudexingqiu, the Skulls had returned to Samsara Fleet's location in the open space immediately outside the system and transmitted the dossier of intelligence information the Silver Hand had provided them. The Nasi plans for building new ships were a stark reminder that the war wasn't over.

"I've looked over the intel that the Hand shared. It's just hard to believe that the Nasi are able do this," Samaha said.

Nicole had looked through the information briefly before they'd opened the video link. The ability to construct large capital ships on a planet's surface rather than in space would give the Nasi an almost insurmountable advantage. Normally, capital ships had to be constructed in orbit with the workers and materials ferried from the surface. It could take years to complete a single ship and required countless engineers, bots, and raw materials. By building their ships on the planet's surface, the Nasi could drastically increase the speed of production and make it much more difficult for their enemies to attack the ships while under construction.

Inside the Silver Hand's files were photographs of open-air construction sites on Wudexingqiu where the large modules were being built. There were also documents and messages that outlined the Nasi construction process. They sourced raw materials from the other species' worlds they'd conquered and had it delivered to their construction facilities on the Human colonies. They built modules on the planets' surface and then launched them into orbit where they could be quickly put together. The Nasi had taken a process that should take at least a year and reduce it to a couple of months or less.

"This changes a lot of things," Kal said. "Apologies for stating the obvious, but we have to put an end to this quickly."

Samaha sighed and rubbed her temples. She had been more tired than usual lately and Nicole could have sworn that the woman had more gray hair each time she saw her.

"Ma'am, when will Ancient Wang be here?" Nicole asked. "The Jadid may have some ideas on how we can stop this."

"We expect him to arrive any day," Samaha replied.

Ancient Bao Wang had been Samsara Fleet and Humanity's biggest ally among the Council of Ancients. He'd helped to convince the council to join with the fleet and had also led the mission to rescue Kal and Nicole from a rebel faction. Nicole didn't think it would be a stretch to say that the man had saved both Samsara Fleet and the galaxy through his actions.

The Council of Ancients had selected Bao to command the Jadid fleet several months ago. A month later he'd arrived in their universe. Since then, he'd worked on getting the Jadid fleet retrofitted so they could operate in the Human's universe.

"Did you ask Bo about this?" Samaha asked.

Bo, or Bowen Nguyen, was a Jadid scientist that had been held hostage by the Nasi. The Skulls had freed him from captivity. Since then, he'd become a valuable member of both the Skulls and Samsara Fleet. His knowledge of fold drives and Nasi technology made him invaluable.

"Yes," Nicole answered. "He said that there wasn't enough information to draw any conclusions other than the obvious."

"Sounds like Bo." Samaha smirked.

"He suggested we talk to the Jadid fleet as well," Nicole said. They would at least be able to say if what the Nasi were doing was even possible.

"As much as I hate to agree," said Samaha, "I do. It'd be foolish to do anything until Bao and the fleet arrives."

"We'll still prepare to strike those construction facilities though," Kal said.

Samaha nodded. "Yes. I already talked with General Zhou." Major General Frederick Zhou was the fleet's executive officer.

Samaha bent down and rubbed her forehead. She was older than Kal but looked at least ten years younger—until recently. Now, her aging appeared to have accelerated dramatically. The lines on her face had grown deeper, and he had noticed that she was more and more fatigued in meetings.

"Ma'am..." Nicole faltered. "I just wanted to say that we'll get through this. We've been through worse."

Samaha took a deep breath and plastered on what Nicole thought of as her meeting smile. "Thank you, Nicole. I appreciate that. Now, you've just come off a tough mission and doubtless I'll be sending both of you into harm's way soon. Enjoy the time you've got."

"Roger, ma'am," Kal replied stiffly. "We'll wait for your call." He turned off the video feed.

"She's got a lot on her plate," Nicole said. The initial shock of the Nasi surprise attack over a year ago had worn off for many of them. Now they were in the daily slog of the war; it was a marathon.

"Everyone does." Kal stood up and stretched. "Hell, I've already got so much on my plate I'm stuffed."

Nicole's stomach rumbled. "Speaking of that..."

❖

The *Ofira's* lounge was nothing special compared to the few high-end restaurants Kal had been to. The only differences between it and the galley were the calming nature scenes displayed on the viewscreens, the slightly nicer tables and chairs, and the bot waitstaff. All the food and drinks were the same—except the lounge had alcohol—and came from the food fabricators that they used in the ship's galley.

The room was full of people laughing and drinking. They were soldiers like Kal and Nicole, enjoying every second as if it were their last. After the Jadid had agreed to join Samsara Fleet, General Samaha had suspended all offensive operations, deciding to lie low until their reinforcements arrived. For scout units like the Skulls, the mission tempo had increased. Samaha and her staff were determined to get as much intel as they could, so they'd ordered the scout teams behind enemy lines to distribute weapons and supplies and meet with various rebel leaders for information.

"Sir, ma'am, over here!" shouted Chief Taisha Kanumba, the Skulls' chief engineer. She'd been temporarily reassigned from the team since she was several months pregnant and beginning to show.

Chief Kanumba was sitting with Sergeant Kimathi at a table loaded with several empty glasses near the center of the large room. Kal knew the glasses all belonged to Kimathi; the sergeant had once informed him that he always told the bots to leave them so he could keep track of his drinks.

"How are things?" Kal asked as he took a seat at the table.

"Boring," Kanumba replied, "Pregnancy sucks. I can't believe I won't be with you."

"I would love boring," Nicole replied, patting Kanumba on the back. The chief smiled warmly, her cheerful expression and warm eyes a stark contrast to the jagged scar across her face.

"Sure," the chief replied with a roll of her eyes, "that's why you're training all the time."

"I would hate to be cooped up on this ship," Kimathi said as he finished what looked to be his fifth drink. He glanced at Kanumba. "No offensive."

"Yeah, almost getting killed by a giant jellyfish sounds great," Kanumba smiled wryly.

"How is Private Ricci by the way?" asked Nicole.

"Shaken up." Ekon shrugged. "Who can blame him? He was pretty torn up about Nenge too. He'll get used to it." A vision of Private Nenge's lifeless face smashing against the Hand's control room floor flashed in Kal's head. He wasn't sure you ever got used to it.

"I guess," Kal said. *Should soldiers get used to the violence and killing?*

"We'll have the ceremony tonight," Kimathi said. He was referring to the fleet's funeral ceremony, a holdover from when they'd been in the EDF. They'd gather around a pair of Nenge's boots by one of the landing bay doors and tell stories about the soldier. The stories could be anything—funny, happy, sad—but they had to be true. Finally, they'd send the boots into space, to drift forever. Normally, it would be the soldier's remains and not just her boots, but they hadn't been able to recover Nenge.

"Let us know when it is," Kal said.

"Of course, sir."

The conversation died down for a moment. Samsara Fleet had been fighting the Nasi for over a year though it felt much longer. At first, they'd barely been able to survive, beaten down by the Nasi's surprise attack against Earth. They'd been on the run, desperately looking for ways to fight a force that seemed almost invincible. At least now that the Jadid had agreed to assist them, they had a chance. Still, every death hurt.

"Did you hear about Hrodar?" Kimathi asked. Hrodar was a former Kurz planet, conquered by the Nasi in the initial days of the war.

"No, what about it?" Kanumba asked.

"The Nasi destroyed it," Kimathi replied after he took a deep sip from his glass. "The planet rose up and destroyed the Nasi garrison. So they came in with one of their dreadnaughts and wiped the entire system out." Dreadnaughts were enormous ships capable of destroying entire systems through disrupting the star's fusion reaction. They were the same ships that had destroyed Earth and several other planets.

"I can't say I'm surprised," Nicole said. The Nasi were ruthless. They'd stationed small garrisons on each alien world they'd conquered with the promise that the planet could remain self-governing as long as the resources continued to flow, and the garrison was left alone. Any deviation, and they would destroy the system. As far as Kal knew, no one had taken them up on it until now

"Damn them," Kanumba swore under her breath. "I'd like to kill every single last one of them."

"Get in line," Ekon said as he downed the last drops of his beer.

"You'll both get your chance, unfortunately," Kal said. "But remember, we're not here to kill Nasi. We're here to save the galaxy from them."

"There's a difference?" Ekon asked as he beckoned to one of the server bots idling at the edge of the room.

"A big one," Nicole said. Kal knew she had more of a right to be angry with the Nasi than the rest of them. They'd used her, disgraced her, and killed her entire family. But she hadn't succumbed to the bloodlust that many others in the fleet suffered. Kal suspected her own guilt played a part in that.

"They sound the same to me," Kimathi said. "Killing—"

*Kal. Nicole.* General Samaha's voice appeared in Kal's head. *Get to the Gedorhan's Return. Ancient Wang has arrived.*

"Brigadier General Norman and Lieutenant Colonel Bergeron," Ancient Bao Wang said as he bowed. "Great to see you both."

The man was several hundred years old but looked

younger than Kal. The only sign of age was the wings of gray hair that spread from his temples and through his black hair. When Kal had first met the Wang, he'd spoken in an archaic form of Human Standard, but his time in their universe had changed that.

"Glad to see you too," Kal said as he gave a slight bow back. Nicole simply smiled and nodded before sitting down on the bench in General Samaha's conference room. The room was intended to be used by Tounous, who normally sat on the ground, not Humans. The only seating were the benches that lined all four walls of the room. Viewscreens decorated the walls above, displaying a looping video of a forest.

Nicole wasn't sure of what to think about the Ancient. She knew Kal trusted the man implicitly. Why wouldn't he? When they had been on the Jadid's home world of Altterra, Wang had led the rescue mission to save the two of them from the Isolationists, a rebel group that wanted no part in the war between Samsara Fleet and the Nasi. At the same time, Nicole felt there was something off about him. She attributed it to the fact that he'd grown up in another age than them. His worldview and his experiences had shaped him in ways they couldn't fathom.

"So we're ready," Wang said, opening his arms. "I bet you never thought the day would come."

"We had faith in you," General Samaha replied. "But it's nice to finally have your fleet ready to assist us."

"The Nasi put up a fight back on Altterra," Wang said. "However, our forces captured the gateways. The Nasi closed them from this side though rather than let us exploit them."

On each Human colony, the city-sized Nasi Foothold contained a gateway which connected to Altterra. They allowed the Nasi to travel freely between the two planets, taking supplies and personnel from one to the other without the use of a ship capable of folding between the universes.

"That should slow them down a bit at least," Nicole said. The Nasi had used the gateways to bring supplies to their fleet in this universe. They'd captured so many planets that they probably didn't need them anymore, but at least it was one less advantage.

"Not as much as you might think," Wang replied with a shake of his head. "When we finally broke through their lines, we found they'd already brought their people and materials here. It's a victory, but a hollow one."

"At least we've cut off one of their supply lines," Kal said diplomatically.

"True, but they're established in this universe now," Samaha replied. "They're self-sufficient."

"I think they always figured this day would come," Wang said. "Esma never intended to remain in our universe. She only needed to stay there long enough for the Footholds to be completed."

"Which they are," Kal said.

Samaha paged through the tablet she had perched on her leg. "Ancient Wang, I want you to look at this," she said.

A grainy aerial shot of one of the Nasi construction facilities appeared on a viewscreen. It looked to be a large circular disc with a bulbous mass resting on it. Small buildings were scattered on the periphery.

Wang stood up and walked closer to the screen, his hand cupped under his chin as he studied the image. "Where is this?" he asked.

"Wudexingqiu," Samaha replied. "Some of our allies gathered these images and some supporting information. It looks like the Nasi are building more capital ships. The interesting thing is they're doing it on the planet's surface." Bao looked back at her, surprised. "They build several modules on the surface then stitch them together in orbit."

"Like our weaves," Wang said thoughtfully. They were prefabricated panels that were mass produced and then strung together over a frame. Despite their appearance, weaves were not only light but incredibly strong and could withstand missile and weapons fire. "I'll need to get my staff to look at this. If they can get it to work, it's ingenious, makes it much easier to build the ship and makes them less vulnerable during construction. Our engineers had proposed things like this before, but no one had ever figured out how to do it."

"Looks like *they* did," Kal observed.

"Have you had Bowen look at it?" asked Wang.

"Yes," Kal replied. "He couldn't provide any more information than what we already have."

"That's too bad. If this is what your people think it is, we've got to strike," Wang said. His face darkened and jaw clenched angrily for a moment. "If Esma can increase the size of her fleet, we're doomed. That woman is pure determination. If she gets too far ahead, then there'll be no coming back."

It was sometimes easy for Nicole to forget the Ancients had known each other for hundreds of years. They'd been friends, enemies, and lovers for longer than she'd been alive. They'd raised families and fought wars together. She saw it in the way Wang mentioned Esma Baykara. There was a deep personal relationship that the others in the room knew nothing about.

"We're still going through the intel," Samaha said. "I'll include anyone you want in the analysis."

"Thanks," Wang replied. "Send everything you have to my fleet." It sounded more like an order than a request.

General Samaha pressed her lips together. "I'll tell my staff to send you what we've got."

Ancient Wang sat back down on the bench and smiled. "Thank you. Your fleet has performed admirably, considering what you've faced. Now that we are here, we can win this war despite this setback. But we'll need to be decisive. Esma will not rest, and neither can we."

Kal picked up his spoon and let the clotted soup drip back into the bowl. The fabricator said it was egusi soup, but it certainly did not look like it. He debated how hungry he really was as he looked down at his bowl.

There weren't many people in the *Ofira's* galley right now. Long white tables filled the large room, but only a third of them were filled. The room was nondescript; viewscreens showing a life feed of space, utilitarian metal tables in the center, and food fabricators filled the far wall of the room.

"I could use some actual food," Kal said, as he sat his spoon down.

Nicole looked up from her plate of what was supposed to be chicken with a look of surprise. "This isn't bad," she replied. "The fabricators on the *Ofira* are a lot better than the ones on the *Salamis*."

Food fabricators were machines that took raw nutrients, textures, flavors, and other materials and combined them to mimic real food. The chicken Nicole was eating was a concentration of protein and flavoring designed to simulate a piece of chicken. The fabricators allowed them to eat a variety of foods, all from the same basic ingredients, while in space. Kal wasn't sure what was in his soup, but it definitely wasn't authentic.

Unfortunately, fabricated food never tasted quite right to Kal. After traveling through space for the last thirty-plus years, the flavors of all the fabricated meals had blended together. One tasted just like another. Although he wasn't unique in his distaste for fabricated meals, some liked them. Veteran soldiers had favorite dishes from the fabricators that were completely different from the food they enjoyed planetside.

"My soup's tasteless," Kal replied as he tried a spoonful. "I'll take a cheap meal of real food any day of the week."

"It's better than what I had back on Earth," Nicole replied. She'd grown up in the communes back on Earth. Kal didn't want to know the food she'd had there that made her like this stuff.

Nicole rubbed the starfish pendant dangling from her neck—she often did that when talking about her life on Earth. It was a gift from her younger sister, Sylvie. Nicole had told him about the family that she'd left when the UEG had assigned her to be an attaché on the Kurz home world of Gorash. She'd intended to return to see them again but had never had a chance before the Nasi destroyed Earth.

"If nothing else, we need to win this war so I can get a decent meal," Kal said as he pushed away his bowl. "I should file a complaint with General Samaha."

"She looked rough over the viewscreen," Nicole said as she ate an enormous piece of her chicken. Kal would have sworn the woman had never eaten before.

"Can you blame her?" Kal asked. "She's dealing with the fate of Humanity. Hell, more than that really, the fate of the galaxy."

"Maybe." Nicole pursed her lips and gently placed her fork down on the plate in front of her. "I've been meaning to mention something to you."

"What?"

"While you and the rest of the team were on Patagonia, I visited the Nasi prisoner, Salah." Salah was a low-level Nasi soldier the Skulls had captured during a raid on New America. After questioning, they'd kept him in the brig on the *Ofira*. There wasn't any other place to put him.

Kal raised an eyebrow and kept silent.

"Samaha had ordered him *tortured* for information," she continued. "A guard told me and Samaha herself confirmed it."

Kal wouldn't have wanted to be there for that conversation. He'd assumed Samaha would have used what they called "enhanced interrogation techniques" on the prisoner though he'd never really thought too much about it. When the fate of the galaxy rested in their hands, they had to do what they could. How could they risk the lives of everyone by not using every tool in their possession?

"You disagree, I assume," Kal replied.

"Of course. How could I not?" Nicole leaned forward. "Did you know about this?"

"I didn't know for sure, but I'm not surprised." Nicole's face fell as he talked.

"So you're just fine with it?"

"I don't really think about it." Kal placed his hand on Nicole's. "We're fighting a war for survival. I don't think it's right, but in the end, what other choice do we have?"

"We could fight honorably."

"Like they did?" Kal felt himself growing annoyed. "Coming out of nowhere and killing entire planets? Or round up people to be executed like they did with the Z'Ta?"

"I'm not saying what they did is right, but—"

"You found out about this, when? Months ago?" Kal asked. "But you didn't mention it until now. Why's that?"

Nicole glanced at the viewscreens on the wall. "There were other things going on. There wasn't time."

"Maybe because you realized that your morals and your survival aren't aligned."

"What's that supposed to mean?" A red flush crept up Nicole's face.

"You know exactly what I mean," Kal said, trying to keep his voice down. "You're a soldier now, and you see the decisions we have to make. There is no right or wrong. We make the best choice we can, and we have to be satisfied with it."

"What makes us different from them?" Nicole asked. "There's got to be more to this than survival."

Kal sighed. "For one, we actually care about doing the right thing. But we aren't perfect. We never were. You grew up in the communes. You saw what Humans are capable of. But we never came close to doing the things the Nasi did."

"If we decide everything is relative, then we can justify anything." Nicole placed her hands on the table. "We can make excuses for any depravity or crime we commit. You say that I avoided talking about it, but it's clear that you avoided thinking about it. You never even questioned what they'd do to Salah even though you knew full well. There's so many things one can get away with if you don't worry about the consequences."

Kal closed his mouth. That one was close to the mark. Nicole was new to all of this; she'd been a diplomat that worked in a world of ideals. Kal had fought against the Torgham, and he'd done things he didn't want to think about. As an officer, he'd sent soldiers to certain death because it was what needed to be done. He didn't want to revisit those decisions, the ones that made him uncomfortable. If he did, he worried he wouldn't be able to make another one.

"What about Bo?" Nicole asked.

Kal often wondered what Bowen thought about the

51

decisions they made. They were fighting his species, his comrades. But he rarely voiced any sort of disapproval and was tight-lipped when Kal asked him his thoughts.

"What about him?" Kal shot back. "He'd agree with me."

"You don't think seeing a fellow Jadid suffering would cause him to question us?" Nicole raised her arms in the air. "What about the Jadid Fleet? You don't think they would wonder if they've made the right decision in joining with us?"

"No, I don't…" Kal sighed. "Look, can we stop?" He grabbed her hand. "I don't want to argue, not now."

Nicole studied him with cool azure eyes. "Why?"

"Because. Because I'm tired. I keep…" Kal paused, he couldn't tell her about his nightmares or the visions that swam in his head. "I just want to rest."

Her face softened. "Okay, we'll pause this for now." She smirked. "I don't want to take away from you enjoying your soup."

❖

A cacophony of burbles, squeaks, and words assaulted Kal as he entered the large briefing room on the *Gedorhan's Return*. The senior military officers in the room represented ships from the six species that made up the fleet: Tounous, Z'Ta, Kurz, Qudoru, Human, and Jadid. The room was a larger version of Samaha's private conference room with a bench running along all four walls with viewscreens above it. Faces of officers forced to listen to the briefing through video because of space constraints filled the screens and several strange-looking pieces of furniture sat in the middle of the room to accommodate the different species' physiology.

Normally, they did not hold briefings like this in person. Although they were in deep space, light years away from any planet, there was always a risk in having this many senior officers in one location. General Samaha had ordered it to be held in person since it would be the first time that Ancient Wang and the Jadid commanders were taking part.

"Sounds like the bar in some deep-space mining station," Major General Zhou said as Kal sat down next to him on the bench.

"Did you bring any drinks, sir?"

Zhou laughed. "Next time. I promise." The general had relaxed significantly since Kal had first met him. Kal liked to think that Zhou's time with the Skulls had changed him for the better though he wasn't sure they could claim full credit. Either way, Zhou's rise had been meteoric since leaving their team.

"Have you seen their fleet?" Kal asked. The Jadid fleet comprised about thirty ships, less than the estimated fifty Nasi ships but still a vast increase from the nine they'd had before. There was one question that needed to be answered: how capable were the Jadid ships? Could they stand against the Nasi?

"Their stats are good," Zhou admitted. "Who knows what they'll be like when they actually fight?"

"They'd better be good," Kal replied. "They used up all our resources getting retrofitted." Samsara Fleet had provided almost all the resources they had to the Jadid as they were rebuilding their ships for this universe. Many of their primary systems had to be modified or completely rebuilt, which required supplies and time. Unfortunately, Samsara Fleet had little of either, and now they had none.

"We'll find out soon. This battle will be the test."

"Welcome!" General Samaha's greeting to the room cut off Kal as he was about to respond. "Today is the beginning of a new era for Samsara Fleet. I would like to congratulate every single officer here and commend you and your soldiers. We survived the initial Nasi attack, we created this fleet, and now, with the Jadid Liberation Fleet, we will wipe out the Nasi." Sounds of approval greeted her statement.

"We've discovered that the enemy has started the construction of new capital ships on the planet of Wudexingqiu." Images of the construction sites appeared on the viewscreens as she talked. "Based on the intelligence we've received, the Nasi will have one complete in the next week. After that, they can build a new one every month." The alien species' implants would automatically translate the unit of time to their equivalent.

"What about the other Human planets? Are they building ships there as well?" asked General Mirana Nervaan, the Qudoru Commander.

"It's something we're still investigating," Samaha replied. "But—"

"But we're here, next to Wudexingqiu," interrupted Ancient Wang, stepping toward the center of the room. "We've all seen the intel. We know what's going on. And we know we have to stop it."

Samaha shot the Ancient an annoyed glance. "You've already seen the order. We'll be sending the fleet to Wudexingqiu to liberate the planet. This is the beginning of the end for the Nasi, and the start of our return."

Kal felt like pinching himself. Could it be this simple? Would they finally be able to free a planet from the Nasi's grasp?

"We are ready to fight," Kurz Field Marshal Krunalt said. A chorus of agreement met his declaration.

"That's good to hear," Ancient Wang said with a smile, "because that's exactly what we're going to do."

Zhou leaned over to Kal and whispered, "Something about this feels off."

Kal nodded, his stomach fluttering. He knew he should be excited but couldn't shake the feeling that nothing was ever this easy with the Nasi. Samsara Fleet was on the attack, and Kal worried they may be heading right into a trap.

# Chapter Four

To Nicole, the plan seemed simple enough. The entirety of Samsara Fleet, almost forty ships, would simultaneously fold as close to the Wudexingqiu as they could and unleash hell. They'd already sent scouts ahead and knew the enemy's displacement and numbers. General Zhou had detailed the exact location for each ship so they would already be in missile range when they arrived. If everything went according to plan—a big if, Nicole had to admit—they'd destroy the Nasi fleet before it had a chance to react.

"I can't wait for us to take it to those bastards," Sergeant Kimathi said as he checked his rifle. The Skulls were in the *Salamis'* cargo bay, going through their last-minute checks before the battle.

"Sergeant, we're just gonna be sitting on the ground," scoffed Sergeant Bhatt. "Maybe we'll get to see a pretty light show or something."

The Skulls' mission was to enter the planet's atmosphere as needed to take out any anti-orbital weapons. Nicole had heard the Tac-I squad talking amongst themselves; they thought it was going to be simple, and Nicole couldn't argue with them. The battle should be over quickly, and the fleet wouldn't be in range of any planetary defenses anyway.

"Sergeant Bhatt," Kal said, his voice stern. "Make sure you and your soldiers are ready. We don't know what'll happen."

"Yes, sir." The team leader kept any sarcasm from her voice. With a swish of her long green hair—Nicole was impressed how she always had a new hair color every time she saw her—the woman turned back to her battle suit and continued to go through her checks. Nicole was sure that if anyone else had spoken to Bhatt that way, they would have gotten more than just an acknowledgement. Sergeant Bhatt was not one to bite her tongue.

The team's gray battle suits were sitting in the docks that lined the bulkhead of the *Salamis*. When the suits were not in use, the docking stations replenished their ammunition and batteries and performed routine repairs. Nicole quickly ran through the checks for her suit—fuel, seams, ammunition levels—everything looked to be fine. She hadn't expected anything else, but the Skulls tried not to leave anything to chance.

"Get ready, everyone," Chief Ramos called over the intercom. "The fleet is about to fold."

Folding was the miracle technology that had enabled Humanity to escape the bonds of Earth. Using their fold drive, a ship could travel by going through a Minkowski wormhole, instantly changing their location in space. Theoretically, there was no limit to how far they could travel in one fold, but in practice, gravity and several other factors limited the distance that a ship could change position in a single fold. To compensate for this limitation, every ship had an advanced computer which allowed them to string thousands of folds together to effectively travel faster than light through the galaxy.

Samsara Fleet was only a single fold away from Wudexingqiu. Despite only being a single fold, it was still over a light-week away.

"I'm heading to the cockpit," Kal said, resting a hand on Sergeant Kimathi's shoulder. "Be ready for anything."

"Suits on?" Kimathi asked with a note of uncertainty. Despite leading their Tac-1 squad, Ekon Kimathi was still a kid in many ways. The last mission had rattled him; it wasn't like Ekon to ask for permission for a simple thing like when to put on battle suits.

"You decide, Sergeant." Kal climbed up the ladder and toward the cockpit.

Nicole walked to the ship's galley and took a seat at the table. The viewscreens were playing a live feed from an external camera of the ship's hull. They were inside the landing bay of the *Ofira*, so all she could see were other ships and the maintenance personnel and bots performing last-minute checks. No military ship, and only a few civilian ones, had windows; they were too fragile and dangerous. Instead, they had cameras on the outside of the hull which piped a live video feed to the viewscreens inside, making them appear exactly like a window.

Nicole adjusted the screens with her implant so that one was a feed from the *Ofira's* external camera, and the other was the tactical map. There were only the green icons of Samsara Fleet on the tacmap, but that was about to change when they folded.

The stars around the ship blinked and changed position in space; they'd folded. It took a few seconds for the tactical map to adjust, but soon red icons showing Nasi ships appeared.

Nicole felt the slight pressure of the *Salamis* lifting off the landing bay floor and changed the viewscreen to the ship's external camera feed. The scout corvette slid through the energy field holding the atmosphere in the bay and sped at the planet with their optical cloak enabled to avoid notice by the Nasi fleet.

Nicole reviewed the tactical map. So far, everything was going according to plan; Samsara Fleet had the planet and the Nasi fleet surrounded. They enjoyed at least a three-to-one numerical advantage and should make quick work of the Nasi.

Samsara and Liberation Fleets' capital ships disgorged their fighters in giant swarms and maneuvered to lock on to the Nasi ships orbiting the bright blue planet. Once they'd moved into place, the ships fired salvos of missiles, which appeared as small green dots on the tacmap, at the Nasi ships. It was impossible to see everything that was happening through the live feed from the ship's external cameras. Instead, Nicole relied on the detailed tactical map which was already becoming a clutter of icons. She used her implant to scroll through the map and adjust the zoom on the video feeds to fully understand what was happening to the fleets.

Nicole tapped into the Fleet's command net using her neural implant. Although intended only for commanders and their staff, Samaha had granted Nicole access as the executive officer of the Skulls. Their notoriety and reputation came in handy sometimes.

*L'kor and L'rok, move to positions blocking target echo,* General Zhou commanded over the net.

*No, wait,* Ancient Wang called out. *I've already got two*

*ships going that way.*

*Sir.* Nicole could hear the annoyance in General Zhou's face words. *General Samaha has given your fleet its orders. Please execute.*

*Her orders are wrong,* Wang said calmly. *Let—*

A burst of static blasted over the net, cutting off the Ancient. A shaft of solid light, brighter than the star at the center of the system, shot out from the planet's surface and struck the center of one of the Jadid battleships. The vaguely spherical brown ship continued to fire its kinetic cannons at nearby Nasi ship. Seconds later, it exploded in a blinding flash, sending large chunks of the ship careening away and leaving behind an expanding cloud of small debris.

*What the hell was that?* Samaha asked, her voice tinged with anxiety.

*We're checking, ma'am,* reported the *Ofira.*

Another beam of light lanced out from another location on the planet's surface and bore through a second Jadid ship, leaving it lifelessly drifting through space.

*General Norman,* Zhou called out through a private net. *Get down to the planet and take out those weapons.*

Nicole held onto the galley table as their ship flew in the direction the planet. The ship quickly dove through the exosphere, rattling and bending metal sounding as they plunged. Two more beams of light erupted from the surface, annihilating Jadid ships, as the *Salamis* sped toward the surface of Wudexingqiu.

*It's some sort of plasma stream,* Ramos called out. *It's coming from underneath the ocean.*

*Sergeant Kimathi, get ready*, Kal instructed.

Nicole leapt from the galley table and ran to the cargo bay. The Tac-1 squad were already in their battle suits and donning their helmets. Some of them were already pairing off to conduct last-minute checks.

Nicole placed her feet in the boots of her battle suit. The back was split open along the arms, legs, and back. She placed her hands in the gauntlets and activated the suit with her implant. The suit constricted around her body, adjusting to her shape, and clamped down on her joints. The seams stitched closed around her body in an airtight seal. As Nicole was grabbing her helmet off the docking station, Kal ran into the bay and began putting his suit on as well.

*We're thirty seconds out from the drop zone*, Lieutenant Sampson said. The cargo bay door opened, and Sergeant Kimathi walked out to the edge of the ramp. All Nicole could see out the back of the ship was an endless expanse of sparkling blue ocean.

The *Salamis* decelerated as they neared the drop zone. For a moment, all Nicole could feel was a sense of panic, a feeling of desperation as she wondered what she could do to get out of her current situation. Then her training took hold, and she joined the others standing on the ship's cargo ramp, waiting for Kimathi's orders to drop.

*Squad, our objective is approximately four kilometers under the ocean's surface*, Kimathi said. Nicole could see the estimated location in the heads-up display of her suit. *General Norman, you'll be with Chedjou in Alpha Team and Bergeron and me will be with Bravo team.*

*Go!* Chief Ramos called over the net.

Kimathi waved them forward and the squad dropped, single file, out the back of the speeding ship and dove straight into the water below.

❖

Kal tried to focus on the task in front of him. Whatever those cannons were, they needed to be destroyed immediately. He was sure that Zhou had sent teams to take out the other ones, but the Skulls had only one mission right now and they had to succeed.

The water grew darker as they plunged through its depths. Kal's suit's display automatically compensated, switching to night vision as the light from the sun disappeared. Aquatic creatures darted about their group as they descended. They came in all shapes and colors, and after the Skulls passed two kilometers in depth, most of them had a natural bioluminescence that made Kal feel like they were speeding through a field of stars.

*Coming on the target,* Sergeant Kimathi said. *Alpha team, approach from the east. Bravo from the west.*

Kal followed Sergeant Sandra Chedjou, Alpha Team leader, as she angled away from the other fire team and continued to descend. They reached three kilometers under the surface, and the life began to thin out around them, leaving only the dark shapes of the battle-suit-clad soldiers around Kal.

*We've got several inbound fighters,* Ramos said. *We'll*

*need to take evasive action.*

*Can they see through the cloak?* Kal asked.

*Not sure, sir,* Ramos replied. *I think they know we're here but not exactly where we are.*

*Okay, get out and we'll let you know when we are ascending to the surface.*

Kal's display suddenly went completely and painfully white as a plasma blast overloaded the night vision. He closed his eyes, still seeing the afterimage of the lance behind his eyelids. His suit registered a spike in the water temperature as the beam flash-heated the ocean water around him.

*They just destroyed another Jadid ship,* Ramos said. *The fleets are retreating.*

It was like a punch to the gut. By Kal's count, they'd lost a tenth of their fleet in less than thirty minutes and had nothing to show for it. The Jadid, who were supposed to save them, were instead being cut down, their ships useless against the planetary defenses built by the Nasi.

*Think we should return to the surface, sir?* Kimathi asked.

*Salamis, what's your situation?* The battle may be lost, but they needed to salvage any success they could.

*Nasi fighters are patrolling the area,* Ramos said. *They know we're here, just not where we are.*

Kal thought about it. This was the best chance they'd get to inspect whatever was destroying the fleet up close. If they got near enough to scan with their suit's sensors, perhaps they could figure out a way to destroy it.

*Sergeant Kimathi, keep going. We're going to see what the hell this thing is,* Kal said.

The ocean floor appeared in front of Kal. It was a lifeless expanse of rainbow-hued sand as far as he could see. The four members of Alpha Team glided a few meters above the bottom, moving toward the estimated location of the plasma cannon.

*Don't get too close,* Kal warned. *We don't know if that thing will fire again.*

*Roger, sir,* Sergeant Chedjou replied.

Private Ricci stopped and began drifting almost aimlessly along the ocean floor. Kal checked the private's status icon. It was green—he shouldn't be having any technical issues.

*Ricci, you okay?* Chedjou asked.

There was no response except the sound of gasps of air being sucked in; the kid was hyperventilating. Kal muted his microphone and tapped into the private net between Chedjou and Ricci.

*—get moving.* Chedjou sounded annoyed.

*I... can't... breathe.* Ricci delivered each one of his words between agonized gasps. Kal double-checked the suit's systems in detail—air supply was fine. Battle suits could last for hours in space and were able to extract oxygen from the water as well. It wasn't his suit that was the problem. *It's too... much. What's down... here?*

*Bolin.* Chedjou's voice had softened. *It'll be okay. You're in the most advanced fighting suit ever created. We're going to go a little bit farther, take some scans, and head to the surface.*

*What was... that?* Ricci's voice squeaked in fear. *I saw something. Jellies! There're Jellies down here. We gotta get out of here!*

*No, there aren't,* Chedjou said calmly. *You can use your sensors. Look around there's—*

*Is Ricci okay, Sergeant?* Private Scott Chadha asked over the Alpha Team net.

*He's got some suit issues,* the team leader lied. *Sir, can you and Private Chadha continue? We'll catch up.*

*Sure,* Kal replied, *Chadha, on me.*

Kal continued forward, with the private trailing him. He continued to scan the ocean floor. Nothing was showing up on any of his suit's sensors. Whatever was firing the beams was well hidden.

*Anything?* Kal asked the private.

*Nothing, sir,* Chadha replied.

Kal's suit only detected solid rock beneath them. There had to be something down there. He couldn't imagine what could generate the beams of pure energy that he'd seen, but it had to be enormous.

*Sir, we've found something,* Sergeant Kimathi called over the net.

*What is it?* Kal asked.

*Something melted the seafloor. The sand's been fused into glass.*

As Kal got closer to the sergeant's location, he saw what he meant. A circle, about half a kilometer in diameter, of melted sand lay on the ocean floor. It wasn't obvious at first— particles of sand had settled on top, partially covering it—but it was unmistakable on his suit's sensors. Kal quickly trained every single sensor he had on the center of the ring, trying to see if he could see anything else.

*We've got company,* Chedjou called out. *At least ten Nasi heading toward our location. They know we're here.*

*I'm going to get a visual on the weapon,* Kimathi said.

*Wait, that thing could still go off.* Kal worried they were too close already.

Kimathi ignored Kal's warning and sped into the center of the circle. Kal swore under his breath, but there was nothing he could do about it right now.

The red icons of the Nasi soldiers appeared on Kal's tactical map as they came within range of the team's sensors, speeding toward their location. Kal still wasn't sure if they knew the Skulls were there or were guessing that they would go to the weapon. Either way, the result was the same; the Skulls had to get out of there.

*Kimathi, we've got to go,* Kal shouted. *Chedjou, is Private Ricci's suit fixed?*

*It'll hold for now,* she replied, continuing the lie. *But I don't think it can withstand any action.*

*Okay, head to the rest of the team,* Kal ordered. *We'll protect Ricci.*

*Got what I could,* Kimathi called out. *Let's get out of here. Both teams, start ascending and head away from the Nasi.*

As they rose, the dark ocean water pressed in on Kal. Normally, when he wore a battle suit, he felt superhuman, like a god from the ancient stories. Now he felt helpless. There was nothing they could do except flee—engaging the Nasi would be suicide. The fleet had retreated out of the system and Kal couldn't see anything except the darting lights of ocean creatures around him.

The *Salamis* had evacuated the area and was being harassed by several of the Nasi fighters. Unfortunately, some of the Nasi fighters were still circling in the air above the Tac-1 squad. The two teams continued to travel to the surface while moving laterally away from where they'd entered the water. They would have to hope their advanced battle suits' cloaking devices would keep them hidden from the Nasi sensors.

Kal swore as he realized that a dozen more Nasi soldiers had jumped from the ships above on his heads-up display. They'd split into four groups, and each entered the water several kilometers from where the Skulls had, effectively encircling them. *They're going to close in on us*, Kal realized. The water and their cloaking devices could make it difficult for the Nasi to track them, but if the soldiers got close enough, they couldn't help but find the Skulls.

The enemy was too close for them to communicate; they could triangulate their signals even if they couldn't intercept them. Kal and the rest of the team followed Kimathi silently as he continued to move up and away from the Nasi weapon. The four Nasi teams rapidly circled around the drop site, staying near the surface. Abruptly, they stopped their circling motion and began moving directly at the Skulls.

*Full thrust straight up*, Sergeant Kimathi called over the net. The need for radio silence was over. *Salamis, get ready. It's gonna be hot and heavy.*

The ocean water buffeted Kal's suit as he shot upward at full power. The darkness began to recede, replaced by the soft glow of the sun. He shot through the water's surface and into the air with three Nasi closing in on him. His suit sputtered for a moment as it adjusted from water to air and then the atmospheric thrusters took over, and Kal felt a jolt of acceleration.

An alarm blared in his suit; one of the Nasi must have a lock on him. He didn't bother to look where they were and instead quickly dove back into the water to avoid the missile surely coming his way. A muffled thump sounded around him as it exploded against the ocean surface above him, the water absorbing the blast.

*Salamis, you need to get here now!* Kimathi's voice sounded ragged and desperate.

*We're working on it,* Sampson replied angrily.

Kal examined the tacmap in his heads-up display. One of the other clusters of Nasi had reached their location, meaning they had six Nasi soldiers trying to kill them. The Skulls were good, but the Nasi had the distinct advantage of superior weaponry.

Kal flew back out of the water and a large plasma bolt sizzled across his field of vision, missing him by centimeters. He turned to see one of the Nasi assault ships hovering over the ocean water, its thrusters generating small rippling waves on the surface. The ship's two side-mounted plasma guns strafed across the area.

A cutoff scream tore across the net, and Kal turned just in time to see Private Ricci dive into the ocean, smoke trailing from where his legs had been. The private's icon changed to yellow on the tacmap as his suit registered the hit.

*Sergeant Kimathi, where are we heading?* asked Chedjou.

There was no response. *Kimathi,* Chedjou repeated. *Should I get Ricci?*

Still no response. Sergeant Kimathi was frozen, circling over the water. If the squad didn't move, they'd be dead in seconds.

*Ekon!* Chedjou gave a full-throated yell.

*I... I.* Kal could hear the man's labored breathing through the net. *Salamis, where are you?*

*We're heading your way now,* Kanumba said. *ETA is ninety seconds.*

*Okay... okay...* the young sergeant muttered to himself.

*Sandra, go get Ricci,* Kal ordered. *We don't leave people behind. Not when they can still survive.* He set a rally point to their east on the shared tactical map. *Everyone else, head to this point. Salamis meet us there.*

Sergeant Chedjou dove into the ocean and a plasma bolt hit where she'd entered the water with a gout of steam. The rest of the team flew to the rally point, weaving in and out of the water and through waves to avoid the Nasi fire. The Nasi assault ship turned and sped past them and then slowed to a hover.

A bolt barely missed Kal as he dove under the water and beneath the hovering ship. When he resurfaced seconds later, his suit's alarm went off—more missiles inbound.

*We've got to do something about this assault ship,* Nicole said. Kal could sense the desperation in her words. *They're going to tear us to pieces.* The ship hadn't hit any of them yet, but it had slowed their process, allowing the armored Nasi soldiers to get closer to the Skulls.

*We've tried,* Bhatt replied. *None of the weapons on our suits will damage it.*

The assault ship chased after Kal focusing most of its fire on him. He swung up and down, sometimes skimming off the waves as he dodged the missiles and plasma fire.

*Sir,* Sergeant Bhatt asked, *can you fly straight ahead?*

*That seems like pretty certain death,* Kal replied.

*Just for a second,* Bhatt cajoled. *Promise I'll make it worth your while.*

*Fine.*

Kal stopped his evasive maneuvers and flew straight ahead, as fast as his suit would go. At first, the Nasi assault ship appeared confused and continued to sweep its fire to either side of him, expecting him to dodge left or right. When the pilot realized he was flying straight, they moved in for the kill, speeding up and unleashing an almost continuous stream of plasma fire.

*Dive now!* Bhatt called out.

Kal cut his thrusters and dropped into the ocean, turning himself in the air. Sergeant Bhatt emerged from the ocean behind him with her arm pointed directly up, blade extending out of her gauntlet. It pierced the underside of the Nasi assault ship in a shower of sparks and flame, cutting through a portion of the ship's underside before snapping off her suit. The impact flipped the sergeant head over heels and sent her careening back into the water with an enormous splash.

*Ugh.* Bhatt grunted as her icon turned yellow.

Flames and smoke billowed from the assault ship's underside as it crashed into the water in a blast of water and steam.

*My thrusters are out,* Bhatt said. *Could use a hand.*

*On my way,* Kal replied as he flew to where the sergeant crashed in the water. He grabbed her by the ankle and activated his thrusters, dragging the sergeant by her ankle. The *Salamis* was almost at the rally point and wouldn't be able to stay there. Kal needed to get to the ship immediately.

*This sucks,* Sergeant Bhatt said conversationally as Kal carried her over the water, dangling upside down.

*Take advantage of the rest and see if you can hit anything,* Kal replied.

Bhatt pulled her plasma rifle from the holster on her back and began firing at the Nasi following them, still hanging upside down by her ankle.

*Got one of the bastards,* Bhatt cheered. Kal didn't bother to look back but saw one of the Nasi icons disappear from the tacmap.

The *Salamis* hovered over the water in front of Kal. Chief Ramos was manning the ship's side machine gun and sending a seemingly unending supply of rounds at the Nasi soldiers that were trailing him. As the squad neared the ship, the plasma fire from behind tapered off, the Nasi beaten back by Ramos.

Kal pivoted to one side and then quickly swept back into the ship, landing on the cargo bay floor with a crash and tangling himself up with Sergeant Bhatt.

Sergeant Chedjou came crashing in behind him, holding on to the arm of Ricci's suit. Seconds later, the other Skulls entered the cargo bay, landing smoothly with a quick whiff of their thrusters.

*Get us out of here,* Kal ordered as Sergeant Kimathi touched down on the cargo bay floor.

The rear door closed as the *Salamis* climbed away from the planet.

*What do we do now?* Kal thought to himself as he lay on the floor. Even with the Jadid, the Nasi had routed Samsara Fleet and crushed their hopes in a single battle.

# Chapter Five

Kal stepped into a battle-suit dock, took off his helmet, and deactivated his suit. The back unzipped, starting at his neck and going down to his feet and hands. Someone had already retrieved the ship's medbot and the squad set it up next to Private Ricci. The bottom of the private's suit had been melted away, leaving charred and melted stumps where his legs had been.

"Someone help me get him out of his suit," called out Sergeant Chedjou as she knelt next to Ricci configuring the bot. Private Chadha ran from where he'd docked his suit and rolled Ricci onto his front, the suit making a metallic thunk as it hit the cargo bay floor. Chedjou activated the suit's emergency release, and the back sprang open. They carefully extracted Ricci from the suit and placed him on a stretcher next to the medbot. Sweat covered his face, and he moaned softly as they extricated him and attached leads and tubes from the rectangular bot to his body.

Kal turned his head, his stomach turning at the sight of the private's charred stumps. Sergeant Kimathi stood behind him, his jaw locked and eyes wide as he watched what was going on.

Kal had seen it before—the man was in shock. Ekon had seen a lot, but he was still very young, barely into his twenties. It could be hard to remember, but less than two years ago, Ekon Kimathi had just been a civilian kid, away from home for the first time, when Kal had met him.

"It'll be okay," Kal said to the sergeant. "You and I have had similar injuries. The medbot will fix him up."

Ekon flinched and looked at Kal without saying a word. He opened his mouth and then closed it slowly. His bravado was gone, the confidence and bluster of a young kid in his twenties crushed with the realization that he had responsibilities to more than himself. Kal knew he'd put Ekon in a tough spot. Sergeant First Class Asif Jones had been the team's first Tac-1 squad leader and taught Ekon everything he knew about being a soldier. When Sergeant Jones had died, Kal had promoted Ekon to replace him. The kid had wanted it and Kal had given it to him despite his misgivings.

"Go check on your soldier, Sergeant Kimathi," Kal said softly as he gently pulled Ekon toward the injured private lying on the bay floor. "Remember, you've done all of this before. It's nothing new."

Ekon trod to where Ricci lay on the floor and knelt next to him. Kal could see him whispering something to the private, who had his eyes closed and jaw clenched in pain.

"I'm heading to the cockpit for the fold back to the fleet," Kal said to Nicole as he walked to the ladder separating the decks of the ship. She gave a quick nod in response without looking away from the private.

Kal flopped down into his chair behind Lieutenant Sampson and Chief Ramos in the cockpit. The two pilots were studying the tactical map and the fold computer on the ship's viewscreen, looking for a spot to fold out of the system. Fold drives were extremely susceptible to the gravity of planets and ships; if they tried to fold from the wrong location, the *Salamis* could implode.

"We're at eight nines," Chief Ramos reported, meaning

they had a 99.999999 percent chance of surviving the fold.

"Go ahead," Kal instructed.

Sampson activated the ship's fold drive, and the stars blinked in the viewscreen in front of them, changing positions. They were now at the fleet's contingency rally point a light-week from where they had been a second ago. Blue and green icons popped up on the *Salamis'* tacmap as it registered the Samsara and Liberation Fleet's ships. Sampson hailed the fleet and then set the *Salamis'* path toward the *Ofira.*

"What are we going to do now, sir?" asked Sampson as he turned around in his seat to face Kal. "Every single time we think we're getting somewhere it goes to hell."

"We're going to keep fighting," Kal replied, putting his hand on the pilot's shoulder. "That's all we can do."

Sampson shrugged his hand off. "I just don't see the purpose. We can't keep going this way. Why don't—"

"Stop it!" Ramos glared at her co-pilot. "Damn it, Hitesh. You're an officer. Show some backbone."

"I'm just saying what everyone is thinking," Sampson replied unapologetically. "How many more people need to die in a futile war?" The words were dangerously close to treason.

"Watch yourself, Lieutenant Sampson," Kal warned.

Sampson had the grace to at least looked embarrassed. "I didn't mean we should surrender or give up. It feels like we're banging our heads against a wall, is all."

"That's exactly what the Nasi want us to think," Kal said. "I've thought it a few times myself. Truth is, we're winning this war."

Sampson gave a sour chuckle. "How d'you figure?"

"The Nasi had all this figured out years ago," Kal replied. "They were planning, gathering supplies, and plotting what they'd do. For them to succeed, they needed to end all resistance in one blow. Destroy the Earth and all those other worlds and beat us into submission. It almost worked, except some of us escaped and continued to fight." Kal held his raised index finger in front of Sampson's face. "Every day we survive, we get a little closer to winning. We started this war with nothing; now we have a fleet. Give it time and we'll defeat them."

The pilot looked back at Kal earnestly and shook his head. "Sir, I just think we're putting off the inevitable."

Kal wanted to shake the man. Many pilots were odd, but Hitesh Sampson was strange even for a pilot. He was excellent as his job, one of the best, and Kal had seen him do things in the cockpit he hadn't thought possible. But personality wise, the man was a coward, always looking for a way to get out of things.

"Just get us back to the *Ofira*," Kal said. "I'll prove to you we still can win."

Nicole watched from the side of the landing bay as several medical technicians loaded Ricci onto the mobile medbot. During the entire flight back to the ship, the private had been in a state of shock, drifting in and out of consciousness.

Sometimes he would call out asking for his parents or scream for help, thinking he was still in the grips of the Jelly. She knew the doctors could replace his legs but wasn't sure if he'd ever be on a mission again. Internal scars could be much deeper than external ones, and they often didn't have an easy fix.

"Get better soon," Nicole said lamely as the medbot floated down the *Salamis'* cargo ramp. Ricci didn't register, or at least didn't respond to, her words.

"I'll stay with him," Sergeant Chedjou said. "He's my soldier." She walked out the back of the ship with her hand resting on Ricci's shoulder.

"Sergeant Kimathi," Kal called out as he entered the cargo bay.

Kimathi jumped and turned from the departing bot to face Kal.

"Check on the soldiers," Kal said. "We had a rough mission. We've lost two people and morale is low."

"I know, sir," Kimathi responded angrily. "I'm sorry."

"Ekon, it's not your fault," Nicole said. "This happens." She tried to place her hand on his shoulder, but Kimathi shrugged it off.

"No one could have prevented what happened today," Kal said. "Not even Sergeant Jones."

Kimathi flinched at the name. Sergeant Jones had been a reluctant legend before Samsara Fleet had even existed. When he'd died, Sergeant Kimathi had had to step into enormous shoes.

"Let the team get some rest," Kal ordered. "Then get

some rest yourself."

Sergeant Kimathi nodded dumbly and then walked past Kal to talk with the remains of the Tac-I squad.

"Think he'll be okay?" Kal asked Nicole softly.

"Of course," she lied. "He's young, but he's strong. He'll bounce back."

"Chief Ramos will take care of the ship and hand it over to the *Ofira's* maintenance team. We've been cordially invited to one of General Samaha's staff meetings."

"Oh boy," Nicole said sarcastically as she mimicked a clapping motion. "Just what we need." Samaha's staff meetings were interminably boring. With a fleet made up of ships from six different species, getting consensus or agreement on anything was always a drawn-out process.

"I already talked with Colonel Petrov," Kal said. "We can attend from her office."

As they walked through the ship, Nicole could feel the cloud of gloom that hung over the *Ofira*. The maintenance crews examined the assault craft and fighters with plasma burns and pieces of fuselage blown away that filled the landing bays. The ships' crews numbly shambled out of the bay with their shoulders slumped. The hallways were mostly empty, and the people Nicole did see walked slowly with their heads down, not bothering to even look her and Kal in the eye as they passed.

"There's nothing more depressing than having hope and getting it crushed," Kal said as they exited the lift to the command level.

"We've been through worse," Nicole replied. "We just

need to focus on our next steps and make sure people know we're not giving up."

Colonel Petrov had already taken her seat at the head of the table in her conference room when Kal and Nicole arrived. General Zhou sat next to her, his face solemn. The officer had to feel a measure of guilt with how their operation had gone; he had been the one to devise their plan.

"Glad you made it back," Zhou said. "You're the only ones that did."

"The Nasi were on us almost as soon as we hit the water, sir," Kal said.

"I was just looking over some data from your mission." Zhou held up the tablet in his hand. "That weapon is impossible to destroy from space."

"It looks impossible to take out from the water as well," Kal replied. "It's too deep in the ocean and is heavily guarded."

"Our sensors recorded at least six of them on the planet," Petrov said. "Wudexingqiu is a fortress now. The beams' range is significantly greater than anything our fleet has."

"Let's see what the fleet commander has to say," Zhou said as he connected them to General Samaha's conference room.

A viewscreen transformed from the live video feed outside the ship to an image of Samaha's conference room on the *Gedorhan's Return*. The commanders of all the species in the fleet, each wearing a version of the Samsara Fleet uniform tailored to their physiology, flanked the general. The other viewscreens in the conference room displayed into the faces of the various command teams that made up the fleet and Ancient Bao Wang.

"General Zhou, how bad is it?" Samaha asked without preamble.

Zhou launched into an update on the damage from the battle, using his implant to pull up relevant charts and diagrams as he talked. The bottom line wasn't pretty. In less than a half-hour, the Nasi had destroyed five Jadid ships and damaged two more in the attack. Samsara Fleet had made it through the encounter relatively unscathed. They had destroyed two of the Nasi ships in the opening salvos, a relatively small amount considering the Nasi's numerical disadvantage.

"Those plasma beams decimated our fleet, and there's no way to get to them. Ancient Wang, have you seen those things before?" General Samaha asked.

"I've never seen those weapons before," Ancient Wang said. He was visibly angry, with narrowed eyes and a flush to his face. "Esma's kept them from the rest of us."

Nicole assumed he meant the other Ancients.

"We must send out teams to see if they're installed on other planets. These defenses are impenetrable from the information we've gathered so far," said the Kurz Commander, Field Marshall Krunalt.

"We're already preparing scouts to go to the other Human colonies," Zhou reported.

Nicole flashed a look at Kal. *Had he tapped the Skulls for this mission?*

Kal surreptitiously shook his head, understanding the look.

"We lost every assault force we sent onto Wudexingqiu except the Skulls," Samaha said. "We can't hit them from orbit and they're almost impossible to reach for even the best of our assault teams."

"We can't let Esma and her children build those capital ships," Wang's voice rose. "We're in a race against time. She'll overwhelm us."

"What about the Jadid?" asked Nicole. "Why can't you just build more ships?"

Ancient Wang paused for a moment, seeming to be surprised by her question. To Nicole, it seemed like the obvious question. If the Jadid had built their current fleet, why couldn't they build more?

"It's not that simple," Ancient Wang replied. "There are several reasons." He held up a finger for each reason as he spoke. "We can't build our fleet as fast as Esma can, and we don't have the resources she does to build them. We would have to fold them into your universe and convert them, during which time they'd be vulnerable. I also have to say that I don't know if the Jadid citizens have the will to do it." At his last statement, the Jadid officers around the Ancient shifted slightly and looked at each other with inscrutable glances.

"We should not do anything right now," said General Nervaan. The Qudoru commander was the most deliberate and thoughtful member of Samaha's staff in Nicole's opinion. "We need to wait and fully understand if they have built these beams on the other planets. Action without knowledge is folly."

"We can't sit around," countered Krunalt.

"We gotta fix our ships," said the Z'Ta Rebel Council. The three Z'Ta that made up the council—Y'dari, Y'torak, and Y'kiran—always spoke as one, each one picking up the thought where the other one left off. "There's no point in attacking or going somewhere else."

"Enough," Ancient Wang said, "we'll wait here until the scouts come back from the other Human colonies. My fleet needs to recover, anyway; it is the first time the Jadid have fought in decades, and we're still adapting to this universe." He closed the line, and the viewscreen with the Ancient's image on it blinked back to the feed of the stars outside the *Ofira*'s hull.

The Ancient's sudden departure clearly surprised Samaha, who quietly whispered to her aide. Nicole doubted she was used to others ending meetings. "You heard the Ancient," the general said after she'd recovered from her surprise. "Get your fleets ready. As soon as we hear more, we'll decide on our next actions."

"I don't think we're going to learn anything we don't already know," said Colonel Petrov after she'd closed the line.

"No, but we're more damaged than we'd like to admit," said Kal. "We need time to regroup."

"And I need time to plan," said General Zhou, stepping up from the table. "The war has changed once again. And we have no idea what we'll do next."

# Chapter Six

"How is he?" Kal asked as he sat down on a chair in the *Ofira's* medical center.

"Recovering," Sergeant Bhatt replied, running her hand through her green hair. She'd sat in the medical center for the past twelve hours keeping Private Ricci company while the medical staff treated his wounds. "But I think he's done."

Kal took a sip of the warm tea in his hands. He figured the kid'd had too much thrown at him too quickly. Kal had seen it before. Sometimes they came back; sometimes they didn't. You couldn't force an unwilling soldier to fight. They'd be a liability to themselves and the team.

"I'll talk to Zhou and see what candidates we've got." Because of their notoriety, the Skulls had soldiers lining up to join them. The trick was figuring out who'd be a right fit. Too many of them were looking to prove themselves or just kill Nasi. They wanted to be the baddest kid in the fleet and thought joining Kal's team would make that happen.

In reality, Kal wasn't looking for bravery as much as he was looking for determination and smarts. There was no end to the soldiers who wanted to sacrifice themselves to be the hero. He needed professionals, not heroes. Sergeant Jones had understood that and had been the person to pick recruits for their team. Kal feared Sergeant Kimathi was still figuring it out.

"Has Kimathi been by?" Kal asked.

"Not yet." Bhatt shook her head. "He wasn't in the right state of mind. I'll talk to him, but it might be good if you did as well."

Although she was one of his team leaders, Koula Bhatt was older than Sergeant Kimathi and had seen as much, if not more, fighting. She'd been a leader in the Patagonia Front, a guerrilla group on the Human colony of Patagonia dedicated to bringing down the Nasi occupation. When the Skulls had attacked the Nasi Foothold on the planet, she'd assisted and had returned to Samsara Fleet with them.

"I don't know if he wants to hear from me," Kal replied. Ekon Kimathi had first met Kal when he'd been at his lowest. Their initial meeting, when Kal had been a lost soul and Ekon still naïve, had always strained their relationship now that Kal was an officer with Ekon under his command. Kal didn't really know what Ekon thought of him, but he never forgot the kid had tied him up and held him at gunpoint shortly after they'd met.

"You might be the only person he'll listen to," Bhatt said. "War makes people grow up fast, but he's still young. You've been there with him the entire time, and I know he respects you."

"I'll talk to him."

"General Norman." A young woman stepped into the waiting room and looked around.

Kal stood up from his chair, feeling the age in his legs, and raised his hand. "Here."

"Sir, the procedure's finished and Private Ricci's recovering. Would you like to see him?"

"Yeah," he turned to Sergeant Bhatt, "you want to join?"

She shook her head. "Nah, I've talked to him, and I'll talk to him again after you leave."

Kal followed the doctor into the ship's medical center. Curtains hung from the ceiling, separating the bunks and their medbots from each other. It was quiet, and empty bunks sat at regular intervals against each wall. Kal spotted one with the curtain drawn around it, about halfway down the length of the room.

"Private Ricci, how are you?" Kal asked as he stepped through the curtain and stood next to the private's bed.

Ricci looked up with rheumy, unfocused eyes. Kal could see a small sheen of perspiration covering the young man's face.

"Thanks for visiting, sir." He smiled weakly. "I've been better."

Kal returned the smile. "I can imagine." He glanced down at the soldier's legs.

"You want to see them?" Ricci asked. "They're operational though the doctors said they'll still need to camouflage them."

There were two stages to getting fitted for cybernetic limbs. The first was installing the metal limb itself and wiring it to the patient's neurological system. The second, camouflaging, was adding a protective exoskeleton and the subtle touches that made it appear as if the new limb had always been there.

Ricci pulled his covers up, exposing a gleaming pair of cybernetic legs. The shiny metal appendages were just a skeleton with small servos, tubes, and wires wrapped around them.

"Very nice," Kal said. "Soon you'll forget you even have

them. My arm"—he pointed to his right arm—"and feet are all cybernetic as well. Takes a day or two to get used to them, but you do."

"Sir…" The private hesitated.

"Don't worry. I know. You need time. After all you've been through, you need a break. We're going to put you on ship duty for now."

Ricci smiled gratefully and eased back against the pillows by his head. "Thank you, sir."

"No need to thank me," Kal replied as he placed a hand on his arm. "You've sacrificed a lot for us. Take some time to recover."

Kal found Sergeant Kimathi lying on the bunk in his small cabin. As a mid-grade noncommissioned officer, the NCO rated a small bunk and fold-out desk in his room, much humbler than the stateroom that Kal had. Still, his quarters were better than most; enlisted soldiers had to sleep in large communal rooms, at least six to a room.

As Kal walked through the door, the NCO pushed himself up from the bunk and turned his head to regard Kal with a pair of bloodshot eyes.

"How's it going, sir?" Ekon slurred.

Kal could smell the stench of alcohol from across the room. Theoretically, the food fabricators had controls to prevent soldiers from being able to get drunk aboard the ship. However, there were ways around it if you knew the right people or had enough friends.

"I went to see Private Ricci," Kal replied as he sat on the single chair by the fold-out desk.

Kimathi's face fell for a moment, and he dropped his head back onto his bunk.

"He's doing well," Kal continued. "They've operated on him already and got his cybernetic legs working. He'll be getting the final touches in a few hours."

"Poor kid," Kimathi said, staring up at the ceiling.

"You have cybernetic legs as well. They're better than the real thing in many ways. He'll make it at least."

"You know that's not what I'm talking about," Kimathi said.

"Ekon," Kal said softly, "what happened out there?"

The sergeant sat up in the bed and leaned into Kal, emitting a cloud of alcohol as he spoke. "I know what you're going to say, sir. You're going to say I froze, but it's okay and that it happens to everyone. You're going to say that you're sure even Sergeant Jones—"

"No," Kal cut in sharply. "What I'm going to say is pull yourself together. It's not okay; you've got the lives of every single member of your squad riding on your decisions. You're sitting in your cabin drunk as hell when you should be figuring out how to be better."

Ekon's eyes flashed. "Kal. You of all people are lecturing me? I remember when I first met you, you were so wasted you couldn't stand. You were passed out while the Nasi destroyed Earth."

"I was a civilian!" Kal yelled back, unable to control

himself. "And you were a punk kid. I'd already lost more than you'd ever had."

Ekon took a deep breath, seeming to realize he'd gone too far. "I'm doing my best," he said.

"Look, Ekon, you knew me before everything happened. I was broken in so many ways. But I pulled myself together. That's what you've got to do. You're a good soldier, but now you've got to figure out how to be a good leader."

Ekon snorted. "Yeah, and you're doing great. We'll win any day."

Kal stood up; he needed to leave before he lost control or said something he'd regret. He knew that he'd asked more of Ekon than was fair. Unfortunately, the concept of "fair" was for children.

"Sergeant Kimathi, you need to do better," Kal said as he stood up. "Bottom line. If you can't figure this out, then I'll replace you." Kal pressed the button next to the door, and it slid open. "And go see Private Ricci in the med center. We're going to need to find his replacement."

Kal walked out of the room, his mind still on the conversation. Ekon had first met a different version of Kal, a man who hadn't cared about anything and had wallowed in his own sorrow. Kal liked to think that it was a completely different person, but Ekon's words hit an uncomfortable truth: that man was always there—waiting.

A week had passed since they'd faced the Nasi at

Wudexingqiu, and the fleet was still licking its wounds. On the *Ofira*, maintenance crews continued to work around the clock—fixing ships when they could or breaking them down for parts to use elsewhere. They were running out of materials, and the desire to do something was palpable.

Nicole looked around the conference room on the Jadid battleship. The *Galaxy's Edge* was the flagship of Bao Wang, a fleet commander and an Ancient, which made him something between a king and a god to the Jadid. She would have thought it would be enormous. Instead, it barely fit the dozen or so officers they had in there now. The room was built using the same fibrous weaves that the Jadid and Nasi used for all their ships.

Nicole had difficulty seeing the other officers in the dim room since the only light was coming from incandescent threads embedded in the walls and ceiling. A roughly circular table, seeming to sprout from the floor, dominated the center of the room with benches surrounding it. Blank viewscreens were affixed to every wall of the room, furthering her feeling of sitting in a cave.

"The scouts have returned," announced General Zhou.

"And?" asked Ancient Wang with a raised eyebrow.

"We can't confirm with absolute certainty that the anti-ship plasma beams we saw on Wudexingqiu are on the other planets. However, it seems likely that they are or are in the process of being built." He turned to one of the Jadid staff officers and nodded. Three of the viewscreens on the wall popped to life, each showing an image of a different former Human colony: New America, Patagonia, and Mariga. Yellow boxes highlighted areas on the planets' surface. "These are deep surface scans from each of the three other planets. As you can see, there are several potential sites that the scans identified. We have no idea which ones are actually weapon sites."

"Without information, we must assume all of them are," said General Neervan. The Qudoru's body shook slightly in a gesture of concern and uncertainty.

"Can't we get any more information?" asked Wang, his annoyance evident in his voice.

"If we want to wait additional weeks or months and potentially lose several precious scout teams in the process, sure." General Zhou regarded the Ancient coolly. "We also confirmed that they have started construction on capital ships on the three other Human worlds as well. It looks like they are using the same construction techniques."

Nicole felt the blood drain from her face. If the Nasi could get their construction process up and running, it would be impossible to stop them. They could launch a ship almost every week and would overwhelm Samsara Fleet and the Jadid in less than a year. She could see the others in the room realized this as well; the conversation had stopped and each of them was staring at the screens. For a moment while she sat in a room full of high-ranking officers amidst one of the most powerful forces ever assembled, Nicole felt vulnerable and powerless. This was the Nasi end game, impenetrable planets that could quickly produce new fleets in months.

"We can't wait for additional information," Field Marshal Krunalt declared. "We must take the initiative and attack before the Nasi build another fleet. I suggest we send in ground units to disable their defense from the surface. Then we send the fleet in and bombard the construction sites."

"That would be suicide," Grand Admiral Zzyrian chirped. "You Kurz always are on the attack. That won't work here."

"They'll never expect it," Krunalt shot back.

"Because it's a bad idea," the Z'Ta Rebel Council replied.

As the commanders continued their exchange, Nicole looked at Samaha. The general scanned the room, independent of who was speaking, watching the others' reactions.

"We can't attack any of the planets directly," Nicole said, cutting through the chatter of the commanders' cross-talk. "Even if we get a single planet, we'll lost the fleet and the war."

"Exactly!" Zzyrian chirped.

"However, we don't need to," she continued. "The Nasi must get the resources they need to build these ships from their other planets. The tributes that they are taking from your planets"—she motioned to the officers around the table—"are being used to build these new capital ships."

"Liberate our planets and cut off the supplies," the Torgham Emissary T'Kalu said.

"It would be a change in our strategy," Samaha said as she considered the idea.

"I like it," declared General Zhou. "We need to attack our enemy where they are weak."

"It requires us to spread our forces thin," Krunalt said. "The Nasi still have their dreadnaughts and numerical superiority. It's better to concentrate our forces at a decisive point."

The Qudoru brought up the idea of raiding the Nasi shipping lanes. After discussion, the group deemed it too risky and inefficient since the only place where they could intercept the Nasi supplies would be at the source or destination. The destination was already impenetrable, thanks to the planetary plasma cannons, and if they were going to attack the source, they'd need to liberate the planet anyway. Their only workable solution was to recapture the planets the Nasi had taken and stop their pipeline of resources altogether.

The conversation shifted, and they reached a consensus that the only way to face the Nasi was to avoid the Human planets for now and focus on the source of their materials. With Ancient Wang and General Samaha steering the conversation, they settled on a broad strategy. Samsara Fleet would split into four fleets of around nine ships each. They would cut the Nasi supply lines by recapturing their planets and cutting off the supply of raw materials that had to be fueling the Nasi construction efforts on the Human worlds. The risk was that the Nasi would already have a significant stockpile of materials on the Human planets, but the Jadid thought it unlikely since they had only recently started construction of the ships.

The group arranged their ships into four fleets: Kappa, Theta, Tau, and Zeta. Each one was a combination of the Samsara and Liberation fleet ships with about ten ships per fleet. As part of Kappa Fleet, the *Ofira* was under the command of the Kurz Field Marshal Krunalt. Theta Fleet was led by Qudoru General Nervaan. Tau Fleet was led by Tounous General Zzyrian. Finally, the Z'Ta Rebel Council would lead the Zeta Fleet.

The two flagships, the *Galaxy's* Edge and *Gedorhan's Return*, would act as a centralized command and control between the fleets, communicating information and providing "strategic guidance." Nicole was surprised at how easily Ancient Wang had been willing to relinquish his own role as the Liberation Fleet commander. Wang had quickly understood that the fleets needed to have commanders that were the same species as the citizens they were freeing. Overall, the Jadid were willing to follow the direction of Samsara Fleet's leaders though Ancient Wang sometimes overstepped. It wasn't surprising considering he'd been part of a ruling council for hundreds of years.

After several hours of planning there was one question left. Where would the Skulls and the *Ofira* go? Though no one said it, every fleet wanted the scout team with them. With each mission, their legend had grown, and no commander would willingly give up such a valuable asset.

She stole a sideways glance at Kal and could see the discomfort written on his face. He hated being the center of attention.

"Okay, stop." Samaha rubbed her face in exasperation. "General Norman, where do you want your team to go?"

Kal seemed surprised by the question. *This is probably the first time that someone had asked him what he wanted in years,* thought Nicole.

"Well, we don't know where the Nasi fleet is," Kal began. "But the Skulls are used to operating on Human worlds. Our executive officer is an expert on the Kurz. So, I think we'd be most effective with Field Marshal Krunalt's fleet in Kurz space." Nicole had been an attaché to the Kurz government on their home world of Gorash before the Nasi had destroyed it.

"Very well," General Samaha said. "I can't think of any better idea." She turned to General Zhou. "You've got the strategy, General. Get the operations teams together to figure out how to make this work."

"Seems like we're a hot commodity," Nicole said as she blew on the soup in front of her.

Kal sat across from her, also waiting for his dish to cool. They were in the ship's lounge grabbing something to eat after their marathon session with the assorted senior officers. Images of serene landscapes from Earth and its colonies played over the viewscreens.

"Yeah, I guess every fleet wants the lucky scout team," Kal replied, shifting in his seat.

"Kal, it's more than just luck," Nicole replied. "Do you know how many scout teams there are in this fleet?" She didn't wait for him to answer. "At least a hundred of them. Of those teams, the casualty rate on deep infiltration missions is something like fifty percent. We've not only single-handedly accomplished more than those other teams have combined, we've remained alive."

"Not all of us," Kal said as he looked down at the tendrils of steam rising from his food.

Nicole wanted to lovingly smack the man on his head. He was horrible at accepting praise or responsibility for things that went well. He was great at accepting the blame, but there was some wall in his head that went up as soon as anyone said anything positive.

"You nervous about returning to Kurz space?" Kal asked.

Nicole gazed at a viewscreen on the wall as she felt her own defenses going up. His question reminded her of a life she'd rather forget, of being an attaché in a dead-end position on Gorash. It reminded her of the decisions she'd made in another life, to funnel what she'd thought was innocuous information to a nameless buyer for money that she sent to her family on Earth.

"I guess that's a yes," Kal said.

"It's going to be strange," Nicole admitted, taking a tentative sip from her bowl. "I don't even know how the Kurz will react if they find out what I've done." The Kurz had a very strict sense of morals and honor. If they knew what she'd done, even though it had been giving away Human secrets and not theirs, she wasn't sure how they'd react.

"We'll keep it to ourselves. There's few people who know anymore," Kal said, a frown flickering across his face. There weren't many people who knew because so many had died already. "I'm more worried about General Krunalt. He's liable to just go charging straight at the Nasi."

The Kurz were known for their overly aggressive tactics.

Their aggressiveness in combat often made people forget they were a relatively peaceful species. They didn't seek conflict, but when it occurred, they charged straight into the battle with all weapons firing.

"I've heard some of their officers talking," Nicole said. "They say he's too cautious which I take as a good sign. Besides, we need to be direct. The longer this campaign lasts, the more time the Nasi have to build ships for their fleet."

"Have you spoken to Taisha?" Kal asked.

"Yeah," Nicole replied, "her morning sickness is subsiding, finally." Chief Kanumba had spent a good portion of the past two months bent over a latrine.

"I remember when... Li Na was pregnant." Kal always hesitated when mentioning his deceased wife. Nicole never pressed the issue. She knew there was a part of the man she'd never reach. It was a part that belong to Li Na and his two children: Stephen and Lan Fen. "She hated it. Wouldn't eat anything from a food fabricator."

"Kanumba's got it rough. I'm glad she's doing whatever secret project they've got her on."

"About that," Kal leaned over the table, "have you heard anything about it?"

"No," Nicole screwed up her mouth, "and Taisha won't say anything either. Just told me it's a big deal. Any luck with Samaha?"

"No, she's said she won't tell any field soldiers about the project, just in case." In case they got captured and the Nasi torture them for information.

"Well, if it's half as great as what Taisha says, then it could change the entire course of the war. Though I don't think it's going too well."

"I keep telling myself that things are getting better," Kal said. "I keep telling the soldiers that too."

"They are," Nicole said. "I used to wonder if we'd still be alive the next day."

Kal raised an eyebrow as he took a bite of his meal. "And you don't now?"

"I wonder less." Nicole laughed.

"Well, we've got a day until the fleet departs and several more days until we reach Kurz space," Kal said. "Let's make the most of it."

Nicole raised an eyebrow suggestively. "What'd you have in mind?"

# Chapter Seven

Kappa Fleet was en route to Kurz space, a five-day voyage. While folding, the *Ofira* couldn't communicate with any other ships, so the Skulls traveled the five days completely isolated from the other ships in the fleet. This meant that many of the regular meetings with senior commanders weren't possible, giving Kal more free time than he was used to. Kal spent most of it in his cabin, rarely talking to the other members of the Skulls outside of their regular standup. The flight crew conducted repairs and maintenance on the *Salamis* while also spending a significant amount of time in the simulators. Chief Ramos sometimes ate breakfast with Nicole or played on a game console she'd been able to get from the Z'Ta.

Sergeant Kimathi spent the days trying to find replacements for Private Ricci and Nenge. There normally wasn't any sort of interview or trial process for most units in Samsara Fleet. However, there were a lot of soldiers that had asked to be transferred to the Skulls. The vetting process was a combination of tactical exercises in the simulators and an interview with the squad leader. Before, Sergeant Jones had handled the entire process himself, but Kal joined Kimathi during the interview process and final decision. The sergeant had refused to say a single word beyond what was necessary while they were judging the candidates.

Colonel Petrov held a daily standup similar to the Skulls', but Kal only attended twice. He occupied a strange place within the hierarchy of Samsara Fleet. He was a general officer but also led a scout team, a role which normally would have been filled by a major. This strange dichotomy was a result of an understanding between Kal and General Samaha, and only added to the legend of the Skulls and their commander.

Kal and Nicole spent countless hours together while they were folding, making up for the time they'd lost while she'd been with the fleet in Z'Ta space and Kal had been leading their infiltration on Patagonia. Nicole made them spend much, but not all, of that time in the combat simulators. She was determined to be every bit as adept a fighter as the soldiers in the Tac-I squad. She already was better than Kal at everything except marksmanship. Kal had been an instructor in the Earth Defense Force and had trained for decades.

Once the *Ofira* arrived in Kurz space and established contact with the rest of Kappa Fleet, Colonel Petrov called them into her conference room.

"Fun time's over," Petrov said with a smirk as they entered. "Time to get down to business."

"Let's do this." Kal could see a knowing gleam in the colonel's eyes.

Petrov snickered as the viewscreens blinked, and the images of the Kappa Fleet's ships' conference rooms appeared on the surrounding walls. At the end of the table was the fleet commander, Field Marshal Krunalt, aboard the Kurz carrier *Frygr*.

The Kurz commander's insect-like face peered from the viewscreen. As he began talking in the high-pitched Kurz speech, which was inaudible to humans, Kal's implant translated the words to Human Standard.

"We have arrived with all personnel and equipment

accounted for," General Krunalt began. "Our goal is simple: destroy the Nasi forces in Kurz space. During the voyage, I have been conferring with my strategic staff around our courses of action." The Kurz spoke like they fought-—direct and without subterfuge.

"We will draw the Nasi ships in this area to us, specifically to the planet of Tamulk. To do this, we will send out ground forces to investigate the Nasi garrison and establish contact with the planetary government. On my command, we will destroy the Nasi garrison, which will alert the Nasi to our presence. They will send a fleet to respond, and we will engage and destroy them."

"Fleet Chief Aksoy, send your scout ships to conduct reconnaissance of the planets in the area and determine what Nasi ships are in Kurz space." The brown-eyed Jadid commander nodded to acknowledge the order. "The rest of the fleet will remain here and prepare for combat. Once our scouts have returned, we will commence the ground phase of the operation and draw the Nasi from hiding. General Norman, you will report to Colonel Hermalk, commander of my ground forces." Kal knew that Colonel Hermalk's title was second hunt commander, but his implant automatically adjusted the ranks to the closest Human equivalent.

Kal suppressed indignation at the orders. He'd maintained his autonomy the past year; to have to report to someone else, and a junior at that, rankled him. But it was war; he had been an officer long enough to know that his pride meant nothing compared to the mission. Nicole must have suspected how he'd feel about the fleet marshal's orders and shot him a sympathetic glance.

"We will accomplish this mission through quick and decisive action," Krunalt continued. "The Nasi have imprisoned all of our people and together we will choke the life from their empire."

The field marshal turned the conversation over to his executive officer, who went through the specifics of the mission, outline timetables, contingencies, and everything else that was critical to their success but was also incredibly boring to Kal. He sat straight in his chair as he tried to let the mundane information flow over him, knowing that it would also be available via the mission file in his neural implant if needed.

"It will be interesting to see what the Kurz do," Colonel Petrov said as the viewscreens flickered back to displaying the stars outside. "This mission may fail if they pursue their normal straight-ahead mentality. The Nasi are tricky."

"The Kurz can adapt," Nicole said. "It may be tough, but they can do it."

*General Norman.* Kal could see that the synthetic voice from his implant was coming from Colonel Tyrgoral Hermalk, the ground forces commander. *I have a meeting with my staff now. You need to attend. Immediately.*

Nicole and Petrov looked at Kal expectantly, seeing that he had received a message on his implant. "You mind if we use the conference room?" Kal asked. "Colonel Hermalk wants to meet now."

"Of course, sir," Petrov replied, standing up. "You want to make sure you make a good impression with the new boss."

She smiled.

Kal used his implant to activate the viewscreens. The image of the Kurz colonel and his commanders appeared on the screens. Like the previous meeting, they were spread across several ships.

"General Norman, I've heard much of your exploits against the Nasi," Hermalk said. "It will be good to have someone of your stature on my team."

"Thank you." Kal inclined his head.

"My understanding is that you have experience on Tamulk," Hermalk said. At the beginning of the war, the Skulls had tried but failed to secure help from the Kurz leader, Chief Planetary Counselor Rohr, on the planet.

"Yes," Kal replied.

"Good. Then you will support our Honor Force when the ground phase commences in a week. I want to make sure that you are all clear on our strategy so that your soldiers have time to train while we wait for our scouts to return. Your mission will be to meet with local officials, brief them on our mission, and find out what they've agreed to with the Nasi. They are surely bound by some agreements, and we will need to understand exactly what." Despite having entered into the agreement under duress—Counselor Rohr had agreed to the Kurz terms after they'd killed a third of the planet's population—the Kurz still saw it as binding.

"The Honor Force is our most effective ground unit and will act as the main effort for this mission. They will scout the Nasi base while you are meeting with the government."

"Shouldn't *they* talk with the government?" Nicole asked.

"We're not Kurz."

Colonel Hermalk's tan skin darkened in annoyance. "No, we shall have the honor of killing the Nasi. They have captured our planet, and the Kurz will be the ones to liberate it."

"I've worked with the Kurz before, but—" Nicole began.

"There will be no more questions or discussion," Hermalk said, cutting her off. "General Norman, I will send the data files we have on the planet and mission to your team. You have between now and when the scouts return to train and prepare for the mission."

The screens blinked and returned to the peaceful image of the stars outside the ship.

"Well, I guess we've got our orders," Kal said, shrugging.

"This seems like a bad idea," Nicole declared. "Cross-species communications—especially when so much is on the line—is tough."

Kal stood up and patted her shoulder. "That's why we've got you."

"Any questions?" Kal asked as he stood by the viewscreen in the *Ofira's* galley. Nicole leaned against a viewscreen next to him, tea in hand, watching the rest of the team. Kal had reiterated the details of the Skulls' mission on Tamulk for what felt like the thousandth time. The plan remained identical to the one that Colonel Hermalk had briefed his leaders on five days prior. The Skulls were tasked with a way to establish contact with Counselor Rohr or another representative of the planet's government. The Nasi would be watching for them, so they had to establish contact in a way that wouldn't tip their hand.

While the fleet waited for the scouts to return, they went through almost constant battle drills. The Kurz leaders were laser-focused on the mission and drove their soldiers hard. Unfortunately, but not surprisingly, their scouts had returned empty-handed. It made sense for the Nasi to remain in deep space away from any planets so they couldn't be ambushed. The Kurz didn't seem to care that they hadn't been able to find the enemy, but it made Nicole nervous.

"Sir, why are the Kurz not meeting with their own leaders?" asked Bo, his head turned quizzically.

"I asked the same thing. They want the honor of freeing their own people," Nicole replied. She just hoped the decision wouldn't come back to bite the Kurz. The Honor Force might be fierce fighters but did not have the track record the Skulls did.

"Seems simple," Sampson said as he cracked his knuckles. "Finally, an easy mission."

"You're going to regret saying that," Chief Ramos said. "Mark my words."

For once, Sampson appeared to be a good mood. Instead of his normal sour expression, the man just laughed. "Don't be afraid to enjoy it when things go your way, Chief."

"Sergeant Kimathi, questions?" Kal asked.

Kimathi had been quiet the entire briefing. As the team's squad leader, he was critical to the mission. Normally Ekon liked to interrupt during mission briefings, sometimes to make an observation, sometimes just to tell a joke. During this one, he'd remained silent and watched from the end of the galley's bench without saying a word.

At the mention of his name, Kimathi slowly turned his head to regard Kal. His face remained cold and solemn without the normal smirk or twinkle of mischief in his eyes. "No, sir."

Kal returned the gaze for a moment and then switched off the viewscreens. "We leave in an hour. Get the squad ready."

Everyone cleared out of the galley until it was only Nicole and Kal left. He hadn't moved a muscle since the rest of the team had left and remained standing at the end of the table, staring at the spot where Kimathi had sat.

"You think I'm too hard?" Kal asked.

"No," Nicole answered truthfully. "I think this entire war is hard. I have faith in Ekon. He'll figure it out."

"I hope so," Kal said.

"You want me to talk to him?" Nicole asked.

Kal shook his head. "He's got to figure it out himself. If he can't get used to the responsibility, then I don't think there's anything we can say to him."

Nicole didn't think was true. There were things that Kal could say, but he wouldn't. Kimathi had lost his confidence in himself and was looking to his commander, a man he respected for a gesture of faith. For some reason Nicole couldn't understand, the man wouldn't provide it.

❖

The *Salamis* slowly rose off the plate metal landing bay floor and glided through the energy shield keeping the atmosphere inside of the bay. Nicole sat on a bench in the galley watching the video feed from the ship's exterior camera. All the members of the Tac-I squad sat next to her, having already done all the checks on their battle suits.

The two new soldiers, Privates Sato and Fischer, sat nervously at the far end of the bench looking around the room. Nicole knew that Kal had been involved in vetting them for the team, something he'd never done when Sergeant Jones had been the squad leader. She had to imagine that Ekon had noticed as well.

"You ready?" Sergeant Bhatt asked Private Fischer.

"Yes, Sergeant."

"Good. Remember, do exactly what I say. If you have questions, ask them, but ask me. Leave Sergeant Kimathi alone; he's got more than you to worry about." Bhatt leaned toward the young private. "And whatever you do, don't talk to an officer unless you have to." She smiled. "That one's more for you than for them."

"Hey," Nicole protested. "You can always talk to us."

"You *can*... but you shouldn't." Bhatt punctuated her statement by lightly jabbing Nicole's arm.

"Prepare to fold," Lieutenant Sampson called over the intercom. Kappa Fleet was only a couple of folds away from Tamulk. They would be there in less than a minute. "Folding."

The stars blinked in the viewscreen. Nothing happened for a second, and then the viewscreen blinked again. This process repeated itself a couple more times until Tamulk appeared in front of them. From this distance, it looked like a dirty brown ball of clay—the bright colors of the planet's surface mingled into each other. A tacmap on the wall showed nothing orbiting the planet except its orbital station.

Nicole used her implant to zoom in on the station. Clearly, someone had been conducting repairs on it. When she'd last seen it, the station was destroyed, a pile of twisted and melted metal floating around the planet. Now there were ships traveling to and from the station as well as several large commercial freighters docked next to it connected with cables and conduits.

Almost every inhabited planet had an orbital station. Large warships, like the *Ofira* and commercial freighters, couldn't land on a planet. Instead, they docked at the orbital station to on- and offload supplies and passengers. Smaller cargo shuttles would then take the materials and passengers to and from the planet's surface. It made sense that the Nasi would rebuild the station—or force the Kurz to—since it allowed them to get supplies off planet much faster than if they just had to use their own ships.

"Looks like they're definitely shipping supplies out," Nicole said as she watched the Kurz transport vessels landing and departing the station on the screen.

"The Nasi are just building up their war machine," Sergeant Kimathi said. "They just keep going. Every time we think we've got them stopped they find some new way to screw us over."

Both team leaders turned and shot a look at the squad

leader. Talk like that was never okay from a leader, especially right before a mission.

"We've beaten them at every turn," Nicole said quickly. "They're on the ropes, trust me."

"Yeah," Ekon snickered, "they really seem that way considering they're—"

"Sergeant Kimathi, perhaps we should get to the cargo bay and check the equipment," Sergeant Chedjou interrupted. She kicked her feet over the bench, stood up, and grabbed Ekon by the arm, leading him out of the galley.

"Don't worry," Nicole said to the two new recruits. "It's just nerves. You'll find this happens when you're starting a mission."

"Ma'am, this isn't my first mission," Private Fischer said, looking at her with his large dark brown eyes. "Sergeant Kimathi's shook. I've seen it before. I just hope it doesn't bite us in the ass."

"Me too," Nicole whispered to herself.

# Chapter Eight

Tamulk was every bit as colorful as Kal remembered from their first mission there. Kal sat on his seat in the back of the cockpit and examined the planet on his console. Vast swathes of brightly colored forest covered much of it, reminding Kal of Altterra, the Jadid home world. When they'd last been there, craters from Nasi orbital bombardments had dotted the landscape. Now as he studied the surface from space it looked untouched. As they entered the atmosphere, he noticed that even the cities—where the Nasi had concentrated their fire—looked as if nothing had happened.

Sampson had activated the optical cloak before folding to the planet, and so far, there was no sign that the Kurz government or the Nasi garrison on the planet had detected their presence. The *Salamis* would land close to the capital city of Shridahz, and the Tac-I squad, along with Kal and Nicole, would attempt to contact Chief Planetary Counselor Rohr. Nicole knew some Kurz officials on the planet from her time as an attaché, and they were relying on them to make a discreet connection. They just had to find them.

"Found a spot here," Chief Ramos said, placing a mark on the tacmap.

"Heading over," Sampson replied as he turned the ship toward the designated landing area.

Kal used his implant to send a short and untraceable coded message over the planet's network to the Kurz Honor Force. Every planet had a network that was used for communication and to distribute news and information. Citizens could access it through any computer, including their neural implant, to perform a variety of tasks. The problem was that although the messages were encrypted, the network was open to all. Kal couldn't be sure, but thought it was how the Nasi had discovered them during their last mission there. This time they weren't taking any chances—there would be no direct communication over the net, only small coded messages like the one Kal just sent.

The *Salamis* slid through the treetops and touched down gently on the forest floor. Underneath the rich canopy, the spray of gray bushes scattered across the blue ground appeared dull.

"I'll get the projectors," Ramos said, getting out of her chair.

"I'll join you," Kal said as he stood up. "Sampson, I'm not sure how long we'll be, just stay alert."

"Roger, sir," the pilot replied without looking up from his console.

Nicole and the Tac-1 squad were already waiting in the cargo bay with their battle suits on. Bo would remain with the ship. Tamulk was a relatively cosmopolitan planet and seeing Humans on the planet would not be out of place. But a Jadid would certainly raise eyebrows.

Ramos grabbed a small case from the corner of the bay and stepped down the ramp. She began to pull small holo projectors out the of the container and place them on the ground around the ship. They would generate a holographic projection that would hide their location to anyone outside their perimeter.

"Get last checks done," Kal said as he walked to his battle

suit. "I'll be ready in a minute."

Sergeant Kimathi gave a thumbs-up in reply.

Kal stepped into the boots of his suit and placed his hands in the gauntlets. The interior supports clamped down on his joints as the exterior knit itself closed, starting at his feet and hands and moving its way up his back. Once the suit was fully sealed, Kal grabbed his helmet from the dock in front of him and placed it on his head, sealing it shut with a click.

"Ready to go?" Kal asked through his suit's external speaker.

"Ready, sir," Kimathi replied.

Sergeant Kimathi stepped down the ramp and onto the moss-covered forest floor. The rest of the squad followed, fanning out into two teams. Kal and Nicole remained in the center of the squad next to Kimathi as the team secured the perimeter and ran long-distance sensor sweeps.

*Alpha and Bravo Teams, is the area secure?* the squad leader asked over the net. At this range they were communicating directly to each other, avoiding the planetary net.

Both team leaders responded in the affirmative, and the nine battle-suit-clad soldiers rose through the air until they were hovering above the treetops. They launched forward, flying in the direction of Shridahz, their feet almost touching the canopy beneath.

*Head to the location marked on the tacmap,* Kimathi said as the city's low skyline formed in the distance. It appeared as a sprawling mass of gray and brown spilled across the bright forest that surrounded it. Kal could see transports flying above the streets and between the oblong buildings, forming narrow lanes of vehicles in the air directly above the buildings.

They touched down in the middle of a small hollow encircled by a wall of gray bushes and covered by an umbrella of multihued trees. The space was more open than Kal would have liked, but there was no way they could scout the area looking for the perfect place to stow their suits.

As Kal lifted off his helmet, the pungent floral perfume of the forest embedded itself in his nostrils. Several squad members rubbed their noses or sneezed as they tried to adapt to the fragrance. Kal joined the others in exiting their suits and then activating the anti-tamper protocols. They were all dressed in the free-merchant outfit—a loose blouse above cargo pants—that had become the unofficial uniform of the Skulls. It allowed them to pass through most planets unnoticed as just another group of merchants there to drop off and pick up cargo.

"Chedjou, your team will take lead and Bhatt will cover the rear," Sergeant Kimathi said. "Remember, don't fire unless fired upon."

If they got into a firefight with the Nasi or Kurz security, they were in deep trouble. The only weapons they had were small plasma pistols in holsters strapped to their thighs. They wouldn't do much against military-grade high-powered rifles and armor.

The fire teams staggered their departure from the small hiding area so that they would travel independently of each other while remaining close. They could communicate directly through their neural implants without transmitting over the planetary net if they stayed close together. Kal walked with Nicole and Kimathi, trying to appear relaxed while also watching everything. The colorful forest gradually gave way to small maintenance yards and industrial buildings.

Kurz workers milled about the area loading cargo, talking to each other, or directing pallet lifters. Even from hundreds of meters away, Kal felt a small shiver when he saw the enormous creatures. At around three meters tall, the Kurz towered over Humans. They walked on two feet with a slight hunch and had wickedly long claws sprouting from their wrists and over their hands. Kal had heard that the first Humans to see them had believed they were meeting mythological daemons. He wasn't sure if that was true but could understand why they would feel that way.

One advantage to their relatively small size was that the Humans could remain inconspicuous as they crept through the industrial area. They slipped through alleyways and between transports and the warehouses and factories turned into homes and shops. Kurz families walked the streets, animatedly talking to one another while transports flew overhead. If Kal hadn't known any better, he would have thought the Nasi had never been there. As they neared the city proper, Kal saw several ramshackle developments that stood out from the hard-walled buildings around them. Kal realized that they were the craters from the Nasi bombardment. The Kurz had filled them in and erected tents and makeshift buildings on the site.

*Keep close,* Ekon called to the other teams through their local net. *We're approaching the objective.*

They were heading to a small restaurant in the middle of one of the open markets that dotted the city. When they'd landed, Nicole had sent an anonymous encoded message to the two Kurz senate emissaries that they'd talked to before, asking to meet there. They hoped that the two officials would be willing to take them to Counselor Rohr. It was a risky maneuver but the best they could hope for.

The market was as busy and chaotic as Kal remembered it. Creatures of all species—Kurz, Human, X'Ado, Nordlok, and more—walked, crawled, or slithered through the area, many of them pushing sleds filled with goods. The stalls and tents were arranged in no particular order, their entrances facing in every direction without any noticeable pattern. Kal could smell the stench of fresh Kurz cooking wafting over the crowd, making him want to gag—though he'd heard some Humans liked it. What was remarkable was how normal the scene felt to him, just a typical, if chaotic, market.

As they wove through the crowd, occasionally stopping to inspect a stall, Kal monitored their progress using the map in his neural implant to make sure they stayed on task. Although he couldn't see them, Kal knew the other teams were in the market as well, looking for any Kurz or Nasi listening devices or soldiers. After they'd surreptitiously inspected the area around the restaurant, Nicole tugged Kimathi toward the door.

"Let's grab something to eat," she said with a small pout.

"We've gotta get the supplies loaded," Ekon protested, pushing her arm off.

"We got a little time," Kal said. "With everything going

on, it's better to eat while you can."

"Fine." Ekon stomped into the restaurant, with Kal and Nicole trailing.

A wave of stench assaulted them as they walked through the door. Racks, partially filled with multihued carcasses, were attached to the wall. The last time Kal had been there, Kurz had sat at almost every table in the place, yelling over one another while they ate the rotted flesh. Now there were plenty of open spaces, and the patrons had a resigned air about them, leaning toward each other as they spoke, their skin shifting colors with their emotions.

The three Skulls sat down at a table in the corner, keeping their backs to the walls. They had no idea if and when their contacts would show. Unfortunately, that meant they'd need to sit down and eat some of the food while they waited.

"So that shipment turned out to be worthwhile," said Sergeant Kimathi, as he continued to scan the room.

"Yeah, uh." Kal realized that a career in espionage may not be in his future. "It sure was."

"We'll have to check the ship's computer when we get back to the landing pad, but I think we cleared enough to last several months," Nicole boasted. She gave a theatrical laugh and slapped the table.

"I think we've earned ourselves a nice meal," Kimathi slapped Kal on the back. "Right, Skipper? You said you love Kurz food, right?

Kal eyed the sergeant. "Uh, yes, I guess I did say that."

"Where's an attendant bot?" Nicole asked dramatically, all the while continuing to scan the room.

"We do not use bots," said a Kurz server as he walked up to the table. The enormous creature towered over the three Humans. "We're strictly low-tech. What can I bring you?"

"I'm full," Ekon patted his stomach, "but the skip over here is as hungry as can be. What do you have?"

"Most Humans don't like the food here, but I always enjoy the Emperor's Feast. It has several cuts of our finest aged meat."

Kal groaned and waved his hands in front of his face. "You know—"

"I think he'd love that," Kimathi interrupted. He pointed at Nicole. "She may want some as well, so please bring an extra plate."

The server tapped his tablet twice and walked away before the others could protest.

"Thanks," Kal said. He wanted to throttle the smiling NCO.

"Yes, thank you," Nicole said flatly. "If you'll excuse me." She stood up and made her way toward the Kurz bio room. As she walked through the sparsely populated restaurant, the former attaché made a show of studying the dried meats along the wall while also surreptitiously scanning the room's occupants.

Ekon extolled the virtues of Kurz cuisine and complimented Kal on his "refined taste" and commitment to eating his entire meal; the corner of his mouth ticked up the entire time.

"Well, I guess *we* deserve to eat well after our haul," Kal said, hoping to change the subject.

"Yes, it was a good run," Ekon replied. "I hope we can find something here to take back with us. I hate empty runs."

Kal nodded his head. "Yeah, it's a waste of energy." Kal remembered when he really had been a merchant pilot. Much of time he'd been stuck in a backwater station or market like this because he didn't have two credits to rub together and couldn't afford to leave without the deposit for a cargo run.

Nicole walked back to the table and sat down in her chair giving them both a small shake of her head.

"The food here looks great, but I think we should leave soon," she announced. "We've got a lot of work back on the ship."

"You're right," Ekon said as the server returned and set a plate filled with a heap of rotting meat in front of Kal. "We should go right after skip gets his meal."

"I didn't give you a full portion, but I believe this should be enough for a Human," the Kurz said.

Kal used an anonymous credit chit that the fleet had provided him to pay the server for the meal. Normally he'd use his neural implant, but the Nasi or local security might trace the funds. "Enjoy your meal," the server said after checking his tablet to ensure the transaction went through. He walked away without another word.

Kal groaned inwardly as he looked at the odorous plate set before him but held his tongue. He didn't see a way out of the trap Ekon had set without making a scene or blowing their cover. In a place like this, he was sure the other patrons could hear what they were saying.

Kal took a bite, and the meat dissolved in his mouth. It

wasn't as bad as he was expecting. In fact, it was pretty good. The meat itself was relatively bland with a hint of saltiness, but the marbling of fungus gave it a rich tanginess that Kal hadn't experienced before. The meal had a complexity of flavor that was not like anything he'd ever had before. He wasn't sure if he'd feel the same way in an hour, but for now, Kal felt pretty good.

Nicole pulled a piece of meat of the plate and popped it into her mouth with a smile. Ekon looked disbelievingly at both of them as they ate. When he realized they weren't going to vomit, he took a small piece of the meat himself— then a much bigger portion. Between the three of them, they finished the plate in a few minutes.

"Either we've been in space too long, or this food isn't as bad as I thought," Kimathi said earnestly as they stood up to leave.

As they were weaving their way through the restaurant, Kal felt something pull on his sleeve. He turned to see a female Kurz sitting at a table, her head turned toward him. The flowing blue tunic she wore implied she was a government official or a well-to-do merchant.

"Greetings," she said as she splayed her fingers in the traditional Kurz greeting. "I thought I heard you say you are looking for cargo?"

Kal returned the gesture. "Yeah, that's right," he replied. "We got a deal too good to be true to come out here and figured we'd scrounge up something for the return trip when we arrived." Although he was playing a part, this was exactly the type of situations Kal had found himself in before rejoining the EDF. Normally new jobs hadn't come this easy though, which made him nervous.

"Interesting," the Kurz responded. "Where are you returning to?"

"Human space," Kal said. "Not too concerned with which planet." Best to be vague.

She tapped her claw on the table. "I have an opportunity for you." She gestured to the chairs next to her. "I am Minister Tkar Froush Qum of the Tamulk Government. We are looking for independent merchants to supplement our regular cargo fleet."

"We're listening," Kal said, as he slid into the seat. This was not according to the mission, but he had learned to not throw away opportunities because they were inconvenient or unplanned.

"My government's beneficiary—"

"You mean the Nasi?" Ekon interrupted.

"Yes." Her skin changed to a dark olive color. Kal wasn't sure what emotion that meant. "They need assistance transporting minerals and supplies from Tamulk to their planets in the former Human space. They've instructed me to find merchants willing to help."

"How much?" Kal asked.

"Depends on how big your ship is," she replied. "But a standard C class vessel can make up to five-hundred thousand credits." Kal didn't have to pretend to be shocked. That was half a year's wages right there.

"I don't know, Skip," Nicole said as the pulled on Kal's sleeve.

Kal shot her a look. "Let's hear more." He turned back to Minister Qum. "What kind of things would we be transporting?"

"Like I said, just minerals and supplies. It changes based on the day. We're trying to get any ship we can, and the cargo changes based on what's available at the time." She placed her clawed arms onto the table. "I can tell you're used to working with...undesirables. That's not what this is. It's a chance to make a lot of money doing something that is perfectly legal."

"Why's the pay so good?" Ekon asked.

"Because we need *every* ship we can get," Qum replied as her skin shifted to a more reddish hue. "You don't have to answer now. I know some Humans still have qualms about working with the Nasi." She transmitted the unique identification mark of her implant to Kal's. The mark allowed Kal to contact her directly via implant in the future. "You now know how to reach me. Think it over and let me know if you decide you want the business."

Nicole's mind raced as they stepped out of the restaurant and into the market.

"That was interesting," Ekon murmured beneath his breath.

Kal's brow was furrowed, and he was lost in thought. Nicole knew that in a previous life, he would have taken the deal without a second glance. It was enough money to buy a new ship, albeit a small one. Though they had no use for money right now, it still could be a way to get intelligence on the Nasi supply chain.

*We're taking up an overwatch position,* Nicole reported to the rest of the squad. She couldn't see them but knew they were close enough for direct communication. At least one of the teams would have eyes on them.

*Roger,* Sergeants Bhatt and Chedjou acknowledged simultaneously.

She led the other two through the market, attempting to seem interested in the goods being provided. Minister Qum or one of her agents might be trailing them, so Nicole headed in the general direction of the landing pads.

Nicole hadn't been in a Kurz marketplace for a long time and felt exposed in all the chaos. Many of the sounds and smells reminded her of Gorash, the Kurz home world. Although the Kurz spoke in a pitch too high for Humans to hear, the rest of the merchants and customers did not. The smells, sounds, and visuals made it impossible for her to process everything going on around them.

*It's an ambush. We need assistance immediately.* The urgent message came through Nicole's implant as an even synthetic voice. It was from the Kurz Honor Force on the other side of the planet. They would only have requested help in the direst of circumstances.

*What assistance do you need?* Kal asked. *What's happening there?*

The net was dead.

*Back to the rally point,* Kal instructed over the net as he started sprinting through the market. Nicole and Sergeant Kimathi were right behind him, weaving through the large Kurz and brushing aside the smaller creatures in their way. That call meant the time for being inconspicuous was over.

Nicole scanned the market as she ran through the crowd. There was no way she'd notice an ambush with everything else going on around her. What could have happened for the Honor Force to contact them?

*Salamis, head to these coordinates.* Kal transmitted the location of a nearby public landing pad. They didn't have time to make it all the way out of the city. Whatever the Kurz needed, they needed it now.

"You sure about this?" Nicole asked.

"Yes," Kal yelled back breathlessly. "We'll have to get the suits on the way."

Ekon had taken lead. His cybernetic legs allowed the noncommissioned officer to outpace them easily. Nicole was sure he was holding back so that they could keep together. As the market gave way to the tan and brown low-slung buildings of the rest of the city, she caught small flashes of the other teams running parallel to them.

The public port was close to the market on the edge of the city. As they neared, Nicole saw the *Salamis* already sitting on one of the crumbling pads. The ship had its optical screen activated, altering its sensor signature and making it appear as a mid-level merchant ship that had seen better days, the *Queen Anne's Revenge*. The only way Nicole knew it was their sleek corvette was because her neural implant was tied to the ship's computer.

The three teams arrived at the base of the ship's ramp and ran into the ship. If anyone from the port was watching, it would appear as if they'd magically disappeared as soon as they stepped foot on the cargo ramp because of the optical screen.

*Sampson, get us to the garrison,* Kal called over the net. *We'll need to circle around and get a good sensor read before we do anything.*

"Kimathi, Bergeron, join me in the galley," Kal ordered. "Everyone else, find whatever weapons you can and get ready. We don't have time to retrieve our suits."

Nicole followed him into the galley and sat at the table, watching the tacmap and video feeds from the hull. The Nasi garrison was about a fifteen-minute flight from the Shridahz for a normal atmospheric ship. For the *Salamis,* it would be a third of that time.

"Thoughts?" Kal asked.

"I wish we had our suits," Nicole said. "Even with whatever weapons we've got onboard, we'll be sitting ducks against a Nasi garrison."

"Agreed," Kimathi said as he put his hands against the table and leaned over it. "Why haven't they said anything more?"

"I'm hoping operational security," Kal replied.

"Maybe they're already wiped out."

"I hope not." Kal rubbed his temple. "We'll need to be ready for anything. Once we get close to the base, we can try to contact them again. Our implants will be within direct communication range."

The Tac-I squad remained in the cargo bay arming themselves while the three of them watched the sensor readouts, searching for any clue as to what happened. So far, all Nicole saw was almost unending forest with mining facilities rising out of it here or there. Occasionally, she'd see a city or built-up area on the horizon, but Sampson adjusted their path to avoid them.

The red icon of the Nasi garrison appeared at the edges of the map. According to the mission brief, it was an abandoned mine that the Nasi had converted into a hardened bunker system, estimated to be about five to six thousand square meters in size. Like many things in war, it was an estimate. The base's actual size was unknown.

"We're circling the base from this distance," Sampson announced over the speaker. "Ramos is scanning them with everything we got."

"Why didn't we just blow the garrison up from space?" Kimathi asked. "It would've been a hell of a lot simpler."

"The Kurz wanted to recover the Nasi equipment and records," Kal replied while keeping his eyes on the viewscreens. "Also, we don't know if it would destroy the base. The thing is a mine after all. It didn't seem like the worst idea at the time."

"Well, I bet they're rethinking it now," the sergeant replied.

"We've got casualties outside the facility," Ramos announced as several yellow boxes appeared over the video feed of the base. Nicole switched the viewscreen from optical to full sensor camera, revealing the slight discoloration of bodies lying on the ground outside the front entrance to the structure. She zoomed the image in; they were clearly Kurz and clearly dead.

*Honor Team,* Kal said over the net. *What's going on?*

No response.

"We've got to assume they're all dead," Ekon said. He wiped the sweat off his brow with his sleeve.

Kal regarded the screen, tapping the table with his index finger. "We'll need to get closer. We've got to figure out what happened." Nicole wasn't sure what was going on, but their mission was certainly shaping up differently than she'd expected.

"Are you sure you want to keep investigating, sir?" asked Lieutenant Sampson. "We can go back to the fleet, and they can bombard it from space. We're here to destroy the Nasi fleet, not capture a small garrison." Kal knew the pilot was right, but he couldn't shake his uneasiness over the Honor Team's warning that it was a trap. What was a trap?

Kal had climbed up to the *Salamis'* cockpit, trying to reach the Kurz force through his implant the entire time. He hoped he could get more information via his command console than through the galley's viewscreens. Unfortunately, they still knew nothing. There had been no movement, heat signatures, or anything else from outside or inside the Nasi garrison. It was as if they'd abandoned the entire building.

"Sir, what *do* you want to do?" Chief Ramos asked.

*I have no idea*, Kal thought to himself. What was there to do? There was no way they could take on the entire Nasi garrison, not one that had wiped out a Kurz ground unit. Still, they needed to find out more.

"If we get closer, will our sensors be able to pick out anything else?" Kal asked.

"Maybe, sir," Ramos said. "But we risk them detecting us as well."

"We can't just return to the fleet with no idea of what happened to their soldiers," Kal said. "Not without at least trying to get closer."

Sampson slowly banked, pulling the ship to within a few hundred kilometers of the base. At this distance, Kal could make out every detail of the Kurz bodies scattered in front of the base on the viewscreen. They were wearing their version of a battle suit, an exoskeleton with thrusters and weapons affixed to it. The bodies had large plasma burns across them that were too big to have come from a rifle.

"Turrets?" Ramos asked as they studied the sensor feed.

"Must be," Kal replied. "I don't see anything on the exterior of the building though." The garrison itself was a simple oval-shaped structure made from the Nasi weaves.

"We've got company," Sampson called out. Five red icons had appeared at the edge of the tacmap—Nasi aircraft approaching fast.

Kal knew what they had to do but hated to give the order. They were hopelessly outgunned and doing anything but leaving the area would be suicidal. In the end, the Skulls were meant to be a scout force, not an assault force.

"Get us out of here," Kal said. "Let's get back to the fleet."

# Chapter Nine

"You don't know what happened?" Colonel Hermalk asked incredulously.

The *Salamis* had evaded the five Nasi aircraft around their garrison, recovered their battle suits, and left Tamulk without trouble. As soon as they had returned to Kappa Fleet's location a few folds away from the planet, Colonel Hermalk had demanded to speak with Kal. Knowing what was coming, Kal had elected to take the meeting from his stateroom. No need to get chewed out in public.

"No, we don't," Kal replied. "All we know is what we told you. We received a distress call, and when we got to the garrison, there was no response."

"Then the Nasi fighters came into the area, and you left?" Hermalk's normally tannish skin was a deep shade of red.

"Yes," Kal replied. His implant could interpret some of the colonel's angry tone and added it to the Human Standard translation that was fed to his auditory nerves.

"You didn't think to land and inspect?"

"I *thought* of it," Kal replied. "But it was a wasn't possible. We had no suits and were walking into an obvious trap. Your team even warned us."

"I can't believe that the infamous Skulls I've heard so much about left comrades to die." As he was talking, Hermalk had continued to lean into the camera and his face filled the screen.

"We didn't leave them to die," Kal protested despite the pang of guilt. "They were already dead." Kal outranked the colonel and could have reprimanded him. But for what reason? He had to admit that perhaps there had been some of the Honor Force still alive in the area. He'd never know.

"Well, we'll never know for sure," Hermalk stated. "But we won't let your dereliction change our course of action. Without hearing from their garrison, the Nasi will send ships to Tamulk to destroy the planet. We'll be ready for them."

"Colonel, I wouldn't do that," Kal said carefully. "Something's off here."

"Well, neither of us makes that decision, and Field Marshal Krunalt has already decided anyway." The screen clicked off abruptly.

Kal let out a deep breath he hadn't realized he was holding in. The Honor Force had warned them of the trap but hadn't been able to avoid it themselves. The mission was not turning out as they expected. That was often the case with the Nasi, but still... Kal couldn't put his finger on it.

He stayed seated and watched through his stateroom's viewscreen as the *Salamis* glided into one of the *Ofira's* landing bays. The mechanics were still conducting repairs on several of the ships in the bay, but they looked much better than they had after the battle at Wudexingqiu. It looked like they would be ready for the battle that would inevitably occur around Tamulk.

As Kal left the *Salamis* and stepped onto the *Ofira's* landing bay floor, Kal heard an alert from his implant. Colonel Petrov wanted to speak with him and Nicole in her stateroom. No doubt she wanted to hear what had happened as well. Kal wished he had had time to file a proper mission report; it'd help him make sense of everything that had happened.

"Ready to talk to Petrov?" Kal asked Nicole.

"Yes, we're going to fold into Tamulk soon. Better give her a debrief before then."

The hallways of the *Ofira* had the energy of a fleet about to enter battle. Flight and operations crews strode through the well-lit corridors with a sense of purpose. The soldiers chattered with each other in the forced way that signaled they were nervous but didn't want to show it. Kal had to admit he didn't share their apprehension. He'd been on enough missions that he only felt the fear of entering battle immediately before it started, right as the ramp dropped and he had to jump out.

"Have a seat." Petrov waved them to her sitting area. Her stateroom was every bit as large and luxurious as the one Kal and Nicole shared.

"Hermalk gave me an earful," Kal said as a way of introduction.

"I can imagine, sir," Petrov replied. "The Kurz have to be upset."

"It's a matter of pride to them," Nicole said as she sat down. "Or honor may be a more appropriate word. To have their entire elite Honor Force wiped out by a random Nasi backwater garrison is tough for them to accept."

"I never agreed with sending you down in the first place," Petrov said. "Seemed like way too much to risk on the off chance of finding information."

"Well, I guess you were right," Kal said. "Though that doesn't help us now."

"Any luck finding the planetary government?" Petrov

asked.

"No." Nicole bit her lip. "We didn't even get close."

"Interestingly, a government official approached us about a job," Kal said. "They wanted to hire us to transport materials to the Human colonies."

"Which colony?"

"She didn't know," Kal replied. "Looks like they're hiring every single freighter and merchant they can find."

"Interesting." Petrov drew out the word.

"Definitely," Kal agreed. "It may be a way to understand exactly what they're doing."

"It also may be a way to get killed," Nicole said.

"Once we capture the planet, perhaps we should talk with Field Marshal Krunalt about it," Petrov suggested. "He should at least be aware." She stood from her chair. "I've got to get to the bridge. Krunalt has ordered all scout and fighter crews to be prepared to fold immediately. He's set up a rotation for scout ships to stay in the system. As soon as the Nasi arrive, we're to fold in and destroy them."

"So we have to sit here and be ready for combat," Kal concluded. "That'll be fun."

"Pretty much, sir." Petrov replied. "By the time the Nasi actually arrive, the soldiers will be ecstatic to see them."

As Kal and Petrov had expected, waiting on high alert became a tedious experience.

Kappa Fleet folded as close to Tamulk as they could

without risking discovery. After that, Krunalt set up a rotation, assigning two scout ships to fold and wait near the planet at a time. As soon as the Nasi arrived, the scouts would fold back to the fleet, which would then return to the planet and engage the enemy. It allowed them to monitor the planet while preventing the enemy from knowing they were there. The only problem was the fleet had to be ready to fold at a moment's notice. Any delay could mean losing the entire system.

An hour turned to a day, and then to several days. The state of being constantly prepared for battle wore down the crew. Soldiers had set up cots next to their battle stations and ate field rations to avoid having to go to the galley.

The Skulls remained on the *Salamis* which sat in one of the *Ofira's* landing bays. They treated the entire wait like a long fold. Occasionally, they'd rotate into the area around Tamulk and wait patiently by the planet for hours, their cloak activated. The fear of entering combat gave way to boredom and then annoyance that the Nasi had yet to show up.

For Kal, the delay wasn't surprising. Even with fold drives, space was vast and sending a ship or fleet to another system was no simple task. After a week, Petrov gave in to the mumbled complaints of her crew and ordered a partial stand down. The galley opened, but soldiers were only allowed one meal in a cycle. They also were authorized to sleep in their own bunks every third day.

The lull in activity gave the Kurz operations cell plenty of time to war-game every scenario. Kal took part in some of their sessions over video but stopped after a few sessions because of the almost naked hostility he received from Krunalt's staff. They clearly believed that Kal and the Skulls were culpable in the loss of the Honor Force.

Kal sat in the corner of the *Salamis'* galley watching Bo play cards with the soldiers on the Tac-I squad. Sergeant Kimathi continued to include the Jadid scientist in his squad's activities since Major Garcia had left. They'd been in the Tamulk system for about two hours, waiting for any sign of a Nasi fleet.

"I don't understand this game," Bo said as he threw the cards on the table.

"Careful, Bo," Kimathi laughed, "those are antiques."

"It's all about bluffing," Private Fischer said. "You want the other person to think that they can't beat you."

"So you lie?" Bo asked.

"Well, yeah. Except in a card game, it's called bluffing." Fischer arched an eyebrow. "Sounds more proper."

"Okay, okay," Bo replied. "Let's try again."

Kal couldn't help but feel a moment of warmth as he surreptitiously watched them play cards. This camaraderie of the mundane was something he'd missed when he'd retired from the EDF. There was no pretense or filter; all of them were in the same ship, literally and figuratively.

"We've got fold signatures, two of them," Ramos called out over the speaker. Kal barely looked up from the tablet he was pretending to read; they'd been seeing a lot of fold signatures from cargo vessels arriving at the planet to transport materials.

"They're Nasi," Ramos said after a moment. "It's a

dreadnaught and battleship."

*Take a quick sensor capture and then fold back to the fleet,* Kal ordered through his implant.

Kal was surprised the Nasi had only sent two ships then realized he shouldn't be. The Nasi's success had forced them to spread their fleet thin. They'd captured five species' colonies; even for a fleet as powerful as theirs, it was a lot of territory to control.

Ekon grabbed the cards off the table, stuffed them into a pocket in his trousers while the rest of the Tac-1 squad rushed out of the room and into the cargo bay to get in their battle suits. Kal ran to the cockpit, climbing the ladder to the second deck two rungs at a time. By the time he reached it, they'd already folded back to the fleet.

"—two Nasi ships, one of them a dreadnaught. Sending the sensor captures from the planet." Sampson finished. Kal could see he was speaking to the Kappa Fleet communications center on the *Frygr.*

Seconds later, a general call went across the fleet's net for all ships to get to battle stations and fold in ten seconds. They'd sent destination coordinates for each ship to fold to. Six of their ships would fold around the dreadnaught and the other three around the battleship.

"Folding into system in three… two… one." Sampson activated the ship's drive and Tamulk appeared in the main viewscreen.

"Where are they?" asked Ramos as she scanned the area. The Nasi ships had disappeared from the tacmap.

The tight knot in the pit of Kal's stomach exploded. Where

had they gone? Had the Nasi developed the same type of cloaking technology for their capital ships?

"Run full optical scans," Kal said. If the Nasi had a cloak of their own, there should at least be some sort of optical signature.

The Kurz ships were already disgorging their fighter squadrons. The Human, Kurz, and Jadid ships exited the bays and formed into large clouds, clearly unsure of where to fly next.

Without warning, the *Salamis'* proximity sensors went off and their tacmap filled with a mist of red icons.

"What the hell?" Sampson said breathlessly. "They're all around us."

Almost twenty Nasi capital ships had appeared, surrounding Kappa Fleet. Swarms of fighters erupted from their bays and headed at the ships. Because of the proximity of the enemy ships, none of Kappa Fleet could fold to safety—they were much more likely to destroy themselves than successfully escape.

"Take evasive action and get us the hell out of here," Kal shouted.

Ramos had kept their optical cloak activated, and Sampson pushed their ship's acceleration to the max. But several Nasi fighters still pursued them. Either they were close enough that the cloak didn't work or the Nasi had spotted them using their optical sensors.

"There're two dreadnaughts in the system," Ramos called out breathlessly. It dawned on Kal: the attack on the Nasi garrison hadn't been a trap; the entire mission had been one.

A broadcast came across the open net, and the round face of Esma Baykara appeared on their viewscreen. "Oh, Bao, are you there?" the woman asked in a purr. "Still think you've got the upper hand?"

She'd become obsessed with returning to the Human universe and extracting punishment for the wrongs she felt she'd suffered at their hands. Looking at the woman's gleeful smile as her ships pounded Kappa Fleet, Kal wondered how much humanity was left in the woman. Had time and anger driven her mad? It certainly seemed that way as she giggled over the net.

Field Marshal Krunalt's image appeared next to her on the viewscreen. Kal could see Kurz working at their stations on the bridge of the *Frygr* behind him. "I am Field Marshal Hurkot Krunalt. I assume you are Ancient Baykara," he said, his skin a dark red. "You will not find Ancient Wang here, only death."

Esma laughed quietly. "Adorable." The laughter stopped and her voice grew deadly serious. "You can still surrender."

"That will not happen," Krunalt said, his skin turning an even deeper shade of red.

"Ah, I thought not," Esma said dismissively. She cut the line, leaving Krunalt alone for a second before he gestured for his communications team to cut their transmission.

The *Salamis* was the fastest ship in Samsara Fleet as far as Kal knew, but the Nasi kept up with them as they weaved through a swarm of fighters. Nasi ships pummeled the Jadid fleet with plasma fire while the clouds of Nasi and Kappa Fleet fighters met in between. The Nasi focused their fire on the Jadid ships, leaving the *Ofira* and *Frygr* relatively unscathed.

The *Salamis* was almost in the direct center of the mass of ships, the worst place for a relatively small scout ship to be. Kal could already see the writing on the wall; this was a battle that was lost before it started.

"*Salamis*, this is the *Ofira*," came a voice through the net. "We are moving to disengage from the Nasi. You are *not* cleared to land. We will meet you at the rally point."

"Roger," Kal replied. "Meet you there and good luck."

There had been no way to get to the *Ofira* anyway. He'd already planned on the Skulls folding away on their own.

He could see that Kappa Fleet was quickly fading, their shields wearing down to critical levels, and their armor plating shattering as several Jadid missiles broke through their point defenses. Initially, the *Frygr* had remained in the center of the mass of ships, focusing its fire on one or two of the Nasi ships. Now it had joined the *Ofira* in trying to escape from the center of the battle, traveling toward the planet in the opposite direction from the Human ship. Apparently, they'd decided to abandon their fighters, leaving them to crash land on the planet's surface—very unlike the Kurz. As Kal studied the map, he realized with a jolt what the Kurz ship was doing. They weren't leaving the battle; they were going to use the planet to slingshot away from the Nasi. Something about their approach looked wrong though. If they did what he thought they were going to do, they'd end up...

It was a suicide run, not an escape.

The *Frygr* was going to ram one of the Nasi dreadnaughts on the opposite side of the planet.

"They're going to crash into the dreadnaught," Kal said to

himself.

Ramos turned back in her chair, "Who?"

Two Jadid ships went critical in quick succession, the bright orb of one explosion blossoming forward before the afterimage of the first one had left Kal's eyes. After only minutes, they were down to seven ships.

"The *Frygr*," Kal said. "It's going to slingshot around Tamulk."

Ramos studied the map. "It's going to have to make it through these fighters," she said, highlighting a cluster of Nasi fighters on the far side of the planet. "That's going to be tough at that speed."

Kal looked at the map. "Perhaps we can help them out," he said. "We'll need to engage the fighters from the other direction."

"Sir," Sampson shouted. "You're insane. We're being chased by three Nasi fighters and you want to engage a full squadron. What you're talking about is suicide. Guaranteed."

"I don't care," Kal said. "We're going to do what we can to help them. Get over there *now!*"

The pilot shook his head slowly. "I'm sorry, sir, but no."

"Dammit, Sampson, stop being such a damned coward," Kal shouted. "For once, think of something other than your own ass and get us over there. They're sacrificing themselves for us."

"That's their choice, sir" Sampson said. "What they're doing is stupid. We've lost this battle, but we can still fight again. We don't have to make the same idiotic mistake."

Kal took a deep breath and forced himself to keep his

voice level. He needed the pilot to understand exactly how serious he was. "I'm not going to argue with you. This is my last warning. Adjust course to the far side of Tamulk and engage the Nasi squadron."

"I said *no*, sir." Sampson said defiantly.

Kal pulled out his pistol and shoved it against the back of the pilot's head. "Chief Ramos, you have the controls. Lieutenant Sampson, I'm relieving you of duty. Get out of that chair."

*Sergeant Kimathi, send two soldiers to the cockpit immediately and take Lieutenant Sampson into custody,* Kal ordered through his implant.

*Roger.*

Sampson got out of his chair and turned to face Kal with his hands up in the air. The middle-aged man's face was bright red, and his mouth was twisted into a snarl as he stared at Kal. A few seconds later, Sergeant Kimathi rushed into the cockpit with Sergeant Bhatt on his heels.

"You realize you're going to kill us, right?" Sampson asked. He tilted his head at the two Tac-I soldiers. "Sergeant Kimathi, I've told the general here what he wants is suicide. Now I'm telling you. For god's sake, listen!"

"Come on, Hitesh," Bhatt said. "We'll figure this out when we're not in the middle of a goddamn battle." The woman cautiously walked around Kal and Sampson, stepping behind the pilot. She grabbed one of his upturned arms and quickly twisted it behind his back, then did the same with his other arm and slapped a restraint on his wrists.

"Get him out of here," Kal said. As the words came out of

his mouth, the ship pitched forward, and several alarms went off. A Nasi missile had detonated extremely close to the aft of the ship.

"Don't you see?" Sampson's eyes were wide, and his face had a crazed look. "We haven't even made it out of this mess, and you're talking about attacking. We're going to die."

"Sergeant Kimathi, place the pilot in one of the cabins and seal the door," Kal said. "We'll figure out what to do with him later."

The two Tac-I NCOs pushed the pilot out of the cockpit, and Kal dropped into the vacant seat. Chief Ramos had already adjusted their course so they would meet the swarm of the Nasi fighters near the planet.

"He's a *really* good pilot, sir," Ramos said.

"It doesn't matter if he won't fly us where we need to be," Kal said. "Besides, you haven't seen me fly." Ramos raised an eyebrow skeptically. "Simulators don't count."

The three Nasi fighters continued to chase the *Salamis*. They were far enough away that their plasma cannons would be basically useless, but they were still in missile range. Kal knew they needed to get them off their tail before the *Salamis* engaged the Nasi fighters in front of them. Otherwise, they'd never be able to line up their shots.

Kal had an idea. A bad one, but still an idea.

"How many countermeasures do we have?" he asked.

"We've used about half of them," Ramos replied.

"On my command, launch all of them."

"*All* of them?" Ramos asked. "You sure?"

"Yes," Kal replied. "And put all our energy into the front

shields and forward weapons."

"Sir, Sampson was right. You are insane."

"Maybe," Kal agreed. "Just do it anyway." Ramos' hand flied across her console as she complied with the order.

"One… two… three. Do it!"

Ramos unleashed their full complement of countermeasures and cut off their thrusters. She turned the ship 180 degrees to face their pursuers. As soon as they were oriented, she applied the rear thrusters, slowing their momentum. The countermeasures continued forward, their speed unchanged.

Kal waited for the tone that signaled their systems had locked onto the three Nasi ships. Several missiles were on paths still heading directly at the *Salamis*. He waited impatiently for the ship's systems to lock onto the Nasi ships while the missiles streaked closer.

"We've got lock," Ramos said as the ship's computer locked onto all three Nasi fighters almost simultaneously.

"Fire as many missiles as we can get out of the tubes," Kal ordered.

Missiles streaked from nacelles on the ship's fuselage and wings, corkscrewing toward the three approaching fighters. Kal followed them up with plasma fire, overriding the system's regulator to shoot as many bolts at the enemy as he could.

The Nasi missiles were almost upon the *Salamis*. They suddenly changed heading, speeding past the scout ship, fooled by their countermeasures.

The three Nasi fighters faded from the tacmap within seconds of each other as the *Salamis'* missiles struck home.

On the viewscreen, the only evidence of their demise was three small flashes that blinked in the far distance, looking almost like stars.

"It's official. You're insane, sir," Ramos said.

"If you think I'm insane now, wait until you see what we do next," Kal said with a crazed grin on his face. "Get us to those fighters."

As they sped at the Nasi fighter cloud in the *Frygr's* path, two more Jadid ships exploded, leaving only five remaining in Kappa Fleet. Kal felt his heart lighten somewhat as he saw the Jadid destroy one Nasi ship and disable another. They would not go down without a fight.

The Nasi dreadnaught remained in the same position, its crew seemingly unaware of the *Frygr's* plan for them. The other dreadnaught remained on the opposite end of the Nasi formation, away from the fighting.

The *Ofira* had taken some hits but was still operational, and Kal's heart lifted as their sensors registered the ship folding away. At least some of them would survive this battle.

"When we get within missile range, I'm going to fire every single missile we have left. When I say go, put every bit of power in our plasma cannons and front shields," Kal said. "Fire everything you can at the Nasi. By the time this is over, our weapons systems should be slag."

"Guess the *Frygr* isn't the only one going out in a blaze of glory," said Ramos in a stoic tone.

Kal hadn't realized it until then, but she was right; his plan was suicide. He felt a pang in his chest. Should they do this? Maybe Sampson was right. Was it better to fight another day? After the ten years he'd spent drugged and wasted following his family's death, he had been too afraid to put himself out of his misery. Kal was willing to do it now though. Why?

Because he was doing it for something.

"Maybe," Kal admitted to himself. "But I'm not trying to die, I'm just trying to save something."

Ramos shrugged in a comical manner for the situation. "Good enough for me, sir."

Tamulk's gravity began exerting more and more force on the *Salamis*, increasing their speed as they hurtled toward the Nasi. The cluster of Nasi fighters on the other side of the planet were oriented at the *Frygr* and flew toward it on an intercept course. There was no way the *Salamis* could take a squadron of Nasi fighters on alone, but Kal only needed to ensure that the Kurz ship made it through.

He waited for their targeting computer to let him know they were in missile range of the Nasi squadron and lock on. One by one, the Nasi fighters came into range. Kal waited. They were going to have one chance at this, and he needed to make sure their shot was a good one. Ramos' phrase "blaze of glory" popped into his head as he pressed the firing square on his console, and missile after missile began launching from the *Salamis'* tubes. Kal had left the ship's safeties overridden, and the tubes rapidly heated up as missiles continued to pour forth. He manually adjusted the rate of fire, keeping their temperatures at critical but not so hot that they melted.

"Do it," Kal ordered.

Ramos fired their front plasma cannons as the first missiles detonated in the swarm of fighters. Kal monitored the tactical map, looking for a sign that any of them had hit their mark. The Nasi had countermeasures of their own, and they were relatively effective, sending many of the *Salamis'* missiles careening away. One, then two, then three of the Nasi ships exploded, their icons disappearing from the tactical map. One of Ramos' shots clipped a ship, sending it lurching into the one next to it in a brilliant flash. Several of the Nasi fighters turned around, realizing they were facing an attack from their rear.

The *Frygr* barreled into the Nasi formation. Several of the fighters scored direct hits on the carrier and the ship's point defense system destroyed several more that were in its path. Kal sighed in relief as the Kurz ship made its way past the fighters and continued around the planet, heading at the dreadnaught.

"It worked!" Ramos sounded as if she couldn't believe it. Kal could have sworn it was the first sign of emotion he'd seen from the woman the entire battle.

"You doubted it, Chief?" Kal asked.

"Yes," she replied matter-of-factly.

Plasma rounds flew past the *Salamis*, interrupting their moment of triumph. Kal hadn't planned on anything beyond getting the Kurz ship past the Nasi and scrambled to think of what to do next.

"Keep going full thrust," he instructed. "Maybe we can

get out of here."

Plasma bolts continued to stream past them, and several hit their front shields, gradually eroding its power levels. By this point, Kal had tuned out the alarms blaring throughout the ship, warning of incoming fire. The Nasi fighters were in disarray—half their squadron had turned around and were fruitlessly chasing the Kurz ship while the other half focused their fire on the *Salamis*.

"Sir, if we continue going this direction, we're going to end up dead," Ramos said. "We did our part, and there's nothing left for us to do. We need to land. If we get into the atmosphere, we might be able to escape."

Kal studied the tacmap. Leaving battle now felt like cowardice. There must be something else they could do. Kappa Fleet was broken, and its ships were maneuvering to escape the planet. Large swarms of Nasi fighters mopped up what remained of the fleet and strafed the capital ships, concentrating their fire on critical systems.

Kal grunted in frustration. "You're right. Do it."

"Finally," muttered Chief Ramos as she turned the ship toward Tamulk.

Kal watched the *Frygr's* progress toward the dreadnaught. The large Nasi ship's crew had finally realized what the Kurz were doing and were turning to escape. Changing course for a ship that large was a slow process, and the Kurz carrier was traveling incredibly fast.

"They're going to miss," Ramos said, disappointment tinging her voice.

"It'll be close enough," Kal said with a smile.

The Kurz ship exploded in a brilliant ball of light that instantly consumed the dreadnaught. *Krunalt had ordered his engineers to overload their reactor*, Kal thought. Large pieces of both ships shot out from the explosion. The debris collided with other ships in the area, smashing into their hulls with gouts of flame and decompression. A Nasi and Jadid battleship were rent in two by the force of sections of the ships colliding with them. Another large piece of the dreadnaught flew into a cloud of Nasi fighters, smashing them.

With the *Ofira* now having folded out of system, there were only three ships left in Kappa Fleet and Kal could tell they were about to go critical.

A blast pitched Kal forward in his seat and smashed his head against the console. As he pushed himself off the console, he could feel a trickle of blood work its way down his forehead. The entire cockpit was pitch black. They were hurtling toward Tamulk in a ship that was completely dead. He tried to call out but was stopped by a wave of pain as he lost consciousness.

## Chapter Ten

Nicole rubbed her hands on her trousers but a sheen of sweat still covered them. The battle had been intense, and watching from the *Ofira's* galley had only added to her sense of impotence. However, she knew there was nothing that could be gained by rushing to the cockpit no matter how badly she might want to. For a moment, it appeared they might make it to the planet, then she'd felt herself slammed against the galley wall and darkness covered everything as the ship's power failed.

Nicole groped her way through the galley trying to reach the cargo bay. As she neared the door, the ship's emergency lighting popped on, coating everything in a crimson glow.

*What's going on?* she asked Kal through their direct net. Nothing.

Nicole climbed to the second deck and burst into the cockpit. Ramos had pulled several panels from underneath the console and was frantically flipping small toggles underneath.

"The blast took out our main power system," the chief said, "and the general's out of commission."

"How much time do we have?" Nicole asked.

"Before we slam into the ground?" Ramos asked. "Perhaps a couple of minutes."

Nicole hoped it was enough time. They had life packs aboard the ship, but the *Salamis* was one of a kind, a skip ship that could travel between the universes. It would be devastating if they couldn't save it.

*Bo, our power's out. Can you fix this?* Nicole asked.

*I'm already trying,* the Jadid responded.

*Okay, hurry. We've got a couple minutes, max.*

Without the viewscreens working, the cockpit appeared much smaller. The red emergency lights cast everything in a foreboding glow, reminding her of the caves in the Z'Ta home world of T'kor'nuk.

*Okay, I found it,* Bo announced. *Our primary conduit is fried and most of our weapon's systems are done for as well. But the good news is we can bypass most of the problems using the auxiliary power harness.*

*Then do it,* Nicole called back.

*Chief Ramos, on my mark I need you to adjust the relays at delta-charlie-one and echo-bravo-six to the aux position.*

*Okay,* Ramos replied breathlessly.

*Now.*

A shower of sparks erupted from the small opening where Ramos had been working. The explosion threw the pilot back into the far bulkhead of the cockpit, where she slumped to the floor. At the same time, the viewscreens and consoles in the cockpit flickered back to life, revealing the dense multicolored forest of Tamulk rushing at them.

Nicole jumped into Ramos' seat and stared at the controls. She'd never flown the ship before, but she'd watched Ramos and Sampson do it many times. How hard could it be? The touchscreen beneath her was a jumble of boxes and circles, each with small letters or abbreviations indicating their use.

Nicole cursed to herself as she scanned the controls. She knew their salvation was there somewhere. She muttered and cursed as her finger hovered over the screen. The flight controls had to be there. Then she saw it: a yellow circle labeled "YOK." Nicole pushed it and a yoke appeared from beneath the panel. She slowly pulled the trembling yoke toward herself, and the nose of the *Salamis* immediately lifted.

Metal shrieked as the ship began to level off. Shouts and the clanging of equipment rang out from the cargo bay as the inertial dampeners overloaded, unable to handle the strain of the sudden change in direction. Finally the ship was level, and they streaked over the Tamulk countryside, the forest rushing below them in a blur of reds, oranges, and violets.

*Bo, can you get up here?* Nicole asked. *I have no idea how to fly this thing.*

*I'd noticed,* the Jadid replied. *I'm coming.*

Bo arrived in the cockpit and took a seat next to Nicole. As the ship was descending, Kal and Ramos slowly regained consciousness, calling out in confusion. Bo was able to find a clearing that was far away from any built-up areas and set them on the ground with a solid thunk. Nicole helped Kal up, while Bo helped Ramos, and they slowly made their way out of the cockpit.

The mood in the cargo bay was somber. Equipment lay scattered on the floor while the Tac-I squad stood in the center waiting for direction, having already exited their battle suits. Kal was still recovering from the blow to his head. He mumbled to himself as he carefully made his way down the ladder and into the cargo bay. She was just grateful for their medbot, which could treat his concussion and prevent any long-term brain damage.

"Get the soldiers on something," Kal whispered to her, his voice unsteady. "We can't have them idling around. Not after the setback we just had."

"Of course," Nicole said. "Just rest and get treated."

She called over Sergeant Kimathi, who sheepishly walked toward her with a look of partial disbelief.

"How are you? How are the soldiers?" From what Nicole could tell, not good.

"We'll be okay, ma'am," Kimathi said. "It's just tough, is all. The soldiers, they thought… well you can imagine what they thought was going to happen. Now with Lieutenant Sampson"—she'd forgot about the pilot, another issue to tackle—"acting the way he did, they're shook."

"I understand," Nicole said in a voice she hoped conveyed reassurance, "but we need to get everyone up and working again. We'll have to figure out how to get off this rock and back to the fleet."

"What do you want us to do, ma'am?" It wasn't a question she could imagine Sergeant Jones asking. He'd have already told her what they needed to do.

Nicole thought for a moment. They needed to get the ship fixed, decide what to do about Sampson, and get back to the *Ofira*. "Get two squads to conduct patrols around the ship. See if there's anything around here. Ramos and Bo will get the ship working again." There really wasn't any purpose to sending out the patrols. But getting out of the bay would help get their heads straight.

"Roger. What about the prisoner?"

Nicole groaned as she realized who he was talking about. That damn pilot. "Keep the room sealed," she said. "We'll settle on what to do with him later."

The sergeant nodded, turned around, and called over his team leaders to relay the orders.

Nicole walked to where Bo crouched by the bulkhead. The Jadid had pulled off an access panel and was inspecting the ship's circuitry. "How is it?" Nicole asked.

Bo whistled ruefully—a very un-Jadid-like thing to do. "We've got multiple issues here," he said. "The explosion completely overloaded the ship's primary power system. Right now, we've got our critical systems—engines, life support, gravity, things like that. But the weapons, shields, and all the other ancillary systems are offline."

"So we can't leave the planet," Nicole said.

"Oh, we *can* leave the planet," Bo replied, "but not the system. And I haven't even looked at the damage to the armor on the outside. It's gonna be bad."

"Better get started fixing it then."

The sun was setting, but underneath the canopy of the forest, it was already night. Nicole hadn't given herself time to process exactly what had happened. Instead she focused on what the others were doing. She sat in the cargo bay next to Kal and Chief Ramos as the medbot evaluated them. The device used its biometric sensors to analyze their condition and then injected a cocktail of nanobots, medicine, and painkillers. Once the bot finished, Nicole walked to the galley and watched the Tac-1 squad search the area, finding nothing. She also trailed Bo as he inspected the ship trying to determine the full extent of the damage.

As she watched the Jadid examining the hull, Nicole received a message on her implant from Kal asking her to come to the galley. He was bringing the crew together to discuss what they would do next.

"So good news first. We're alive." Kal remarked dryly once everyone had sat down. "We've got a *few* things to figure out, but I'm sure it won't take long." Sarcasm dripped from his last words.

"Sir, even with our fabricator, we need several parts for the ship," Bo said. "I can't fix it here. We'll need to get parts from the local economy and a landing facility."

"Parts that are almost certainly going to be hard to find," Ramos added. "This is a cutting-edge ship. I can't imagine that any part, much less the ones we need, will just be laying around."

"We'll need to head in to Shridahz," Nicole said. "Before the Nasi, it was the main open port for the planet. If there are parts that would work on a ship like this one, they'd be there." The Kurz had allowed trade between their worlds and others but had always kept it tightly under control. They had a few "open" ports on each planet where outside ships could land.

"How long will the repairs take?" Kal asked.

Bo shrugged. "Not sure, sir. You torched the entire weapons system. I doubt we'll be able to find the parts here to fix that. For the other systems, it will depend on how much

I need to alter the ship to make them work."

"Right now, the question is how much can we save, sir," said Ramos. "Then we can tell you how long it will take."

"We need to get back to Samsara Fleet to warn them as fast as possible," Kal said. "The other fleets are in danger. Somehow the Nasi knew what we were going to do."

"It's Esma Baykara," Nicole said. "Somehow she anticipated what our plan was." The two Ancients, Bao and Esma, had worked together for years. She couldn't imagine what they'd been through but knew there was a familiarity mixed with contempt between the two.

"We faced off against half their fleet here," Kal said. "My guess is the other half is waiting to attack one of our other fleets. They must've recalled their ships from their expansion and consolidated them while we were waiting for the Liberation Fleet to stand up."

Nicole remembered the few lessons she'd received in military strategy at university. In interstellar conflict, distances were large, and communication lagged or was nonexistent. Fleet commanders had to lure the enemy from the relative safety of deep space and destroy them in a single decisive move. The trick was figuring out a way to get your enemy to commit against a superior force. Esma had managed to do that at Tamulk, and Nicole guessed she was going to do it again to one of the other fleets. If successful, they'd be outnumbered two or three to one.

"Our next steps are clear," Kal said as he leaned back with a small sigh. "We need to get off planet. Let's focus on that and then worry about the rest."

"What about Sampson?" Kimathi asked. "What are we gonna do with him?"

"I'm not sure." Kal took a breath. "We can't let him go, but I don't enjoy having him locked up."

"Sir, what he did was treason, at least under the EDF regulations," Ramos said. "Hitesh is a damn good pilot and not as much of a jerk as he seems at first. But actions have consequences, and he knows that."

Kal tented his fingers and seemed lost in thought for a moment. His bent frame reminded Nicole of Samaha and the effect that their decisions—that the war—had on their bodies. Kal hadn't been young when she'd met him, and he looked much older now. She still loved him though, loved him for caring enough to bear the burdens he did.

"I'll go talk to him," Kal said. "Others can speak with him as well. Chief Ramos, you especially. You're the one who knows him best." The truth was none of them knew Sampson very well. He'd always been a recluse, eschewing their offers of camaraderie to spend time in his cabin.

Chief Ramos nodded.

"Bo," Kal said. "Get whatever repairs you can done in the next few hours. We're going to Shridahz as soon as we're able. After that, we'll see."

Kal stood in the hallway outside Ramos' cabin, staring at the metal door and wondering what he was going to say. What was there to say? Sampson had always had a chip on his shoulder, and no one knew why. Until yesterday though, he'd done as he was told, and he deserved a chance to defend himself. Kal wasn't going to lock the pilot away without talking to him. Ignoring the debt Kal felt he owed to Sampson as one of his soldiers, Samsara Fleet was already short on personnel, and a skilled pilot wasn't something that could just be thrown away. Kal opened the door with his implant and stepped through.

The pilot lay on his bunk, his gray hair tousled into a nest on his head. His head faced his feet and the door, the loose skin under his neck bunched up, making him look like he had more than a few double chins despite his relatively skinny frame. Sampson was the only person aboard the *Salamis*, except Bowen, who was older than Kal. The difference was that Kal didn't look his fifty-plus years, whereas Sampson looked older than his.

"What'd you need, sir?" Sampson asked bitterly.

"I just came to talk," Kal said, remaining by the door. He hadn't brought his sidearm with him. If Sampson tried anything, Kal was pretty sure he could take him, and he didn't want the pilot with access to a weapon if he'd gone that far.

"At least we survived."

"True," Kal said. "We're stuck here for now though."

Sampson gave a mirthless laugh. "Figures."

"How so?" Kal asked.

"You are the luckiest person I ever met, sir," Sampson said as he sat up. "It's like you're in a holo or something."

Kal couldn't disagree. At this point, he'd lost count of how many times he should have died. He still hadn't though—or at least he didn't think so. Where he thought the pilot was off was that it wasn't all luck; there was some skill in there too. Not his own, but the skill of his team.

"I don't know what to do with you," Kal said as he leaned against the bulkhead. The words came out of his mouth before he had time to second-guess himself. "You're a great pilot, perhaps the best I've ever seen. But there's something wrong with you. Something that prevents you from being a great officer."

The pilot dropped his grin. "Yeah, I've heard that a lot. I can be the best damn person at my job, but it never seems to matter." He slammed his hand against the bunk. "I've been a lieutenant for six years now. I joined late in life, and they weren't going to let me get commissioned. But they couldn't stop me because of my flight rating. I joined the EDF because they told me it was a meritocracy. If you're the best, you'll be treated like it." He shook his head ruefully. "But it's just the same as everywhere else."

"Sampson, I'm going to be honest." Kal took a deep breath. "Your problem is that you're an ass. No one wants to be around you, and we can't promote you because you don't seem to care about your fellow soldiers."

The lieutenant looked up, shocked. Kal doubted either of them had realized that this was where the conversation was heading. "That's the reason you're still a lieutenant. You do a great job at being a pilot, but you've made it painfully obvious you'd be horrible as anything more."

Sampson was still too shocked to respond. He just stared at Kal, licking his lips. Kal could imagine that the officer had planned on telling him off, on saying that he was trying to save the ship and they'd survived, but that was just luck. Kal doubted he'd anticipated his outburst. Hell, Kal hadn't anticipated it himself.

"Look," Kal continued. "I need a pilot and, like I said, you're good. I'm not willing to let the fleet lose you. When we get back, I'll get you transferred off combat status. You can spend the war transporting high-ranking officers around." Kal hoped the scorn in his voice wasn't apparent. It was a waste of the man's talents. "I've told the crew they can come visit you. Perhaps that'll help you make sense of all this."

Kal opened the door and walked out. Let him chew on that for a while.

Repairs to the *Salamis* took another day to be finished. When they were done, Bo and Chief Ramos swore it was the best they could do. They'd been able to get everything back online except the weapons, shields, and fold drive. Nicole tried to find out what Kal had said to Sampson, but he wouldn't say more than that he'd promised to transfer the pilot. Ramos and Sergeant Kimathi also visited him and told her that the pilot was depressed, which didn't surprise Nicole. She would be too in his situation. Hell, they all were depressed.

"Okay, let's try it out," Ramos said as she spun up the *Salamis'* main engines. Nicole was sitting in Kal's chair since he was seated in Sampson's console.

The engines came online, and Nicole felt the gentle vibrations of the ship coming to life. From what she could tell, everything was working fine. All the ship's diagnostic markers were in the green.

"Good to go?" Kal asked.

"Yes, sir," Ramos clicked her tongue. "We can take off."

"Do it then. Next stop Shridahz."

The capital was on the opposite side of the planet. Their sensors indicated the Nasi fleet had left the system, but they still stayed low to the ground to avoid detection, adding hours to their flight time. It also gave Nicole a chance to appreciate the planet. As a child, she'd never known anything except the cramped communes of Earth. Her interest in other planets and cultures was one of the things that had attracted her to the United Earth Government's diplomatic corps.

The forest spread out beneath them, covering the planet in a patchwork blanket. Tamulk was one of the few planets that had no oceans. All the water on the planet was in large subterranean aquifers beneath the soil. It meant that there were no rivers, lakes, or oceans breaking up the colorful foliage as they sped along. Nicole wondered what creatures were living underneath the dense cover provided by the trees. There must be an entire complex ecosystem that she couldn't see, living and dying as they sped over. They called Tamulk a Kurz planet, but it was no more Kurz than it was Nasi or Human. It really belonged to the creatures underneath them, the true natives of the planet.

The *Salamis'* path was relatively straight though they took a few turns to avoid cities and mining hubs. In the distance, the forest disappeared, replaced by the straight lines and angles of Shridahz's skyline. Nicole could see small transports flying over the city as well as larger interstellar ships like the *Salamis* landing and departing from the landing pads at the edge of town. They'd discussed trying to land in the forest on the outskirts of the town, but there was no way they could fix the ship without being in a port facility. Since Bo had fixed the optical screen, they could disguise the ship as a small freighter. It should fool the Kurz though they weren't sure it would fool any Nasi if they were still there.

"Shridahz port two oh nine, this is *Queen Anne's Revenge*," Kal called out over the net. "Looking for a pad to set down." Nicole smiled. Kal had used the name and registration of his old civilian freighter.

"Roger. Head to the location shown."

Ramos touched down while Kal transferred the landing fee from their credit chit. Since they didn't know how long it'd take to get the ship fully repaired, he'd set it up to auto-renew daily. There was enough money on it to pay landing fees for decades.

"Let's go make some friends," Kal said with a smile. Although he often talked about his time as a free merchant with an air of regret, she could tell there was a bit of nostalgia. He was looking forward to pretending to be a merchant once again.

# Chapter Eleven

As Kal walked through the market, he couldn't help but feel his spirits lift. The mélange of voices and the vibrancy of the traders made him feel alive. Places like this were what had called him to the stars so long ago, and he still loved them.

Kal pushed open the flap of a tent and sidestepped through. Large display shelves formed walls underneath the fabric roof, and several small chests were scattered throughout the open area in the center. Ship parts were stacked on every surface and piled on every shelf with no discernable organization. Despite the clutter of the tent and the shelf walls lining the sides, a breeze made its way through, cooling the interior and carrying the brackish scents and chaotic sounds of the food vendors in the surrounding market.

"Hey!" Kal called out as he looked around. The interior appeared completely empty. "Anyone here?"

"One sec," a voice chirped from behind one of the large display crates—a Tounous. "Keep your friggin' hands to yourself."

Kal stood by the flap patiently as he waited for the proprietor to appear. Finally, an orange-skinned creature popped through a small gap in the shelving and scuttled toward Kal on his three legs.

"Whatdya need?" the creature asked, looking up to meet Kal's eyes.

"Parts," Kal replied, holding out a tablet. "How many of these do you have, and how much do you want for them?"

"Lemme see," the Tounous grabbed the tablet from Kal's hand with one of his bifurcated arms and held it centimeters from his face to review. Tounous were subterranean hive creatures with horrible eyesight.

The creature studied the tablet, making small whistling sounds. Finally, he—at least Kal thought it was a he—handed the tablet back to Kal. "This is a crazy list, Human. Good luck finding most of those parts. I've got this and this"—he pointed to two of the relatively low priority items they needed—"but these other ones are real deal military grade parts." He looked up from the tablet at Kal. "Who are you? Why do you need these? They're military grade."

He'd prepared for this question. "Our ship is an old retrofitted EDF scout ship," Kal lied. "We stole it when the Nasi came."

The Tounous chirped in what Kal thought was disapproval. "Well, I guess you gotta take while the taking's good, eh? Anyway, you want the two parts?" He tossed the tablet back to Kal.

"Sure," Kal replied. At least he had something.

The Tounous scrambled to one of the display shelves that made up the wall and rooted through the parts, chirping to himself too softly for Kal's implant to pick up. As he sifted through the pile, several of them fell to the floor with a clang, but the shopkeeper continued his search uninterrupted.

"Hey, you got any idea where I can find the other parts?" Kal asked.

"Catch!" The Tounous lobbed a small cylinder over his head to Kal. "No, man. Like I said, those parts are super hard to find. The Kurz have put a lockdown on them anyway. They want them all for themselves. The only way to get parts like these is to talk to the Tamulk government." The Tounous darted over to a bin and rifled through it. Parts cascaded down onto the ground, making a small clatter. "Catch," the shopkeeper called out as he threw a second part at Kal, a small box that Kal thought belonged to an air filtration system.

The shopkeeper scurried toward Kal, pulling a small tablet out of a pocket on his vest. "Let's see, my friend. For a man as opportunistic as yourself, it'll be twenty thousand." That was about three times more than what it should cost.

Kal let out a mock laugh; it was time to haggle. "You seem to have me mistaken for someone else. Otherwise, why would you be trying to cheat me like this? Three thousand." They went back and forth before finally settling on a price that was higher than Kal planned on, but in the end, the Skulls had plenty of credits loaded onto their chit, enough to buy a new ship if they wanted.

He headed back to the *Salamis* with the two parts to find that Nicole and Sergeant Kimathi had also returned from their trips to hunt for the necessary parts.

"Got these," Kal said as he handed the two parts to Bo. "We seem to be out of luck for the rest."

"Thank you," the scientist responded. "Colonel Bergeron was also unsuccessful in the market. Sergeant Kimathi also tried all the salvage yards with no luck. The drive on this ship is military grade. There's nothing available outside of the government."

"Yeah, I gathered," Kal replied. "I still have another idea."

"The Alliance?" Nicole asked.

The Alliance was a criminal organization that spanned the galaxy with fronts on almost every planet and station, at least before the Nasi had arrived. They mainly dealt in smuggled drugs but were not averse to getting their hands dirty with other jobs if the price was right. The Alliance had cloaked themselves in mystery, an organization that everyone had heard of, but no one knew how to find. The Nasi had seen their anonymity and ability to operate outside the law as a threat and tried to eliminate them from every planet they conquered.

Kal nodded. "They've helped us before. Maybe they can do it again."

Because of the Nasi, the Alliance had agreed to help Kal and Samsara Fleet as much as they could. Unfortunately, the Nasi had been successful in their campaign against the Alliance and their power had waned. The Nasi were systematically destroying their fronts and agents every chance they got.

"I activated my chit back in the market," Kal said. "Maybe they'll contact us like before."

"Maybe," Nicole said. "I'm going to still reach out to my government contacts for help."

"Until we find something, we're not going anywhere," Bo said.

❖

Kal had spent the good part of an afternoon walking through Shridahz, hoping the Alliance would contact him. He went down every dark alley and secluded space he could find but never received a message or chit slipped into his palm leading him to a secret front. He had to accept that the Nasi had wiped the Alliance from the planet.

After accepting defeat, he joined Nicole in the market. She'd been roaming through the area, circling the restaurant where she'd asked to meet the Kurz emissaries with no luck. When she saw Kal approach, her face told him everything he needed to know about her state of mind.

"I'm beginning to get worried," Nicole whispered to Kal as they looked at a display of Qudorian cloth.

"Beginning?" Kal asked. "What does it take to get you fully worried?"

"I'd worked with Torkav and Noram for years on Gorash," Nicole said. "The fact that they're not responding is a really bad sign."

"What about going to Counselor Rohr directly?" Kal asked. "Her palace is not far." The chief counselor's palace was on the outskirts of the city. It was a risky move, but they were running out of options.

Nicole considered it. "The Nasi have to be monitoring her." She shook her head. "It's too dangerous." She was probably right.

"I think we may need to take a job," Kal said.

"Minister Qum?" Nicole asked.

"She's the best hope we have." She was the only person they knew who might be able to get the parts they needed. The question was, how badly did she need cargo ships?

Nicole sighed. "It's the best we've got," she agreed. "And

the restaurant's not far."

They walked to the restaurant, not bothering to disguise their intentions or blend into the crowd. For all intents and purposes, they were merchants looking for a job.

The smell of the rotting carcasses felt like a smack in the face as Kal walked in the door. He looked out over the tables, searching for the Kurz minister. Finally, his eyes spotted her in the corner, dressed in a fine red blouse with small metallic devices sewn into the fabric. She was sitting with a small glass in front of her, studying a tablet.

The two Humans weaved through the tables and sat in the chairs facing the minister. The large chairs were intended for Kurz, and Kal felt like a little kid as he hopped onto one, his feet dangling off the floor.

"Hello?" the minister's tone betrayed a hint of confusion.

"Greetings," Nicole said as she raised her arms and splayed her fingers in greeting. "We're interested in the job."

The Kurz returned the gesture. "Apologies, but I talk to many people here in the market. It can be quite overwhelming with all these different species." Her skin took on a greenish hue. "So hard to tell all of you apart."

"Not many crews taking you up on your offer?" Kal asked.

Qum's skin changed to a slightly reddish tinge. "Many haven't realized that there's good money to be made here. They're too afraid of the Nasi to see an opportunity."

"Well, we've considered your offer and wanna hear more." Kal said. "It's not the best we've received, but we don't want to dismiss it out of hand."

"Glad to hear it," Qum replied. "Our benefactors will pay

more than any other contract you can find, and we've got shipments leaving the planet all the time."

Kal pretended to be considering the offer. "Well, we're ready to leave," he said. "I think we could take you up on your offer, considering how badly you need help. There is one minor consideration though."

Qum turned her head. "Really? What would that be?" Her tone was skeptical.

"Well, our fold drive is down," Kal said. "Just up and died on us. It's a top-notch drive—we don't skimp on anything— and we've been looking for a few repair parts, but apparently the Kurz government—"

"The Tamulk government," Qum interrupted.

"The *Tamulk* government," Kal continued, "has restricted all high-priority parts. There's nothing to be found."

"Ah, now it makes sense," Qum laughed. "You don't *have* any other options. You can't get out of here without me."

Kal didn't bother to respond. She knew she was right.

The minister's demeanor had changed—she had them where she wanted them. "Give me the list of what you need, and we'll take it out of your commission." Kal's implant added an undercurrent of smugness to her tone. Although she called herself a minister, Kal could tell that Tkar Qum was a merchant at heart. She reveled in their negotiations and in getting the upper hand. "But first, we need to see if we even want you. What type of ship do you have?"

"A Shreen Quark," Kal said. He'd known that she would ask. Quarks were some of the fastest and most able merchants' ships around, with a payload around the same size as the *Salamis'*. Its fold drive was also extremely similar to theirs and could be modified, so it was plausible they'd need the parts they were asking for.

"Impressive. Any modifications I should know about?"

"Why do you ask?" Nicole arched her eyebrow suspiciously.

"Guessing this is her first time hauling cargo," Qum said to Kal with an inclination of her head. She turned to regard Nicole. "There are certain modifications that can set off compounds. Also, some materials need special equipment, like isolation containers, to be transported."

Nicole blushed. "I just took her on," Kal said. "She's new to the business but a whiz with finances. We've got the base model." He could feel their commission dropping every second they talked. Now they were an inexperienced crew desperate to get off planet in Minister Qum's eyes.

Qum picked up a tablet sitting on the table next to her and paged through it with slow sweeping gestures. After half a minute, she looked up. "I've got a shipment that needs to get to its destination in the next standard week. I can get these parts to you today. Now you tell me, what's your price?"

"I think you'd mentioned five hundred thousand," Kal said. It was an outrageous offer—he knew it, and so did Qum. But it was part of the dance they played. Anything other than a high figure would set off even more alarms than they had already.

"Ah, I forget how funny you Humans can be," Qum laughed. "You're lucky I don't just call it even with the parts.

Stop acting like you have a choice." She tapped her claws on the table. "But I'm fair and perhaps you'll come back for more work. Twenty-five thousand."

Kal and Qum went back and forth like that for a good ten minutes while Nicole furtively glanced around the restaurant. Finally, they settled on seventy-five thousand credits, payable upon delivery. It was a lot of money, but he knew they'd given up at least a hundred thousand to get the parts. By the time they'd finished, Nicole was practically vibrating in frustration. Kal could tell that Qum was not an ordinary government bureaucrat. She was a merchant. He had to haggle and extract every credit he could in the deal, otherwise she'd know something was off. Nicole hadn't lived as a merchant before. She didn't understand.

"Take this to the depot at the landing port," said Qum as she handed Kal a chit. "You'll get the parts you need. Good doing business and remember," she put her hand over Kal's, "my clients do not tolerate anyone who double-crosses them."

"Pleasure doing business with you," Kal replied with a smile as he pulled his hand away.

"We got the parts," Kal announced triumphantly as he strode up the ship's ramp.

"That's great, sir," Bo replied. "Where are they?"

"They're here in the landing port at the government's parts depot," Kal said. "We agreed to haul some goods over to Human-controlled space in exchange."

"Which means we need to look like a Shreen Quark," added Nicole.

"Well, it might seem strange if our ship suddenly transformed into a different model on the landing pad," Ramos said dryly. "I'll go fire up the engines. We can do a lap around the planet and adjust our optical and sensor signatures during our little joyride."

"Everyone already on board?" Kal asked.

"We're ready to go," Ramos shouted as she climbed the ladder. "The Tac-I squad has been focusing on playing cards and picking their noses."

She laughed at her own joke and disappeared into the cockpit as the squad members shouted after her.

An hour later, the *Salamis* returned to the same landing port appearing like a Shreen Quark named the *Goliath*. As soon as they landed, Kal and Nicole walked over to the depot to retrieve the parts they'd requested. They'd only asked for the parts Bo said were necessary to get their fold drive up and running again. The weapons and shields would still be inoperable, but there was no way Kal could've explained why they needed military grade armaments on a civilian merchant ship.

After inspecting the parts and doing some quick calculations on his comeca, Bo estimated it'd take him and Ramos two days to repair the fold drive. Sergeant Kimathi wisely restricted the Tac-I squad to the ship during that time despite the mutters of protest from some of the younger soldiers. Letting soldiers roam a port, even highly trained ones, was a recipe for disaster.

Kal was crouched down in the cargo bay watching Bo work when his implant pinged with an incoming message. *Sir, can I speak with you?* asked Lieutenant Sampson. Kal hadn't realized the pilot could still reach him over their neural net.

*Sure, I'm heading over,* Kal said.

He found Sampson standing in the center of the cabin, his lieutenant's insignia glittering in his open hand. "Sir, I've given it a lot of thought. I'm resigning my commission."

Kal was dumfounded. "What do you mean, resigning your commission? We need pilots like you." He wasn't sure what to do with Sampson yet. The guy was a piece of work, for sure. But the only thing he had to offer the Skulls and Samsara Fleet were his abilities as a pilot.

The soldier threw his rank at Kal's feet. "After we spoke, I talked with the other soldiers, told them to ignore rank, and just tell me the truth." He chuckled dryly. "And boy did they. Do you know what it means to have a carbon rod stuck—"

"I get the idea," Kal said. He could imagine several of the soldiers had been eager to give the man a piece of their mind. "The soldiers are unhappy with you. That's something you can change eventually. Why would you leave the fleet and throw everything away?"

"I'm not leaving the fleet, sir," Sampson replied, his back straight and eyes focused on Kal's. "I'd like to join the Tac-I squad as a private."

"What?" Kal was even more confused.

Now that he'd made his announcement, something deflated inside the pilot and Sampson crashed down on the bunk. "I've had time to think, and I realized that maybe there's something to what you said. Maybe I'm just selfish. I don't know. But what I realized is that things like rank and privilege don't really matter anymore. Respect is the only thing that you or any other officer can't give me. It's something I need to earn."

"So you want to earn the Tac-I squad's respect?" Kal asked dubiously. "I mean, I just heard them bragging about who could clog the bio recycler."

Sampson took a deep breath. "I hate to admit it, but yeah, I do. I want to earn their respect. But more than that, I want to earn my own. There's something missing with me. I've been doing the same thing now for years with the same result. It's time to change. I know I'm a good pilot—hell, I'm a great pilot—but that doesn't seem to make a difference. For too long I've assumed that everyone else is broken or corrupt, but really, it's me. And this is the only way I can think of to fix myself."

"You'd be throwing away your skills," Kal protested. "Putting you in the Tac-I squad would be a waste of your talent."

"If I don't change, I'll just end up here again," Sampson said, spreading his arms wide.

"What about Sergeant Kimathi?" Kal asked. "Have you even asked him?"

"I have," Sampson met his eyes. "He actually had an idea about this that might make it work."

"I'm guessing you two have been hatching a plan?"

"I wouldn't say that, sir. I just checked in with him and he had some thoughts about opportunities for one of his soldiers."

"Which soldier?"

"Sergeant Chedjou, sir."

Of course, Sandra Chedjou had dreamed about becoming a pilot since she was a girl. Sergeant Kimathi was looking out for his soldier. It was an interesting idea, certainly one that Kal would've never expected from Sampson. He couldn't decide what he thought about it. He didn't like the thought of losing an expert pilot. Ultimately, if he didn't agree though, he'd lose Sampson altogether. The man was right, there was something wrong with him, and the same issue they'd faced a few days earlier would come back again.

"I'll let you know," Kal said.

"Thank you, sir," Sampson said as he executed a perfect salute. "That's all I ask."

Kal returned the salute and walked out the door to find Sergeant Kimathi.

Two days later, Kal stood in the cargo bay watching the newest Tac-1 member Private Sampson's first training exercise. The squad had converted the bay to a training facility and set up a portable simulator and several calisthenics stations throughout the space. The soldiers took turns "motivating" Sampson as he alternated between physical training and tactical exercises. As a former EDF officer, he knew how to fire his sidearm, but that was the extent of his basic soldier skills.

He was out of shape and in desperate need of exercise and training, and the Tac-I squad was more than willing to give it to him. "Fresh meat" was the term Kal had heard them use.

"Dammit, Private! That's not at all what I said," Sergeant Bhatt bellowed as Sampson dodged behind a makeshift barrier.

To his credit, Sampson had yet to complain. Even when he slipped on his own vomit and landed in a heap on the metal bay floor, the man said nothing. He got up and continued the drill. Kal wondered how long the man could keep going like that.

In exchange for Sampson, Sergeant Kimathi had given up Sergeant Sandra Chedjou to be trained as a pilot. Kal had known Sandra since she before she'd joined Samsara Fleet, when she'd been traveling the stars as a civilian, and dreamed of becoming a pilot in the EDF. Kal was glad she was getting the chance to realize her dream.

In the old Earth Defense Force, none of this would have been possible. Officers could not simply give up their rank and become enlisted soldiers, and NCOs couldn't be assigned to pilot training without going through a rigorous selection process. But there were no rules or regulations in Samsara Fleet, and there certainly weren't any in the Skulls. He was willing to give this new arrangement a go. If it didn't work, they'd figure something else out.

Bowen had taken over the portion of the bay that was not taken up by the Tac-I's training. He'd disassembled much of the ship's fold drive, installed the replacement parts they'd picked up at the depot, and put the incredibly complex equipment back together. The *Salamis* was a skip ship, meaning that not only could it fold between different points in the same universe, but it could also fold between universes, allowing it to travel to the Jadid's universe. Bo was one of a handful of individuals who actual knew how the drive worked and how to repair it. He'd disassembled the drive, installed the new parts, and placed it back in the ship's hull. All they needed to do now was to pick up the cargo and leave the planet.

Nicole had proposed they leave without the cargo. Minister Qum had demanded they put two hundred thousand credits in an escrow account specifically to discourage such behavior, but the lost credits wouldn't matter to the Skulls or Samsara Fleet. However, Kal turned down the idea. This mission was an opportunity to get an insight into the Nasi supply apparatus, and they could inspect the cargo to see what materials the Nasi were shipping from Tamulk. Finally, there was always the off chance that the planetary government would stop them before they could fold.

Getting the cargo onto the ship would be a problem though. The *Salamis'* optical screen projected a holographic image around the *ship*, making it appear to be a civilian Shreen Quark. As soon as the Kurz stevedores tried to load the cargo into the bay, they'd see that the ship was not at all what it appeared to be from the outside. Even if the Skulls loaded it themselves, it would seem as if they had disappeared as soon as they entered the ship to bystanders.

To get around the problem, Bo had adjusted one of the small optical projectors they used to hide the ship, so it would project an image inside the cargo bay. Tied to a set of external cameras, the setup would create the illusion that they were walking to the ramp of a Quark as long as no one looked too carefully.

The Kurz landing port had remained busy the entire time the *Salamis* had been on Tamulk. Civilian ships of all types and sizes continued to land and take off at all hours. At the center of the port was the large complex of buildings that were used to store cargo going off planet. Streams of pallet lifters and hover sleds floated to and from the landing pads, leaving the large complex filled to the brim with crates and boxes and returning almost completely empty. A lot of material was leaving Tamulk, but nothing was coming in. The Nasi were slowly bleeding the planet dry.

"Where's your chit?" asked the Kurz supervisor as Kal stepped to the counter.

Kal handed over the chit Qum had given him, and the stevedore quickly scanned it with his tablet.

"Hm," she remarked, turning a shade of yellow, "hope you have a fast ship."

"What are we carrying?" Kal asked.

The Kurz made a shrill tone. "You should know not to ask that. We tell you what you need to know, and your discretion is part of the bargain. You'll be carrying the cargo to Mariga. Once you get to the planet, contact the port control and they'll provide further instructions. Take this" —she handed Kal a small chit— "just press the sensor on the side to find the cargo. You need help with loading?"

"No, we can take care of it," Kal said, relieved that they

175

had the choice.

"Excellent. Good luck." The Kurz motioned for the next person in line, Kal and Nicole already out of their minds.

The chit was a flat card, only four centimeters long and two wide. It felt cool like metal but had a glossy white enamel surface. When Kal pressed his finger to the sensor, a holographic arrow hovered over the card. It led them to a tunnel that descended into the ground, away from the storage area and into a large subterranean hangar. An enormous metal cube, at least ten meters tall, took up at half the hangar. Two Kurz guards stood on either side of the wide door at the center of the cube, their weapons at the ready. Kal was impressed; the door and walls of the cube had to be at least two meters of solid metal. Whatever was inside was either incredibly valuable, incredibly dangerous, or both.

After she inspected the chit, a guard led Kal and Nicole into the cube. The interior was filled with rows and rows of shelving that reached to the ceiling. Bright phosphorescent white lights hung from the ceiling, casting long shadows across the room. Large bots clung to the sides of the shelving and slid horizontally and laterally as they pulled containers off and deposited them on the floor.

The guard pressed a few buttons on a display panel near the wall and one of the cargo bots zoomed to the top of the shelves and came back down with a dull black container that looked like it could have fit at least one of their battle suits.

"That's it?" Kal asked when he realized the bot was done. He'd been expecting something larger or several crates at least.

"That's it," the Kurz replied. "You can use one of the pallet lifters to transport it to your ship." She turned and walked back to her post outside.

Kal grabbed an unused pallet lifter from the side of the cube and placed it under the box. After they secured the box, they activated the lifter's thrusters, and it floated upwards until it was at their knee level. Despite being a relatively simple bot, the pallet lifter was smart enough to follow them out of the storage area and to the *Salamis*.

When they got to the ship, Kimathi and the Tac-I squad were waiting. They acted as a sort of Human screen, preventing anyone from getting a clear look as Kal guided the bot up the ramp. The distraction and Bo's holo worked well enough. No one paid them a second glance as they secured the cargo onto the bay floor and brought the empty pallet lifter back out.

"We're loaded and we've got our instructions," Kal said after he'd dropped the lifter off by the central storage area. "Let's get going."

"Where to?" asked Kimathi.

"Mariga."

"Heading home then, sir?"

Kal shot the man a look. He should know never to talk about personal details in public. They had to assume they were being listened to, and any information they provided, no matter how innocuous, could be used to trace them later. "No. I'm from Earth. Now get in the ship."

Less than thirty minutes later, Sergeant Chedjou activated the *Salamis'* fold drive, and they left the space around Tamulk, heading to meet the fleet.

# Chapter Twelve

The *Salamis* arrived at Kappa Fleet's contingency rally point to find it empty. Nicole wasn't surprised that the *Ofira* wasn't there. Colonel Petrov must have assumed that every other ship in the fleet had perished in the battle and folded back to the *Gedorhan's Return* to warn General Samaha about what had happened.

Fold drives allowed ships to effectively travel faster than the speed of light. However, there was no way to communicate at that speed. When the fleet needed to send out ships like the *Salamis* to conduct missions, they also needed a way for them to return without risking the entire fleet's safety. Since the fleet was always moving, they'd created a schedule that detailed where there would be a scout ship with the fleet's current location.

The schedule led the Skulls to a rendezvous point in the center of Human-controlled space. Normally, it would take them at least a week to fold there from Tamulk. But the *Salamis* could travel to the Jadid's universe, where the laws of physics were different, and they were able to fold over much longer distances, drastically decreasing travel times.

Entering the Jadid universe was always a shock to Nicole. After Chief Ramos activated their fold drive transporting them to the Jadid's universe, the ship's systems went silent and the interior was shrouded in darkness.

After a few seconds, the ship came back to life, and the lights and viewscreens popped back on. A low thrum filled the cockpit as the equipment on the ship designed to work in this universe began to operate. Nicole looked out at the amber-hued stars that surrounded them, wondering what strange species and wonders were out there. They'd only visited one planet, Altterra, the Jadid's home world, but she'd heard stories from the Jadid's history about the strange and powerful creatures that lived in this galaxy. It would be amazing to see them. One day, would Humanity fold between universes like they folded between systems now? What would they discover?

The oscillating push and pull of the universe's gravity had replaced the ship's constant Earth-like artificial gravity. Nicole bounced off the top of the cockpit, quickly dragging her back to reality. She looked up at her hand as she pushed herself back toward the floor. Her formerly pale hand was now a bright yellow.

Ramos and Chedjou quickly checked all the ship's systems and entered the rendezvous coordinates into the fold computer. After setting their course with Ramos' supervision, Chedjou announced it would take twenty-two standard hours to reach the coordinates.

Nicole pulled herself out of the cockpit and glided to their stateroom. "So what do we do?" Kal asked as Nicole entered. The general was floating upside down, his body bobbing in the small waves of gravity that penetrated this universe.

"The Skulls or Samsara Fleet?" asked Nicole.

"Both, I guess," Kal said, gently pushing his tablet toward the desk in the corner of the room. She could see the weight of their defeat written on his face. It was something he tried to hide from the soldiers, but here, in the privacy of their stateroom, she could tell he was feeling lost and uncertain.

"It's such a pain," Nicole said. "There're layers upon layers of ambushes. We ambush the Nasi, then they just do the same to us."

Kal signed resignedly. "True. It's the nature of fold warfare. Ultimately, it's a judgement call that fleet commanders have to make, when to commit all your forces."

"We need to figure out a way to break this cycle," Nicole said. "One more battle like the one we just had, and we're done."

"Luckily, we don't have to figure it out right now," said Kal. "We just need to survive." He pulled himself upright and glided along the ceiling until he bumped into Nicole and wrapped his arms around her. She returned the embrace, enjoying the feeling of his warmth next to hers.

"How are you?" Kal asked softly.

It was a good question, and one that she had avoided asking herself. "Same as anyone else. Been better I suppose." She laughed hollowly. "But we're still alive and kicking."

Kal seemed satisfied with the answer, or at least he didn't want to pry, and pulled her close again.

"Did you see the Tac-I squad?" he asked after what felt like an eternity.

"No."

"They've got Sampson doing zero-G calisthenics." He chuckled. "Wonder if he's regretting his decision yet."

Nicole couldn't imagine what zero-G calisthenics were but laughed anyway. She'd been shocked at Sampson's request but impressed by the grit he'd shown so far. The Tac-I squad were not taking it easy on him.

"Want to go watch them?" Kal asked. "We can also inspect the cargo and find out exactly what we're carrying while we're at it."

"Sure," Nicole replied. She was curious on both counts.

Zero-G calisthenics looked much more intense than Nicole had expected. The Tac-I squad had set up several obstacles throughout the bay and tethered them to the walls, floor, and ceiling using cargo ties. Private Sampson wore a battle suit with his helmet removed and the servos disengaged. Sergeant Bhatt and Kimathi floated near the top of the bay, calling out instructions to the middle-aged private while the rest of the squad cheered him on.

"Push off and one-eighty midair," Kimathi ordered.

Sampson pushed off the cargo bay door and floated across the bay, trying to flip his torso so he was facing the way he'd come. The private wriggled around, flailing his arms and legs as he gently soared. To Nicole, it looked like someone had poured a cup of fire ants into his suit. The other soldiers laughed and then exploded in a roar when Sampson collided into the far bulkhead with a metallic clang as his armored shoulder hit off the wall.

"It's impossible," Sampson declared furiously. He looked at the other soldiers. "Shut up!"

"Private Sampson, what's my goddamn rank?" Sergeant Kimathi's smile had vanished, and a scowl had replaced his smile.

"Staff sergeant, Sergeant," Sampson called.

"And you will address me as such." Kimathi commanded as he pulled himself along the wall toward where Sampson had pushed off from. "Now watch."

The sergeant pushed off from the wall and immediately raised his arms above his head while sticking his legs forward so that his body made an L. He turned his upper torso to the left and then pulled in his arms and legs, sending his body turning the opposite way. When he'd turned fully around, he mimed shooting a rifle. Then he stuck his arms in front of his body while extending his legs downward and twisted his upper body to the right, stopping his rotation immediately before gently contacting the far bulkhead. The Tac-I squad broke out into scattered applause and cheers.

"I thought they taught physics in flight school," Sergeant Kimathi said with a smile. "Try again."

"Yes, Sergeant."

Beads of sweat were already pouring down Sampson's face. Despite his apparent exhaustion, he didn't hesitate to get in position to try again. The man was nothing if not determined.

While Nicole had been watching the Tac-I squad, Kal had pulled himself along the cargo bay bulkhead and was floating next to their cargo. Bowen floated gently next to him, tapping on his comeca—the wrist-mounted computer all Jadid and Nasi had in place of an implant. Nicole used the wall to pull herself to them.

"Any luck?" Kal asked.

"Well, sir. The Nasi have wired this thing with at least five different anti-tampering devices and at least two of them are wired to high explosives." Bo looked away from his wrist. "But from what I can tell, none of them are intended to work in this universe. So we can just open it."

"Won't they go off as soon as we enter our own?" asked Nicole.

"Ah, yes, good question," Bo frowned. "That's where it gets a bit more difficult. I can ensure we don't destroy ourselves upon folding back, but there still will be some evidence that someone opened the container."

Kal frowned. "How much risk is there?"

"That they'll find it, sir?" Bo asked. "I'm not sure. I doubt the Nasi will scrutinize every single container that's delivered."

Kal bit his lip for a moment, clearly trying to decide if it was worth it. "Let's do it," he said. "We should know what we're carrying."

Bo pulled a few tools from one of the cargo pockets on his trousers and dug around the seams of the matte-black container. After a half minute, there was a small click, and the Jadid pulled open the lid, swinging it backwards so it rested against the wall.

Nicole wasn't sure what she was looking at. Cylinders, about a meter long and as thick as her wrist, filled the container. There had to be hundreds of them stacked inside the padded interior. "AAA" had been engraved in large red lettering along the length of each cylinder.

Kal let out a whistle.

"What is it?" Nicole asked.

"No wonder they aren't shipping this by cargo freighter."

"What the hell is it?" Nicole asked again.

"Azidoazide Azide Antimatter, I'm guessing," Bowen said. "I'm surprised that it even made it here."

"It's one of the most explosive and volatile substances in the galaxy," Kal explained. "You look at the stuff wrong and it can blow up."

"Do they build weapons with it?" Nicole asked.

Bo shook his head. "Not normally, it's too unstable. I don't know why they have this or this much of it."

"Either way, I'm not going to be sleeping well until we get this off the ship," Kal said. "Get the container put back together and make sure you triple check it. We don't—"

Private Sampson careened into the wall next to them with a thud, cutting Kal off mid-sentence. "I think we need to stop the training for now," Kal said, eyeing the private. Nicole didn't think she'd be sleeping too well either.

❖

"General Norman, what are you doing here?" General Samaha's voice sounded worried to Nicole. "Where is the rest of the fleet?"

After reaching the coordinates and returning to its own universe, the *Salamis* had found Samsara Fleet's scout ship and rendezvoused with the *Gedorhan's Return* at the edge of Human and Z'Ta space. The trip had taken thirty-six hours from the time they left Tamulk until they were talking with

Samaha while sitting at the desk in their stateroom. The *Ofira* probably wouldn't arrive for at least another four days.

"Kappa Fleet was destroyed," Kal said. "We need to talk with you immediately on a private net."

Silence was the only response.

"Did you hear me, ma'am?"

The sound of a deep exhale. "Yes. Yes. I'll activate a private holo between us and Ancient Wang" Seconds later, both Samaha and Wang appeared, each in their conference rooms aboard their flagships.

"What's happened?" Ancient Wang said with a frown.

"We executed the mission according to plan. The Kurz assault force was decimated at the garrison. When the Nasi showed up, it was only a dreadnaught and a battleship." He cleared his throat. "We folded to the planet to destroy them, but when Kappa Fleet arrived, they were already gone. Then half the friggin' Nasi fleet folded around us. It was a bloodbath."

"Damn. How many survived?" General Samaha's head was down, her hand rubbing her temples slowly.

"Just the *Ofira* and us," Kal replied. "The *Frygr* sacrificed itself to take out one of the dreadnaughts and the Liberation Fleet was completely overwhelmed." What Kal didn't say was that it had been evident the Nasi had focused their fire on the Jadid. Nicole wasn't sure if that was because of a personal vendetta or because they feared them.

"Esma's a monster," Ancient Wang said, his face turning red. "She's willing to kill her own children for power."

"She anticipated our move," Samaha said. "We can only

guess that another one of our fleets is about to enter a trap if they haven't already."

"She was there at Tamulk," Nicole said. "She asked for Ancient Wang."

Wang snarled. "She's a madwoman. She's grown bitter and twisted over the years."

"We need to warn the other fleets," Kal said. "There's still time. Our skip ships can reach them and get them to pull back."

"The *New Dawn* is ready," Samaha said. "They, along with the *Salamis*, should be able to reach the other fleets in the next standard day. It should be enough time to warn the fleets not to engage." The *Salamis* had been the first skip ship they'd built using parts retrieved from the Nasi. The *New Dawn* was the first skip ship they were building from scratch. Construction had taken months since they had to find a host of rare materials and build complex components. Nicole knew that Bo had been heavily involved in the construction of the new ship.

"If we can warn them, then perhaps we can salvage an even greater victory from this defeat," Wang said, eyes flashing.

"Yes." Samaha looked up thoughtfully. "Yes, perhaps. We could concentrate our forces and destroy that second fleet. Wipe out half of their fleet. General Norman, can you head to Z'Ta space and warn the Zeta Fleet?"

"There's something else, ma'am," Kal said. "We entered into a contract with the Tamulk government to transport Triple-A to the Nasi on Mariga."

"Triple-A! I am sure there's a story there," Samaha said dryly. "But we'll have to save it for another time."

"We'd like to make the shipment," Nicole said. "It's our opportunity to peek behind the curtain of the Nasi operations. It's a way to get on the planet and see what they're doing."

"A *dangerous* way," Samaha corrected.

"Everything is dangerous," Wang said with a wave of his hand. "This could be a great opportunity."

"There's also an opportunity to sabotage their Foothold," Kal said. "Triple-A is extremely volatile after all." Nicole looked at him; he hadn't mentioned sabotage before. "But we will need to transfer it to a different ship. They're expecting a Shreen Quark cargo ship, and if we arrive in the *Salamis,* they'll be able to figure out pretty quickly that we're not." They'd talked to Bo about this beforehand. He'd confirmed Nicole's suspicions; the ship's optical screen wasn't likely to fool the Nasi at close range.

"I need to think it over," Samaha said. "I don't see any reason that your team needs to be the ones to warn the other fleets though. We should get you *and* the Triple-A off the *Salamis.*"

"Yes, ma'am," Kal replied. "We'll unload the cargo immediately."

Nicole tried to get herself comfortable on the hard bench of General Samaha's conference room on the *Gedorhan's Return* but found it impossible. The two skip ships had already returned, less than thirty hours after they had first been sent out.

"This is turning in our favor," Samaha said with a smile. "We'll be able to crush half the Nasi fleet."

"Yes, ma'am," General Zhao said. "Theta, Tau, and Zeta fleets have all been contacted and are returning to our location."

"Our combined fleets can lay an ambush for the Nasi," Wang said. "We can attack one of the colonies and Esma will only be expecting a portion of our fleet."

"Isn't that what we just did?" Samaha raised an eyebrow. "We lost a quarter of our fleet in the effort. I think we need to take the fight to them rather than waiting for them to attack us."

"I doubt they're orbiting a planet," Zhou said, "and finding them in deep space is impossible."

"Why wouldn't they be near a planet?" Nicole asked. "Don't they need to resupply and refuel?"

"They know we're hunting for them," explain General Zhou. "But you are correct, they will still be resupplying their fleet from somewhere."

"Ma'am." Kal spoke softly, but all the eyes in the room were immediately on him. "I suggest you send out several scout teams, including ours, to see what we can find. We already have an in on Mariga. We can investigate the Nasi forces on planet and see if we can discover anything."

Samaha didn't reply as she leaned back, biting her lower lip in thought.

"I don't disagree with the course of action," General Zhou

said. "But I think we need to be sure that we don't squander a potential opportunity. The Nasi will eventually move on. With their fleets unified, this is the chance to truly crush their hopes."

"Aamina," Wang leaned in conspiratorially. "We're close to perfecting the missiles already. If we wait too long, we risk prolonging this war by years."

"Fine." Samaha said, placing her hands on the bench. "We're going to go ahead with General Norman's plan. But"—she held up a finger—"you'll only have about a week, Kal. That should give you enough time on Mariga to find out information and will give our fleet time to return and prepare."

Kal nodded.

"After that, we'll go with Ancient Wang's plan and attack one of the Nasi garrisons, drawing their fleet to us." Wang leaned back, a contented look on his face. "Now, let's see about getting you a new ship."

Nicole wasn't a large person, but she felt enormous walking through the cramped passages of Samaha's flagship as she walked with Kal to landing bay. She knew from personal experience that the subterranean Tounous had very little need or desire for space, and it showed in the tight confines of the ship.

"Are we sure these work?" Nicole asked as they entered one of the landing bays. It was filled with civilian ships in various states of disrepair; all of them were from refugees who had fled to Samsara Fleet after the Nasi had arrived. The flood of refugees had lessened to a trickle and then completely stopped. By now, commerce in the galaxy had returned to normal and traders had learned that the Nasi were not interested in destroying or capturing their ships. General Samaha had ordered her commanders to keep all the civilian vessels to be used for parts or in case of emergencies.

"Doubtful," Kal replied. "But I'm guessing at least a few of them do." He slapped his hand next to a large hole in the fuselage of the ship next to him.

They walked through the rows of ships, looking for a Shreen Quark or anything that was similar. Nicole found her eyes drawn to small details on the ships as she scanned the rows of vessels. There were so many to take in. Things that made her think about who had owned these ships and wonder how they had arrived there. Small names painted on the fuselage or scarring from atmospheric entry or the small pits of space debris. Many of the ships had burns or pieces melted off from plasma hits. It was amazing that some of them had survived whatever hellish journey they'd been through.

Kal let out a yell, causing Nicole to jump. He stood, hands on hips and mouth open, staring at a derelict-looking Shreen. The ship was roughly two-thirds the length of the *Salamis* with several crude patches welded onto its metallic skin. Kal smiled as he walked around its boxy frame and ran his hand along the ship's side.

"I take it you know this one," Nicole said.

"It's mine," Kal said. "This is *Annie*. The ship I owned

when the Nasi attacked."

"I thought they'd destroyed it," Nicole said.

Kal looked up and inspected the underside of the delta-shaped wings. "Me too. I left her on Caracas. I'd assumed she was destroyed or captured with the station." Caracas Station was the civilian port that orbited New America.

"Well, guess not," Nicole said as Kal touched one of the metal panels on the underside of the wing, causing it to fall to the floor with a clatter. "You weren't lying about it needing some work." That was putting it mildly. The thing was a wreck.

"It might be just the right ship for this mission," Kal said, still mesmerized.

Nicole studied the pitted hull and peeling paint. "Let's keep looking," she said diplomatically. "There may be better options."

"Well, it's the only Shreen ship we've seen so far that looks like it might be operational." She hated to admit it, but he had a point.

"It's not a Quark though," Nicole pointed out. In fact, it was a far cry from that top-of-the-line model.

"Taking a trip down memory lane, eh?" asked General Samaha as she made her way around the back of the ship to join them. "I was wondering if this was your ship, Kal."

"It is," Kal replied, his hand still affectionately resting on the ship's hull. "It's probably the closest thing I ever had to a home since I left Mariga. I spent a decade of my life in this wonderful pile of crap."

"Didn't want to put too much money into keeping her up,

eh?" the general asked with a raised eyebrow.

Kal looked away. "I had other things on my mind," he demurred. "As long as she could fold, I was okay."

"Let's check out the rest of the bay," Nicole suggested. She desperately hoped they could find something better than Kal's commune in the stars.

"I was talking with General Zhou," Samaha said as they walked through between the ships. "I want to be clear that we will proceed with the mission if you don't return in time. I'm concerned that we are running into something we don't fully understand."

"I hear you," Kal said.

"General Zhou and Ancient Wang are aggressive," Samaha said. "It's a good quality in a leader. But right now, we need to be careful and understand what we are stepping into. Intel is more valuable than ships and ammo to me. If you're somehow able to sabotage the Triple-A, good. But make sure you get back."

"You've done amazing things," Ancient Bao Wang announced as he strode toward them. Nicole wondered if he'd heard what Samaha had said. His black hair was slicked back with two wings of gray spreading away from his temples, reminding Nicole of a professor in a holo. Albeit a young one—the Ancient didn't look older than thirty. "The Skulls have single-handedly changed the course of this war, and I can say with certainty that my Liberation Fleet would not be here without you."

Bao gave a small bow. "Unfortunately, even your team couldn't save our ships at Tamulk." His expression darkened.

"I can't believe I have already lost almost a quarter of my fleet to Esma."

"At least the *Frygr* destroyed one of their dreadnaughts," Samaha said.

"A minor victory there," said Wang.

"It's not small," Samaha corrected. "The Nasi only have two left. If we can eliminate them, it changes the dynamics of this war. We won't have to worry about the Nasi destroying entire systems in retribution."

Wang looked like he was going to respond then stopped and nodded his head. "Of course you're right." He paused for a moment, rubbing his chin thoughtfully. "I think this tragedy has shown that my officers still need training. It has been a long time since they fought, and they aren't used to combat in this universe."

"Go on, Bao. What are you thinking?" Samaha asked.

"I'd like to suggest that my officers rotate among the other ships in your fleet," Bao said. "I know they're short-staffed. My soldiers can provide needed help, and it will help give them the experience they need. We can't rely on battle to train our soldiers."

The suggestion appeared to catch Samaha off guard. She cleared her throat and regarded the Ancient. "I need to think about it. Your soldiers don't know how to operate the other ships."

Ancient Wang lifted his hands in a sign of surrender. "No worries, Aamina. I can understand if you're hesitant. We've only just joined this fleet. It may take some time for you to get used to us."

"It's a good idea," admitted Samaha. "I want to check with the commanders first though. Each one has a say in who is on their crew."

Wang nodded. "Of course."

Samaha turned to look at Kal. "I noticed that Sergeant Chedjou and Chief Ramos piloted you here. What happened to Lieutenant Sampson?"

"Interesting story there," Kal replied.

He relayed the story of Sampson's refusal to follow orders and subsequent resignation of his commission. Nicole could tell Ancient Wang found the entire story hilarious; a small smile never left his face as he listened. Samaha seemed more perplexed than anything, concluding that "it wouldn't fly in the EDF but in Samsara Fleet we make our own rules."

By the time Kal finished the story, they'd reached the end of the bay. Despite their popularity in the civilian market, there were only a handful of Shreens, and none of them were Quarks. To Nicole's distress, *Annie* was the best of the lot. Every bit of cargo shipped came with an encrypted bill of lading, filled out by the sending party and only readable by the receiver. In commercial shipping, it would contain information about the contents of cargo, its dimension and weight, the price for shipment, and other information. Bo had already tried to decrypt the bill that came with their cargo unsuccessfully. They might be able to explain away a different model of ship, but there was no way they could explain a completely different manufacturer.

"I guess you get to relive your glory days as an independent merchant," Nicole said.

"I wouldn't call them glory days." Kal couldn't keep the smirk off his face.

"General Norman, remember the mission while you're taking a stroll down memory lane," Samaha said. "I'm not sure what you'll find on Mariga. But the Nasi are out there and any information on their fleet could mean the difference between life and death."

# Chapter Thirteen

When he had gone through the interior of the *Queen Anne's Revenge,* Kal thought of all the repairs and upgrades that he had put off while he'd been her captain. The ship was running on equipment that was at least a decade behind the time. It hadn't mattered when he'd been semi-hoping that the ship would explode, taking him with it. But now that he was relying on it to save not only him and his friends but all of Humanity, it was a major problem.

He stood outside the ship and studied the hull. The *Gedorhan's Return's* maintenance crew had been able to patch up the holes and apply a fresh coat of anti-radiation paint on the hull. Bo and Ramos had been busy and spent the last standard day fixing and upgrading as much of the ship's systems as possible. Unfortunately, they couldn't add any of the weapons, shields, or advanced electronics they'd had on the *Salamis.* It would have been a surefire giveaway when they arrived at Mariga.

"Sir, I've been able to upgrade some systems," Bo said as he tapped on his comeca. "But there's only so much we can do in such a short time."

"Thanks, Bo."

"The bones of the ship aren't bad," Ramos admitted. "But you clearly didn't invest a lot of credits in keeping her current—or clean."

When Kal had first opened the rear cargo door of the ship, it had been like opening a portal to a past life. Whoever had flown the ship from Caracas Station hadn't bothered to clean up any of the mess he'd left. Empty boxes, broken equipment, partially eaten food, and other debris were scattered throughout every compartment. Kal had spent the better part of four hours cleaning up the trash he'd accumulated over years. It was a harsh wake-up call to how he'd been living. He hadn't expected the shame he'd felt as his soldiers saw exactly how their commander had lived as a civilian.

Nicole had said nothing, perhaps sensing his discomfort. For that, he was grateful.

"We've been able to upgrade the fold drive," Ramos said. "These Shreens are great with how they modularize their systems. It was a simple plug-and-play fix. Same with the viewscreens and the consoles in the pilot's area."

"The other systems are too complex to replace in whole," Bo said. "But I was able to make some slight tweaks." A small holograph of the ship appeared above the comeca on the Jadid's wrist. A green highlight appeared over several systems on the ship, areas where he had been able to work his magic. "I added some additional components to the electrical and communications systems and upgraded the wiring. The hull needed a significant number of patches, which the Tounous maintenance crew handled, and we replaced the food fabricator."

Ramos made a face. "All it could make was coffee and burritos."

"Yeah, that does get old," Kal admitted.

"There's one other thing," Nicole said. "The ship's not big enough to hold the full crew." *Annie* was a little more than half the size of the *Salamis*. The twelve people they'd had on the scout ship might fit on her, but it would be uncomfortable and the Marigans might be suspicious. "I've talked with Sergeant Kimathi and he's going to leave one of his teams behind." Kal had noticed Nicole stepping more up as the team's executive officer, handling the regular planning so he could focus on their strategy.

"Make's sense," Kal admitted. "I assume it's Corporal Sato's team." With Sergeant Chedjou moving to become part of the flight crew, Kimathi had promoted Private Sato to Corporal and assigned her as team leader in Chedjou's place. It would only make sense to leave her with the fleet and take Sergeant Bhatt's team.

"Yeah, she'll stay back along with Chadha and Ramirez." Kal was sure they wouldn't be happy about it, but they'd understand.

"Well, I guess there's nothing left to do then." Kal slapped the side of the ship. It would be good to be back on his old ship. He hadn't realized how much he'd missed it. "Let's get loaded and get out of here. The Nasi will expect us to deliver the cargo to Mariga soon."

Since they were already at the edge of Human space, the voyage to Mariga would only take a standard day. After the first few hours on his old ship Kal found himself thinking of the *Salamis*, almost pining after her like a jilted lover. *Strange how we get attached to objects*, Kal mused.

He sat on the edge of the bunk in his cabin on *Annie*. It

was smaller—and cleaner now—than he remembered. The décor was purely functional, none of the wood trim and elegance of the stateroom on the *Salamis*. From the frame of the small bunk to the desk in the corner of the room, everything was brushed metal. Despite the room being intended for a single person, Nicole was sharing it with Kal. It made for some uncomfortable nights but helped save much-needed space.

The *Queen Anne's Revenge*, as it was officially named, was laid out similarly to the *Salamis*. It had two cabins and the cockpit on the top level; the cargo bay, galley and crew quarters were on the bottom. Chief Ramos had the cabin across from Kal and Nicole's while the other six members of the Skulls shared the tight confines of the crew quarters.

"Well, we're off," Nicole announced as she walked through the door.

"I'd noticed." Kal had seen the stars flickering rhythmically in the viewscreen.

Nicole hesitated, something she rarely did. It normally meant she had something serious or contentious to say. "What are you planning to do to the cargo?" The question came out in a sort of rush.

"Deliver it," Kal replied nonchalantly. "But I'm guessing that's not what you mean." He'd been dreading this conversation.

Nicole screwed up her mouth. "You *know* that's not what I mean. You mentioned sabotage. What are you planning on doing?"

Kal had noticed her reaction when he'd mentioned that. It

had been the same look she'd given him when talking about the enhanced interrogation techniques.

"We can't just give the Nasi a crate full of super high-explosive material. Not if we can do something about it."

"Are you going to detonate it?"

"The thought had crossed my mind," Kal admitted.

"I've looked into that stuff," Nicole declared. "That amount of Triple-A will wipe out entire cities."

"I've thought about that," Kal replied. "Where will the Nasi have us deliver the cargo? Where will they store it? Their Foothold. We could potentially wipe out their entire presence on Mariga."

Nicole grabbed his hand, her already pale skin white as snow around the knuckles. "Those Footholds are cities, full of Nasi citizens, not just soldiers. And what if you're wrong? What if it kills Humans on the planet? You're tossing a grenade at the planet and hoping it goes off where you want. This is genocide, same as what they did."

Kal slammed his hand against the bulkhead. This *was* their discussion about the prisoner all over again. He loved Nicole, and he loved her compassion. He knew it was something that had been stripped away from him a long time ago. But she failed to see the forest for the trees. If they could defeat the Nasi even if it meant doing something wrong, they had to do it. It would be wrong not to.

"How dare you compare—"

A small chime announced someone at the door.

"Come in," Kal yelled.

Bowen entered the room, ducking his head slightly as his

lanky frame went through the doorway.

"Sir, I had something I wanted to talk with you about." Bo's speech continued to evolve from the stilted Human standard that most of the Jadid spoke the longer he remained with the Skulls. But he still lapsed into the more formal Jadid dialect sometimes, especially when nervous. His gaze bounced between Nicole and Kal, taking in the situation. "I can come back."

"No, sit down. I think it would be good to get your opinion." Kal remained on his bunk and motioned to the chair that was fixed to the floor by his desk.

"Kal—General Norman—wants to rig the Triple-A to explode," Nicole said.

"I see," said Bo, his face impassive.

"And Colonel Bergeron wants us to just hand a crate of explosives to the enemy without taking advantage of the opportunity."

Bo took a deep breath. He slowly shifted in his chair to face Kal, his face unmoving and his violet eyes glowing under the overhead light of the small cabin.

"Sir, I've been a part of this crew for a year now. During that time, I've learned more than I ever did back on Altterra. Not about physics or interstellar travel, but about Humans and Jadid. I like to think of myself as one of your crew, and I hope you share that feeling."

Kal smiled at the scientist. "Of course. That's why you're here."

"You still seem to view the Nasi as a monolith, as a homogeneous collection of zealots. But that is a grave mistake. There are evil Jadid within the Nasi, but there are good ones too. The Nasi are a force of destruction and vengeance in this universe, and in my own. That's why I have helped and fought with you. But not all of them are evil, any more than everyone within Samsara Fleet is good. For you not to understand this is not only wrong but a strategic mistake. You are forgetting about the most powerful foe the Nasi have—themselves."

Kal chewed on the words, thinking through his experiences with the Nasi. They had destroyed so much, killed billions, and shattered the galaxy. But he knew intellectually that they were not monsters from the holos. He'd seen Nasi citizens in their Footholds looking as frightened as any Human. But there were casualties in war, and no action was truly just. The destruction of the Nasi Foothold could cripple them, at least temporarily. Wasn't the price of some civilian collateral damage worth it?

"I see you're conflicted." Bo's face softened. "I will make it easy for you. It's not technically possible for me to sabotage the cargo without either destroying ourselves or tipping off the Nasi. I also will not agree to try."

"I could order you," Kal said feebly.

"You could. But I am not Human nor am I bound by your orders. If I was, then I'd be working with Chief Kanumba on the fleet's secret weapons project. I refused General Samaha as I'm refusing you. You can have my help but only as I see fit to give it."

Kal took a deep breath. "Fine." It surprised him to realize he didn't feel any anger over the Jadid's words. Kal was satisfied to have the decision taken away from him. He could feel Nicole's body relax on the bed next to him.

"I came here with a request though," Bo said. "I think the Nasi will direct us to land within their Foothold, considering the cargo we are carrying. With your permission, I'd like to infiltrate the facility if we have an opportunity."

It meant a lot to Kal that the Jadid was volunteering, but that had been his plan all along. He'd be the perfect operative to get into the Foothold. Who knew if they'd have the opportunity, but if they did, Kal would be a fool not to use Bo even if that put him in danger.

"I'm glad to hear that," Kal replied. No need to let him know it was already being considered. "But do you think you'll be able to blend in?"

"I don't have the Nasi tattoos," Bo gestured at his unmarked violet arms, "but I can still pass as a worker. Even though they are Nasi, they are still Jadid, and I should be able to get around. I doubt they would be expecting this."

"I appreciate you volunteering for this," Kal said, giving the scientist a light tap on his arm. "And I'll take it into consideration. We don't know what we'll find on Mariga when we get there. Just follow my lead and be ready for anything."

Kal had mixed emotions as he looked at Mariga from *Annie's* cockpit. He'd left the planet over three decades ago, not yet a man, to chase his dream of becoming an officer in the EDF. The few people he'd known on the planet were no longer there or long dead, and the person he'd become was nothing like the man he'd dreamed of becoming.

From space, Mariga appeared to be a uniform mass of blue-tinged white ice. It was a savage planet. Anyone caught unprotected on the windblown surface would die within minutes, frozen solid. There were no seasons to speak of, and the temperature was uniformly cold, whether at the poles or equator. Looks could be deceiving though. Underneath the blanket of white were cities and ecosystems that stretched across the entire planet.

"Mariga control, this is the free-merchant ship *Queen Anne's Revenge*, requesting clearance to land," Sergeant Chedjou called out over the open net.

"*Queen Anne's Revenge*, this is Mariga control," a female voice responded. "What is the purpose of your entry?"

"Delivery of materials to Nasi forces." She sent their shipment information.

A pause and then another Nasi voice came on the net. "*Queen Anne's Revenge*, you will land at the coordinates provided. Once you have landed, power off your engines and do not depart from your ship. Failure to comply with these instructions will result in your death." The line clicked closed and a waypoint appeared on their tacmap.

"Cheery lot aren't they," Ramos deadpanned.

"Just do as they say," Kal instructed.

He stood in the cockpit and braced himself by placing his hands against the bulkhead as the ship descended. The turbulence from entering the atmosphere was more severe than it was on the *Salamis*, causing Kal to lose his footing a few times. After having spent over a year in cutting-edge scout ships, the merchant vessel seemed like a relic. Equipment that had seemed modern, or at least passable when he'd first flown in the ship, now felt more like it belonged in a museum.

They flew over the glacial landscape, the ship soaring a few thousand meters off the ground. The reflection of the sunlight off the ice made it difficult to see any sort of detail in the ground until the viewscreens automatically dimmed to adjust. Large chasms, kilometers wide and thousands of kilometers long, fractured the landscape. Transports and ships flew in and out of the gaps, traveling to and from the cities and factories nestled in the canyons underneath.

*Annie* glided down into a wide chasm. Beneath them, the Nasi Foothold rose above the snow-covered ground. The Foothold was enormous, as big as a small city itself, with a large, almost organic tower in its center and irregular concentric circles of oddly shaped buildings radiating outwards. A large spherical building seemed out of place within the evenly spaced circles. It was the gateway, the portal between this universe and the Nasi's—now closed. A tall wall surrounded the entire compound. Although they were hidden from sight, Kal knew antipersonnel and anti-ship weapons sat along the entire length of the wall. He was surprised to see an almost invisible iridescent dome surrounding the entire compound.

The city of Torgut extended outwards from the Foothold, occupying the entire floor of the chasm. The city itself was hidden from view, but the dark roofs of its buildings dotted the ground, spreading out from the Foothold and appearing like small black bumps along the chasm floor. They were low to the ground and rounded as if the sharp winds that coursed through the valley had worn them away. Complex networks of metal tunnels rose out of the ground and arced gracefully between the roofs before diving back beneath the surface. Kal knew they were used to carry larger transport vessels long distances. Most citizens traveled below the surface, walking on the streets of the city without having to face the planet's harsh atmosphere.

*Annie* landed on a large cluster of landing pads near the center of the Foothold, and Chedjou turned off their engines. Hundreds of civilian merchant ships were around them, some being unloaded by Nasi stevedores and bots, others waiting with their engines off. Kal found his eyes drawn to the Nasi soldiers in full battle suits that patrolled the area. They moved like dancers, gracefully walking through the area, their weapons held at the ready.

"Looks like we're going to be waiting a bit," Nicole said. "There's a lot of ships still waiting to be unloaded."

"Well, let's get comfortable then," Kal said. "Bo, you may be in there for a while."

Despite the lack of response, Kal knew the Jadid could hear him. When Kal had been a merchant, he had sometimes accepted an occasional less-than-legal contract. To get past planetary customs, he'd built a special compartment into *Annie*, tucked into the bulkhead between the two decks. It was the only sizeable investment he'd ever made in the ship. Active and passive anti-sensor technology lined the inside of the container, making its contents almost invisible to anything but the most intense scrutiny. There was no way for them to hear Bo from inside, but Chief Ramos had installed a small speaker inside so the Jadid could hear what was going on inside the ship.

After reporting to the port control, they sat around the galley table waiting for word from the Nasi. There'd been no indication of how long it would take, which made time pass even more slowly. After an hour, Sergeant Kimathi went to the crew quarters and brought back his weathered deck of playing cards.

After three hours of watching the others, Kal had given up trying to understand the complex rules of the game and stood at the corner of the galley, silently observing. He could see that most of them—except for Sampson—were clearly enjoying the game, seemingly oblivious to the danger they were in. That ability to compartmentalize, to focus only on what they could control, was the mark of an experienced soldier. They had no option but to sit on the Nasi landing pad and wait for further instructions, so the team wouldn't bother themselves with worrying about getting caught. They'd just relax and wait to find out what was going to happen. Kal couldn't do that. He couldn't stop wondering what would happen when the Nasi finally boarded their ship. Would they discover Bo? Would there be an issue with the bill of lading?

"*Queen Anne's Revenge*, this is Mariga port operations." The stilted voice coming through the speakers caused Kal to jump. "Open your rear cargo bay then have all personnel exit the craft and remain next to your ship. Any deviation from these instructions will be met with force."

"To be continued," Sergeant Kimathi said as he leaned across the table and gathered up the cards. The others reluctantly stood up and glanced around the room. Now Kal could see the flickers of doubt cross people's faces. He was glad he wasn't the only one.

Kal had expected a blast of frigid air when they opened the ship's back ramp. Instead, he only felt a cool breeze waft into the bay, carrying the sounds of the bots unloading ships and the crisp smell of the glaciers around them. Kal looked up at the thin dome overhead with a new sense of awe. The Nasi had somehow developed a way to keep the frigid atmosphere of Mariga out of the Foothold.

"This isn't so bad," Private Fischer said as he looked around the port.

"It must be the dome," Kimathi said, pointing to the iridescent layer above them. "The Nasi must be regulating the temperature and weather inside."

"Impressive," the private replied, echoing Kal's thoughts.

A few minutes later, a team of four Nasi, clad in battle suits, strode up to their ship.

"Documents," said the one in front in a deep voice. Kal assumed he was the team leader.

Kal held out the chit with the bill of lading, and the Nasi scanned it with a small device he pulled from his suit. He studied the screen for a moment and then looked back up at the Humans.

"This document says your ship is a Shreen Quark." Kal noticed his accent was less pronounced than many Nasi—

he'd been in this universe for a while. The other Nasi almost imperceptibly shifted on their feet as their leader spoke.

*Showtime*, Kal thought.

He swaggered forward with a confident grin plastered on his face. "There must have been a mix-up. I told that Kurz minister that the ship was as *fast* as a Quark. She must not understand simple Human Standard." He added a tone of chummy familiarity to the last statement. Not like us Humans and Nasi was the implication.

It was impossible to gauge the soldier's reaction behind his featureless helmet. "We'll need to conduct a full inspection. Your crew will remain outside your ship while you will accompany me."

Kal made sure his grin remained plastered on his face. *Don't show you're worried.* "Of course, of course." He turned to the other Skulls. "Go ahead and wait here."

Kal followed behind the Nasi team leader as he glided up the ramp. Two of the guards remained outside the ship while the fourth trailed Kal and the team leader, ready to intervene if he should try something. The team leader pulled out a rectangular device, about the size of Kal's forearm from another compartment in his suit and swept it across the bay.

"You've got quite the operation here," Kal said, motioning to the Foothold outside the bay. "I'm amazed at how fast the Nasi have been able to establish your presence on Mariga. How long have you been here?"

The team leader ignored him and continued to inspect the cargo bay. It took every bit of Kal's willpower not to look at the part of the bulkhead where Bo was hiding. The hideaway was intentionally in a place where most wouldn't look to scan, behind the ladder and between the two decks. He'd used it several times, and it had yet to fail him, but that hadn't been with the Nasi.

"Well, I've got to say it's good you're here," Kal continued. "Humanity needs the Nasi. We've drifted for too long, stuck in our mediocrity. Powerful enough to survive but not strong enough to thrive." Kal enjoyed how that sounded—like a political slogan. He knew this was exactly what these Nasi soldiers had been told as to why they were there. Esma and the Nasi leadership had spread the idea that they were coming back to the Human universe to help them. That their Human ancestors were like wayward children; they'd fallen from grace but could be redeemed through the guidance and intervention of the more intelligent and disciplined Nasi. It was twisted logic, something that didn't really make sense, but the Nasi were twisted creatures in many ways.

"Seeing what you've already built is amazing," Kal continued. "I mean, I never was proud to be a Human, but you guys have opened my eyes." He was laying it on thick.

The team leader turned away from his scanning and looked at Kal. Finally, he gave a small nod of acknowledgement.

Kal felt a surge of accomplishment. He'd actually gotten a Nasi soldier to behave like something other than an automaton. It was a minor victory, just a nod of the head, but it gave him a flash of confidence to keep going. He needed to distract these two Nasi from the inspection, cause them to be

211

lax. He realized he was considering this because of Nicole and Bo. They'd made him realize that the Nasi, for lack of a better term, were still Human.

"I'm sure it must be tough to be away from wherever you're from," Kal continued. "But it's worth it to me. Sure, there's some that don't agree with it, but they're the same type of people who said Humans shouldn't invent the fold drive." He wondered if the allusion to their origins would resonate. "I've got a family back on Wudexingqiu." He saw the team leader train the device on the ladder between the decks and quickly pulled out the actual picture of him and his family from his jacket pocket. A younger version of Kal stood surrounded by his wife Li Na and children, Lan Fen and Stephen. "This is a picture we took a while ago. I liked it so much I even got it printed." Kal held the picture out to the two soldiers.

After a brief pause, the team leader picked it out of Kal's grip and held it in front of his face mask. "It is a nice picture," he remarked. Kal could detect a hint of something—wistfulness, perhaps—in his voice.

"You want to see the cockpit and cabins on the second deck?" Kal asked. Now time to direct them away from the danger area.

The team leader put the scanner down and nodded. Kal led the two inspectors through the top deck of the ship, talking the entire time. He wasn't normally a talker, but spending a decade as a free merchant had taught him how to carry a conversation even if the other people had no desire to take part. The Nasi warmed up, bit by bit, to him. They were still cold by Human standards but were at least responding with short sentences when Kal asked a question. He remembered something a friend of his had told him a long time ago: conversation was as much about what was not said as what was said. He played the dumb Human and asked questions he knew the answers to. When the soldiers responded, Kal listened to hear not only what they said but where they hesitated or when they refused to answer altogether.

"So I assume they're letting you out onto the planet." Kal was pretty sure that they weren't. "I haven't been to Mariga before. Any recommendations?"

"No." The answer from the team leader was short and final—he'd touched a nerve. The team leader turned around, exited the cockpit, and glided down the ladder into the bay. The two Nasi moved so smoothly even inside the tight confines of the ship that Kal couldn't help but be impressed. He could only imagine what he'd look like in a battle suit trying the same thing.

"You're cleared," the team leader said as Kal turned around from climbing down the ladder. "Remain here and we'll instruct your crew to join you. We will remove the cargo immediately." He paused for a moment. "Thanks for your cooperation."

The other soldier slid near Kal. "Try the Flying Snow Worm," she whispered before turning and trailing the team leader out of the bay.

The other Skulls strode up the ramp followed by two Nasi soldiers and a pallet lifter. The Nasi strode through the room, seemingly oblivious to the Humans, and placed the cargo on the lifter.

One of them turned to face Kal with a small chit reader in their hand. Kal obligingly pulled out their credit chit so that it could be scanned. "The outstanding balance of your payment along with your escrow has been applied to your chit. You are not required to depart Mariga, but you will leave this port facility immediately." They turned around and strode down the cargo ramp, leaving the Humans looking at one another.

"Let's get airborne," Kal said as he slammed the button to close the back cargo door. He'd already pushed it with the Nasi soldiers; there wasn't a way to get Bo off the ship.

No one said a word as Chedjou and Ramos climbed up to the cockpit and the Tac-I squad retreated to the galley. Even with the ramp closed, they were in the Foothold; they could talk later.

# Chapter Fourteen

Torgut's public landing port differed from the ones Nicole had seen on other planets. Rather than a single large pad, or amalgamation of several, Torgut's port was divided into isolated clusters, each containing about a hundred pads. The entire port was enclosed, with a large aperture above each pad that could constrict open and closed to let ships in and out. From above, the nest of landing pads appeared almost like an insect hive, with hundreds of apertures at the top, spaced at regular intervals.

The flight from the Foothold had been over in less than a minute. Kal had stood in the bay, his brow furrowed the entire time. While he'd been inside *Annie* with the Nasi soldiers, Nicole had felt like she was going to explode. Thoughts of the hundreds of ways their plan could go wrong kept floating through her head. All the while, she had maintained the same airy expression on her face, trying to appear unconcerned that the Nasi could find them out and kill them at any moment.

"Okay, we're clear," Kal said. "Bo, you can come out."

Nicole turned to look at the ladder, waiting for the panel near the ceiling to slide open. Nothing happened.

"Bo?" Kal called again.

He waited a few more seconds and then unhooked the ladder, placing it on the ground, and opened the panel. It slid open without a sound, revealing an empty compartment.

"When did he leave?" Kal asked, turning around to look at Nicole.

"No idea." She hadn't seen a thing. Bo had somehow left the ship with none of them noticing, not to mention the four

Nasi soldiers that had been inspecting it. She chuckled. "Good job, Bo."

"Well, looks like we have time to start scouting the city," Kal said. Hu turned to Sergeant Kimathi, who'd just entered the bay. "Let's get a rotation going. We'll need at least two people in the ship at all times. There are a few leads we should chase down while we're here, so I plan on getting out of this port and seeing what we can find out. We don't know when or how Bowen will return, so be ready to leave at a moment's notice."

Kimathi nodded and headed back to the galley.

"What leads?" Nicole asked.

"I actually struck up a conversation with the Nasi," Kal said.

"Really?" Nicole couldn't believe that Kal, of all people, would strike up a conversation with a Nasi soldier. It seemed you could teach old dogs new tricks.

"Well, conversation may be too strong a word. But I got them to talk to me. They mentioned a place I'd like to check out. A chem bar, I'm guessing. Also, we should see if we can reach our Alliance friends. They're our only hope since the Nasi have stamped out all resistance groups on the planet." He held up the chit he used to contact the Alliance.

"So I guess we get our bearings and see if they contact us?"

Kal nodded. "I've already activated the chit. It's like on Patagonia and Tamulk—no response. If the Alliance is here, they'll try to make contact."

"What did you say to the Nasi?" Nicole asked.

Kal shrugged. "Nothing much. Mainly I just let my mouth go. Talked about how great they were and how Humans were so in need of their help. Then I mentioned family and tried to pull on the old heartstrings."

"Guess it worked." She had a hard time imagining any of the four death-dealing Nasi she'd seen as having a family or emotions for that matter. It was also surprising that Kal was willing to even mention his family to the Nasi; he almost never did to her.

"We'll find out," Kal said as he started toward the ladder. "I'll talk with Ramos and Chedjou. Be ready to leave in ten."

The war was good for business. Equipment and weapons needed to be transported and most of the free merchants in the galaxy were happy to do it if the price was right. Nicole heard ships taking off and landing through the portals that connected the clusters of bays within Torgut's port. Walls dropped from the ceiling and ended about five meters above the ground, separating the clusters from each other. The pads were filled with civilian merchant ships of different makes and models while a variety of species walked between the ships, chatting with each other.

"Welcome home, sir," Sergeant Kimathi said as he looked around the landing port.

"Thanks," Kal replied, "it hasn't changed a bit since I was here except for the ads." Like all landing ports, advertisements were plastered on the walls, and kiosks littered the center of the hallways. The only people coming through a landside port like this one were merchants; passengers entered through the orbital station. Brightly colored signs advertised maintenance shops, equipment dealers, bars, and less savory items for a merchant who might be looking for a day or two of rest.

The four Humans joined the flow of traffic and followed the signs toward the exit. As they walked with the crowd, Nicole could hear snippets of conversation.

"—finally get a day's rest—"

"—they've got the best rates, but you hate to think about what they'll do with the cargo—"

"—tried it and they never could stop. It's that good—"

"—but I think Samsara Fleet at least has a chance—"

Nicole had to prevent herself from turning to look at the two Qudoru talking to each other as they slithered past on their way back to their ship; the Skulls operated in the shadows and in deep space. Hearing others talk about Samsara Fleet made her feel good even if it didn't sound like they had full confidence.

The pathway led them to the mouth of a large tunnel lined with velomats carrying pedestrians in and out of the port. Nicole stepped onto one and felt a small touch of wind across her face and realized the walls were now streaking by although she was still walking at the same pace. She looked up to see a bright blue sky bracketed by sparkling white glaciers.

Sergeant Kimathi and Private Fischer looked around the tunnel, smiles on their faces as they enjoyed the experience.

Velomats couldn't handle harsh climates and were expensive to build, making their use relatively rare. This was the largest one Nicole had ever seen.

Finally, the tunnel ended, and they walked out onto a bustling city street. The air was crisp and held a hint of earth while the sun shone down on them from the ribbons of blue sky that peeked between the tall buildings that surrounded them.

"Why isn't it cold?" asked Fischer, still taking in the people and cityscape around them.

"Because we're not outside," Kal replied. "We're about a hundred meters underground. That"—he pointed to the sky— "isn't real. It's a viewscreen."

Nicole looked up and did a double take. It seemed so real. It had to be the largest viewscreen she'd ever seen. She tried to find a flaw, some way to confirm it wasn't actually the sky.

"Look at the buildings," he said, noticing Nicole studying the ceiling. "You can see a small line where the screen intersects with them." Kal pulled her close to him and pointed at a tall building in front of them. "See right there?"

She saw it. Each building had a thin black line bisecting it, all around the same height. The tops of the buildings, like the sky, were just an image on the viewscreen.

"The buildings go up past the viewscreen," Kal said. "They extend through the ground and poke out through the top of the planet's surface. You might have seen them when we were flying from the Foothold."

Now she understood. "So all of those bumps on the

ground we saw when we were landing—"

"Are just the tops of these buildings. They're mostly beneath the ground. It's much more efficient to heat them, and the wind on the surface is intense."

"But the Foothold was completely aboveground," Nicole said.

"Yeah, I don't think the Nasi had a choice," Kal said. "They build using their weaves. It takes decades to build underground, and that was time they didn't have. Besides, they have that huge atmospheric shield. That's something I've never seen before."

Citizens and merchants hurried past them, seemingly oblivious to what was going on around them as they used their implants, their faces vacant. Nicole had expected everyone to be dressed in grime-covered coveralls, but she saw several people wearing fashions that wouldn't have been out of place on Earth.

Kal led them through the busy streets. Nicole recognized the names and logos on many of the buildings they passed. These were the large mining and energy companies that had powered much of the United Earth Government's empire. Countless fortunes had been made on this very planet because of its abundance of mineral wealth. Most of it had been transported to New America or Patagonia to be refined into finished goods.

"I don't know what I expected," Ekon said, looking around, "but it wasn't this."

"It's not all like this," Kal said. "This is the center of the capital. When you get into the deep tunnels and the mining outposts, it's a lot different."

"That's where you grew up, right?" Nicole asked. The stories Kal had told her had been of a hardscrabble childhood. His father had been a country doctor, treating the miners, and his mother, who'd been a teacher, had died when he was relatively young.

"Yeah, though I'd only come to the capital with my father a few times each year either to pick up supplies or just get some culture. I'll call a transport; we're going to go to another part of the city."

Less than a minute later, a small six-seat vehicle glided down next to them. A transparent bubble covered the top and sides of the vehicle where it met a dirt-covered thruster at the bottom. After landing, a door opened on the vehicle's side, and the four of them climbed into the cabin, taking seats on the rows of benches in the middle facing outwards.

"East Arm," Kal called out after they were all seated. The vehicle gently lifted off the ground and sped between the buildings and over the heads of the pedestrians several meters below.

As they made their way through the city, the crowds disappeared, and the viewscreen ceiling gradually descended as they neared the edge of the enormous cavern that contained Torgut. The buildings grew shorter as well, some of them not even reaching the viewscreen. The well-known corporate logos gave way to smaller establishments like grocers, equipment retailers, and restaurants. The people passing them on the street had changed as well. The fashionable neon colors, transparent materials, and sparkling jewelry were gone and had been replaced by stone-faced men, women, and children in utilitarian coveralls and work clothes. They walked with a purpose, not like they were eager to get where they were going but like they knew one way or another they'd end up there. This was the Mariga Nicole had been expecting.

"We're getting into a sketchy part of town," Kal said. "This is miner territory, so keep your wits about you when we land."

Eventually the enormous cavern narrowed until they were traveling through what Nicole would have called a large tunnel—the East Arm, Nicole realized. Several strips of lights replaced the viewscreen sky on the ceiling. Ramshackle buildings and shops nestled against the walls or in a row in the middle. The businesses catered to miners with pawnshops, bars, equipment suppliers, and brothels taking up every available storefront.

"Torgut is shaped like a star or a person," Kal explained. "There's the center and then four tunnels that lead from it: East Arm, West Arm, East Leg, West Leg, and the Head. Everyone enters town through one of the arms or legs. The ends of the arms and legs can be dicey though East Arm is the worst. I almost never went to the center, wasn't much there for average people." Nicole eyed a brothel with several scantily clad men and women standing outside—culture, indeed.

"This is fine," Kal said to the transport's AI. "Let us down here."

The vehicle obediently slowed down and landed on the

hard-packed cave floor. The tunnel had narrowed so much that the stores were close together, forcing the throngs of people to shove past each other as they made their way past. The press of people pushing their way past each other reminded Nicole of the Z'Ta hive on T'kor'nuk where the rocklike creatures crawled over each other as they moved around their nests.

"Before we do anything else, we should eat," Kal said, looking at the other three. "You ever eaten Marigan cooking?"

They shook their heads. "Probably a reason for that," Kal smiled. "But we need to be seen. Besides, you've never lived until you've had ice worm pho."

Nicole took another bite and tried not to grimace as she chewed on the rubbery ice worm meat. Besides the horrible texture, the meat was completely flavorless except for a slightly metallic aftertaste. No wonder Marigans liked spices. She had to imagine they ate it because of the prevalence of the worms rather than any sort of gastronomic desire.

"Interesting place," Sergeant Kimathi said, eying the room.

The Iced Canary was an overload to the senses. Viewscreens hung from the ceilings, dividing the tables and displaying a jumble of entertainment: seminude Humans gyrating, random scenes of carnage, and nature shots from the Marigan landscape. Meanwhile, the viewscreens affixed to the wall cycled through static advertisements for alcohol and designer drugs. Clientele, mostly Human, packed the bar. They sat at the tightly clustered tables or stood by the bar at the far end of the room downing their drinks glumly. A coarse fabric hung over a door in the back which surely led to more illicit activities than in the front. Like many bars on Mariga, the Iced Canary served food, presumably to lure in the workers who were only looking for a meal to eat. Nicole guessed that many of them ordered more than after being in there for a while.

"Yeah," Kal agreed. "You get used to it."

"You used to come to places like this when you were a kid, sir?" Private Fischer asked, his eyes wide.

"Don't call me sir here," Kal replied gruffly. "And yes. Most of Mariga is a cold and harsh place. My father did what he could."

"What are we doing here exactly?" Nicole asked, trying to change the subject.

"We're fishing," Kal replied. "I don't know where our friends are. If they're anywhere, I'd guess it's in the East Arm; it's the shadiest place in the city. Last time, they found us. I'm hoping they will again."

"Don't look," Kimathi whispered as he looked to his left, Nicole's right, "but looks like we're drawing a bit of attention."

Nicole stretched, placing her arms above her head and arching her upper body back as she turned her head slightly to the right. Four people—two men and two women—sat several tables over. They wore dark blouses that covered what looked to be cargo pants. The group was engaged in a conversation, but periodically glanced at the Skulls, studying them. As Nicole's gaze darted over the group, one woman locked eyes with her, and her mouth turned up in a smile. Nicole hastily looked back at her table.

"I said don't look," hissed Kimathi.

"They know we're out of place," said Kal. "We need to avoid trouble. Just eat your food and be prepared for anything when we leave."

They continued to eat quietly, only exchanging brief words between bites and sips. Nicole kept her eyes forward, assiduously studying a holo on the far wall for the entire meal. After Kal had transferred the credits to the attendant bot, they stepped up from the table and brushed through the crowd to get back into the street.

Nicole casually brushed her hand against her thigh, reassuring herself that her pistol was still there. The hair on the back of her neck rose as she saw the group at the other table leave the bar behind them.

The situation reminded her of her childhood, of carefully sneaking out of her family's small room in the commune to go play with friends. She remembered padding through the hallways and looking around corners to make sure that she didn't stumble upon any of the people her parents warned her about.

The crowd had thinned out some though there were plenty of pedestrians still walking through the area. *They wouldn't try anything here,* Nicole reassured herself. She wasn't afraid of the four Humans—she'd taken on Nasi and survived, for goodness' sake. She was worried about the attention that facing them might bring. In the communes, the only thing worse than the criminals who lived inside were the criminals who patrolled the area. Nicole didn't know what information the Nasi or the local security had on them, but the last thing she wanted was to find out.

*Time to end this,* Nicole said to the rest of the team. There was no use in waiting for the thugs to jump them.

She spun around and leveled her pistol. The rest of the squad was a split second behind her, their plasma pistols aimed directly at the four toughs. Their pursuers stopped in their tracks and slowly raised their arms, warily looking back at the Skulls.

"Whoa, easy," said one of the men. He smiled, the tattoo covering half his face making the expression seem sinister rather than reassuring.

Kal nodded to an alleyway a few shops down. "We need to get out of the street."

"Head over to the alley," Nicole instructed with a flick of her head. "Move slowly. Anything strange and we shoot all of you." It wasn't an idle threat.

Their would-be assailants moved slowly toward the alleyway, hands up. Pedestrians walked around the eight of them, diligently looking away as they tried to stay out of the situation. Nicole could tell from their reaction that this was not uncommon in East Arm.

"Look, we're just walking down the street, same as you," said the man with the tattoo.

"Stop," said Kal. "Why were you following us?"

"We weren't," said a woman, "we're just enjoying some rest and relaxation. You know, R&R."

Kal fired his pistol. The plasma round hit the ground between the woman's feet. "Enough bullshit," Kal said. "Speak, or this will get a lot worse for you."

"Fine. Fine." The woman took a step back. "Look we need to eat, same as anyone else. We thought you might be able to help us out."

*I doubt they know who we are,* said Nicole. *I think we just take the weapons and go. We can't stay here long.*

*Agreed,* Kal said.

"Put your guns on the ground and kick them to us," Kal ordered.

Two of the group members dragged out their pistols, obediently placed them on the ground, and then kicked them toward the Skulls. The weapons clattered against their feet. Kimathi and Fischer bent down and picked up the weapons, placing them in the waistband of their pants.

"Any more?" Nicole asked.

The four shook their heads.

"Kneel down," Kal commanded. "We're going to walk out of this alley." Kal's voice wasn't loud, but it was firm, leaving no doubt of his resolve. "You'll stay like this for five minutes. If you move or if you leave this spot, we'll put a hole in each of your torsos. We're not—"

He stopped speaking as a wall of ear shatteringly loud noise filled the alleyway. Nicole dropped her weapon and slammed her hands against her ears, trying to stop the sound. The shrill noise filled her head and dropped her to the ground, writing in pain. Finally, it stopped. She lay on the hard packed dirt for a moment, trying to catch her breath. She heard boots behind her, coming near her. She opened her eyes to see two security patrollers in armored black uniforms, rifles pointed at the Skulls.

"Don't move," said a woman, her face expressionless, "or I will open fire."

The other patroller holstered his rifle and moved between the four Skulls, roughly pulling their arms behind their backs and attaching restraints. There was a faint smell of something medicinal on his breath, some sort of drug—Zip, perhaps? Their four assailants pulled themselves off the ground, dusting themselves off and shaking their heads slowly, trying to clear them.

"Thanks," the tattooed man said. "But damn, you know I hate the sound cannon."

"Shut up," said the female patroller. "You should've been more careful. Now we gotta clean up your mess. Get outta here."

The toughs walked past the Skulls toward the mouth of the alley. Two of them bent over and pulled their weapons from the Tac-I's waistbands while another planted a kick directly into Nicole's ribs. She groaned as a knife of pain stabbed through her torso.

The male patroller had pulled out his pistol and had it trained on them as well. "Get up, and get into the transport," directed the man.

*Should we rush them?* Kimathi asked over the net.

*What would that do?* asked Kal. *No, just keep quiet and*

228

*do as they say for now.*

The woman pulled out a small device from her vest pocket and walked over to Kal, pressing it against the back of his head. Nicole heard a small sound, like the puff of an air gun and saw a small metal disc attached to his scalp. The man pulled out the same device and was walking toward her and Kimathi.

*They're disabling our implants,* Nicole thought to herself. She tried to reach their crew on *Annie. We need help. We're at—* The implant went dead as she felt the small pinch of the disc embedding itself into her skin.

"No calling for friends." The patroller smiled patronizingly down at her. "Now like I said before, get into the transport."

Obediently, Nicole rolled herself over, stood up, and trudged into the jet-black police vehicle at the mouth of the alley. The vehicle's oval-shaped interior was bare except for a strip of lights on the ceiling and gray padding on the walls, floor, and ceiling. She climbed into the back of the vehicle and flopped into a seated position on the floor next to Kimathi.

As he was about to close the door, the male patroller stopped, eyes going distant for a moment. Someone was contacting him over his neural implant. "Seems like someone wants to meet you," he said. "Guess it's your lucky day."

The door hissed shut, and seconds later, Nicole could feel them take off.

# Chapter Fifteen

Kal looked around the bare cabin of the patrol vehicle, searching for anything that might help them. The feeble cabin lights glared from above with a ghoulish light, casting dark shadows down the other's faces.

"Well, you said you wanted to be noticed," Kimathi said in a lighthearted tone as he tested his restraints.

"Quiet," Kal hissed. "I'm sure they're listening to us. Just do as they say." He hoped the team could infer the "for now" added to the end of that statement.

He could feel the patrol vehicle winding through the arm—probably away from the center of the city—and then felt them climb. They had to be above the surface, probably in one of the mass transit tubes that coursed across the planet. Other than the sensation of movement, he didn't know what was going on. There were no viewscreens or windows for him to see out of, and the chamber seemed to be soundproofed. Who were these people and who were they taking them to see? Kal had never been a fan of the police in Mariga, but he'd never known them to be this corrupt. Things had changed since he'd been away.

Kal remembered seeing the Mariga police striding through the passageways of Torgut and being impressed with their black armor and fearsome rifles. They'd been tough but had always acted like they cared about the citizens; he'd even had an officer stop and give him a larva candy once.

Finally, the car descended before landing with a soft thump onto the ground.

"We're *here*," sang Kimathi, earning a dirty look from

Nicole.

The door swung open in a blaze of light. For a moment, Kal thought they were outside. *They're going to leave us out here to die.* However, the air blowing through the open door was cool but not the skin-freezing cold of the surface. There was a whiff of spice and earth in the air, scents not found on the surface. As his eyes adjusted, Kal realized they had landed in a hydropod.

Almost every Human-built structure on Mariga was in the caves and chasms below the ice. It was the best way to protect the inhabitants from the wind and cold and allowed them easier access to the rich minerals in the rock. One exception to this practice were the hydropods, enormous hydroponic farms with heated glass roofs that sat flush with the surface of the planet. It allowed them to use natural light to grow the crops needed to sustain the population.

Kal stepped out of the vehicle at the patroller's command and looked around. Rows upon rows of white towers, slightly taller than Kal, stretched beneath a vast glass dome. Plants sprouted from holes drilled into the towers at regular intervals and cascaded toward the ground. A metallic wall, keeping out the glacier that surrounded them, made its way to either side of them and disappeared behind the towers.

"Kal Norman?" asked a small woman, her head barely reaching Kal's shoulder.

"Yes," Kal replied, shielding his eyes against the harsh glare of the sun pulsing through the glass dome. He searched his memory, trying to recall if he'd ever met her. He doubted it. Her face was smooth, angular, and perfectly symmetrical with dark eyes that seemed both alluring and dangerous. Black braids rose from her head and curled around each other in loops, creating a sculpture that seemed almost too delicate to exist.

"Stay there," instructed the woman. She nodded to a large man, his head glistening under the sun, standing next to her. "Check him out."

The man walked up to Kal and scanned him with a small device, no bigger than Kimathi's pack of cards. "It's him," the man said.

The woman nodded and smiled. "You can release them."

The two patrollers quickly removed the restraints and stepped back to the patrol car.

"What happened?" She looked angrily at the two patrollers.

"Kitzik's crew was going to jump 'em and got jumped instead," the woman replied with a small smirk. "They called us for help."

"Sloppy." The woman's eyes flashed. "That's the kind of shit that will get us noticed. Make sure Kitzik understands."

"You wanna—" the man started.

"You know exactly what I want." Her rosebud mouth pinched in a scowl. "I don't care if he's your mate. Do your job."

"Of course," the patrollers responded in unison.

She smiled perfunctorily. "I always appreciate the understanding we have with the Torgut police. But I need some time alone with our friends." The patrollers quickly walked back to the driver's compartment of their vehicle and got in. Seconds later, it was airborne and glided through a round hatch in the hydropod's side.

"Sorry for that. Come walk with me." She beckoned them with a single crooked finger and turned around, not waiting to see if they followed. This was a woman who was used to being obeyed.

Kal walked next to her as she turned and strode through the rows of hydroponic towers. She reminded him of a Nasi, face impassive with smooth flowing movements as she walked over the spall covered ground.

"General Norman, what brings you to Mariga?" the woman asked.

"We came for the sun," Kal replied, raising his arms toward the dome. "Maybe you tell me who you are and then we can talk more."

The woman turned to look at him, a smile on her lips. "I saved your life, you know. If the Alliance hadn't placed a monitor order on your ship, then you'd be on the surface frozen solid right now."

"So you're Alliance?" Kal asked.

"I *was*." The woman sighed. "Now I'm just me. Name's Gudit."

"What are you now then?" Kal had never heard of anyone *leaving* the Alliance. Sure, he'd worked for them, but only as an independent contractor for a few runs. He didn't know much about the organization but had always had the impression that once you were in, you were in for life.

"Just a woman trying to make a living," Gudit replied. "The Alliance is gone."

"It's not completely gone," Kal said. "I've seen some of your colleagues on other planets." He thought he saw a flicker of concern behind her dark eyes. The Alliance wouldn't look kindly on one of their operatives abandoning them.

"Well, I haven't heard from them in over a year," she replied with a shake of her head. "There hasn't been a single message through the net. I can't sit and wait for instructions like a good little soldier forever."

They walked through the rows of plants in silence with the other three Skulls and Gudit's bodyguard trailing behind, still in earshot. The hydroponic towers stretched in front of them, preventing Kal from seeing beyond either side of the small path they walked down. What or who else was in the hydropod with them? He doubted that someone like Gudit would trust her safety to a single bodyguard.

"So why'd you free us? What do you want?" Kal asked.

"Honestly, I'm not sure," Gudit replied. "Like I said, your ship, the *Queen Anne's Revenge*, is tagged in the Alliance's monitoring program on this planet. I still have some of those protocols running. It's a good way to know who's going on and off the planet. When I heard some of my crew got jumped by a bunch of merchants, I figured you may have a hand in it."

Kal didn't buy the story for a moment. It wasn't pure chance that they'd gotten jumped by four of her goons as soon as they arrived on Mariga. He was guessing she was targeting former Alliance agents and shaking them down. The question he had was why she'd decided not to go through with it. Did she want something? He hoped it was because she wanted to help them but doubted it. Gudit did not seem like a woman who'd risk anything for a cause other than her own.

"You must have some idea of why we're here," Kal said. "What we're fighting for."

She nodded. "I do, but I'm not sure why you're fighting. You're from Mariga, so you know the planet. Has it really changed since the Nasi came? Here on Mariga things are the same; normal men and women go to work and then the corporations take their money. The only change is that the planetary governor reports to the Nasi instead of Earth."

Growing up as the son of a miner, Kal had seen firsthand how accurate Gudit's words were. Although they'd had a house and he'd had a standard middle-class childhood, he'd seen men and women he loved get up every day and work themselves to death in the mines below the surface. Their hard work built the enormous towers in the center of Torgut, and the only thing they got was a premature death from the toxins and chemicals that pervaded the air in the mines. However, he'd left Mariga and seen the rest of the galaxy. Along the way, he'd learned that there was more to the equation than what he'd seen on his home planet. Even though the average citizen of Mariga didn't notice the difference, he knew their work was now helping the Nasi, who would use the planet's raw mineral wealth to create a fleet that would conquer the galaxy. It may seem like it was the same to these people, but it wasn't.

"You know there's a difference," Kal replied. "Maybe the man and woman in the mine shaft don't see it, but people like

235

you and me do. The UEG wasn't the best, but the Nasi are so much worse."

"I'm not here to be a revolutionary," Gudit replied. "I'm a businesswoman. Consider this a professional courtesy. I may not be in the Alliance anymore, but I figured I'd help a former freelancer."

"Fair enough," Kal said. "Then let's do some business. Information for credits."

"I'm listening," Gudit said.

The ground in front of them swung down, revealing a ramp that led to a dark cave. The former Alliance leader didn't break stride as she walked down and into the square opening below.

"Come on, General Norman," Gudit called out, turning to look back at him. "Let's do business."

The door led to a small metal-lined chamber that the six of them barely fit in. On the other side of the room from the ramp stood a reinforced door with a black security panel next to it. Gudit placed her hand on the panel and the door swung open with a small click, revealing a large room lined with viewscreens.

"So welcome to one of my panic rooms," Gudit said as she flopped down on a chair. The four plush chairs were the only furniture in the cold metallic room.

"What is this place?" asked Private Fischer. "You had this built just for you?"

"When they first built the hydropods, the pumps and machinery were housed in these chambers. About fifty years ago, the government retrofitted most of them and never bothered to do anything with the space." She patted the chair next to hers. "So, Kal, what do you want, and how much are you willing to pay for it?"

"Information," said Kal. "We want any information you've got on the Nasi. Specifically, we're trying to find out about their fleet locations. Any word on supply vessels, anything like that. Also, we know the Nasi have been building new surface shipyards and long-range plasma cannons. It'd be helpful to learn more about those as well."

"Oh, that's all," Gudit replied with a hollow laugh. "Just the most dangerous information on the planet."

"I thought you wanted to do business. This is the information we need. If you're afraid, we'll go somewhere else."

"Damn right, I'm afraid. You are too." She motioned around the room. "We all should be. I've seen what the Nasi can do, and I gather you've seen more than I have. I don't want to get on their bad side."

"You must know something," Nicole said. "No one, not even the Nasi, can build these things in total secrecy. There's got to be supply routes, workers, aerial images, something that you can provide."

Gudit put her hands behind her head and bit her lip as she thought. Kal could tell the woman enjoyed the leverage and control she had over the situation. "Perhaps," she mused. "But I'll need time."

"How much time?" Kal asked. Time was much more valuable than credits.

"I don't know." She made an exasperated sigh. "Not like there's some sort of standard timetable for this type of information."

"We can give you a day. Maybe."

"What the hell?" Gudit sat up on the couch. "That's not enough time to get shit."

"It's all the time we have," Kal said. "We may have to leave at a moment's notice. We'll pay for anything you can provide, no matter how small." With Bowen somewhere in the Nasi Foothold, they had to be ready to leave the planet at any time. He wanted to get what information he could right away.

That calmed her down. "You'd better," she said. "And you're gonna need to pay upfront."

"What the—"

Kal held up his hand, stopping Kimathi from saying anything else. Gudit scoffed and looked up at the sergeant. "I could just leave you here. Hell, I could shoot you or turn you in to the Nasi." She stood up. "You're only alive because of me. Remember that."

"Yeah, we get it," Kal said. "But if you work with us, you could be a helluva lot richer."

"Hey, I'm willing to bargain." Gudit opened her arms. "You tell me what you're willing to pay."

"How about this—" Kal tried to remember how much money they had on their chit. It had to be several million credits. Now a bit more with the credits they'd received from delivering the Triple-A. "Two hundred thousand up front and then we'll pay depending on what you bring us."

"What?" Ekon shouted.

Kal saw the small grin creep onto Gudit's face. He'd seen that look in other's eyes, usually before something terrible happened. "The money's encoded in a biometric chit tied to my implant," Kal warned. "You do anything and the deal's off. You won't get anything."

"Oh, but I've got people," purred Gudit. She was playing with him to see what he'd do.

"It's military grade encryption that's been enhanced by the Jadid," Kal lied. "So either take the deal or we're getting the hell out of here."

"Calm down." The moment passed. "I'll see what I can get you."

"Good choice," Kal said, feeling a small bit of control return. "And maybe we can see about making this arrangement more permanent depending on what you find."

Gudit considered the thought. "We'll see. There'll be a transport outside waiting to take you back. You can work out the details with my people. I'll be in touch soon."

"No more than twenty-four hours," Kal replied. He turned around and walked out of the crime lord's panic room, not wanting to stay a second longer. The three others followed him out the door and up the ramp.

Kal felt his hackles rise. They'd have to be careful; Gudit was a wild card. The woman was as equally likely to turn them in as help them.

❖

True to Gudit's word, a transport was already waiting for them by the time they returned to the edge of the hydropod. Two men, dressed in simple black trousers and blouses, were waiting by the vehicle.

The trip back to the East Arm was less eventful than Kal expected. He'd hoped to see a bit of the caves and landscape of the planet, but they spent most of the journey inside one of the large metal tubes that rose above the surface. The only thing Kal could see through the viewscreens was the regular pulse of the pipe's safety lights as they sped through. The transport finally exited the nondescript tunnel at the far edge of the East Arm and touched down outside a pawnshop.

The transport door opened, and the Skulls climbed back out onto the city street. The henchmen efficiently removed the discs from the back of each of their heads before handing Kal a small chit. "Now we just need payment. Two hundred thousand."

Legitimate commerce was done through simple transfers of credits between accounts using neural implants. For people like the Alliance or Gudit, these types of transactions were too public, too easily traced. Chits got around this problem by keeping all the credit encrypted on the card itself. The only people who knew about the transactions were the owners of the cards. It was completely untraceable.

Kal obligingly transferred the money between the chits. "Okay, we'll be in touch," said the man after verifying the credits had transferred to his chit. He turned around and climbed back into the transport, the other man following behind, and lifted off, speeding in the direction of the city's center.

"That was interesting," Nicole said. "Think we'll see her again?"

"No idea, but we should get back to the ship," Kal replied. "We've got to let the others know we're safe."

A transport arrived minutes after Kal called for it with his implant, and they climbed in. As they sped through the East Arm, Kal reflected on what had just happened. Why would the former Alliance boss spare them? The mild sense of nostalgia he'd had when they'd arrived was fading, shoved aside by their encounter with Gudit. Mariga was a hard planet, but its people were harder. The thought that the woman would use her connections in the Alliance to rob former contractors was unconscionable even for a career criminal. Kal thought back to the flicker of fear in her eyes; she knew what the Alliance would do if they found out she'd worked for them. Kal could only imagine.

"Glad to see you're back," Sergeant Bhatt said casually as they walked into the galley. Across from her, Bo was studying the cards splayed out in his hands.

"What the hell," Kimathi said. "We send out a distress call over the *public net* and you just sit here on the ship playing cards."

"Yup, Sergeant," Sergeant Bhatt replied, momentarily glancing up from her hand. "What'd you want us to do?" She drew two of the brightly colored cards from the pile in front of her. "Call the patrollers? We didn't know where you were. Besides, you always manage to escape with everything

241

intact." She glanced down at Kimathi's two prosthetic legs. "Well, *almost* always."

"You took my cards from my storage locker too," the sergeant complained, flinging his hand out at the deck on the table.

"We were bored." From Bhatt's tone, it sounded like she still was. "We wanted some practice."

Sergeant Kimathi muttered a curse and stomped out of the room. Kal could see Bhatt's lip twitch in a barely suppressed smile as he left. She was in Samsara Fleet but still had the heart of a rebel.

"Anything happen while we were out?" Kal asked.

The sergeant shook her head. "Nothing, sir. What happened to you guys?"

Kal quickly gave her the details on the expedition to the East Arm. He knew little about Bhatt but knew enough to suspect that she had had experience with people like Gudit. She knew exactly how things like this worked.

"You think she'll come back with anything? Or at all?"

"Maybe," Kal replied. "It's worth the investment if we can get any solid information."

"Speaking of that," Nicole interjected. "We've got at least a day. What's next?" Kal's mind went to the place the Nasi soldier had mentioned, the Flying Snow Worm. He'd never heard of it, but it seemed like their next best lead.

# Chapter Sixteen

The Flying Snow Worm was nestled between a general store and a pawnshop in a quiet section of the West Arm of Torgut. As Kal had expected, it was a chem bar like most of the surrounding establishments. A cute animated snow worm jumping out of a glacier and flying over the ground flickered on the holo out front. In real life, snow worms were terrifying, at least four meters long and as wide as a person's waist with a circular row of razor-sharp teeth they used to burrow through the ice. There were stories of miners who'd been in the wrong place at the wrong time and been cut in half by a snow worm that burrowed through the tunnel they were walking through.

The interior was smaller than he expected with only a few tables scattered throughout the enclosed dining area. A clearly inebriated woman gyrated on top of a small stage in a corner of the room and screeched the words to a song Kal remembered from his youth. A couple of Human servers walked between the tables, chatting with the customers, taking their orders, and delivering them to the bar along one wall. Overall, it could have been almost any bar on Mariga, perhaps a little smaller and cleaner than most, but nothing out of the ordinary from what he could tell.

Kal and Sergeant Bhatt took a seat and waited for a server to come around. The clientele was more upscale than what he'd seen in the East Arm. Mainly low-level white-collar workers along with some foremen from the mines in town on a supply run. It was the kind of place his father would have taken him to.

"Seems normal," Bhatt said, looking around the room. Kal nodded, disappointed.

A large woman sauntered over to their table to take their orders. Kal had already studied the menu displayed on the tabletop screen. The food looked more appetizing than Kal remembered from the places he'd frequented as a kid. It was mainly traditional Marigan fare: snow worms, algae, and the like. They had drugs and alcohol of course. How else would they stay in business? But it looked like the owner put some effort into the food as well.

"Better food than most chem bars," said Bhatt after the woman had left.

"The definitely seem to take the food pretty seriously here," Kal agreed. "I see nothing else out of place though. This could be anywhere."

"What were you expecting?" Bhatt asked.

"I don't know," Kal replied. "There's got to be some reason that Nasi soldier suggested we go here."

They talked while they ate their food. It had been ages since Kal had eaten any dishes from home. Between bites he scanned the room but saw nothing remotely interesting except for the inebriated woman still caterwauling on the karaoke stage. It was impressive that she was still standing. Watching her became a sort of game. Every time she staggered her way to the edge of the stage, Kal tapped Bhatt's foot. Each time they were disappointed as the woman somehow remained upright instead of falling off the stage and flat on her face. Kal remembered his father saying to him, "Luck favors drunks and children," when they'd visit town.

The two Skulls kept their conversation light and steered away from discussing anything related to the Nasi, Jadid, or Samsara Fleet. Unfortunately, that eliminated virtually everything they had in common. After several minutes of awkwardly asking what holos the other had seen, they found some common ground in talking about their childhoods.

"I'm worried about Ekon," Bhatt said, changing the subject. "Seems like he's having trouble at work."

Kal peeked at the other tables. The conversation was awfully close to reality. "He'll pick it up," he replied. "Jobs like his are high stress. Leading a drilling crew is tough work."

"He's young," Bhatt replied, running her hands over her stubbled scalp. She'd picked up the habit since she'd shaved her head recently. "It's a lot of responsibility."

"You're young," Kal replied. He saw her mouth twist in annoyance. "Drilling is a young person's job." Kal looked her in the eyes. "Are you saying this because you want his job?"

She laughed. "Nope. No way. I'm saying it because his entire squad—team—is depending on him. His boss will have to decide if he becomes a liability."

Kal cocked his head. "What do you think?"

"Not yet, but he's not getting better."

"It takes time to—"

The woman on stage fell to the ground with a shriek, knocking over a nearby table and sending the glasses and plates flying across the synthetic floor.

Kal could see the glee in Bhatt's eyes. "Finally!"

A server rushed to help the woman, who was laughing hysterically, onto her feet. The table she'd crashed into was on its side, and the two men that had been sitting at it were looking down at the woman with expressions that straddled anger and amusement.

"I can't believe I missed that," Bhatt crowed. "This entire—" She stopped, and her gaze froze. Kal turned to see what she was staring at. Another employee had entered the dining area from a door at the end of the bar, trailed by a knee-high cleaning bot.

"What?" Kal whispered, leaning closer. "What'd you see?"

Bhatt looked at him with raised eyebrows. "There's a whole other room back there, and there's Nasi inside."

Kal's mind raced. What was this place? A sting operation? Some sort of clandestine base? Granted, he hadn't been around the Nasi too much, but he'd never heard of them leaving their Footholds for anything except a mission. He couldn't imagine anything requiring them to be at a bar on the far end of the West Arm of Torgut. Since the door was behind him, he couldn't observe it without being completely obvious. But Bhatt had a good view and watched it as they continued to talk about their respective planets and youth.

"Anything?" Kal asked after a few minutes.

She shook her head. "Nothing. No one's gone in or come out."

"But you're sure you saw them?"

"Yeah, I saw a bunch of the big purple bastards back

there."

There was only one thing Kal could think of that made sense. The Nasi weren't here on any orders; these were soldiers who'd somehow left the Foothold and snuck down here to get plastered. It was an extremely Human thing to do, but he'd thought of the Nasi as too disciplined for those kinds of shenanigans. Apparently, not.

"Why would a Nasi tell me about this place?" Kal mused to himself.

"Isn't it obvious? She wanted you to join them," Bhatt replied softly. "According to Bo, the Jadid and Nasi are fascinated by us. Who knows why. But either way, I'm not surprised a few of them got together to create a speakeasy where they could meet with the locals."

Kal felt himself sweat at the thought of going into a room full of Nasi. He felt pangs of terror just knowing they were on the other side of the door. They were genocidal killers, heartless machines that crushed anything that stood in their way. How could he go into the lion's den?

"I've gotten to know our scientist friend pretty well," Bhatt said. "Dude's pretty weird—I'm not going to lie. But he likes to have fun, and he can make jokes. He's just as *Human* as we are. So I'm not surprised that a bunch of Nasi soldiers found a way to get out and party."

"They're still the same creatures that destroyed entire systems and committed genocide." Kal could not reconcile the two images in his mind. "They killed Ruiz, Park, and so many others."

"Yes," she whispered as she leaned over the table, "but

not the ones in that room." She looked up. "I mean, probably not those ones. Everything the Nasi did has been done before. Almost every species has crimes like that in their history, including Humans. I'm not saying they're good, but I *am* saying they aren't necessarily the monsters in the holos. Either way, it would be a good idea for us to get in there."

"So, what? You think we should just get up and try to get in?" Kal asked.

"Haven't you ever crashed a party before?" Bhatt asked. "We don't ask. We just go in."

She stood up from the table and walked toward the nondescript door with Kal hastily following her. The bartender eyed them warily as he prepared a drink.

"Door's not opening," Bhatt said loudly as she unsuccessfully tried to pull it open. "Hey, can you open this up?" She asked the bartender, who had left his station and was rushing at them.

"That's a storage area," said the man, running his hand over his slicked back hair. "If you're looking for the bio recyclers, they're over there." He pointed to a curtain across the room.

"Don't worry," Bhatt said with a smile. "We've been invited. We're friends." She grabbed Kal by the shoulder and pulled him close. "Go inside and ask them. They'll tell you to let us in." Kal stole a glance at the sergeant. She couldn't have seemed more certain of anything.

The man paused and stared past the two of them, obviously accessing his neural implant. After a few seconds, he gave a perfunctory smile and pressed his hand against the security plate next to the door. "Go on in."

"Told you," Bhatt said as she opened the door and stepped inside.

Kal pulled back a flimsy fabric curtain to find the back room of the Flying Snow Worm packed with Nasi. They clustered in groups near the bar and sat at makeshift tables, murmuring to each other. Strands of work lights hung from the ceiling, illuminating the room with faint golden light.

Kal could tell they were mostly low-level by the lack of tattoos on most of them. Nasi, as opposed to Jadid, often had ornate black tattoos over their body. Called Sishen, they were indications of rank and detailed much of the wearer's personal history. Only a few of the Nasi in the room had them and none were more than a single line.

Kal realized there were other Humans in the room as well, talking and laughing as they looked up at their occupiers. He was surprised then realized he shouldn't have been. Weren't there always collaborators in war?

"Hey," a Nasi male walked up to them, shoving his hand out. "Welcome. Always glad to have more Humans. How did you hear about this place?" He was wearing a loose-fitting tunic and breaches that wouldn't have looked out of place on a Human.

The tension building in Kal's chest made his throat go dry. He stared back into the dull brown eyes of the Jadid, wanting to speak but not being able to.

"Hello." Bhatt stuck her arm in front of her. "I'm Airi and this is Hakim. We're here on a trading run. The patrollers at the Foothold landing port recommended we come here."

"I am Kiz. It's always great to have Humans here." He grinned. "Good to know the word's getting out."

"What is this?" Bhatt motioned around the room.

"Ah, yes. I can imagine this may seem a little strange to you." He took two drinks off the bar and handed them to Kal and Bhatt. "It started as a small thing. Just a couple of us sneaking into the city. But more and more Nasi heard about it, and it's just grown." He smiled contentedly, obviously proud.

"Aren't you worried about getting caught?" Kal asked.

"Worried? I guess," Kiz replied. "But I've been studying you from afar for years. I can't pass up this opportunity to learn more now that we are here among you. If our leaders find out, they will punish us. But what is this entire war about if not reuniting Nasi and Humans?"

His response, that the wholesale slaughter of billions was about reuniting the Nasi with Humanity, was almost infuriatingly naïve. "What about the people who died?" Kal asked as he set the drink Kiz gave him back on the bar.

Kiz's smile faded. "That is a sad thing. I can't say that I agree with everything that has happened. But you're here, so you surely understand what this is all for." He interlocked his fingers together. "Humanity and the Jadid were separated for such a long time. We Nasi are uniting the two together, and it will make it better for all."

Bhatt shot Kal a look. "So are you one of the Nasi soldiers

we hear so much about?"

"Ah, that's funny." Kiz laughed. "I'm a settler. I was one of the first brought here."

"Settler?" Kal asked. "What's that mean?"

"Well, if we're going to make this universe our home, we need people who can do things beyond just shoot. I—" he paused for a moment. "Does it bother you? The thought of us settling here?"

*Damn straight,* Kal thought.

"No, of course not. I think we can learn a lot from you." Bhatt said reassuringly.

Kiz frowned. "I used to think that as well. I don't think I expected how much I'd learn from you Humans though. Not science of course. You're almost primitive. But when I arrived here on Mariga I realized perhaps there has been something missing from the Jadid and Nasi." He motioned around the room. "This sort of thing doesn't exist back on our planet, Altterra."

"It should though," slurred another Nasi as she rested her arm across Kiz's shoulder. "There's so much the Ancients didn't teach us."

Kiz pushed her arm off his shoulder and glared. "You'd better stop there. Having fun is one thing. Openly disrespecting the Ancients is another."

The other Nasi just laughed and walked away. Kiz looked back at her, a tight frown on his face.

"Great meeting you, Kiz," Bhatt said, stepping back. "We're going to circulate a little, get to know people."

They quickly walked away before the Nasi could reply. As

they wandered through the tables and groups, Kal listened to the conversations going on around them. Several of them were what Kal would have expected to hear from Human soldiers: complaints, talking trash about their commanders, or asking each other if they'd heard some piece of news. After he'd been wandering for a while, Kal realized the one thing he didn't hear was any sense of longing to return or nostalgia about Altterra.

Many of the Nasi were wasted. Several were drunk and shouting to each other across the room. Others, clearly high on something, found everything funny, laughing at whatever was said to them. A handful were almost catatonic, slumped to the floor, staring ahead with a small smile on their face. From what he understood, drugs didn't exist on Altterra. These Nasi were not prepared for addiction and the evils that came with them. Thinking of his own daemons, Kal had to admit he felt bad for them.

"Hello!" A man stepped in front of Kal and Bhatt. "Nice to see some other Humans here." He was young, maybe mid-twenties, with close-cropped black hair. "Name's Aiguo." He held out his hand.

Kal took it. "Yeah, uh, nice to meet you."

"How'd you learn about this place?" Bhatt asked.

"I do some work for the Nasi, transporting stuff from the planet to their Foothold. Lots a people won't give me the time of day anymore, but the pay's good. I got to talkin' with some of 'em." He took a sip of his drink. "They're not bad once you get to know them." He elbowed Kal. "Hell. You're here, you understand."

"Yeah," Kal agreed. "I mean, they can be a bit...odd. But they're funny too." He thought of Bo. "They're damn smart as well."

"Well, not all of 'em," laughed Aiguo. He pointed to a female Nasi with shoulder-length black hair. "Gita over there isn't the brightest pixel in the viewscreen."

Aiguo launched into a detailed story of his life. He was the kind of man who was alone but didn't want to be. He wasn't built for society, at least not like most people. The more Kal and Bhatt tried to get away, the more Aiguo continued to talk. Like Kal, he'd grown up in the countryside of Mariga. He'd come to the city only months before the Nasi captured the planet looking for a job that didn't involve working in the mines. When the Nasi looked around for Humans to ship goods for them, the man figured, why not?

As they talked, Kal could understand why Aiguo found himself drawn to the Nasi. He hadn't lost a thing when they'd taken Mariga, and contrary to what some of Kal's soldiers thought, many people on Mariga didn't hold Earth in the same high regard they did. Its destruction had meant the same to many people as the destruction of the Qudoru home world. It was sad, sure, but not the end of the galaxy. In the somewhat backward and awkward Nasi, Aiguo had found friends he could relate to.

As they talked, several Nasi came by and introduced themselves, slapping him on the back and introducing themselves to Kal and Bhatt. Often, they'd ask questions about what they did or what they thought about the Nasi. There was almost a childish eagerness to their questioning, kids trying to fit in and seeking approval. It was a far cry from the genocidal species that had laid waste to so many worlds and that Kal had fought.

The Nasi grew even more inebriated. Their talking grew louder and more insistent, and a few fights even broke out. The bar had placed a miserable Human bouncer inside the room to break up anything serious, but he must have realized as Kal did, that these Nasi could easily disable and kill him if they wanted.

Although the Nasi rarely talked about what they did or the Foothold, Kal heard a few interesting snippets as he circulated through the room. There was a lot of conversation about something big that was going to happen. No one would say it outright, but whatever was going to happen, it would require a lot of them to be gone for a while. Kal tried to pry out details, but his efforts came to nothing. Even the Nasi that were too wasted to stand balked at saying anything more.

The Nasi crowd had thinned, and the ones that remained were less than coherent. Kal and Bhatt decided it was time to leave before anything happened. The only Nasi remaining in the bar were too high or drunk to even speak. They'd noticed that the Nasi left through a different door than the one the Humans used. Bhatt tried to peek in and see where it led, but the bouncer hurried her away.

After they said their goodbyes to the few Nasi still coherent enough to understand them, they walked through the door to the front room. The viewscreens were off and the room was completely empty except for an elderly woman sitting behind the bar with a tablet in front of her. She sneered when she saw Kal and Bhatt step out of the room.

"Damn Nasi lovers," she spat, then looked back down at her tablet.

# Chapter Seventeen

It had been two days since Kal and Sergeant Bhatt had gone to the Flying Snow Worm. Hearing their stories of the Nasi bar had awakened the academic in Nicole. The Nasi had changed the galaxy forever, but the concept of the Nasi behaving like Humans intrigued her. She realized she shouldn't have been too surprised; she'd seen the same behavior in Bo over the course of the past year. The Jadid scientist had taken on so many Human mannerisms so easily that it was hard to realize he was the same taciturn scientist they'd rescued.

Bowen still hadn't returned from the Foothold. Nicole worried for him but there wasn't a thing they could do. They continued to maintain a watch on the ship, waiting for him to return. They'd talked about rescuing him but had no clue where he would be, and the Foothold was completely cut off from the rest of the planet. Instead they continued to gather information and search for information about the Nasi fleet, plasma cannons, and shipbuilding facilities.

Nicole and Sergeant Kimathi had taken a public transport to a small town named Jena to follow up on intel that had been given to them by Gudit. The underground town sat at the edge of one of Mariga's vast glacier-covered oceans. Despite being under the ice, the oceans were home to underwater mines and an important part of the planet's economy. Jena was a consolidation point where minerals were offloaded from the carts used in the mines to large hopper transports which made their way to Torgut and other cities for shipment off planet.

Unlike Torgut which had been built in an enormous naturally occurring cavern, Jena was completely manmade, having been carved out of the rock near the ocean hundreds of years earlier. The city consisted of several square caverns connected by smooth circular tunnels. Automated public transports circled through the various chambers of the town despite it being small enough to walk across in an hour. Large square lights on the ceiling radiated faux sunlight and heat down on the squat metal buildings and streets below, making the small town seem less cavernous. Unfortunately, Nicole didn't get the sense of being on the surface that she did in the capital.

After arriving in the city, Nicole and Ekon had located a store that sold tunnel crawlers, no questions asked. Locals used the bullet-shaped vehicles to travel through the caverns and tunnels around the city. The slate gray crawlers had two rows of heavy-duty wheels on their top and bottom, allowing them to traverse almost any subterranean cavern, primarily for inspection and maintenance of the mines but also for recreation.

"What are we doing here again?" asked Ekon, through his chattering teeth. Outside of the town, the caverns' temperature remained just above freezing and the crawler's heater wasn't working. They'd purchased some cold-weather gear at Kal's suggestion but not nearly enough as they'd come to realize.

"Gudit said there were several shipments going to this area," Nicole said, shivering. "So we're checking it out."

The former Alliance member sent one of her goons to

*Annie* each day with information for them. Nicole had no idea how much Kal was paying for it, but it was probably too much. The information they'd received had either been obvious or so broad as to be unusable. This was the first time they'd gotten anything that Nicole would have considered a clue. Between waiting for the Alliance goons and hoping for Bo to return, they'd walked around Torgut getting to know the lay of the land and talking with the locals to gather intel. So far, there'd been no mention of Nasi fleets in the area and Nicole got the sense that the people of Mariga had become resigned to the Nasi occupation.

They'd left the town and had been traversing through the network of naturally occurring caverns that radiated down to the ocean. Carts filled to the brim with rocks and debris passed them occasionally, headed toward Jena, but otherwise the caverns were empty and completely pitch black. The only light they had was from the headlamps at the front of their vehicle.

"This feels like a wild-goose chase, ma'am," Ekon said, rubbing his hands together next to her. "I don't know what the hell we expect to find."

"It's the best we got. Now keep an eye out. This is the area where the shipments have been spotted." Gudit's runner had given them a set of coordinates where someone had spotted Nasi soldiers driving large transports filled with equipment. It certainly was odd, but the equipment could have been replacement parts for the mines as much as any sort of weapons materials. They needed to investigate.

As they sped through the tunnels, Nicole continued to

check the map on her implant. It was hard to follow the three-dimensional representation of the tunnels since she had to turn and manipulate it in her vision as they sped along. The tube crawler's AI was doing most of the driving, automatically adjusting for the tunnel's winding path and uneven terrain, allowing Nicole to devote most of her time to studying the map superimposed over her vision.

"Wait. Stop." Ekon called out. Nicole obligingly brought the crawler to a halt with a small grinding of gravel and dirt.

"Look here," Ekon said as he pointed to a small tunnel on the crawler's display. "That tunnel's off."

"What do you mean?"

"It's perfectly straight for one," Ekon said, "and it's perfectly round. That's been drilled into the rock."

Nicole compared the sensor readout from the vehicle to the map in her implant. The tunnel wasn't on the public maps. "You're right. That shouldn't be there. Let's check it out."

She drove to the mouth of the small tunnel and then stepped out of the vehicle through the door in the windshield and onto the cave floor. Nicole turned on her light and studied the mouth of the tunnel, her feet crunching on the sandy floor. It branched out from the cavern, heading at a steep angle downward to the ocean. The walls of the tunnel were smooth, at least smoother than the cavern they were in with grooves that spiraled down its length—clear signs that it had been drilled into the rock.

"So maybe Gudit's information wasn't completely useless," said Ekon as he traced a gloved finger along a groove in the tunnel.

"Nope," agreed Nicole, "this is something."

They climbed back into the vehicle, and Nicole drove into the tunnel. It stretched on forever, extending beyond the limit of the crawler's sensors. As they drove farther into the ground, the temperature rose and Nicole pulled off her coat, unable to take the heat anymore.

"Guess we don't need to worry about dressing warmly anymore," Nicole joked as she saw the beads of sweat trickle down Ekon's forehead. The sergeant grunted as he struggled to remove his coat in the tight confines of the cabin.

The tunnel leveled out but continued to stretch forward in a straight line. According to Nicole's implant, they were underneath the ocean. She wondered what they'd find at the end.

"Looks like it's opening to something," Ekon said pointing at the screen on the dashboard. The tunnel ended in a large rectangular chamber about the size of Jena—certainly something that should have appeared on the public map in Nicole's implant.

"If there are Nasi there, they'll see us for sure." The crawler was extremely loud, and although not the size of a transport, it wasn't small either.

"Let's get out then and check it out," Ekon replied.

Nicole thought about it. The crawler barely fit in the tunnel, and there was no way to hide it or pull over to allow other traffic. If someone else came down the passageway, they were stuck. On the other hand, they were already there. Who knew if they'd get another chance?

"Okay," Nicole said as the crawler came to a stop. "I can't

help but think this is a terrible idea."

"Aren't those the best?" Ekon asked as he swung himself out of the vehicle.

❖

They crept quietly toward the tunnel exit. Without any light to guide her, Nicole had to use the wall to steady and orient herself as she walked. She spotted several small lights in the cavern ahead of them and pointed them out to Ekon.

"They look to be attached to a building," he said.

Nicole squinted. He was right; she could see the glimmer of naked metal underneath the glow of the lights. It appeared to be a lattice structure of some sort. As they kept walking to the tunnel exit, more of the structure was revealed.

The building took up the entire cavern and reminded Nicole of images she'd seen of Human factories taken hundreds of years ago. The vaguely rectangular structure was made from the Nasi weaves but had a spiderweb of glistening metal pipes of varying diameters coming out of it and embedding themselves into the ceiling, walls, and ground. A faint cloud of steam surrounded the top of the structure. Several transports sat in front of the structure, near a circular door set off to a side.

*Looks like someone is home.*

"Capture everything," Nicole whispered to Ekon as she turned on the record function in her own implant. She looked around trying to get every aspect of the cavern and the plant. Later, she could transfer it to *Annie*'s computer and take it back to Samsara Fleet for the intel cell to examine. The only problem was the implant's memory was woefully small.

The circular door at the front of the building opened and two Nasi dressed in worker's coveralls strode out of the building and got into one of the transports.

"Crap," whispered Ekon, jumping backwards.

The transport lifted off, but rather than gliding to the tunnel where Nicole and Ekon were hiding, it went through an opening in the far side of the cavern.

"Interesting," Kimathi said. "So there's at least one more way in."

"Not sure about in," Nicole said. "But out at least." She remembered that their vehicle was still behind them blocking the tunnel. This facility, whatever it was, was occupied, which meant that a Nasi transport could find their crawler at any time. "We'd better head back."

They walked back toward the crawler, again using their hands to guide them as they crawled through the pitch-black tunnel. With the cavern behind them, the tunnel was completely black. It was unsettling, and Nicole could feel a sense of panic clawing its way into her head. Occasionally, she looked at the faint glow of the factory behind them to reassure and ground herself.

She yelped as she banged her shin into the side of the crawler. The stab of pain was quickly followed by a sense of relief since she wouldn't have to walk through the featureless tunnel anymore.

"We're on the wrong sides," Ekon said. He was on the driver's side of the crawler now.

"No worries, you can drive," Nicole said. She just wanted to get back into the vehicle.

The soft glow of the tunnel crawler's screens was a welcome sight. It illuminated the cabin so she could see Ekon's face next to hers as he bit his lip and oriented himself to the controls of the vehicle, quickly testing the steering yoke, brakes, and accelerator.

"I just realized we can't turn around," Ekon said.

Nicole groaned inside; he was right. They'd have to back out. She looked in the cabin for a place to get sick should she need it.

"No way we're going in that cavern. We'll have to go in reverse."

Ekon began to back them up slowly then gradually increased their speed as he got more comfortable at the controls. After a few minutes of trying to look behind them using the small window at the back of the vehicle, Ekon gave up and looked at the viewscreen as he operated the vehicle based on feel. Nicole's stomach began to do flips as they traveled backwards, but she held onto the flimsy armrests on her seat, steeling herself to keep it together.

"Wait. What's that?" Nicole asked, pointing at a white dot on the sensor map.

Ekon slammed on the brakes, and they both watched as the dot moved closer to them. "Dammit," Ekon swore. "Nasi."

Nicole looked back and could see the faint glow of headlights against the tunnel walls. She tried to think of what to do. The tunnel crawler was designed to go almost anywhere underground. Perhaps they could somehow go *over* whatever was coming down the tunnel.

Kimathi pressed the accelerator to the floor, launching the crawler forward and throwing Nicole against her seat. The engine roared and Nicole could feel the vibrations in her bones.

"What are you doing?" Nicole asked, bracing herself against the vehicle's frame.

"What do you mean?" Kimathi looked at her with wide eyes. "I'm getting us the hell outta here. They're chasing us."

Ekon was right. Whatever was behind them was keeping pace as they sped through the tunnel. The light from the factory grew ahead of them. If they were lucky, they'd be able to turn around in the open area in front of the building and evade whatever was chasing them.

They shot out into the cavern and several plasma bolts splashed against the wall next to them. A group of Nasi in workers' coveralls stood outside the factory with their plasma rifles raised.

"Here goes nothing," Ekon shouted as he yanked the steering yoke to the right. The front of the crawler started to turn, but a wheel caught, and they began to flip sideways. Thankfully the crawler was designed for this, and the wheels that had been above them grasped onto the floor and propelled them forward. The interior of the crawler remained upright, rotating within its frame. The Nasi continued to fire at them, their bolts hitting the ground near them and the walls behind.

"Neat." Ekon chuckled.

"Yeah, great," Nicole said. "Just drive." She felt the bile rising in her throat.

They shot into the other tunnel, ricocheting off the wall as they entered. Nicole glanced backward and saw another crawler enter the cave. Several of the Nasi who'd been outside the building were entering the transports that had been parked outside the facility.

The tunnel swept upward, and she felt like they were almost completely vertical as they climbed toward the surface. Nicole looked over to see how Ekon was doing. His mouth was fixed in an almost maniacal grin, and she could see a shine in his wide eyes.

"You're enjoying this, aren't you?" she asked in disbelief.

Ekon laughed. "I can't help it. I've never driven before."

The crawler slammed against the ceiling as the tunnel abruptly ended in a level cavern. Ekon tried to control the vehicle as it careened from side to side, bouncing back and forth on the tunnel walls.

"Where the hell are we?" Ekon asked.

Nicole checked her implant. According to the public maps, this tunnel shouldn't exist. They were deep in the Marigan countryside, away from any town.

"No idea," said Nicole. She could see the three Nasi vehicles following them on the sensor screen. As the cavern widened, the two transports flew past the Nasi tunnel crawler.

"We've got two transports inbound," Nicole said. Seconds

later, plasma fire lit up the surrounding tunnel walls with sea-green flashes.

"Dammit," Ekon swore. "We can't outrun those things."

Nicole studied the vehicle's sensors display. The tunnel branched ahead. "We're going to have to lose them," she said. "Tunnel splits in a few hundred meters." Plasma fire from the two transports punctuated her words. Thankfully the tunnel's undulating path prevented the Nasi from getting a direct shot, but the Nasi continued to close the gap between them.

Ekon glanced down at the sensor display. "Okay, well, hold on." He turned the yoke to the left, and they swept up the wall before gravity brought them slamming back to the tunnel floor. The gyroscopic motion of the internal cabin kept them level while the vehicle flipped over inside the tunnel.

"Sergeant Kimathi, what are you doing?" asked Nicole, her voice close to a scream.

"Trying to dodge the shots, ma'am."

"You're going to kill us."

"Not if they kill us first," the sergeant responded as he twisted the yoke to the right, sending them flipping over the opposite wall just as several bolts slammed into the tunnel floor in front of them.

Nicole could see the tunnel branch ahead of them in the glow of the crawler's headlights. They sped along the left tunnel wall, the crawler barely remaining upright as it hurtled forward. The two Nasi transports had taken positions on either side of the widening tunnel, ensuring that whichever way the crawler went, one of them could follow. As they were about to enter the left fork of the tunnel, Kimathi slammed the yoke to the right, causing the vehicle to flip once and then soar across the stone divider that separated the two tunnels.

Nicole's head slammed into the console, causing her vision to blur for a moment as they crashed into the right tunnel wall. "Sorry," Ekon yelled as he tried to regain control of the vehicle which continued forward at a breakneck pace.

The maneuver had worked though. The transport on the left shot down the tunnel, leaving the other transport and the crawler.

"That won't slow them for too long," Ekon said.

"We've got to lose them somehow." Nicole looked for an avenue of escape on the sensor map, but their only option was to continue traveling down the twisting cavern.

"I know, I know."

Ekon continued to swerve through the tunnel as it rose and fell. The tunnel's windy path forced the Nasi transport to slow, but it was still close enough to fire the occasional plasma blast, some shots landing only centimeters in front of them. The crawler kept pace as well but was too far back to fire at them.

"We're coming up to another fork," Nicole said. "Take the left this time." She could see the right fork was a dead end on the sensor map.

"Roger." Ekon kept his eyes on the windshield. His hands gripped the yoke so tightly Nicole wondered if he'd be able to let go when this was all done.

At the next branch, Ekon pulled the same maneuver as before, steering the crawler so it was straddling the far-left wall. At the last moment, he pulled the yoke right but quickly turned it back to the left and kept going. He gave a guttural yelp of triumph as the other transport shot off into the right branch. Unfortunately the Nasi crawler was still on their tail and Nicole knew the transports would catch up soon.

The ground beneath them abruptly dropped, causing the crawler to soar through the air for a few seconds before landing several meters below with a crunch and sending dust flying around them. Nicole's restraint saved her from hitting her head against the console a second time.

"There something up ahead," Nicole said. "I can't tell what it is."

Kimathi glanced at the viewscreen. "Weird. It looks vehicles or something."

The tunnel ahead of them was glowing softly. The walls widened until they were in an enormous cavern filled with azure blobs casting eerie halos of light on the walls and ceiling. As the crawler's headlight illuminated one of the blobs, Nicole felt her breath catch in her throat. Tylwyth. According to Kal, the creatures were a legend among the Marigans. The half-plant, half-animal creatures inhabited the most remote caves on the planet, shying away from Human interaction. Nicole watched, her mouth agape, as they slowly floated through the cavern like bioluminescent balloons.

"What are those?" Kimathi asked as he dodged through the creatures.

"Tylwyth," Nicole responded softly. "Kal—General Norman—told me about them. They're incredibly rare."

"They're amazing."

As they raced through the creatures, Nicole watched in wonder. They were larger than Nicole had first realized, easily the size of several transports. Their skin was a lattice of small rainbow-colored veins enclosing what appeared to be a wafer-thin skin bladder. Up close, she could see intricate patterns and swirls coating their ephemeral exteriors, more elegant than the finest art.

A bright fireball erupted in the cavern behind them; a Nasi transport had crashed into one of the gorgeous creatures igniting its gas-filled bladder. Nicole felt a moment of sadness for the Tylwyth, another innocent casualty of this war. One of them descended in front of their crawler, forcing Ekon to swerve abruptly and bringing her back to the present.

They continued to lurch between the creatures, barely missing several until gently bumping into one, sending it floating off into another portion of the cave. The remaining Nasi transport had fallen back, unable to fly through the dense network of creatures in its path. Nicole and Ekon finally reached the other side of the cavern and entered a tunnel with the Nasi crawler still following.

The tunnel led them to a cavern several times larger than the landing bays on the *Ofira*. The floor dipped in the middle, the shape on their sensor display reminding Nicole of a bowl. In the center was a hole that dropped into a nest of caverns below. Kimathi turned the yoke and traced around the outside perimeter of the room, looking for a way out.

"We're going to have to go down," Nicole said.

Kimathi eyes the sensor display. "That's a free fall. We're liable to kill ourselves as much as get away."

"I know," Nicole replied. "But there's no other way." She pointed to the Nasi transport on the map; it was almost through the Tylwyth cavern and was still chasing them. "We can't get past them and they're catching up." The Nasi crawler had entered the room and was trying to cut them off as they circled the perimeter.

"Fine." The sergeant gritted his teeth as he slammed on the brake and turned the yoke hard to the left, flipping the crawler end over end as their momentum continued to carry them around the room.

He pressed the accelerator as the Nasi crawler shot past and sped toward the hole in the center of the cavern. Nicole's stomach rose to her throat as the ground gave way beneath them and they fell through the shaft. The crawler bounced back and forth between the sides of the cavern as they fell, sending them spinning in multiple directions. They finally landed with a crunch of cracking metal on the floor of one of the tunnels leading from the central shaft.

"Damn." Kimathi rubbed his hands over his face. "That must be what it feels like to go through a bio recycler."

With a grinding of gears and shriek of metal, the crawler moved forward. They gradually picked up speed, and the dots of the Nasi vehicles on the sensor display faded into the distance behind them.

"We lost them," Nicole said after they disappeared. "Now we just need to find our way back."

# Chapter Eighteen

"There you are," Kal said as he placed his tablet on the galley table.

"We ran into some trouble." Nicole walked to the food dispenser. She needed something hot. "We found something but barely made it back."

"Something like?"

"Like a power plant, maybe. I don't know for sure." The machine hummed as it prepared her tea. "We recorded everything we could on our implants."

"Where's Sergeant Kimathi?" Kal glanced out the galley door.

Nicole shrugged. The sergeant had been avoiding Kal for a while now. He'd show up to the leadership meetings but studiously avoided the general any other time. She didn't know what the two had said to each other, and Kal wasn't too forthcoming about it. Either way, it was something they'd have to work out for themselves.

The video recording of the Nasi underground facility appeared on a viewscreen. Since Nicole had recorded it using her implant, the holo appeared as an elongated circle that faded at the edges, mimicking her field of vision. Kal stood up and studied the screen as he fast-forwarded, rewound, and zoomed in on key details of the holo.

"Strange," Kal said. "It must have something to do with the plasma cannon near there, but I have no idea what it does."

"Bo would know," Nicole said, feeling a stab of worry as she mentioned their friend's name. Although Kal had mentioned how Human the Nasi he'd met were, she knew that if they captured their friend, they wouldn't hesitate to torture and kill him. She'd experienced what it was like to be a Nasi captive firsthand.

"I'm sure he'll be back soon," Kal said, placing his hand on hers. "Until then, we've got to continue to get as much information as possible. Let's see if Chief Ramos can tell us anything about this."

Kal called for the chief, and she appeared in the doorway a few seconds later. As the ship's chief engineer, she needed to not only be able to fly it but also be familiar with every system, including their plasma cannons. Without Bo there, she was easily the most technical person aboard.

"Thanks for coming." Kal motioned at the viewscreen. "This is the video from Colonel Bergeron's expedition out to Jena. They found something in the caves near the city. We just don't have a clue what it is."

"It was located under the ocean floor," Nicole added. "We think it has something to do with the enormous plasma cannon that's near there."

Ramos studied the video, rewinding it several times, before speaking. "You're right; it's definitely something with the plasma cannon. There are a few things you'd need to make a weapon like that. A lot of power, a way to make the plasma, and finally, a way to propel it into space. This building could be any of those things." She traced the pipes leading from the building into the surrounding rock. "These pipes go in all directions. My guess is that it's using energy from the planet for power." She tilted her head. "It might use gas and minerals to create the plasma as well."

"Whatever it is," Kal said, "it's a target. Getting to the actual plasma cannons will be next to impossible. But if they each have these power plants, then we can disable them that way."

"It'd be nice if Bo was here," Ramos said. "He could tell us more."

Kal sighed. "That's what we've been saying too."

"Maybe you mention the area to some of your friends at the Flying Snow Worm and see if they say anything," Nicole suggested. Kal and Bhatt had been back to the Flying Snow Worm every night for the past three days and were becoming regulars.

"Friends may be a stretch," Kal replied. "But I'll mention it."

The bartender gave Kal and Bhatt a sly nod as they walked through the door of the Flying Snow Worm. They returned the gesture and grabbed seats at their customary table near the back. The chem bar was busier than normal and filled with the typical countryside crowd—people wearing the cheap fabricated clothes they'd bought specifically for coming into the capital. Kal could remember doing the same thing with his father. His dad would pull out the clothes he'd had made just for the occasion and wipe them down before they headed to the public transport. Nothing too expensive but something that would let people know they weren't the deep cave yokels you saw in the holos—despite being exactly that.

A few minutes after they sat down, a server came by and took their orders. It was the same woman who'd spat at them on their first night. Her face remained locked in a hostile frown as she tapped their orders onto her tablet and walked away.

"Why does she work here if she hates them so much?" Bhatt asked after the woman walked away.

"Hard to find a job here if you can't work in the mines." Mariga was a rough planet. People who didn't work tended to either leave the planet or end up in the East Arm.

"I guess."

While they waited for their food to arrive, Kal and Sergeant Bhatt returned to the same conversation they'd had during the previous nights—talking about their childhoods. They had to be careful, no mention of the EDF, Samsara Fleet, or anything else that could implicate them if someone overheard. The omissions meant there were a lot of gaps in the stories they told.

Kal continued telling her about growing up the only child of a miner on Mariga. It wasn't something he normally talk to anyone about—there wasn't much to say—and a lot of the memories had faded into nostalgia. He'd lived several lives since then as a soldier, merchant, and now as some sort of resistance fighter. He talked about exploring the area around his town as a kid and finding strange and wondrous creatures in the labyrinths of caves under the surface. Humans had settled Mariga centuries ago, but they were still finding new creatures and phenomena that expanded their understanding of what was possible.

On previous nights, Bhatt had talked about her life on Patagonia. She was the middle child in a large family. Her parents had owned a small shipping company, transporting materials around the Human colonies. She'd grown up in the commercial and shipping ports of her planet, learning the trade from them.

"How'd you end up here?" Kal asked.

"Long story." Bhatt smiled. "Me and my siblings were port rats. We hung out listening to the crews and running around cargo ports while my parents did business. I'd always figured I was gonna be on a crew or a stevedore and then join my parents' business. One day in Tertiary, I met a teacher who changed my life." She meant Tertiary School, the last step of schooling before university. "He was a professor who opened my eyes to the universe and made me realize that there could be more for me beyond Patagonia. You've met him before." She must've meant Kinkaid, the commander of the Patagonia Front, the guerrilla organization she'd been part of before she joined the Skulls. "He inspired me to join up. So I did some things and then got my free ride." She meant the guaranteed scholarship that service in the EDF provided.

"Here." The server dropped their plates down on the table with a thud and walked away.

"We come for the food but stay for the smiles," Bhatt said as she scooped the food back onto her plate.

"You got out"—of the EDF he meant—"and then went to university?" Kal asked.

"Yeah, I was in my fifth year. I was working on my

dissertation on Classical Music and Poetry." Bhatt chuckled. "Seems kind of useless now, but I had a plan. I was going to teach on Earth and see all those sights I'd read about. Go to Long Beach and Brooklyn to better understand what they were talking about."

"A lot has probably changed since people first started recording those songs and poems."

She shrugged. "Probably. But places retain something. They hold on to their history even if it's hard to see at first. You and me, we're colonists; everything we've got is brand spankin' new in the grand scheme of things."

Kal supposed she was right. Growing up, he'd thought of Torgut as an old city; it was the first city the Human settlers had established on Mariga. But it was a baby compared to the rest of the galaxy. Earth and the other home worlds had been around for millennia with entire civilizations growing and dying before Humans had ever known of Mariga's existence.

They dug into their food, talking only sparingly. Kal relished the mixture of spices that warmed every inch of his body. It was something he hadn't realized he'd missed these long decades. All too soon, his dish was empty, and Bhatt looked across the table expectantly.

"Ready?"

"Ready." Kal stood up and looked at the bartender, who gave a nod in return. The two Skulls strode to the door that led to the Nasi bar in back, and the bartender pressed his hand on the security panel and the door swung open.

As soon as they were through, the door clicked shut behind them. The room was more crowded than previous nights and there was barely space for Kal and Bhatt to make their way through. The underground bar was full of energy and peals of laughter rang across the room. A crowd had already formed around the bar, and the two Humans behind the bar seemed overloaded as they poured drinks.

"Airi! Hakim!"

They turned around to see Kiz beaming at them. He'd learned the Nasi's name was actually Deniz but he'd taken on the "friend name", as he called it, of Kiz. The Nasi found the concept of nicknames especially interesting, and most of the Nasi they'd met had given themselves a friend name they preferred. Kal hated to admit it, but he'd formed a friendship of sorts with Kiz. He told them about his job as a transport technician and his impressions of the planet and Humans in general. He'd peppered them with questions, asking about Earth and Humans and what they thought of the Nasi.

"Hey, Kiz." They both slapped his hand in greeting.

"Pretty full tonight," Kal said. "What's going on?"

Kiz's smile evaporated. "Why're you asking?" He grabbed both of them by the arm. Kal gasped in surprise and futilely tried to pry the Nasi's fingers off. Kiz pulled them close and leaned down at them, the warmth of his alcohol-laden breath smacking Kal in the face.

"You shouldn't be asking questions like that." His eyes studied Kal.

"Kiz, let go," Bhatt said. "He meant nothing by it."

The Nasi's grip tightened. "You seem awfully interested in what we're doing." He cocked his head. "It seems very strange. Two merchants start coming in here and asking questions."

Kal couldn't speak. His mind raced. As soon as the Nasi started asking questions and digging, they'd figure it all out. The entire team was compromised. Should he warn them over the net? It would risk getting them discovered, but weren't they already there?

Kiz's smile suddenly returned, and he let out a loud laugh. "What a prank, I totally got you." He let go of their arms and gave them both a slight shove. "You two were so scared!"

Kal felt confusion and then a wave of relief course through his body.

"Goddamnit, Kiz!" Bhatt belted the Nasi in the face. He was too busy laughing to even register the blow. The Nasi was almost doubled up with laughter, holding his hands to his sides.

After several seconds, his laughter died down and he looked back at them. "Pretty good, yeah?" He looked at them for approval, his eyebrows raised.

"That wasn't funny," Kal replied. He wanted to hit the bastard himself but knew it wouldn't do any good.

"Why not?" Kiz's smile faded.

"Because you acted like you were going to kill us!" Bhatt shouted.

"Humans don't joke about stuff like that," Kal explained. "Perhaps try something a little less high stakes."

"Hm." Kiz nodded his head as he processed their response. Kal imagined a computer trying to analyze a new set of variables. "I've tried that joke on a few Humans now and that seems to be the consensus—not funny."

"I swear, Kiz, someone's gonna kill you," Bhatt shouted. The Nasi chuckled.

"I am sorry." He didn't appear to be though. The smile was still spread across his face. "About your question, though. Several of our teams are going to be on double duty the next couple of days, so everyone's taking the chance to get out while they can."

"Do your leaders know that you're here?" Bhatt asked. They made sure to never press on issues like this so as not to arouse suspicion.

"No." Now the smile vanished. He looked away. "It would be unpleasant if they were to find out."

"Why do you come here then?" Kal asked. "Why risk it?" It was a question that still bugged him. Nasi were normally so rational, and this bar was the complete opposite.

The question confused Kiz, and he scratched his face as he thought. "It's not something I can put into words. It's just something I need to do." He was put off. "If you will excuse me for a moment, I need to talk to someone over there." He waved to the far corner of the room and walked away without another word.

The two Humans exchanged glances and then continued to walk through the room, listening carefully for any clues. Part of their routine now was to always be circulating through the room to overhear any conversations.

The number of Humans in the back room had increased over the past few days. They had to be careful when talking to them. The Nasi couldn't read their facial expressions or understand the subtle tones and subtext behind their speech.

But Humans could tell when they were lying or if their stories didn't make sense. Kal's opinion of Humanity had taken a nosedive in the past few days. Most of the people they met in the bar seemed to have an almost religious view of the Nasi.

On the other hand, his opinion of the Nasi had changed as well. He'd heard several conversations where the Nasi questioned what they'd done and why they were there. Their leaders' decisions confused them, and they were trying to make sense of how their actions made sense with their goals of helping and leading Humanity. Bo was right: they weren't a monoculture. There were differences of thoughts and opinion. The starkest ones were between what Kal thought of as the "regular" Nasi and the military commanders and soldiers. There was a weariness in the creatures at the bar, a desire for peace—and even acceptance—that he wouldn't have expected a week ago.

"Split up?" Bhatt asked.

Kal nodded in response and headed toward the bar. One thing he'd learned in the past few days was that Nasi could not hold their drink. Several slumped at their table or leaned over the bar, jabbing their long fingers in each other's faces as they yelled at each other.

"—you're not going to be able to come back down," a female with long blonde hair shouted. "It's going to be at least a few months before they'll rotate you out." Kal drifted closer, not wanting to miss anything that was said.

"I'll be okay," the male said, "I'm bringing my stash with me."

"Risky," she replied, "you get caught by the officer and

you'll be executed."

The man shrugged casually. "If I'm going to spend the next few months in orbit, I'm going to bring something to ease the pain."

"Hakim, what's going on?" Kal jumped in surprise. He turned around to see the smiling face of Dill, aka Diallo. She was a clerk in their private landing port and one of the more Human Nasi that Kal had talked to. Many of them were like Kiz, methodically trying to mimic the mannerisms of Humans. To her, it seemed to come naturally.

"Nothing much. Heard there's some big thing going on and everyone's getting here while they can." He looked around the room.

Dill rolled her eyes. "Nasi are talking more than they should."

"Drink'll do that," Kal said.

She nodded. "What about you? When are you getting off this rock?"

"Still waiting on parts. You know how it is." He smiled. "We're thinking of heading out to the countryside. A friend mentioned Jena. Said there are some nice tunnels out that way."

Dill's eyes narrowed for a moment. "Yeah?"

"You been out there?" Kal asked. "On any of your runs?"

She grabbed Kal by the shirt and pulled him close. Her yellow eyes looked down on him for a moment. "Listen, I'm telling you this cause I like you. Don't mention Jena again." Kal tried to reply, but she overrode him. "Don't go there. And don't mention that place around here."

"Okay, okay." Kal didn't have to pretend to be scared.

Dill realized was she was doing and released him. "Sorry." She reached out and hastily straightened Kal's shirt. "I'm guessing that's not how Humans normally speak to one another."

He tried to laugh it off but could still feel her steel grip and see her eyes flashing. They were playing with fire by going to that bar. Eventually they'd talk to the wrong person or ask the wrong question. There would be no way to escape if something went wrong.

Kal retreated and looked for Bhatt. He didn't have the stomach to stay there any longer. She was drinking shots of ice water, a local liquor, with a couple of Nasi at a table on the other side of the room. Judging from the glasses scattered across the table, they'd been going for a while.

"Airi, we'd better get back," Kal said, resting his hand on her shoulder.

Bhatt looked up at him with a genuine look of disappointment. Her eyes took a second to focus on him, but she knew enough not to question when it was time to leave. She said her goodbyes to the Nasi and stood up.

"I was havin' a good time," she said as they walked to the exit. "What's up?"

The bouncer opened the door to the bar as they approached. "Just time to leave." He looked back at the crowded room; the party was still going on. The Nasi clinked glasses together and laughed. Conquerors trying to understand what they had conquered and why.

"General Norman?" Gudit's singsong voice echoed from *Annie's* cargo bay to the galley where Kal was sitting.

Kal had been waiting for one of her goons to show up. He was surprised she showed up herself; it exposed her, not something an Alliance boss would normally do.

"Gudit," Kal said. "To what do I owe the pleasure?"

"What? You don't want to hear about how my day is? My feelings about life?" She sauntered through the cargo bay, idly examining the screens and equipment on the bulkhead. "Straight to business, eh, Kal?"

"I figured you'd appreciate that. You're a businesswoman, right?"

She spun on her heel, her flowing dress fanning out around her, and turned to Kal. "Indeed. That I am."

"So why are *you* here, Gudit?"

"I'm guessing you wouldn't believe me if I said because I wanted to enjoy your sparkling wit." She smiled, showing her perfect white teeth. "I've come to tell you our arrangement is at an end."

"Why?"

"Seems like the Nasi have locked down the town of Jena. Someone was snooping around the area and went places they shouldn't have." She raised her eyebrows. "I imagine I don't need to tell you how important secrecy is in my profession. Your people tromping through classified areas tend to get the Nasi concerned."

"What about the fleet?" Kal asked. "Any word on that?" It

was the reason they were there, but so far none of their sources had a word about it.

"I checked to see if I could identify anything around resupply destinations. Nada." She clicked her tongue. "The Nasi fleet locations would only be accessible inside the Foothold. And only to select group of their top leaders." She waved her hand. "It's not something you're going to find on Mariga. Not unless you got a helluva lot more firepower than I see here."

Kal had suspected as much, but he'd hoped for a different answer. The information they'd gained on Mariga would be valuable. Understanding the Nasi cannons would be incredibly helpful, but if Samsara Fleet was destroyed, it was useless.

"I do have *some* good news," Gudit continued. "We received some information about a site near the surface that looks to be one of the Nasi construction yards. Consider it a parting gift."

"Gift?" Kal asked. "Does that mean it's free?"

She laughed. "Maybe gift is not the right term. How about gesture of goodwill?" She clicked her tongue. "Nothing's free, at least not from me."

By the time they finished haggling, Kal had cut down the price of the intel by half. It still was a lot of credits for a little information, but information was the only currency Kal dealt in now. He estimated they'd spent a million credits of the chit that the fleet had given them for the mission. Samaha would consider it money well spent if Kal could get this information back to them.

"One other thing, Kal." Gudit turned mid-stride as she was walking down the ramp. "Some advice from a colleague. You need to leave. Soon. I don't know what's keeping you here, but the Nasi know that there are spies on Mariga. You stay much longer, and they'll find you."

❖

"So what're we looking for, sir?" Sergeant Kimathi asked. "If we know where the site is, then why scout it out?"

Kal took a deep breath. He had to remind himself that Kimathi questioning his orders was a good thing. It meant the soldier was thinking at least. "Two reasons. One, we need to make sure that *is* the site. So when the fleet comes back, they'll know exactly where to strike. Two, we can see what these ships will look like and maybe find some info that can help us in battle." Kal had served on a general officer's staff before and knew what happened behind the scenes. The intelligence cell processed a lot of intelligence. One or two bits of information may be meaningless, but combined with others, they could make an enormous difference.

"What about Bo?" asked Nicole.

Kal looked at the faces around the galley table. Nicole, Ekon, Ramos—they all had the same thought: when do we accept that Bo's not coming back? He knew in his head the Jadid was gone, captured, or killed, but his heart couldn't accept it. He couldn't say the thing they were all thinking, not about his friend. Unfortunately, they'd run out of time. After this final mission, they had to leave to make it back before the fleet folded to engage the Nasi.

"Bo'll come back," Kal said. "It's been a week, but he'll make it. In the meantime, we execute. If the Nasi force our hand, then we'll figure it out. Until then, we continue to gather as much information as we can." He turned to Ramos. "I want you or Chedjou in the pilot's seat at all times. If the Nasi do come for us, who knows how much time we'll have."

The chief nodded.

"Bhatt and I are going back to the Flying Snow Worm," Kal said. He had to take one last chance to find out any information they could about the Nasi fleet.

"Sir, I don't think that's a good idea," Nicole said.

"We've got to go back," Kal replied. There was nagging voice in the back of his head that he refused to acknowledge. He wanted to go back. Just to see the Nasi like that once more, not as soldiers and enemies but as regular sentient creatures. It was puzzling yet reassuring somehow.

"It's too dangerous," Bhatt said. "They're already growing suspicious of us. We've been warned multiple times. It's just not worth it."

"I understand," Kal said. What he was asking them was crazy. But it had to be done. He couldn't explain more than that—how could you explain a feeling? "But we need to take advantage of this final opportunity before we get back to the fleet."

"Sergeant Kimathi and I can go," Nicole offered. "It's not like the Nasi there care which Humans come. You and Bhatt were able to just walk right in. They won't know who we are."

Kal didn't like it. He was the one making the stupid

decision; he should have to live with the consequences. But Nicole was right, there would be a lot less suspicion if they went. The Nasi wanted Humans there, so it wouldn't be hard for them to get in. "Okay. Bhatt and I will go with Sampson and Fischer to the shipyard," Kal said. "We can give you a rundown of the Nasi we've talked with before. Just be on alert. Either of us could be walking into a trap. Be ready to run."

"We'll be on standby," Ramos said. "For whatever happens."

"Good," Kal replied. There were a lot of moving pieces, they'd be spread thin across the planet and still had a soldier—because that's what Bo was at this point—missing behind the enemy line. "Because whatever happens, we leave soon."

## Chapter Nineteen

The coordinates that Gudit had provided Kal were on the other side of the planet. The closest city to the location was Neu Heidelberg, the largest city in the western hemisphere. Kal took a public transport with Sergeant Bhatt and her squad from Torgut to the city. After leaving the public transportation hub, they walked through the streets looking for a shop that would sell them a tunnel crawler without ID; they'd need the vehicle to get anywhere outside the city.

Kal knew the city was larger than Torgut, but it didn't look like it while he was walking through the streets. Torgut's huge central cavern allowed it to have a bustling downtown filled with skyscrapers, making it seem much larger. Neu Heidelberg sprawled across multiple small caverns connected by an interweaving fabric of tunnels. The ceilings had large light panels interspersed at regular intervals rather than a viewscreen, making him always cognizant of the fact he was underground. The buildings, though modern, were shorter as well with only a few extending to the rock ceiling overhead.

He quickly got lost as they walked through the crowded streets trying to find a neighborhood equivalent to the East Arm where shopkeepers knew enough not to ask questions. He continually had to call up the city map in his implant in order to check that they were going in the right direction. Bhatt and the Tac-I soldiers probably could have gotten them there faster, but they all clearly enjoyed watching him fumble around.

"I can hear what you're thinking," Kal glowered at the three soldiers as they made their fourth turnaround.

"Doing great, sir," Sampson replied, straight-faced. "I can tell you're a local."

"I'm glad we're taking time from our mission to take a tour of the city," added Bhatt. "We never get to appreciate the planets we visit." She looked over at the young private. "Don't you think?"

Kal ignored them and made his way through the street. Most of the surrounding buildings were family dwellings. Children ran through the streets yelling to each other while their parents sat on the small balconies overhead calling out to them. He had to imagine scenes like this one had been playing out for millennia. It was a core part of Humanity. He remembered doing the same when he'd been a father. Sitting in their yard with Li Na and shouting for the kids to be careful.

Small general stores and electronics shops appeared as they made their way from the port. They continued to walk trying to look inconspicuous, merchants in town for a day. The shops become seedier, and the garish glow of chem bar holos appeared on either side of the street. This was the area where you could get something, no questions asked. Kal led the group into several stores. It took about a dozen tries before they found a small pawnshop with a sign advertising a used crawler willing to take their credits and look the other way.

Less than thirty minutes later, they were speeding through the tunnels leading from Neu Heidelberg to the surface. After they'd left the squat metal structures on the city's periphery behind, Kimathi pulled over so they could remove any identifying marks and disable the transponder.

"Sir, what should we be on the lookout for?" Private

Fischer asked as Kal did a final once-over of the crawler's systems. "Anything specific?"

"All we've got is coordinates," Kal replied. "Just keep sharp. If it is the shipyard, then we'll know soon enough. We'll have to play it by ear when we get there."

"Make sure your restraints are tight," Bhatt added. "Whatever's there, we can assume security'll be there too."

They drove through one of the caverns that was a major thoroughfare into Neu Heidelberg. Transports and tunnel crawlers sped past as they rolled over the densely packed road, kicking up a small cloud of dust in their wake. The crawler's engine was too loud for them to talk. Instead, each looked out the window, lost in their own thoughts. As they entered the back tunnels small rest stations appeared on the side, adorned with holos advertising food and refreshments. Occasionally cargo transports passed them with a roar, the air from their thrusters causing the crawler to shiver. Most of the vehicles were mineral transports, bringing raw ore into the city or leaving the city loaded with repair parts for the drilling rigs.

Kal turned into a small cavern—barely wide enough to fit two transports—that branched off from the main road. The floor of the tunnel rose, and he could hear the crawler engine's pitch increase as it adjusted to the slope.

"We're getting close to the surface," Kal said, pointing to the small tendrils of ice that hung from the light strips on the roof of the cave.

As they continued upward, the ice grew thicker and began to snake down the tunnel walls in a shimmering curtain. The rock abruptly gave way to a dirty blue ice; they were driving through a glacier. The overhead lights disappeared, and the only light was from the tunnel crawler's headlights. A soft glow appeared in front of them, and light seeped from the deep blue glacial walls as they neared the mouth of the cave.

Their crawler burst onto the surface, and Kal had to stop the vehicle and shield his eyes. Sunlight came at them from everywhere, streaming from the sky and sparkling off the snowy hills of the undulating landscape around them.

"Damn," Bhatt cursed.

After a few seconds, Kal squinted and looked around. They were at the bottom of a valley. Large white hills with patches of blue ice rose around them. Tire tracks marred the otherwise pristine snow ahead of them, twisting over the mountain in front of them.

They slowly ascended the mountain, following the crawler tracks in front of them. As they climbed, Kal glanced around, looking for any evidence of Nasi activity. They were still relatively far out from the coordinates that Gudit had provided. Bhatt and Kal had agreed that it was safer for them to exit to the surface farther away rather than next to the coordinates.

As they climbed the hill, gusts of wind rocked the small crawler back and forth. Icy jets of wind worked through gaps in the vehicle's skin and swept into the cabin, causing the temperature to drop precipitously. His breath puffed out before him in a cloud, and he closed every flap on his cold-weather suit.

"Sir, do we have heat?" Bhatt asked, shivering slightly.

Kal studied the console and paged through the various

screens until he found the climate controls. When they'd bought the vehicle, the merchant had assured him it worked—the last thing he wanted was to be on the surface without a working heater. He flipped it on, and almost immediately, warm air blasted from several vents throughout the cabin.

As they crested the ridge, the Marigan landscape spread before them. Hills covered in virgin snow rolled beneath them. Small patches of blue ice and the occasional boulder dotted the otherwise featureless landscape. The small path they had traveled on merged at the summit then disappeared, and everywhere he looked, Kal could only see untouched terrain.

"That way." Bhatt pointed to the east.

Kal turned in the direction Bhatt pointed, and they rolled down the hill, the wind dying down as they got lower. As they continued along, the seemingly barren terrain revealed that it was teaming with life. Several small creatures ran across the landscape, their fluffy white tails trailing behind them. Worms, at least two meters longs, swam through the snow, their bodies weaving up and down. The wind picked up and dropped off as they crested small hills and then continued into the valleys beneath.

"Sir," Bhatt said, "look."

Kal stopped the crawler, strapped on a pair of tactical goggles, and used their magnification to study the area in the distance the sergeant was pointing at. It was a large gash of gray covered by a shimmering dome on the otherwise immaculate surface of the planet. An elongated lump the goggles estimated was three thousand meters long rose in the center. It looked the same as the aerial images they had seen on Wudexingqiu—a Nasi shipyard. The bulbous ship component was so large he couldn't fathom how the Nasi were ever going to get it off the planet's surface.

Kal scanned the perimeter of the yard and examined the landscape ahead of them. They were too far away for him to make out any security systems or Nasi. He had to assume that there was an advanced security perimeter. Was there a way to get closer without getting noticed?

"Sir, we can circle around and approach from here." Bhatt pointed to a route on the crawler's display. They would have to go out of their way, but several large hills would obstruct them from the view of the Nasi.

"Okay," Kal said. "Remember though, if we can see them, they can see us."

Kal struggled to understand what he was looking at. The shipyard itself was relatively straightforward, a circular pad encircled by a wall made of Nasi weaves. Small towers which most likely contained the defensive systems dotted the perimeter at regular intervals. Inside there were several small buildings with a regular flow of Nasi and equipment moving in and out of them. Clearly the buildings led under the surface; there was no other way to explain the large volume of traffic. It was what was sitting on the pad inside the facility that confused him. It looked like an enormous tent, irregularly shaped with a high peak on one end.

"What do you make of it?" Kal asked, turning to look over at the covered faces of the others. The others were indistinguishable, except for their height, under their cold-weather gear. The wind continued to blow, forcing them to yell as they spoke to each other.

"They're smart to cover it," Sampson said.

Kal realized that the thing that looked like a tent *was* a tent. The Nasi were covering the ship from observation.

"I don't know if there's anything we can use—"

A high-pitched alarm wailed from the Nasi base, echoing across the landscape and cutting off Sampson's words. The former pilot jumped up and ran to the crawler.

"Get the hell down!" Bhatt shouted at the private.

Sampson dropped onto a knee. "We're going—"

"Your first reaction is to run?" Bhatt asked, cutting him off. "You don't know what the hell is going on. Sit tight and let's see what they do."

Sampson obediently crawled back to their position on the hill and got back into the prone position. Inside the yard, streams of Nasi trailed by their equipment made their way from the tent to the buildings on periphery of the compound. The siren stopped and the entire yard was empty and motionless.

The four Skulls exchanged glances with each other. *What was going on?* Kal didn't think the Nasi had spotted them but nervously scanned the hilltops around them just in case.

The surface of the tent moved, and the fabric slid across the top of ship underneath, slowly unveiling it. It was so slow that at first Kal wasn't sure if he was just imagining it, but as the fabric continued to move, he became certain. The module was a long black cylinder with a white pointed cap at one end. It was as tall as the skyscrapers in Torgut and longer than any capital ship Kal had ever seen; he guessed at least four thousand meters.

"This is just part of it?" Bhatt whispered.

"That can't get out of the atmosphere," Sampson said. "There's just no way."

It took a quarter of an hour for the fabric to be pulled off the ship module. After it was completely revealed, several vehicles glided out of the buildings and stopped near the mountain of fabric at the end of the ship and towed it away in pieces. The Nasi rocket—Kal thought of it as a rocket since it looked exactly like the old Human rockets from when they'd first started exploring the stars—sat alone on the pad.

"Are you getting this?" Kal asked.

Bhatt nodded. "I'm recording it. Still waiting to see what they do next." Kal had to agree. How would the Nasi get the enormous spacecraft upright and into orbit?

A small hatch opened on the pad and light gray drones swarmed out, landing on the underside of the Nasi rocket. They continued to pour out in a small cloud until they completely covered the bottom of the rocket near the cone.

As he sat entranced, Kal idly realized that he was losing all sensation in his toes and wriggled them in his boots. His suit's internal heater was already at max, but he needed to see how the Nasi launched the rocket.

Again, the facility's klaxon rang across the white

landscape. The drones emitted a small hiss and small jets of blue flame shot from each of them. They acted in concert, gradually lifting the pointed end of the ship from the ground until it was standing vertically. As they worked, the drones seamlessly moved around the outside of the rocket, stabilizing it and adjusting the movement through their positioning.

When the rocket was almost perpendicular to the ground, an enormous blue-orange flame shot out from its thruster. Flames shot across the pad and engulfed the buildings and wall. The drones perched on the outside of the rocket rearranged themselves, spreading across its surface as the deep rumble of the main thrusters reached the Skulls' positions.

"Interesting," Bhatt said. "Using the drones to lift and adjust the ship."

Kal remembered back to his engineering classes at the academy. What they were seeing shouldn't be possible—the drones, the stresses on the ship, the enormous thruster, all of them were things that Humanity had never thought possible. Yet here were the Nasi, doing it despite having only been in their universe for a few years. He hated to admit it, but there *was* something Humanity could learn from them.

As the rocket inched upwards, gathering momentum as it rose, the exhaust spread beyond the shipyard and melted the snow. It continued to accelerate as it arced into the sky and the drones fell off, dropping toward the ground like flies. The four Humans craned their necks as the ship streaked above them, a trail of spent drones cascading down to the surface in a straight line.

"Aw, damn," Bhatt swore as drones rained around them in a chorus of wet thumps. Kal thought about running to the crawler, but they'd never make it back down the hill in time.

"Sir, we've got a problem," Fischer said as he pointed back at the shipyard.

Kal followed his gaze to see a small fleet of cargo transports streaking out of the yard toward them. The transports glided over the ground, stopping occasionally as they retrieved the drones.

"We've got to get out of here," Bhatt said, "before we're discovered."

"If we leave now, they'll see us," Sampson said. He pointed to the path they'd come from. The Nasi transports would have a clear view of them if they tried to go back that way. Unfortunately, they couldn't go the other way either; they'd be completely visible to the shipyard.

Kal's mind raced. Perhaps they could dig under the snow? Were there any tunnels near them? Nothing he could think of would help. They were completely at the mercy of luck.

"Sampson's right," Kal said. "Our only option is to wait here and hope they don't find us." He watched the Nasi transports as they combed the icy surface picking up drones, the wind howling in his ears. The closer they came to the Skulls' position, the farther the transports spread apart as the drones spread increased.

Kal felt his stomach flip as he heard the whine of a transport engine behind them and the crunch of it setting down on the snow. As he scrambled to his feet, a voice cried out. "Freeze!" Kal turned around to see a Nasi, completely encased in white cold-weather gear with a plasma rifle pointed at his head.

## Chapter Twenty

*Kal was right,* thought Nicole, *the West Arm is nicer than the East.*

Kal and the others had left for Neu Heidelberg several hours earlier but not before they'd given her a detailed description of the secret bar and the Nasi they had met there. They'd provided names, backgrounds, their tells, and likes and dislikes. It should help her to establish a quick rapport with them.

She walked through the busy streets studying the stores and establishments. Although grungy, the West Arm didn't have the same patina of grime and aura of danger as the East. Sure, there were chem bars and pawn shops—it was a mining planet after all—but there were also a few residential buildings and general stores. She didn't see as many people passed out on the ground, some sure, but not as many.

"Bite to eat?" Nicole asked, pointing to the glowing holo of the Flying Snow Worm. Kal had said they served snow worm meat in the bar. If they were anything like the sign, she'd feel terrible eating such an adorable creature.

"I guess so," Kimathi responded, playing the part of a reluctant merchant hand.

They strode into the chem bar at sat down at a table. An elderly woman, tablet in hand, strode up to the table and took their orders. Nicole ordered the cave rat stew. She always believed in the importance of trying local dishes; a planet's a species culture comprised so many things, and their food was one of them. Sergeant Kimathi found something from his home planet and played it safe rather than trying "to eat a strange ice creature".

As they waited for the food to come, they passed the time idly chatting about their impressions on the planet. For Nicole, it was fascinating seeing how the constraints of living on what was essentially a giant ball ice made them change their society. Ekon missed the warm open spaces of New America and the feeling of the sun on his skin. He said the planet made him feel they were still on a ship or in a mining station. Nicole remembered hearing that Mariga had the highest enlistment rate of the Human colonies. She wondered if it was because the citizens were accustomed to living in the confines of a ship or because of the relatively low income of its residents.

The waitress brought their food. Nicole could smell the tangy spices in the stew as soon as the server set it down on the table. As she took a bite, an onslaught of heat and flavor overwhelmed her senses. The meat itself was mushy with a relatively bland flavor, reminding Nicole of tofu. But the spicy broth more than made up for its lack of flavor. As she took small bites, she felt like her tastebuds were being seared out of her mouth. *How could Marigans eat this dish regularly?*

Kimathi chomped on his fried tofu strips, a contented smile on his face as he watched her, sweat beading on her forehead. "Tofu strip?" Ekon held it aloft with a grin.

"Shut up," Nicole said, shooting the young sergeant a glare. "You just stick with your same old New American dish and leave the culinary exploration to those of us who are truly brave."

"Okay," Ekon replied, his smile widening. "You're

drooling by the way."

Nicole was done. She wiped her face with her napkin and pushed the bowl away from her. "Shall we?" she asked, eying the door by the bar.

"Sure, Chyou," Ekon replied, using the alias she'd given him before the mission.

They stood in unison and made their way to the door. As expected, the bartender walked toward them, waving her hands. "This is a storage closet," she said. "The bio recyclers are over there." She pointed to a curtain on the other side of the room.

"We're here to see some friends of ours," Nicole whispered. "They invited us."

The woman frowned at them. "Ah, you're one of them 'eh?" She paused as she spoke with someone through her neural implant. "Okay, you're cleared," she said, pressing her hand against the security plate.

Nicole felt her stomach twist as she pulled open the curtain and entered the back room. There were only a few Nasi in the space—talking quietly to each other at the tables. It was strange to see these creatures that she had learned to hate even while being fascinated by them doing something as normal as sitting down to drink and eat. Despite knowing what they would find, her first reaction was to run back out the way she came.

"Well, here we are," Nicole said. She looked back. Sergeant Kimathi was still standing at the doorway, his eyes wide and body halfway through the curtain.

"Ivar," she said, "come on in."

Kimathi didn't move, so Nicole reached back and pulled him through by the arm. Ekon stumbled forward, his eyes darting around the room. She could sense the tension rising from the man. They were face-to-face with the creatures that had killed so many people, including their friends.

"Welcome," said a Nasi male with several bands of Sishen scrolling their way across his skin as he extended his hand. "My name is Tristan." His gave a broad, genuine smile that made his blue eyes shine in his violet face. He wasn't someone that Kal and Bhatt had mentioned.

"Chyou," Nicole replied. "And this is Ivar." She elbowed Ekon and the man slowly extended his hand as if reaching for a vat of something acidic.

"Where did you hear about us?" Tristan asked.

"We met some Nasi at the landing port," Nicole lied. "They mentioned this place."

"I imagine you must be nervous. Perhaps a drink?" He motioned at the bar with his head.

"Not nervous at all," Nicole bluffed. "We're not like some of those other Humans. We realize that we're lucky to have our long-lost brethren back. It's just so hard to get to meet and get to know the Nasi."

Tristan shook his head. "So true, so true. It is nice that we can have this location to meet." He pulled out a chair. "Would you like to sit down?"

"Sure," Nicole said as she sat down.

"So do you remember the name of the Nasi who told you about this place, or what they looked like?" Tristan asked as he placed drinks—beer by the smell—before Nicole and

Kimathi. "Just wondering if I know them."

Nicole took a small sip of beer to be polite. "They never said," she replied. "To be honest, I never got a good look at them since they were in battle suits." She looked around the bar. She couldn't see any other Humans.

"Oh well." The Nasi shrugged. "Too bad. I am a settler. What is it you said that you did?"

"We're merchants—well, I'm a merchant and Ivar here works on my ship." She turned to Kimathi, hoping the man would say *something*. But he only stared solemnly with a small sheen of sweat on his face. She wasn't feeling too hot herself. She took another sip of the beer.

"What ship?" Tristan asked.

"A small freighter called the *Richardson*," Nicole lied. She'd seen it on the landing pad a few days ago.

"You come to Mariga often?" Tristan's smile had remained on his face, but his voice had a sense of urgency, of expectation.

"When there's a contract here," Nicole replied, blinking her eyes rapidly.

Nicole tried to access her implant but found nothing—a piece of her was missing. She couldn't reach the other Skulls; her implant was blocked. She shot a worried look at Ekon and could see he was making the same discovery. There was no one who could hear them. *This is a trap.*

Nicole stood up and felt her legs give slightly. She placed her palms on the table to steady herself. Ekon jumped up and placed a hand around her shoulders. "We'd better go."

Despite the nausea and her issues standing, Nicole felt

clearheaded. A fuzzy wave of numbness had started at her feet, and was slowly climbing up her legs and arms, making its way to her core. Thankfully whatever was doing this didn't affect her mind. She could still clearly register how terribly wrong everything was. The warnings had been right, and the Nasi had caught on.

Tristan's smile had disappeared. "I think you'll need to come with us." He didn't hold a weapon, didn't need to. Nicole could barely stand, and a single Human wouldn't be able to do anything against a Nasi, much less a room of them.

Hands grabbed Nicole from behind, pulling her arms back and she was roughly tossed onto a Nasi's shoulder. She heard a few shouts and a quick struggle before hearing the whir of restraints being applied and the sound of a pistol being dropped against the table in front of her.

Nicole looked to the side and watched the room as the Nasi carried her to a far corner. There was the small click of a door opening and she was carried into a metal-lined utility corridor. The door clicked shut behind them.

"Sorry," whispered a voice.

Nicole barely had time to register it before the Nasi carrying her flung her forward. She hit another Nasi, knocking them to the ground. As she lay on the ground she saw the face of Bowen, looking down at her.

"Bo, you're alive. Thank—"

Bowen jumped over her and brought his knee crashing

304

down next to Nicole's face, cutting her off. The Nasi underneath her rolled to the side just in time, leaving Nicole and Kimathi sprawled on the ground underneath Bo.

Bo rolled forward milliseconds before the Nasi's kick swept through the area where he'd been—Nicole could hear the whoosh of the leg as it swept over her head. She tried to move, but her muscles wouldn't respond. Instead she lay there as Kimathi crawled from underneath her. Thankfully she was on her side and could see the Nasi and Jadid facing off against each other at the end of the hall.

"Hey, you okay?" Ekon asked as kneeled next to her, his hands still restrained behind his back.

"I can't move," Nicole replied. "But otherwise, yeah."

"Yeah, I kinda figured." He looked up as the Nasi slammed Bo against a metal conduit that ran the length of the hallway with a clang. Their friend slid under the Nasi's grip and backed to the center of the hallway with his back to the door to the Flying Snow Worm. A small trickle of blood streamed from his forehead and dripped down his cheek. The Nasi turned to face him. His body hunched slightly as if he was injured, but he was still moving with the same sinuous movements that all Jadid did. They performed a deadly dance, feinting back and forth as the Nasi tried to reach the door to call for help, and Bo held him back.

"Stay put," Ekon whispered as he stood up into a crouch, hands still restrained behind him.

Nicole held her breath as the sergeant ran at the Nasi, his steps slow and clunky compared to the flowing movements of the two Jadid. Without warning, the Nasi spun, his foot streaking out toward Ekon's head.

Somehow the sergeant expected the movement and ducked. The bony foot slid above the top of his head as he dropped to the ground. The Nasi was thrown off balance for a split second; it was all Bo needed. In a single flowing movement, he leapt forward and brought his knee up to connect directly with the Nasi's forehead. As the Nasi dropped to the ground, Bo's hands were already slamming into his face, knocking his head backwards as he landed on the ground with a hollow thud.

Nicole glanced at the door, expecting it to open any moment as the Nasi still inside the bar checked to see what the commotion was. Nothing happened.

Bo stood up and rushed to Ekon who was still on the floor, staring at the ceiling.

"You okay?" Bo asked as he lifted him by his shoulder. He reached toward the unconscious Nasi, pulled a small device from his pocket, and used it to remove Ekon's restraints.

"I am now," Kimathi replied. He lightly punched the Jadid in the ribs. "Glad to see you again. You had us worried."

"I am glad to see you as well." Bo strode to Nicole and knelt so his face was hovering over hers. "Any tightness or numbness in your chest?"

"No." She wanted to hug the awkward genius. "I thought you were dead."

"No, not yet." Bo touched her shoulder affectionately. "You only ingested a small amount of the drug. The paralysis should wear off in an hour or less, I think. It's hard to say how it will affect you Humans though." He picked her up, cradling her in his arms like a baby.

"I am *really* glad to see you," Nicole said with a smile.

"Me too." Bo returned the smile quickly, then turned to Kimathi. The sergeant had already gone through the unconscious Nasi's body and retrieved several items including a plasma pistol and his comeca, his wrist-mounted computer that functioned much like a neural implant.

"How do we get out of here?" Nicole asked.

"This tunnel is a direct connection between the Foothold and the bar," Bo replied, pointing away from the Flying Snow Worm. "But there are branches that have been blocked off. We'll need to find a way through."

"Well, no need to sit here talking," Ekon said. "Let's go."

The sergeant took the lead, the pistol held close to his side as he rushed forward. Kimathi's cybernetic legs gave him the ability to run almost as fast as a Nasi or Jadid. Despite carrying Nicole, Bo could easily keep up with the Human. *We're faster with Bo carrying me*, thought Nicole.

As they ran, their footsteps clanged against the tarnished metal floor announcing their progress to anyone who might be waiting ahead of them. Nicole guessed the tunnel had been there before the city of Torgut, which was built by the original settlers, existed. A musty odor saturated the air and rust covered several dented sections of the metal walls. The tunnel had several sharp ninety-degree bends. At each one, Kimathi stopped, bent low, and leaned his head around the corner.

"The tunnel splits left up ahead. It's blocked off but is the only way out before the Foothold," Bo said.

The panels covering the branch looked as if someone had riveted them to the wall in a hurry. They sat jumbled at various angles allowing Nicole to see small spots of black between the wall and the rust-covered panels.

Kimathi activated the light on the comeca and tried to peer through the holes. After a few seconds, he turned to the two of them with a groan of frustration. "I can't see anything in there," he said. "It's too dark."

"We'll have to risk it," Nicole said. "Bo, can you pry those open?"

"I'll try." The Jadid gently set her against the wall and walked to the plates. He stuck his fingers in a hole between a plate and the wall and began pulling. His jaw clenched as he used his entire body to pry the plate off the wall. After a few seconds of trying with no success, he changed his position and tried the other gaps between the wall and the plates, all without success.

The sound of feet running across the metal floor rang through the tunnel. Nicole reflexively tried to turn her head with no effect. The acoustics of the metal corridor made it impossible for her to tell how close they were.

"Bo, stand back," Kimathi yelled. He pulled the Nasi pistol from his waistband and pointed it at the plates. Bo jumped back just as Kimathi unloaded the contents of the pistol on the plates, causing a rapid stream of plasma bolts to splash against the edges of the rusty metal plates; the last few bolts sailed through the small hole he'd created.

Bo reached back into the large hole and pried at the plate again. His face was locked in a grimace of pain as the still hot metal burned itself into his hands. The shots had melted several of the rivets that had held it to the wall, and it slowly gave with a shriek of metal. Finally, the plate fell to the floor with a clatter, leaving a gaping hole in the wall's side.

Bo scooped Nicole off the floor and followed Sergeant Kimathi, who'd already climbed through the opening, with his comeca's light glaring before him. They were in an abandoned shaft, with dust covering the stone walls and the uneven stone floor.

The tunnel led straight ahead. Nicole was so turned around that she didn't have a clue where they were going. As Bo carried her, her eyes darted around looking for a place to hide or escape ahead, but the tunnel continued forward without bending or any branches or alcoves.

Kimathi disappeared through the floor in front of them with a small shout and a shriek of metal. Bo was fast behind and quickly dropped through the hole while cradling Nicole in his arms. They landed in what appeared to be an old storeroom. Someone had abandoned the circular chamber in a rush; packaging and crates littered the dust-coated floor in a haphazard manner. Several portals led from the chamber. Though it was impossible to see farther than a few meters into the openings, they all appeared to be more tunnels.

"Tracks," Ekon said as he shined his light on a sinuous trail that crossed through the center of the room. A trail of large claw marks with the telltale line of a tail crossed through the room and into one of the portals.

Nicole tried to remember what Kal had told them about the creatures on the planet. Whatever had made the trail in the room was large—very large. She couldn't think of anything he'd mentioned that would have made something like that.

The metal steps of their Nasi pursuers grew louder. They were almost upon them. "This way," Kimathi said, rushing to an opening without tracks leading into it. Bo followed, and they plunged into the ink-black opening.

A few meters in, a staircase appeared in the halo of light in front of them. The sergeant ran down them, taking several steps at a time, with Bo following right behind. The stairs circled back several times before finally ending in another dirt-covered hallway.

Kimathi came to a complete stop, causing Bo to stumble into him. Two glowing eyes appeared in front of them, accompanied by a low raspy sound that was something between a growl and a rattle. A face like something out of a nightmare appeared in the halo cast by Kimathi's light. It was almost completely white except for a faint hint of blood red around the enormous muzzle which occupied at least half of the creature's face. Its eyes peered at them, sizing them up in a bone-chilling intelligent manner. Below the eyes were small pits that led to the mouth with large buck teeth, each as long as Nicole's forearm, sticking out like two scimitars. As the creature stepped forward, Nicole realized its full size—it was easily as tall as Bo and at least five meters long. The creature was low to the ground; its six legs splayed out from its body as it slinked forward. Its claws, as long as Nicole's hand, clicked on the rock beneath with each step it took forward.

As the creature approached them, its tongue darting out

of its mouth tasting the air, Bo and Kimathi remained frozen in place, whether by fear or deliberate was unclear to Nicole. It raised its snout as if sniffing the air around. Were they friend, foe, or food to the creature?

The shriek of Nasi footsteps on the stairs behind them pierced the stillness. The creature's head shot up for a moment before darting toward the stairs, knocking them aside as if they were nothing. Seconds later, screams rang through the stairwell and tore at her ears. A few blaster bolts sizzled in the stairwell, and then all was quiet.

"Run, dammit!" Kimathi hissed as he pulled himself up.

They rushed through the hallway, their steps quiet against the packed ground. After several minutes of sprinting, Kimathi moderated his pace. He glanced around as he ran as if expecting something to jump out of the tunnel's rock walls and attack them.

They arrived in another large storeroom that was something from Nicole's nightmares. Metal racks extended from the floor to the high ceiling, covering the walls. Skeletons of all kinds hung from the racks by small bands of wires, small bits of darkened skin and flesh still clinging to the bones. At the far end of the room, metal plates covered what looked to be another doorway.

"What is this place?" Ekon asked, sweeping his light across the rows of animal skeletons. He stopped as it came across a large skeleton hung from the ceiling that looked like the creature they'd seen in the hallway. It reached from the ceiling to floor where its clawed front paws rested on the dirt-covered ground.

"A pantry of sorts, I'm guessing," Nicole said. "From the first settlers on this planet."

"It's creepy as hell," Kimathi said, shivering slightly. Nicole couldn't disagree.

"I agree. This is fascinating," Bo said. "I'm afraid we don't have time to study this room more. We need to get out of here before that animal we saw earlier or the Nasi arrive."

The metal plates that covered the far door to the room looked to be in even worse condition than the ones that Ekon has melted with his pistol. Several of the rivets that held them to the wall were rusted through—more dust than metal. Bo sat Nicole on the ground and pried at the corners of the panels, grunting in pain as he grasped them with his burned hands.

The bolts gave way abruptly, and the panel dropped to the ground with a clang. Light spilled through the opening. Nicole felt a surge of gratitude. She might not know where they were, but at least they would have light.

"This way," Kimathi said, pointing to the left of the small utility corridor. "This meets up with one of the transport tunnels that go in and out of Torgut." Nicole had a moment of confusion before realizing that their implants were working again. Whatever the Nasi had used to block them was localized around the Flying Snow Worm. She smiled slightly and felt a surge of pleasure as she accessed her implant to find out where they were.

Ekon was right. The network of tunnels had taken them to right outside the city of Torgut. It was too dangerous to call for a transport since they had Bo with them, so they began walking along the tunnel back toward the city. Nicole happily realized she was even able to move her legs slightly.

"We missed you, Bo," she said with a smile.

The Jadid looked down. "Me too."

# Chapter Twenty-One

Kal slowly raised his hands, his eyes focused on the barrel of the plasma rifle pointed at him. The other three Skulls picked themselves from the snow-covered ground and did the same.

The Nasi were completely encased in cold-weather gear, making it impossible to see their faces or eyes. The transport behind them had an open bed filled with gray drones in the back and an empty crew compartment in the front. A mechanical arm was perched at the end of the vehicle, ready to pick up any equipment from the ground.

"Keep your hands up and turn around," the Nasi commanded.

*Should we rush them?* Bhatt asked as they complied with the Nasi command.

*No,* Kal replied, *there's no way we'll get to them in time.* The Nasi were too fast.

*What if we all go?* Sampson asked.

*Wait, but be ready,* Kal replied.

"Hey!" Kal shouted, turning his head behind his back. "Wait, we weren't trying anything. We just—"

"Quiet!" The howling wind almost completely drowned out the command.

"We're just a merchant crew. We were at the Flying Snow Worm—"

"What's your name?" Interrupted the Nasi. They adjusted their grip on the rifle.

"Hakim," Kal replied, shouting to be heard over the wind.

"Hakim?" There was a note of recognition in the voice.

"What are you doing here?"

Kal hesitantly turned around, half expecting a plasma bolt to catch him in the chest at any time. "Who is that?"

"It's Kiz." The Nasi who'd first let them into the back room of the bar. "Why are you here, Hakim? You shouldn't be here."

Kal shrugged with his hands still raised. "We got a contract and are leaving tomorrow. We'd heard that there was some big to-do out here today and wanted to check it out before we left."

"It's a restricted area!"

"We didn't know. No one told us that." Kal tried to project as much regret as he could in his voice. "We're partners, right? I thought there wouldn't be any harm in just seeing what was going on from a distance."

"*Who* told you about this?" Kiz kept his rifle raised. "You shouldn't even know about it."

"Kiz, we're sorry," Bhatt added. "We didn't think anyone would mind."

"Airi?" Kiz asked. "I should've figured. Who's that with you?"

"Two of our hands," Kal replied. "They're loyal to the cause. Our entire crew is. You know that."

Kiz slowly lowered his rifle. "You almost got killed, Hakim. I was so close to shooting you."

Kal slowly lowered his hands, keeping his eyes on the Nasi the entire time. "I'm sorry, Kiz. We'll go. We didn't mean to cause trouble."

"I already called this in," Kiz replied.

Kal's heart skipped a beat. "Will they do anything to us?" Kal knew the answer to that full well.

"Yes, I fear they will," Kiz replied. "Wait." He gestured at his transport. "Get in the bed, quick."

Kiz ran over to the transport and dug through the pile of drones, pushing them to the side. "You're gonna have to all climb in there."

Each of the four Humans climbed over the edge of the transport's bed and dove inside. Kal tried to dig through the large metal drones, but could only dig his arms in. "Go sideways and pull them on top of you," shouted Fischer. Kal looked over to see the private almost completely buried in the drones with only few parts of his white suit visible.

Kal jumped on the bed and lay down near the side of the pile of drones. Through a combination of wiggling sideways and pulling the drones on top of himself, Kal embedded himself in the pile of metal. Each time one of the devices landed on him, he felt a sharp pain, but continued to shimmy his body trying to ensure that no part of him was showing. Before the drones completely covered his vision, Kal saw Kiz running back to where they had been standing, kicking at the snow with his feet.

The whine of at least two transports sounded over the wind whistling through the drones covering Kal. He made a final effort to cover himself and then went completely still, praying that his white suit wasn't showing. The crunch of booted feet came near them—it sounded like two Nasi.

"Technician Mensah," shouted a voice over the wind. "Where are the intruders?"

"Sergeant Li, I was mistaken. There were no intruders."

"Mistaken? How could you be mistaken?"

"I called it in too soon. It was just a trick of the light."

Kal heard a muffled thump and a short groan. "You have wasted our time. Do you think that our soldiers have nothing better to do?" The voice was even, without a hint of anger.

"What are these tracks in the snow then?" asked a female voice.

"I must apologize again." Kiz sounded winded. "I had some trouble with the transport and then looked around to investigate the area."

"Perhaps we should investigate, Sergeant."

Kal felt the pang of fear dig deeper into his chest. Their crawler was sitting in the valley below them. If the Nasi soldiers found it, there would be nothing Kiz could do to save them. He sized up their situation. *Was there any way to get out of this?* For a moment, he wondered if this would be what it felt like to be in a coffin surrounded by darkness and unable to move.

"We need to talk with the vehicle technicians," Kiz said quickly. "They are always acting up. I believe you had some issues with the vehicles too, Sergeant."

"I had more than some issues." Kal could sense a hint of anger in the voice. "We cannot do our jobs if we do not have proper equipment. I have talked with Officer Stevens multiple times about this issue."

"I do not know if they understand the importance of the situation," Kiz agreed. Kal could have hugged him; the man was egging on the Nasi soldier.

317

"We will head back," said the voice Kal assumed belonged to Sergeant Li. "Finish your duties. I am going to talk with Technician Aziz when we return. We will discuss your punishment later."

"Yes, Sergeant," Kiz replied.

The two Nasi soldiers walked away, snow crunching under their feet. Kal could hear the transports lift off with a low growl and then streak away with a whoosh. A minute went by and then Kiz called out all clear.

"Thank you, Kiz," Kal said as he lifted the mask from his face. "I think you might have saved our lives."

Kiz lifted his mask as well. He furrowed his brow over his dark brown eyes and pressed his lips tightly together in a small frown. "I am certain that I saved your lives, Hakim." He paused for a moment. "But I'm not sure why I should need to." He curled his lips inward in a pensive expression. "I've enjoyed our times together, no matter how brief they were, but you should leave. And I would recommend that you don't return there."

"Thank you," Bhatt said. "Maybe when we return to Mariga, we can meet you at the bar. When things calm down."

Kiz shook his head. "No, Airi, never return there. Perhaps we will meet again, but that place is no longer safe for Humans or Nasi."

Nicole flashed through Kal's mind. *What did Kiz mean?*

"Did your leaders find out about it?" Kal asked.

"Yes." Kiz nodded. "They try so damn hard to keep us away from the Humans that we're supposed to be helping."

Kiz seemed shocked by his angry admission. He looked around for a moment before pulling the mask back over his face. "You'd better leave," he said. "We're in the middle of the first recovery pass. This is your window to escape. Best luck to you." He seemed melancholic for a moment.

"You too," Kal said. He reached out and put his gloved hand on the Nasi's shoulder. "Thank you."

Kal ran down the hill as fast as he could in the bulky cold-weather suit with the others right behind him. Several times he almost lost his footing and pitched forward but recovered at the last moment. In his mind, there was only one concern: getting out of the area so he could use his implant to call the other members of the team and warn them. The Nasi would be on alert for any signals this close to the shipyard.

"Get in," Kal yelled to the others, holding the windshield door open so that Sampson and Fischer could climb in the back.

As soon as they climbed in, he jumped through himself and pressed the button to start the crawler's engine. Kal pulled off his gloves and mask and hit the accelerator while turning the yoke hard to the right.

"Sir," Bhatt said, "be careful. They're still Nasi in the area, and I doubt we're friends with all of them."

She was right. They'd have to be very careful in making their way back to the tunnel; there were still many Nasi transports in the area picking up the drones. Kal pulled his foot back on the accelerator. "Everyone keep an eye out," Kal said. "We'll be traveling through the valleys, but it'll still be risky. Let me know if you see or hear anything."

"Sir, if we hear anything over this," Sampson gestured to the rear of the crawler where the engine was, "we're screwed anyway."

"Just keep an eye out." Kal turned to focus on the path ahead of him. The sides of the glacial valley were relatively shallow, allowing the bright Marigan sun to shine on them and making it difficult to spot anything above through the glare. The gusts of wind that blew from the hilltops and into the valley had already swept away the path they'd made earlier.

As they traveled back to the tunnel, Kal could only think about one thing: Nicole. Against his better judgement, he'd sent her into a trap. He shouldn't have risked it. They already had as much information as they were going to get, and asking a few questions at an underground bar would not change much. In hindsight, it was such a foolish decision.

The other Skulls kept their eyes glued to the tops of the hills around them as Kal weaved through the shallow canyon. Thankfully, no one raised the alarm. After they'd passed what Kal estimated to be the last point where drones had fallen from the Nasi module, he pressed his foot to the floor and moved in a straight line to the tunnel entrance. The crawler flew over the hilltops and landed with a soft crunch as they sped from hill to hill, getting closer to the tunnel. Kal could feel the time counting down in his head and tried to avoid thinking about what might be happening in Torgut right now.

Finally they reached the crest of a hill and he saw the dark cave below them. As soon as they entered the blue-tinged darkness of the cave, Kal reached out over the net using his implant.

*Nicole? Annie? Can you hear me?* Kal cried out. There was no response.

As they descended into the ground, he continued calling out and waiting for some sort of response.

"Sir, we're too far out from the city," Bhatt said. "There's no connection here."

Kal checked his implant and then slammed his hand against the yoke in frustration, causing them to swerve for a moment. She was right. Mariga's planetary net was much smaller than other Human colonies. It was almost impossible to get a signal this close to the surface.

As they rushed through the tunnel, Kal periodically continued to call for the others. Each time he felt the same sliver of hope grow and then melt away as there was no response.

*This is Annie.*

Kal wanted to scream with joy. *Annie, we believe the other group is in trouble,* Kal said. *Have you heard from them?*

*Negative,* came Chedjou's reply. *Nothing so far. They left for the mission about thirty minutes ago. As soon as we hear anything from them, we'll let you know.*

*Nicole. Ekon,* Kal called out. *Can you hear us?* Nothing.

*Meet us on Neu Heidelberg,* Kal instructed. *Pick us up and we'll head back to find them. We'll storm the Foothold if necessary.*

"And do what, sir?" asked Bhatt. Kal turned to look at the sergeant. She regarded him with a cool gaze, her green eyes seeming to drill holes. "You've been to that bar. If the Nasi have captured them, there's absolutely nothing we can do."

Her words were like a punch in the gut. She was exactly right; if the Nasi had taken them to the Foothold, they were beyond his reach. They had a merchant ship and a few plasma pistols. Even if they'd had the *Salamis* and a host of battle suits, there was nothing they could do. The Nasi Foothold was completely isolated from the rest of the planet and had enough defenses to hold off an army. Kal knew because he'd seen them do it on Patagonia.

"They need to stay there," Bhatt continued. "We don't know what happened, but if Kimathi and Bergeron are being chased by Nasi, they'll need a quick getaway. We've just got to get back to Torgut and see what we can do from there."

Damn if she wasn't right. *Belay that,* Kal said reluctantly. *We'll meet you back on Torgut. Get the engines spun up. They may come in hot.*

*Will do,* Chedjou replied. *Do you have an estimate—*

She stopped. There'd been a small click. To most people, it would have meant nothing. But Kal knew exactly what it meant. Someone had just breached their encryption. The Nasi had heard them.

"Damn," muttered Sampson from the back seat.

They entered the caverns of Neu Heidelberg a few

minutes later, and Kal almost jumped at every sight or sound as they rolled through the street. There was no way to know how much the Nasi had heard or how well they'd triangulated the signal. The only thing they could assume is that the Nasi would be on the lookout for anything suspicious. The question was whether they'd been able to get the unique identification number of their implants as they communicated.

There was a discussion over what the best course of action was to do with the crawler: destroy it or just leave it on the street. In the end, Kal had sided with Bhatt—destroying the vehicle would raise a lot of questions and confirm suspicions that something was wrong.

Kal found a large parking lot near the transport hub and tucked the vehicle in a corner. They removed their cold-weather gear which fit neatly into their backpacks. They went through the crawler's cabin, wiping down surfaces to destroy any DNA, and ensuring it was spotless.

Kal split them into two groups—him and Sampson in one, and Bhatt and Fischer in the other—and walked to the transportation hub. The entrance to the building was one street over and to the right. As Kal passed the intersection where they needed to turn right to enter the hub, he spotted two Nasi soldiers in battle suits standing outside the entrance to the squat building and a small drone hovering above them; its camera was scanning the groups entering the building. Kal kept walking straight, eyes fixed forward as he passed the guards. This was bad. Finding a way back to Torgut outside of the transit hub was going to be hard.

They walked through several more intersections until

darting into an alley between two warehouses. They ducked
behind a large container, waiting for the Bhatt and Fischer to
join them.

"They've got the transport hub blocked," Bhatt said.
"They must have some idea of who we are."

Kal tried to think. They had to get back to Torgut and fast.
"They can't know everything," Kal said. "Otherwise, we
wouldn't have even made it into the city. We have to assume
that we're only persons of interest." It wasn't likely the Nasi
realized the conversation they'd intercepted was between a
Samsara Fleet scout team.

"We go into that transit hub, and we're as good as done,"
said Sampson. "We—"

"Dammit, Sampson," Kal swore, turning on the private.
"Not again. We're not running or waiting. We're going to get
back to *Annie*."

"I was going to say that we have another option,"
Sampson said. "Isn't there a constant stream of mineral
transports that go from here to Torgut? What if we jumped on
one of those?"

Kal thought about it. The private was right, and he should
have thought of it himself. There was a constant stream of
mineral transports that flew between the two cities—raw
materials from the mines around Neu Heidelberg that were
being sent off planet. The only problem was that the
transports traveled on the surface through the planet's
freezing atmosphere. Even with their cold-weather suits, they
risked dying from exposure before ever reaching the capital.
He'd heard stories as a kid of port workers finding frozen

bodies on the intercontinental cargo haulers.

"It's a good idea," Kal said, feeling a pang of regret for snapping at the former pilot. "But they're open air and travel thousands of meters above the ground. It'll be even colder than on the surface."

"We've already got the cold-weather gear." Bhatt pulled her small backpack off and patted it.

"It's not enough," Kal said. He bit his lip as he tried to think of where they might find anything to help them. The Nasi clearly knew something was up. The question was if they'd thought of watching the cargo port.

"There's got to be something we can find, sir," Sampson pleaded. "We go into that hub and we're as good as dead. They might have your implant's ID. We get on a cargo transport, and we have a chance."

There may be some supplies they could get in the general stores that were so plentiful in Neu Heidelberg. Miners sometimes had to brave the surface to repair machinery or get to distant mines. Sampson was right; there was no better option.

"Let's do it," Kal said. "The cargo port is in across the city from here. We need to get there fast before the Nasi lock it down." He brushed past the group and walked back out of the alley. "Split up. We'll see what we can find on the way."

# Chapter Twenty-Two

After stopping at some shops to pick up supplemental heating equipment along the way, the four Skulls arrived at Neu Heidelberg's cargo port. It occupied an entire cave of the city, split off from the rest by a ramshackle wall of metal. There wasn't much reason to keep people out of the area. In their unrefined state, the minerals were almost worthless. After nonchalantly walking along the perimeter checking for security cameras and Nasi activity, they ducked through a small break in the wall.

On the other side was an enormous cacophonous cavern filled from floor to ceiling with a web of velomats ferrying bins of minerals. Hundreds of metal carts clanged along on the belts overhead dropping small bits of minerals and dust on the metal floor beneath. Large industrial lights on the ceiling glared down on them, casting undulating shadows of the belts onto the ground.

"Where to?" asked Sampson, eying Kal.

"No clue," he replied. It's not like he'd ever worked in one of these ports.

"There," Bhatt whispered. She pointed at a metal staircase on the other side of the room. The mats were carrying the mineral bins to a large opening midway up on one of the cavern walls. The metal staircase led to a half-open utility door next to the opening. "There must be landing pads on the other side filled with cargo transports waiting to be loaded."

"Looks like it's—" Bhatt's hand clamped down on Kal's mouth.

"Quiet," she whispered, pointing across the room.

He followed the path of her finger and saw several small bots whirring up and down the length of the room. They were almost completely square, with a small brush at the bottom and a round sphere perched on a pole on top. As they moved, the bots swept the debris falling from the velomats into small grates at either end of the floor.

"The thing on top of them is a sensor," the sergeant said. "We run across this floor, and they'll trigger an alarm."

"Can we take them out somehow?" Kal asked.

She shook her head. "No, they're on a failsafe. You take them out and it automatically alerts the maintenance team." She would know; she had grown up in cargo ports like this.

Kal ground his teeth in frustration and studied the room. There had to be some way they could get around the bots. They were too close to let a few brainless machines stop them from leaving.

"Do they look up?" Sampson asked.

"What?" Bhatt shot the pilot a confused look.

"The bots, do their sensors look up?"

She thought for a moment before responding. "As I recall, their sensors have a field of view of plus or minus ten degrees. So they look up, but not far."

Sampson pointed to a metal conduit that ran up the wall next to them. "How good is everyone at climbing?"

Kal studied the conduit. It climbed up the wall before disappearing into the ceiling. One of the velomat belts entered the chamber directly next to it. It was possible they could climb the conduit and hop on the belt; it would just require a bit of sweat.

"I grew up climbing the trees in my parents' orchard," Private Fischer whispered. "Just watch what I do."

A large rectangular charging container stood in the center of the room. The box was about as tall as Kal and had multiple layers of docks partially filled with bots, their blinking green lights showing they were charging. The box would block the bot's sensors if the bots were in the center of the room. They'd have to time it just right and climb the pipe when the container was blocking the bots' sensors.

"Wait," Kal said, pointing at the charging bay. "The bots need to be in center of the room so that charging container blocks the sensors."

Fischer paused for a moment, then scurried to the pipe and stood up safe behind the bay. He faced the conduit and placed his hands on the back of the pipe and tested it to make sure it wouldn't pull away from the wall. After the test, he turned to look at Kal, waiting for his signal.

The bots crisscrossed the room in a synchronized pattern, pushing debris over the edge of the metal floor and into the grates simultaneously, only to turn and cross back the other way. When all of them were reaching the center of the room, Kal pointed his finger at the private.

Fischer jumped up and grabbed the pipe while placing his feet against the wall behind. In a matter of seconds, he'd reached the belt and jumped onto its side, crouching on the side so the velomat wouldn't carry him away. He looked down at them with a smile. The bins were moving past him on the belt.

Bhatt was next. Although not as graceful as Fischer, she still climbed quickly and joined the private on the belt, looking down at the Kal and Sampson.

A look of doubt flitted across Sampson's face as he approached the conduit. He stared at the pipe and then the ground dubiously while compulsively wiping his hands against his pants.

"You've got this," Kal whispered. "If you think you aren't going to make it in time, just fall. You can try again." Whatever happened, they couldn't trip the bots' sensors.

At Kal's signal, the private started climbing. He pulled himself upward, but his feet kept slipping on the stone wall. He pulled himself upward again and was almost level with the top of the charging container before falling backward, crashing into the ground with a sharp grunt.

For a moment, Sampson lay on the ground staring at the ceiling with tears of frustration trailing down the side of his face. He slammed his hands against the floor, whispered an oath to himself, and stood back up. "I've got this," Sampson mouthed to Kal before stepping back to the pipe. He set his jaw as he stared resolutely up at the conduit attached to the wall.

They waited for the bots to make their trip to the grate and back to the center of the room, then Kal pointed to Sampson. The pilot leaned back and placed his legs against the wall. Slowly, but surely, he climbed up the wall, using his grip on the pipe to keep him in place. He wasn't as fast or elegant as Fischer or Bhatt, but he was methodical. Kal's gaze alternated between Sampson and the bots. It would be close.

It was impossible to know if he'd trigger the bots' sensors, but it would be close.

As Sampson awkwardly transitioned from the conduit onto the overhead belt, a bot let out a small chirp and stopped, followed by the others. Kal's heart skipped a beat, and he felt a tingle of shock work its way up his body from his feet. They'd been found out.

The bot that had chirped abruptly turned and made its way across the room to the charging bay and docked, while another bot left the dock and quickly navigated to take its position. Once it was in place, the entire symphony continued, the bots resuming their regular sweep across the room.

At first, it was all Kal could do to breathe. His body still shook from the adrenaline that had been pumping through it just seconds before. They still had a chance. He was the last one who needed to go.

He placed his cybernetic feet along the wall and gripped the pipe. His prosthetic right arm allowed him to have an inhumanly firm grip on the pipe. He looked up at the others on the belt above him, waiting for a signal to climb. Bhatt met his eyes and shook her head. Not time yet.

A few seconds later, she gave Kal the thumbs up and he quickly shimmied up the pipe and onto the belt. Kal felt a moment of foolish pride at how easily he'd made it. He took a quick glance around. There were shoulders on either side of the belt where there was no velomat. Large bins, about two meters long, rumbled past them toward the opening on the other side of the room.

"Let's go," Kal whispered as he stepped off the shoulder and rode the mat to the next room in the port.

The belt carried them into a large tunnel. Almost immediately, it dumped them onto another velomat which carried them up to the planet's surface. The tunnel was dark with only a small pinprick of light ahead. As they rose, the temperature dropped precipitously until it was almost unbearable. They pulled off their packs and put on what cold-weather gear they could. It would have to be enough for now.

The mat led to a large landing pad that was filled with large cargo transports. The boxy ships sat in two rows on either side of a central velomat, their cargo bays open at the top. Bots pulled bins from the mat and dropped their contents into the open ships with a crash of rock before placing them back on the belt which disappeared into the ground. They were at the bottom of a large glacial crevasse, the shimmering blue walls stretched above them, leading to a clear blue sky. Wind blew through the fissure, biting through Kal's cold-weather gear and hitting his face like small daggers stabbing his flesh.

"Which one goes to Torgut?" Bhatt asked.

Kal scanned the transports, looking for some clue as to their destination. At first glance, they appeared identical, the same wind worn metal boxes with only small numbers stenciled on their sides to tell them apart.

As they talked, two of the cargo ships lifted from the pad

and flew out of the chasm, heading in opposite directions. Kal checked his implant, trying to determine what cities they were heading to.

"What are you doing here?" a voice asked from behind them.

Kal turned to see a woman in worker's coveralls, her face coated in a dark film of dust, with a pistol pointed directly at Bhatt. As Kal turned, he quickly pulled off the cold-weather glove on his right hand, his firing hand. A tall man walked out of a door embedded in the stone wall behind the woman. He quickly saw what was happening and pulled out his pistol as well, pointing it at Fischer.

"Looks like we've got some freeloaders," said the man. He motioned at them with his gun. "Get over here." He turned to the woman. "Want me to call this in?"

"Wait!" Kal cried out. "Just wait."

"We're saving your life," said the woman. "You get on one of those cargo ships and you're gonna freeze to death. I've seen my fair share of people who think they can hitch a ride. They all end up the same."

"We *need* to get out of here," Kal pleaded. "Please." He could feel his own weapon in its holster on his thigh. He hoped he wouldn't need to use it, but they had to leave.

"We can't take a civilian transport," Bhatt added. "Trust us."

"What are you?" asked the man. "Criminals or rebels?"

The woman looked at her coworker hesitantly while keeping her weapon trained on the four Skulls. "Look. Either you speak or we call security and let them deal with you."

Kal thought about it. How much should he say? How much could he? "We're from Samsara Fleet"—he saw a flicker of recognition in both their eyes—"and we're here on a mission. We're not rebels, but if the Nasi catch us, we're as good as dead." Kal could feel the skin on his face freezing in the icy wind sweeping through the landing pad. It was a minor problem compared to the two pistols pointed at them.

"Samsara Fleet, eh?" The man spat. "I've heard of you and I don't believe it. I've seen what the Nasi can do. There's no fleet that's gonna save us. You people just run around trying to be heroes, while the rest of us get killed."

"Jannik, I don't know," said the woman. Jannik turned to look at her, while keeping his weapon pointed at them. Kal's hand drifted to his holster outside his suit. Their time was running out. "You know what'll happen to them if we turn 'em in. What if they're telling the truth?"

"I don't care, Taraji" spat the man. "Rebels. Samsara Fleet, if they exist. They're all the same. My nephew was one of them rebels. He died in the street, gunned down by the Nasi. But not before a bunch of innocent folks were killed in the crossfire. I say, let—"

The loud crash of minerals being dumped into a hopper interrupted the man and caused him to jump. He fired and the round grazed Fischer's coat before ringing off the side of a transport.

Kal dove to the side, pulled out his pistol, and fired back. The plasma round hit the worker square in the chest, and he dropped with a gasp. The woman fired at Kal, but the shot went wide, hitting the rock wall behind him with a small ping.

Kal fired back at her, striking her dead center as well, and her eyes widened in shock as she fell to the floor.

For a moment, no one moved or said a word. Kal stared down at the bodies on the ground in front of him. The plasma had burned holes in their chests big enough for him to put his arm through. They'd barely had time to register what happened before they had died. Or at least that was what he liked to believe.

Sampson let out a small whimper next to him. The pilot's face mirrored the look of shock on Kal's two victims. Tears dripped down his face, freezing before they could hit the ground. Taraji and Jannik, two more names to add to the seemingly endless list of people he'd killed or let die. Kal realized his arm was still up, finger still on the trigger stud. He slowly lowered it and placed the gun back in its holster.

"Fischer! Sampson!" Bhatt barked. "Help me get these bodies into a cargo transport. We can't have the Nasi finding them."

The two privates jumped and then rushed over to help the sergeant drag the bodies to a vehicle. One at a time, they awkwardly lifted them up and pushed them over the edge of the transport's hopper. The corpses' arms and legs flopped as the privates pushed them over the side to land on the rock inside with a meaty thunk.

"Sir!" Bhatt yelled. "We got to go." She turned to Sampson. "You're a pilot. Which transport do we go in?"

Sampson looked at her blankly before pointing to the row of transports opposite them. "I—I think over there. The last ones that left from that side were heading to Torgut."

"Works for me. Let's climb in then."

Kal picked his glove from the ground and placed it back on his already numb hand. He moved without thinking, following the sergeant to the transport and climbing over the side to land on the mound of rocks inside.

As Kal sat on the rocks staring at the worn metal sides of the hopper, the face of Private Pudari swam in front of him. He'd killed her too. She looked at him with her petite mouth drawn up in a snarl and her black eyes staring in anger. How many people would he kill? What wouldn't he be willing to do?

"Sir, get your gear on!" Bhatt shouted next to him.

Kal took off his pack and mindlessly put on the rest of his cold-weather gear as they waited for the transport to lift off. Just as he finished, they lifted from the landing pad and soared into the atmosphere, hopefully heading to Torgut.

# Chapter Twenty-Three

Bo carried Nicole through the transport tunnel toward Torgut as Sergeant Kimathi walked in front. The tunnel was barely wide enough for two vehicles to pass each other and was lit by a strip of white lights on the ceiling. Nicole had tried to walk on her own, but even though she could move her limbs, her sense of coordination hadn't recovered, and she'd almost immediately fallen. Thankfully no people or vehicles crossed their path—though they were ready to jump to the side if it should happen. A Jadid walking through a transport tunnel would surely raise suspicions.

"What happened to you?" Nicole asked. "We thought the Nasi had captured you or worse."

Bo looked down at her. "They almost did. Several times. But they were laxer than I'd expected them to be." He screwed up his mouth. "Before the Nasi left the Jadid, when we were still struggling to survive in our own universe, we were almost completely of one mind. Now the Nasi are…" He paused, and looked away, searching for a word.

"Fractured?" Suggested Nicole.

"Yes, that would be an appropriate word." Bo looked down at her. "They're fractured in thinking and process. I am not sure what Ancient Baykara expected when she first planned on her Nasi returning to this universe, but I do not think this was it."

"What does that mean?"

"The collision of our universe and your own has sent shock waves through both. The Nasi's discipline is breaking down. Procedures not followed, soldiers grumbling, backtalk. I think that these are not too uncommon among other species, especially you Humans, but they are unheard of among us Jadid. It made it easy to move around the Foothold. I was able to sneak past guards and infiltrate their systems relatively easily."

"What took so long then?" Nicole was heartened to hear about the change in the Nasi. At least Esma was feeling the ramifications of her own actions. It put the illicit bar at the back of the Flying Snow Worm in perspective. Another sign of their immense change.

"It was easy to move around but hard to find a way out," Bo replied. "As you may have realized by now, the Foothold is isolated from the rest of the planet. It took me a long time to find out about the tunnel that connects it to the rest of the planet and then a little longer to get access to it."

"So was it worth it?" Nicole asked. She didn't want to put too much pressure on the Jadid though she couldn't help but feel a tingle of anticipation. They needed to know where the Nasi fleet was. "Were you able to find anything about their fleet?"

"Yes," Bo's small grin faded into a frown. "But it's not good. From what I could tell, the Nasi have been anticipating everything that we've done so far. Samsara Fleet's actions have been within their planning parameters with a few small exceptions."

"Like?"

"Like us," Bo replied. "The Skulls are the wildcard in the deck as Sergeant Kimathi says." Nicole felt a small sense of pride, something she hadn't felt since she'd funneled information to a Nasi agent. Finally, she'd been a part of something that had made a difference. "Now they're finding out that their own soldiers are changing, which is another thing they didn't expect. The Nasi are getting desperate and have combined their forces and are looking to strike and end the war. If General Samaha tries to draw out the Nasi, she will have the full fleet to contend with."

"Quiet," Kimathi hissed. He motioned for Bo to press against the wall. "We've got people up ahead."

Bo obediently slid to the wall and knelt, still carrying Nicole.

"Let me down," she whispered. "You'll need your hands free if anything happens."

Bo placed her at the corner of the rock wall and the dirt-packed floor. She stretched out her arms and legs; they were working well enough. She hesitantly stooped into a kneeling position next to the Jadid. So far, so good.

"We're entering the city," Kimathi said. "There doesn't seem to be any security. But I don't know how we're going to get to the landing port." He eyed the purple Jadid, who was at least a head taller than the tallest Human.

"Don't worry about me," Bo said. "Are there any Humans in the area?"

Kimathi nodded. "A couple."

"Just distract them," Bo said, "and I'll do the rest. Please make sure that the bay door to *Annie* is open."

"Good luck, Bo," Kimathi said. "We'll meet you back at the ship."

"You too," the Jadid replied with a small smile and a nod.

Nicole and Kimathi walked into the city. They were at the edge of the West Arm. Single-story metal buildings lined either side of the tunnel, their roofs almost reaching the top of the cave. A few people milled around, calling to each other in voices heavy with drugs and drink. Some men and women, dressed in outfits that left little to the imagination, called out to the miners and workers walking by.

As they passed the first row of buildings, Kimathi suddenly turned to Nicole and pushed her hard enough to knock her to the ground. It was showtime.

"You goddamn liar," Kimathi spat. "We had a deal!"

Nicole jumped back up, a small tinge of genuine anger in her cheeks. "You shoulda read the contract, moron. It's not up to me to make sure you understand what you're signin'."

Kimathi struck out with a right hook, but he telegraphed the move so Nicole could react. She automatically ducked under the blow, lashed out with a jab into the man's stomach, and was rewarded by a sharp exhale of air.

They went back and forth, trading blows in the middle of the street. In seconds, a crowd had gathered around them, picking sides and cheering. *Bo had better have found a way past by now,* thought Nicole. She gave a small wink and lashed out, sweeping Kimathi's legs out from under him.

"Stay down!" Nicole said, raising her eyebrows to emphasize the words.

Kimathi jumped up and furiously dusted himself off. "Fine, but I'm going to report you," he shouted as Nicole walked away. She was glad he didn't see the smile on her face. Pounding on the Tac-I sergeant had been fun.

As Nicole strode through the narrow street the crowd was already dispersing, laughing to each other as they walked away. She ducked into an alley and waited for Ekon to catch up.

A few minutes later, the sergeant strode into the alley with a slight limp. His former look of mock anger now seemed very real.

"You're supposed to act," Kimathi said, rubbing his jaw. "You were throwing real punches out there."

"It had to seem real," Nicole said, trying to suppress her grin.

Kimathi wagged a finger at her. "Ma'am, I'm going to get you. I'm not saying when or how, but I will."

She laughed. "Fair enough." Kimathi didn't return the smile. He was dead serious. "But now we've got to head back to the ship."

Nicole and Sergeant Kimathi circled around the port area several times, looking for any signs that the Nasi had security in the area. She could feel the scales balancing in her head—did they risk capture more by returning to the ship or by trying some elaborate attempt to sneak into the port? How much did the Nasi know about them?

In the end, Sergeant Kimathi decided for her. As they were walking past the large entrance to the port facility, the man broke away and purposefully walked through the mouth of the wide tunnel and onto the velomat. After a moment of shock, Nicole hurried next to him and began walking up the incline.

"What are you doing?" she asked in a hushed voice.

"You couldn't decide, ma'am," Kimathi whispered back. "So I did it for you."

Nicole felt like smacking him. Even so, at least a part of the old Ekon was back. The same person who'd led them to his family on New America because he missed them. She'd been in enough firefights and situations to know that leaders had to be decisive and accept that there would be unknowns. It seemed like Kimathi was realizing that again himself.

Merchants and crew members traveling to and from their ships crowded on the mats, talking and laughing with each other as they walked. The war the Skulls were fighting could have been in another universe for as concerned as they all appeared. For a moment she wondered if the Nasi even entered their minds.

Once they reached the main landing pads, Nicole and Kimathi walked in the direction of the landing cluster where *Annie* was. Nicole tried to act casual, just another crew member walking back to her ship, despite the knot of worry that continued to build in her chest.

That knot tightened as she spied a Nasi patrol dressed in full battle suits and carrying their daton plasma rifles. They looked around, scanning the crowd. *Who were they looking for?* She didn't know but wasn't going to risk finding out.

Nicole pulled at Kimathi's sleeve gently, directing him away from the patrol, and then turned to look at one of the small shops that sold spare parts. As they pretended to examine the equipment in the glass-covered shelving, the attendant bot glided up to them, asking if they needed help and reminding them that shoplifters would be prosecuted.

The Nasi patrol passed by, seeming not to notice them. After a few seconds, Nicole and Kimathi left the store and continued walking in the direction of their ship.

The sergeant cursed.

"What?" Nicole whispered.

"Look." Kimathi bobbed his head. Nasi soldiers had cordoned off the cluster where *Annie* was. They stood at every exit and entrance to the cluster of landing pads. Nicole felt a pang of fear as she looked at the soldiers in their sinuous battle suits, their long datons resting on the ground next to them.

"They're bored," Kimathi whispered to her.

"What?" That was not the reaction she'd expected.

"Look at them. They're bored stiff. They'd rather be anywhere but doing guard duty around a bunch of civilian ships."

She looked again, past the ferocious armor and weapons. She couldn't see their faces but could see what Kimathi meant. They *were* bored. The soldiers leaned against support columns or watched the viewscreens on the walls advertising products. They didn't want to be there almost as much as she didn't want them there.

"I see what Bo meant," Nicole said.

They walked around the cordon and entered a small cafe on the far end of the terminal called the Traveler's Oasis. Spacers of all species filled the establishment, talking and laughing with each other. The assorted noises of chatter combined with repetitive music piped in from the ceiling was so loud it was almost impossible for Nicole to hear anything. The cafe had a tropical theme with viewscreens playing holos of a rainforest, and the attendant bots were dressed in grass skirts. At another time, Nicole would've enjoyed the overall kitsch of the place.

"I don't see how we're going to get past them," Nicole said.

"What?" Ekon pointed at his ear.

"How're we going to get past them?" Nicole asked louder than she would have liked.

"They know something's up, but they don't who they're after. They've cordoned off a whole cluster of the port. Who knows? They may not even be after us."

Nicole found that hard to believe, but maybe the man was right. Another thought occurred to her. They could be trying to lure them in.

"Should we just walk in?" Kimathi asked with a shrug.

"No." Decisiveness was one thing. Complete hubris was another. "We need to get to the ship some other way."

They had three options to get past the cordon: over, under, or through. The floor was metal-covered rock, built to withstand the weight and exhaust from interstellar ships. Under was out. Through would require them to either sneak between the Nasi guards unseen or talk their way in. She doubted they had the agility or speed to sneak through and wasn't sure they could talk their way through either. It didn't look promising.

"Is there any way to get over the cordon?" Nicole asked.

Ekon rubbed his hand over his head as he thought. "They've got those doors on the ceiling that the ships go through," he said. "There's got to be some way for maintenance crews to reach them."

"Then we'll just need to drop onto the ship."

Kimathi snorted. "It's at least a twenty-meter fall." He rubbed his head again. "But there's probably more than one way into or out of the maintenance area. If we can find a way in, I bet they have stairs inside the cluster that we can use. We could just walk back down and sneak onto the ship. Those Nasi aren't looking in, just out."

"Let's check it out," Nicole said. "It's the best option we've got."

They walked through the landing pads, stopping at vendor stalls and asking about repair parts. As they made their way, they scanned the columns and rock faces searching for a service door in the rock face. Ekon was right—there had to be a way up to the ceiling for the maintenance crews. With so many doors, maintenance crews would need access. She wished Bhatt was there; she'd grown up in space ports.

Nicole spotted a large door enclosed in a stone column with a security panel next to it. She gently elbowed Kimathi as they walked by. They continued through the area, and she saw a few more. There was at least one door in each landing cluster they walked through. It looked like there was a way to bypass the Nasi cordon and reach their ship; the question was how to get access.

They finished their circuit of the port and ended up back at the Traveler's Oasis.

"Did you get a look at the security panel?" Nicole asked.

"Yeah," Ekon replied. "Standard biometrics and ID lock. We don't have Chief Kanumba with us. I think we'll need to convince someone to let us in." Chief Kanumba had been the Skulls' resident hacker. Without her preprogrammed skeleton keys, they'd need to use their wits.

"How in the galaxy can we do that?" Nicole felt frustrated by their helplessness. They needed to warn the fleet of the Nasi trap but couldn't even get past a security door.

Ekon looked around the bar. "I have an idea," he said. "Follow me."

He led them back toward the port entrance where there was a cluster of shops and bars, all filled to the brim. "Give me some space," Ekon said, "but keep an eye on me." Nicole dropped back and watched him as he scanned the bars, looking for something. Finally, he strode into an establishment called Port in a Storm.

After waiting outside for a few seconds, Nicole followed him in. The bar seemed standard for the port, generic fixtures and lighting with a few viewscreens displaying holos of areas around Mariga. Ekon stood by the bar, a drink already in his hand. He idly leaned against the counter, his dark eyes staring off into the distance, and occasionally looked around. It made it seem like he was waiting for someone but didn't care when they arrived. Nicole grabbed a table on the opposite side of the room and ordered a beer from the attendant bot.

Ekon downed his beer and sauntered to the bio recyclers at the rear of the room. On his way back to the bar, he stumbled and fell against a young woman in a port worker's coveralls. They started talking and Ekon slowly moved closer while the woman, who seemed to have had a few too many, gesticulated wildly.

"This will never work," Nicole muttered to herself. She wasn't ready to trust Humanity's fate to Ekon's ability to seduce a port worker. She looked around the bar and saw a young man in coveralls, perhaps a few years older than the sergeant, sitting in the corner by himself.

Nicole rubbed her eyes vigorously, trying to squeeze at least one tear out. She stood up and walked toward the port worker. As she walked, she panted as if out of breath. The young man looked up at her, eyes wide. His dark brown, almost black, eyes and close-cut hair reminded her of Kal. Could the general have ever looked so young and naïve as the man sitting in front of her?

"E—excuse me," Nicole breathed, placing a hand on her chest. "I'm so so so sorry but I…" She broke down into sobs and covered her face with her hands.

"You want into the maintenance area," stated the young man matter-of-factly.

Nicole kept her hands over her face, hiding her momentary surprise. Slowly, she dropped them and peered into the man's eyes, her lip quivering slightly. "It's just that I have—"

He held up his hand, his face impassive. "I'm gonna stop

you right there. You can drop the act. You aren't that good of an actress, anyway." Nicole felt a pang of indignation at his pronouncement. "I've worked here long enough to have everyone and their mother ask me to get them into the maintenance area so they can avoid the customs scanners." He held up a finger. "The question is, how much is it worth to you?"

She stopped crying and sat down in the open chair at the table. This was even easier than expected. But she had no idea how much something like this should cost. "How much do you want?"

He smiled, showing emotion for the first time. "That's the question I like to hear. Fifty thousand and we can go right now."

Kal had the chit with most of their credits, but Nicole also had one with a small balance. Fifty thousand was basically the entire chit, but it would be worth it. "Deal," she said, holding out her hand.

"Put that away," scoffed the man, eyes darting around quickly. "You gotta chit?"

Nicole nodded. The man pulled out a small tablet and pointed the screen at her. "Okay, transfer the money." For a moment, Nicole wondered if he'd double-cross her. Really, there was nothing she could do if he did. She grabbed the tablet, transferred the money, and handed it back.

"Listen," he said after confirming the credits were on his chit, "you get one shot at this. It doesn't work out, well that's on you. I get the impression you're not the most experienced smuggler, so I'm just makin' sure you understand how this works. We got a bunch of Nasi walkin' around, so you'd best be on your toes. You got it?" The man stared at Nicole, waiting. He didn't seem nearly as naïve now. She nodded back at him. "Good. I'm gonna get up. You wait a few seconds and follow me. I'll pass by a door and open it. You'll have three seconds max to get in before the door locks again. That's your window."

"Okay," Nicole said. "I'm—"

He'd already stood up and was walking out the door. Nicole jumped up and followed him. "Come on," she whispered to Ekon, hitting him on the shoulder. "Let's go."

Ekon followed her out of the bar and into the main section of the port. The worker was already well ahead of them, hurriedly walking away from the port entrance. Nicole had to work to keep up with him. He was tall, and it was a struggle for Nicole to keep up with his long strides without breaking into a jog.

He turned, leading them to one of the distant wings of the port. The crowd had thinned; now there were only a few merchants in the area as they walked through a passageway between the pads. He turned again, this time into a small sally port between two clusters of landing bays. As he walked through the portal, he brushed against a door, slowing long enough to place his hand on the security panel next to it. A small light above the panel turned green.

Nicole broke into a run, counting to three as she did. Just as she pulled the door open, she heard the click of the lock reengaging.

On the other side was a simple metal staircase. The paint

had been worn from the treads by decades of people walking up and down. Kimathi rushed in behind her, and they let the door close behind them.

"Nice job," the sergeant said. "I would've gotten it, but this is faster. Now there's nowhere to go but up."

They began climbing up the staircase, their footsteps clanging against the metal treads. As they clambered up, Nicole wondered what they'd find when they reached the ship. Could it be a trap?

# Chapter Twenty-Four

Murder. The word haunted Kal as he stared at the featureless gray wall of the cargo transport. Gusts of wind howled above them, dipping into the hopper and blowing the smaller particles of dirt and rock around. The specialized heating equipment they'd bought in Neu Heidelberg helped take some of the chill out of the air, but he could still feel his hands and face growing numb as they flew above Mariga.

It was impossible to talk enclosed in layers of cold-weather gear with wind blowing around them. Kal tried to spend the time thinking about what they would do when they arrived at the cargo port in Torgut. Instead, he couldn't focus on anything but the two guards he'd killed—Taraji and Jannik. He'd killed other people on Patagonia while fighting in the civil war there. But they'd been soldiers and firing back at him. This was different. Taraji and Jannik were two names that he added to his list of sins. The list was long—and growing longer.

He felt the transport slow and descended to the surface. The hopper walls were too high for him to see below them, but the massive ice-covered crevasse walls appeared above his head as they lowered into the chasm that held the cargo port. With a small thump, the transport touched down.

Bhatt crawled across the stone to peek over the side of the bin. After a few seconds, she dropped back down and motioned for the others to come to her.

"Coast's relatively clear," she shouted over the wind. "Just be ready to run."

They nodded in response, then Bhatt climbed back up.

She held out four fingers on her hand and dropped them, counting down to zero. As the last finger dropped, she flipped over the side of the hopper and the others followed. Kal was the last one to leave, pivoting his body over the edge after Sampson. As he landed on the metal floor, he felt shocks move up his legs as his blood circulated, warming his ice-cold flesh.

Torgut's cargo port was larger than Neu Heidelberg's. Instead of a single belt with two rows of transports, there were three belts and six rows. At the other end of the belts, a large plate lifted the end of each transport and poured the contents into large bins below, presumably for sorting and refining.

Kal felt a sense of dread as he looked around. If someone caught them, he didn't know if he had the strength to do anything but surrender. Luckily, the entire floor was empty— not even a bot in sight.

Bhatt pulled her gloves off and stowed them in her cargo pocket. She pulled her pistol from its holster and motioned for them to follow her. Sampson and Fischer both followed suit, taking off their gloves and pulling out their pistols. Kal just walked after her dumbly, his gloves still on. He wasn't killing anyone else on this mission.

The door that led to the rest of the cargo port was open, and they quickly crept inside to find a long utilitarian hallway on the other side. Bhatt took point while Fischer dropped back to cover their rear. They strode rapidly down the hall, looking for a way out, pistols held at the ready.

"Get ready," Bhatt whispered as she reached the door at the end of the hallway. She quickly counted down and gently pushed it open. A siren started to wail. "Let's go!" she shouted, shoving the door open.

They ran down the metal utility staircase on the other side, taking the steps three at a time as the siren continued to shriek around them. Every time he turned the corner at a landing, Kal expected to see a door leading out but only found more stairs. Finally, they reached the bottom of the staircase and a door leading out of the stairwell. Bhatt came to a hold and directed Fischer and Sampson to take positions on either side.

Bhatt kicked the door open and dove forward while the two privates streamed through behind her. After a moment, Kal walked through after them, pistol holstered and gloves on.

They were in a large storage room. Everything in the room was metal. Bare metal silos stood in neat rows, stretching from the metal grating on the floor to the painted ceiling several stories overhead.

"This is where they store the minerals," Bhatt said, her voice joining the klaxon in echoing through the room. "If this is like the port on Kasongo, there'll be another stairwell on the other side that will lead into the public area of the cargo terminal."

They crept through the rows of metal cylinders. The loud bang of a door being slammed open cracked through the room, followed by the sound of at least three people rushing into the room, their steps too heavy to be Nasi.

"Come on out, buddy," shouted a man's voice. "You can't go sneaking around on cargo transports. You're lucky to be alive."

Bhatt looked at Kal expectantly. He froze. Was there any way out of this other than fighting? Kal felt torn. Finally, he dropped his gloves and pulled his pistol from its holster.

"Sir?" Bhatt hissed, breaking Kal from his trance. Did he have to fight? No. But was he willing to fight? Was he willing to kill? Yes. Their mission and purpose were bigger than the Skulls, bigger than the guards on the other side of the room. If he was willing to die for it, he was willing to kill as well.

"I don't want any trouble," Kal shouted. Even he could hear the note of weary resignation in his voice.

"Listen buddy," said a woman in a soothing voice, "we get it. You need help. We can help you. Just come on out with your hands up. We don't want any violence."

*Weren't they listening?* "Neither do I," shouted Kal. "That's why you need to get out of here. This is your final warning."

"Let's just all step out and talk about this," said the woman. "We'll all show our hands, and we can just talk."

*Why weren't they listening to him?* Kal slammed his fist into the silo next to him with his cybernetic arm. "I don't have time. You need to leave. Now!" He could feel the anger and shame from Neu Heidelberg washing over him.

Kal paused and waited for a response. He thought he might have heard them talking but wasn't sure over the wailing of the alarm. They needed to get out of there. If the Nasi figured out they where they were, it would be all over.

"I'm going to move forward," Kal shouted. He motioned to the others to take positions in the other rows between the large silos. "If you're still here, I will assume you are hostile."

He motioned for the team to go forward. They crept in a single line, using the silos as shields as best they could, their pistols out and their fingers on the trigger studs.

"We're leaving," shouted the man. A few seconds later, Kal heard the clang of a door opening and closing.

The Skulls continued to creep forward, scanning the room until they were on the other side. There was a closed double door in the center of the wall. It was an old and unpowered, and opened into the room they were in. Bhatt grabbed a handle on a door and stood to the side while Kal knelt behind the other one. He used his fingers to count down from three, then Bhatt pulled the door wide open.

As it opened, the reports of kinetic pistols rang out. The amateurs hadn't even waited to see their target to fire. Something broke inside of Kal; he'd had enough. He waited for the initial burst of gunfire to falter and then leaned over to see the guards' positions. On the other side of the doorway was a corridor with an intersection a few meters beyond the door. The guards had taken up positions on either side.

Kal ducked back just as the port security guards started firing again. He checked his plasma pistol. There were enough bolts left to get the job done. Bhatt tried saying something to him, but Kal waved her off and listened to the pings of the bullets hitting the floor and walls, waiting for his moment. He'd tried to warn them, but they hadn't listened. He wasn't responsible anymore.

Kal rolled through the door, his pistol already pointed where he expected the guards to be. As he came out of the roll, all he saw were blue eyes. He pulled the trigger and looked to the other side. Brown eyes. He pulled the trigger and jumped to the side, already looking for his last target. Another pair of brown eyes, these ones feminine and wide with surprise. He pulled the trigger a final time and rushed to the intersection to check for any more enemy. All the guards were dead. Bodies were heaped on the ground, their faces burned away.

"Let's go," Kal shouted gruffly. The other three walked into the room. Fischer and Sampson's eyes were wide with shock as they stared at the bodies. Bhatt only looked at Kal, a frown on her face. For some reason, her look made him give an involuntary whimper which he muffled with his arm.

He studied the hallways for a moment. They all looked the same—plain, utilitarian corridors that stretched to a double door in the distance. Kal felt a moment of despair. Would they remain in this maze forever? Then he spotted a difference. One set of doors was painted a gleaming white, the same white used in public areas. Kal pointed at it. "This way."

Bhatt peered through the white doors before turning back to the group. "Transfer Room," she said. "It's where the local merchant crews coordinate the transfer of the goods to their ships. I didn't see any guards in there, just civilians. The alarm isn't going off, so maybe we can get out if we blend in with them."

"Let's go," Kal said. He pushed open the doors and entered the Transfer Room. His mind was split. It was a strange feeling. Part of him was back in the intersection, another part on Neu Heidelberg, and another part was here. He pushed down his sorrow and pain and focused on the mission. Compartmentalize. Getting back to the ship and helping their friends, that's what's important now.

A large desk area staffed by Human officials, took up one wall of the room. Kiosks and well-dressed merchants in expensive handmade, rather than fabricated, garments took up the rest. These weren't small-timers like Kal had been. They were employees of the large corporations that shipped most of the materials in the galaxy.

As he strode through the room, Kal tried to project a sense of purpose. Head held high, he walked through the crowd, acting as if he expected it to part before him. Thankfully, the traders and merchants were too focused on their business to notice the four Humans dressed in cold-weather gear walking through the area. Kal could see the busy streets of Torgut through the glass panes of the doors ahead. They were so close.

"Hey, stop," shouted a woman from behind them. The four Skulls kept walking.

"You four in the white coats, stop! You just left a restricted area."

Kal glanced at Bhatt and nodded. Time to run. They sprinted to the door which had opened to let a group of Qudoru in. The creature's large bodies took up most of the doorway, but the Skulls pushed through, shimmying between the metal doorframe and the slug-like creatures as several people shouted after them.

"Let's go," Kal shouted. He ran through the crowded streets, occasionally looking back to see if they were being followed. There was a disturbance in the crowd behind them, people crying out and getting shoved. Someone was chasing them.

They kept running, taking lefts and rights randomly, trying to make sure they stayed in the crowded areas. Ahead, Kal spied a small alley between two large buildings. He checked his implant—it wasn't a dead end—and ran into it, pulling the white coat off as he ran. "Get your gear off!' Kal shouted behind him. He stopped at a large trash receptacle, finished pulling off the heavy clothing, and shoved it into the container. The rest of the team did the same.

Kinetic rounds slammed against the container's metal side, causing the team to scatter against the alley's walls. "Put your hands up," shouted a man's voice. Kal could hear the soft scraping of people creeping down the alley toward them.

"I'll provide cover," Bhatt said.

Kal nodded. As the sergeant fired plasma rounds down the alley, the other three of them rushed to the other end. Kal could hear the sizzling sound of plasma fire, the sound rapports of kinetic weapons, and the heavy footsteps of the privates running behind him. In front of him, people frantically ran past the mouth of the alley, glancing at the chaos that was unfolding right next to them.

Kal dove behind a metal utility box at the mouth and fired back at their attackers. The light from the city's viewscreen sky illuminated the alley and the three patrollers rushing at them, taking turns to leapfrog up the alley. Bhatt jumped up from her position and began running back toward her comrades. Kal fired his pistol sporadically, trying to avoid the patrollers but too tired to care if he hit them. Fischer and Sampson joined him, trying their best to avoid Bhatt.

She let out a shriek and fell to the ground, her body twisting in the air as a bolt hit her. "Cover me," Kal called out to the two privates. As he jumped from behind the utility box, he saw another body on the alley floor. They'd taken down at least one patroller. Plasma bolts flew past him as he ran to the lump on the ground that was his friend. He took well-aimed shots at the two remaining pursuers as he ran; he wasn't trying to miss anymore. The small screen on top of the weapon registered eight shots left.

As Kal fell to the ground, he saw Bhatt moving. At least she was alive. Bhatt looked up at him. "One of you shot me," she said with a note of indignation.

"Yeah, sorry about that," Kal replied as he maneuvered his hands underneath her shoulders.

"I—I can get up," Bhatt said breathlessly, pushing Kal's arms off her. She staggered to a kneeling position, using her left arm; the end of her right arm was now a charred stump.

"Let's go."

They ran to the end of the alley. Sampson's and Fischer's fire streaked way above their heads; the two privates were clearly shook from hitting one of their own. The two remaining patrollers continued to pursue them up the alley, one at a time. Kal turned and got off a few shots while he ran, but they all missed their mark, hitting the buildings or alley floor. Bhatt was able to keep pace with him, holding onto her ruined arm.

"Come on." Kal motioned to the two privates as he ran out of the mouth of the alley and onto the now empty street. He looked in both directions. To their right, a large crowd had gathered, watching the mouth of the alley.

"Help! Help!" Kal cried, rushing at the crowd. He tucked his pistol into its holster and waved his arms in the air. "They attacked us!"

"Who?" asked a man, his brawny arms folded in front of his chest.

"We don't know," Bhatt said. Tears streamed down her scratched and dirt-covered face. "We were just walking, and they came out of nowhere."

The man looked down at her right arm, his eyes focused on where her hand had been burned away. Kal felt a wave of nausea as he saw small bits of white bone amidst the charred flesh. "Wait here," the man said, stepping between them and the patrollers now leaving the alley.

Kal pushed past and kept running. He heard the patrollers crying out for the crowd to stop them, but they were already several people deep. "Don't stop! Don't look back!" Kal called to the others.

They continued to push their way through until the crowd had thinned enough that they no longer had to shove people aside. Kal slowed from a run to a fast jog and then a walk as they continued to put distance between themselves and their pursuers. Finally, he led the group into a small store selling low-quality fabricated clothes. The attendant bot waited patiently as they picked out new blouses and a pair of gloves for Bhatt, then they changed behind a fabric curtain in the shop's corner.

Kal checked his implant. They were only a few streets away from the commercial port. He turned to Sergeant Bhatt. "You okay?"

"I'll make it to the ship," she said through gritted teeth. Kal could tell the adrenaline was wearing off. A sheen of sweat coated her sallow skin. "Okay, let's get back to *Annie*," Kal said as they left the shop. "Then we can figure out how to help the others."

# Chapter Twenty-Five

Nicole rushed up the metal maintenance stairs trying to keep up with Sergeant Kimathi and his cybernetic legs. They corkscrewed through a circular shaft with small sconces affixed to the wall lighting the way.

She wondered how Bo would get past the ships, though she didn't doubt he would. Despite being an academic, the Jadid had superhuman physical abilities. She wouldn't be surprised if the Jadid could simply climb the ports walls.

At the top of the stairs was a long circular metal-lined corridor that was too short for her to stand in. The temperature had dropped significantly, and Nicole could see her breath as they walked through the tunnel.

"Any idea where to go?" asked Nicole.

"Roughly, ma'am," replied Kimathi. "Our pad is delta forty-nine. It's got to be this way." He pointed ahead of them and to the right.

They crept through the narrow corridor, the metal grate floor clanking with their steps. Small signs had been stenciled into the walls at each intersection directing them where to go. As she walked, Nicole wondered what was happening with Kal and the others. They'd have to figure out some way to get to them and get off planet to warn the fleet. Problem was, the Skulls were struggling themselves, split into two groups scattered on opposite sides of Mariga. The bone-chilling cold and pain of having to crouch as she walked through the tunnel did nothing to improve her outlook.

"Stairwell down should be up ahead," Kimathi said. "Maybe a hundred meters or so."

Nicole couldn't wait to get out of the tunnel. She heard the clang of feet on the metal grate floor. Another group of people in the tunnels with them had made their presence known.

"You hear that?" Nicole whispered. Kimathi nodded. The clang of the metal plates was distant but unmistakable. The acoustics made it impossible to say where they were, except that they weren't close.

Nicole and Kimathi picked up their pace and raced toward their ship's location, their footsteps reverberating through the tunnels. No doubt the other people in the maintenance tunnels could hear them, too. Staircases were located at regular intervals along their path, small signs showing which landing pads and clusters they led to.

"Down here." Kimathi launched down a set of stairs, and Nicole followed as close as possible, almost losing her balance as they spiraled down to the ground. She realized she couldn't hear the other group's footsteps anymore. The other group had either left or were listening to figure out where Nicole and Kimathi were.

"Ready?" Ekon rested his hand on the door at the base of the stairs. Nicole nodded. He slowly pushed and peered through the crack of light between the door and frame. After a moment, he launched himself through the small opening and Nicole followed behind.

The landing cluster had at least a hundred pads inside, each with a ship on it. The ships ranged in size from small two-seaters to enormous cargo ships that were ten times larger than *Annie*. From Nicole's vantage point, crouched on the floor, they all seemed enormous. But she couldn't see *Annie*; nothing looked familiar. It seemed Kimathi was having the same problem as his gaze swept across the bay.

The sound of pounding feet on metal, distant but growing louder, came from the door behind them. Nicole turned to Kimathi. "They're coming down the stairs." They needed to get away from the door. "This way." She pointed to a sleek new freighter.

She darted across the open area between the maintenance door and the ship and dove over its large skids. Kimathi followed behind and landed on the floor next to her, already scanning the bay for their next position.

"Dammit, where is she?" Ekon muttered.

They had to get farther from the door. They weren't visible, but they wouldn't be able to move from this position if port security burst through the door behind them.

Nicole's eyes lit on a small Jupiter merchant ship, a three-seater at best. Its wedge-shaped hull and battered red paint seemed familiar to her. "Over there." Nicole leapt up and ran at the ship without waiting for a response from Kimathi; the sergeant would just have to keep up.

She heard the small metallic squeak of the maintenance door behind her. Whoever had been following them was in the landing cluster as well. The ships between them prevented her from seeing who had entered. Nicole and Ekon crawled around the small ship and dove next to the landing skids of the large transport on the next pad over. She fought the urge to stick her head up to see who was in the cluster with them. But if she could see them, they could see her.

"Look!" Kimathi whispered, pointing to their left.

Nicole saw *Annie's* familiar undercarriage peeking out from between two larger ships. Unfortunately, there was a lot of open ground between them and the ship and no way to cross it without being exposed. She heard the muffled thumps of the other group rushing from the doorway.

"We're going to have to run," Nicole said, pointing at *Annie*. "On my mark."

Kimathi nodded.

"Go!" Nicole jumped up and ran across the painted metal floor. She weaved between two freighters and then sprinted across the open area to *Annie*. She saw a Nasi guard standing with their back to her meters away and made a mental note to always wear soft-soled shoes on missions from then on.

The ship's ramp was already down, allowing Nicole to run inside without breaking stride. Hoping that they hadn't been spotted, she slammed the panel next to the ramp, and it lifted off the ground in a stuttering motion.

Halfway up, the ramp came to a stop with a slight squeak and changed direction. Nicole felt a pang of terror as she looked back.

"You weren't going to leave without us, were you?" Her fear melted away as Sergeant Bhatt jumped onto the still descending ramp, followed by Fischer and Sampson. Seconds later, Kal rushed into the cargo bay, his face grim.

"You're okay," Kal said, his eyes softening a touch.

"We are," Nicole replied. "What happened to you?" She eyed the charred stump at the end of the Bhatt's right arm with a look of horror.

"Long story," Bhatt grunted. Her body was bent over, and she cradled the arm close to her chest. "We've got to—"

Chief Ramos came out from the ship's galley, a relieved look on her face. "Thank goodness you're all back."

A muffled thud sounded from outside the ship, barely audible over the low hum of the ship's engines.

"What the hell was that?" Kimathi asked.

As if on cue, Bowen dropped from the top of the ship onto the bay ramp.

There was a small bit of commotion from the four Skulls who had been at Neu Heidelberg. "I'd thought we'd lost you," Kal said as he gave the Jadid a one-armed embrace. "You had us scared."

"Apologies, sir," Bo replied as the others slapped him on the back.

"Sorry to cut this short," Nicole said. "But we need to leave now."

"That's going to be a problem," Ramos said. "They're not letting anyone get in or out of this cluster. They already searched every single ship and have locked down the departure gates."

"Can we somehow override the controls?" Nicole asked.

"Not from here." Bhatt replied. "They're hard-wired."

"Could you...unwire them?" Nicole asked. "Get the door open?"

Bhatt shook her head. "I'm not an engineer, ma'am."

"I may be able to do it," Bo said. "I've been studying how security and bioelectrical systems work in your universe."

"You do know how to party," Kimathi snickered.

"If I can get Chief Ramos and Sergeant Bhatt to give me some information," Bo continued, "there's a good chance I can open the door. Civilian ports like this one are usually relatively simple."

The team looked to Kal for a decision. He stood with a dazed expression on his face.

"Ma'am, what do you think?" asked Bhatt, turning away from the general.

"Go for it," ordered Kimathi.

Nicole wondered what had happened to Kal. The man looked desolate despite all of them making it back to the ship. They'd been in some bad situations, but she'd never known him to freeze in doing his duty.

"Welcome back, everyone. We've got a problem!" Sergeant Chedjou called over the intercom. "The Nasi are conducting searches of the ships in the cluster."

Damn! "How long do we have?" Nicole asked.

"No idea, ma'am" Chedjou replied. "They just started. Based on the last round of inspections, perhaps fifteen minutes."

"I'm on my way," Nicole said as she walked to the ladder that led to the cockpit. She turned to Bo. "Bo, you'd better hurry."

"Where are they?" Nicole asked as she entered the cockpit with Ramos on her heels.

Chedjou pointed to a large freighter at the far end of the

cluster. A group of four Nasi stood in a semicircle around the ship's cargo ramp. "Over there."

"Actually, they're over there too," Kal said as he walked into the cockpit. He pointed to the opposite side of the cluster where another group of Nasi surrounded a small ship. Nicole was glad to see him walking and talking. He still looked like hell, but at least he was talking. He saw her looking and quickly brushed her hand with his own.

"I'm heading out," Bo said over the intercom. "When the doors open, please leave. I'll make it back to the ship."

Nicole watched the cockpit viewscreen as the Jadid cracked open the ship's cargo ramp and grabbed the top of the fuselage, flipping onto the top of *Annie*. Seconds later, he darted through the cluster of ships, his violet body melting in with the shadows cast across the iron floor. Eventually, she lost sight of the scientist. Now they just had to hope that he wouldn't get caught and that he could open the bay.

"Did you know he could do that?" Nicole asked.

Both Kal and Chedjou shrugged. Who knew *what* the Jadid were capable of—even one that was their friend?

Now they had to wait.

The three Humans sat in the cockpit, watching the two groups of Nasi comb through the ships. They'd started on opposite sides of the cluster and were methodically working their way toward the center, where *Annie* sat. Most of the time, the battle-suited soldiers would emerge from the ship after a few minutes. However, it occasionally took longer, and they sometimes left with a prisoner in restraints.

"What are they looking for?" asked Sergeant Chedjou.

"They're scanning IDs," Kal replied. Every neural implant had a unique ID. It was how the planetary network knew where to route messages and information.

"They must have been able to grab your implant's ID when we talked," Kal said.

"I didn't know that was possible." The sergeant was aghast. Under the United Earth Government, it had been illegal to keep records of a person's ID. Nicole knew that there had always been conspiracy theorists that believed the UEG lied about storing the records. But if they kept records, they certainly didn't share them with diplomatic attachés or planetary governments. Word would have gotten out.

"Just be ready to take off," Kal said. "We'll need the bay open for Bo to get back in. Once we clear the city, I'm taking over. I know this area pretty well." Chief Ramos nodded.

His voice had lost some of its depression. No matter what Kal thought of himself, Nicole knew he was a man who thrived when faced with a problem. Their situation had made him forget whatever was weighing him down. She was glad to hear a little of the man she loved in that voice.

The two groups of Nasi soldiers methodically moved from ship to ship until there were only a few remaining. As they cleared the ships, the cordon grew tighter and tighter until Nicole could see the entire Nasi perimeter through the ship's external cameras.

"Where are you, Bo?" Nicole muttered to herself.

"Open your cargo door and have all personnel stand in your bay with their hands up." The command came from a group of four Nasi standing outside the ship. The female speaking sounded bored like she wanted to be anywhere but there.

Nicole glanced at Kal. He ran his hand over his hair as he stared at the screen.

"I say again." The Nasi's voice grew louder. "Open this door now." The other soldiers picked up their datons and held them at a loose ready position.

"Can those things get through our armor?" Chedjou asked.

"With one shot? No." Kal said. "With a few. Yes." He pressed the button to activate the external speaker. "Er…hello…this is embarrassing, but we're having trouble with the door. Even the manual release is broken. We're working on it."

"Fix it now." The soldier's voice was steel. All four Nasi pointed their datons directly at *Annie*.

A metallic thunk came from outside the ship and the Nasi looked up. Bo had been successful. The circular gate in the ceiling was slowly dilating open.

"Let's go!" Kal said as he strapped himself into the co-pilot's seat.

Ramos' finger flew across the console in front of her as she powered on the engines. As soon as they spun up, the Nasi began firing their datons. The ship's limited energy shield—it was only intended to absorb cosmic radiation, not sustained weapon fire—absorbed the first volley of shots and then they hit the bare metal of the hull.

"Hurry, hurry," Nicole said as she eyed the external temperature gauge. It was rapidly rising as the plasma bolts splashed against the outside of the ship.

"Tryin' my best, ma'am." Ramos said, continuing to focus on the screen in front of her.

The engine's low whine turned into a low-throated growl, and they lifted off the pad, knocking Nicole to the floor.

"The door's not fully open yet," Nicole said. It was only open halfway.

"It'll be open enough by the time we get there."

Nicole wasn't sure she shared the pilot's optimism.

"We've got a problem," Chedjou shouted, pointing at the rear camera. One of the Nasi soldiers had jumped and grabbed onto the back of the ship.

"Let me handle this," Kal said. "I know what the ol' girl can do." He activated the ship's intercom. "Everyone strap in. *Now!*"

*Bo, we'll be up in a second,* Kal called out over the neural net.

*Roger, sir,* Bo replied. *There's a Nasi patrol entering the area, so please hurry.*

The engines roared as Kal increased the power to the thrusters on the top and bottom of the ship, causing them to gyrate wildly while they hovered above the pad. The Nasi hanging onto the fuselage was caught in the exhaust and thrown back to the pad underneath while the others slid across the bay floor. Even some of the small ships skidded across the pads as Kal increased *Annie's* engine to its max output. Nicole lurched into the small jump seat on the side of the cockpit and fastened the restraints around her waist and across her chest.

"Ready?" Kal looked back at Nicole, and she nodded back. Kal activated the rear cargo door. She could see eddies and gusts of wind flooding the bay in her console's screen, turning anything that wasn't strapped down into a projectile. He pressed a button and the engines quickly dropped to a hum as they quickly shot through the opening in the ceiling.

When they were level with the landing pad opening, Bo jumped from a small portal near the opening onto the cargo ramp. He strained to hang on as *Annie* continued to rise through the canyon that contained Torgut. After a few seconds, he swung his legs onto the ramp and pulled himself up. As he rolled inside the ship, Ramos activated the controls, closing the cargo ramp.

"We've got several fighters heading toward us," the chief said.

"Don't unfasten your restraints yet," Kal said as he directed *Annie* back into the crevasse.

He flew them along the canyon floor. The sparkling walls surrounding them and the bulbous top of Torgut sailed below. From this vantage point, the canyon looked untouched; Nicole wouldn't have believed there was an entire metropolis beneath the icy planet's surface unless she'd seen it with her own eyes.

Their pursuers were catching up; *Annie* was a merchant ship, not a fighter like the ones chasing them or a scout ship like the *Salamis*.

They continued to soar along the chasm, and its walls closed in on the ship until Nicole felt like they were touching the bulkhead. The narrow canyon twisted and turned, widening and narrowing, as they shot down its length. Looking at the sensor readout, she could see they were heading to a web of canyons spread over thousands of square kilometers—the perfect place for a ship to hide.

"They're getting close, sir," Chedjou warned. "They'll be able to pick us up on sensors even in these crevasses."

"I know," Kal replied with an edge of annoyance. "Just have faith."

The valley branched in several spots on either side. The offshoots' jagged sides and windswept white floors appeared identical to the one they were already flying through. Kal followed the network of canyons, shifting left and right as the fighters closed the distance between them. The fighters abruptly pulled out of the maze and flew above the surface of the planet, allowing them to close the distance in a straight line.

"They're going to be in missile range soon," Chedjou warned. "They'll have a straight shot from above."

"Have faith," Kal said. "We're close to my home. I know this area like the back of my hand."

"Which one?" the chief asked. "I mean, your right hand is pretty new."

Kal grunted. "Just let me know what they're doing. This'll be over soon."

He continued to snake through the canyons as the fighters closed the distance. Despite the inertial dampeners, Nicole felt herself becoming nauseous as they looped back and forth. She wondered how much longer their luck could hold out. Kal was flying like a man who didn't care whether he lived or died.

"We've got missile launch!" Chedjou cried out.

Nicole could see the small red icons speeding at them on the tacmap. There was nothing they could do about it; they didn't have countermeasures or the speed or agility to outmaneuver the missiles. Their only defense was the canyons and the twisting, turning routes they were taking through them.

She watched as the missiles impacted against the walls, their icons fading from the map until there was only one left doggedly following them. It came closer until it was right on them. A loud blast from the explosion rocked the ship forward, and Kal barely kept them from crashing into the frozen wall in front of them by flying over the lip of the canyon and then back down on the other side.

Another cluster of red icons appeared behind them on the map. Leaving the canyon had allowed the fighters to lock onto Annie. They were sitting ducks.

"If you're going to do something, do it now," Nicole said evenly to Kal. She was beyond terrified to where her dominant emotion was a sense of acceptance. There wasn't any way out of the situation.

"There it is!" Kal shouted as he pushed the yoke down, sending Annie toward the canyon floor.

Nicole barely had time to react before they plunged into a small rock-lined hole. As soon as they were through, Kal hit the reverse thrusters and twisted the yoke, desperately trying to ensure they didn't crash against the jagged rocks. Barely fitting in the small tunnel, the ship bounced off the cave walls a few times. The missiles detonated at the mouth of the cave, creating a bright fireball behind them and sending a pile of rock and ice cascading down.

"This is where I learned to fly," Kal said. "Not in a ship this this big. But I'd figured we'd be able to fit in."

He continued to maneuver them through the cave as it wove its way under the planet's surface. The AI emitted periodic beeps as they squeezed through. A few times, the ship brushed against the rocky sides, shuddering slightly as it continued forward.

"Sir, I thought you said you knew how to fly," Chedjou said.

"Quiet," Kal replied in a calm tone. "I've only flown through here in small atmospheric craft. It's harder in an interstellar ship."

"Do you think the fighters think they got us?" Nicole asked.

"Maybe," Kal said, "but they'll figure it out soon enough when they scan through the rubble. We need to make it through here and get off the planet."

They wound their way through the narrow cave for several minutes until Nicole saw a pinprick of light ahead. Kal accelerated as they neared the cave exit, hand on the console in front of him, eyes on the screen, and mouth bunched up as he tried to judge the right approach. Large boulders lined the mouth of the cave, forcing him to sweep the yoke from side to side to avoid them.

They shot out of the cave's mouth, and Kal immediately pushed the ship to max speed. The momentum pushed

Nicole back in her chair as they broke through the thin clouds and exited the planet's atmosphere. Thankfully, it looked like they'd evaded the planetary forces. With the Nasi fleet massing to attack Samsara Fleet, there were no ships in orbit, nothing to prevent them from leaving.

"Look over there," Chedjou said as she adjusted the main viewscreen's magnification.

Four identical cylinders floated next to each other in the space near the orbital station. Several small ships were tethered to their outside and workers and bots floated between the large modules—building tunnels and attaching cabling to join them together.

"Seems like they're almost finished," Kal said. "They probably already started on new modules on the surface."

Nicole felt a stab of worry at Kal's words. What would happen if the Nasi could build these ships with impunity? The only way to stop them was to secure the other colonies, but the entire Nasi fleet stood in their way. Freighters and smaller cargo ships trailed to and from the planet's surface, delivering supplies to the planet. She had to imagine the same thing was happening at each of the four former Human colonies. If they didn't cut off the Nasi supply lines soon, there would be nothing standing in their way.

# Chapter Twenty-Six

Kal had been in a haze for the first day of their voyage to rejoin the fleet. The adrenaline of their escape from Mariga had worn off and left him with guilt and the haunting images of the people he'd killed. He knew everyone on the ship was on edge around him. They'd look at him out of the corner of their eyes when he entered the room or slap on a reassuring smile when he'd ask them a question. Nicole had tried to talk to him once they'd folded away from the planet, but his monosyllabic answers quickly shut her down. He couldn't talk about what had happened—not yet.

The rendezvous point with the fleet was only a day away. As they folded there was a general air of anticipation, like an unseen timer ticking in everyone's heads. Could they reach the fleet before they attacked the Nasi?

Kal walked into the ship's galley to grab something to eat, only to find the room filled. Everyone turned to look at him as he entered, their expressions a tapestry of surprise, concern, and guilt.

"What's going on?" Kal asked. He tried to squash the feeling of betrayal. His soldiers were allowed to meet without him.

No one spoke.

Bowen broke the silence. "I'm debriefing the team on what happened in the Foothold."

"Shouldn't I be here?" Kal felt a trace of annoyance.

"We thought you needed some time to recover," Nicole replied. Kal could sense the Bhatt must have told her what he'd done on their return from Neu Heidelberg. Perhaps she thought he needed some time alone, but she should have known better than to do this without him.

"I'm recovered," Kal said as he activated the food fabricator. "Please go on."

Bo cleared his throat. "Right. So like I said, the Nasi clearly are adapting to this universe in ways we didn't expect. That's what allowed me to operate as freely as I did within the Foothold."

"What are they planning?" Nicole asked.

"They're entering what they call the final phase. They've solidified their hold on the Human planets with their Footholds and are working on establishing their manufacturing base on the four planets. The other systems are primarily for resources and some low-level industrial output. With this framework in place, they will essentially be unstoppable. They can build advanced ships at a rate far beyond anything we've seen before."

"What about their fleet?" Kal asked. "Where is it?"

"It's in Tounous space," Bo replied. "They've got a small fleet of ships on a planet called Ffromar in the J'Kalnik system. That's the bait. The rest of their fleet is a few hours away, waiting for us to fold to the planet."

"When we escaped from Tamulk, they knew they had to adjust their plan," Bo explained. "They expected us to do exactly what we did: combine our entire fleet and hunt for them. If Samsara Fleet attacks that Nasi fleet around Ffromar we'll be bringing the entire Nasi fleet down on us."

The tactic wasn't groundbreaking. Amass your forces, destroy the enemy in a decisive battle, and move on.

377

Continue doing it until your enemy has lost their ability to fight. The Nasi were using Samaha and Wang's aggressiveness against them.

"Even with every single remaining ship in Samsara Fleet, they still outnumber us," Chedjou said. "How do we stop them?"

They looked at each other. None of them knew the answer. "I don't know," Kal said. "But if we can get back to General Samaha and Ancient Wang in time, we'll have the element of surprise at least. We'll get to decide how, where, and when we fight. That'll gives us a chance."

"I should also mention that they're divided," Bo said. "It was one of the reasons I was able to get as much information as I did. As I walked through the Foothold, I heard conversations I had never heard on Altterra. Nasi questioning why they were there and if their goals are the right ones."

"Well, the hidden room at the Flying Snow Worm shows that they've changed," Kimathi said. He gave a small mirthless grin. "Think they'll just pack up their ships and go home?"

"I'm sure it's likely, Sergeant." Bhatt rolled her eyes. After they'd left the planet, they'd used the medbot to heal her right arm. Although she was missing her hand still, the wound was now a smooth stump rather than a charred mess.

"Bo, that's good to hear. But what can we do with it?" Kimathi asked. "I mean, do we ask them if they like us before we shoot?"

"It's already come in handy," Bhatt said. "The only reason we made it out alive from that planet was because one of the Nasi knew me and the general."

Kal hadn't thought about it that way, but Bhatt was right. His smooth talking when they landed and their friendships with the Nasi allowed them to not only gain access to the planet but escape it as well. Prior to their mission on Mariga, Kal had never thought of trying to establish a relationship with a Nasi, but it was a technique that had been easy and effective. Perhaps they didn't have the cynicism and suspicion that Humans did.

"We'll need to make sure we document all of this," Nicole said, perhaps thinking the same thing Kal was. "The other scout teams in the fleet need to know what we did and how we did it."

Chief Ramos looked thoughtful. "How long do you think the Nasi can go on like this?"

"What do you mean?" Kal was confused. To him, the more important question was how long *they* could go on like this.

"If the Nasi are already changing so much, what will they look like in a year? Or two?" Ramos asked. "Most of the Jadid haven't even been to our universe, and they've already undergone a civil war."

"I fear you may be right," Bo said, shuddering. "I do not think the Jadid or Nasi will emerge from this war anything like they were before it began."

"Bo, you *fear* it?" Kimathi asked. "It'd be great."

"Change is not inherently good nor bad," Bo replied. "But it *is* unknown which makes me worried. You assume the change will be for the good, but what happens if someone worse ends up leading the Nasi? Yes, I fear it. I believe we are

379

winning this war, no matter how desolate it looks."

"How can you say winning?" asked Bhatt. "We're barely surviving."

"He's right," Kal said, thinking to himself. "When we first fought the Nasi, we had two ships. Now we have multiple fleets. Our technology has jumped leaps and bounds."

"Their fleet has grown too," Ramos protested.

"No, it hasn't," Kal said. "It has always been the same size, but we just never knew how big it was. They were always going to capture these planets and build the Footholds. I don't know if we're winning now. But if we can stop them from creating these ships, then we will be."

Kal lay in the small bunk staring up at the ceiling. Faces flashed through his head. The war was getting to him. It was getting to be too much. He'd seen it happen to others during the Torgham War but didn't realize it would happen to him. Shellshock, battle fatigue, PTSD—many names for the same thing.

"What happened?" Nicole asked as she sat on the end of the bunk. The cabins on a small ship like the *Queen Anne's Revenge* were tight. There wasn't much room for two people.

"You know what happened," Kal replied. He knew what she was trying to do. But the last thing he wanted to do was to talk about what had happened on Mariga.

She frowned and placed her hand on his leg. "You *can* talk to me. You know that, right?"

"Talking about this won't make me feel any better. Only time will help."

"We'll be there any second. You ready?" It was only minutes until they'd be back with the fleet. Kal would need to act the part of the general or at least a functioning Human.

"I'll be fine." He sat up. "What about you? How are you feeling? You seemed pretty shook up." He knew he was exaggerating. He'd only said it to change the conversation. Nicole was tougher than him; she could handle the stresses that they faced better. Perhaps because she was still relatively new to it or because she hadn't had to pull the trigger as many times as he had.

Nicole raised her eyebrows. She knew what he was doing. "I was just tired. We'd been through a lot at that point." She rubbed her hand over her face. "What do you think they'll do to the Nasi in the Flying Snow Worm?"

"I don't know." He hadn't thought about it. "Execution, maybe? Maybe just a work detail. Letter of reprimand? Who cares?" Kal hated to admit it, but despite his words, *he* did. Against his better judgement, he liked the Nasi they'd befriended in the Flying Snow Worm. Kiz had saved them, for goodness' sake. "Well, we saw Kiz outside the bar. So it couldn't have been that bad."

"Maybe he didn't get caught. Or maybe he was the one who turned in the others."

"He wouldn't do that." Kal's response had more heat than he intended.

Nicole raised an eyebrow. "Perhaps you care about them more than you think."

Kal was about to respond when Ramos' voice came over the ship's intercom. "Final fold is complete, and we've established contact with the *Gedorhan's Return*. We should land in fifteen."

"Thank god they're still here," Nicole said.

"Glad to see you got back," General Samaha said, motioning to the chairs across from her desk. "Ancient Wang will join us via holo." As she spoke, the Ancient appeared on the viewscreen to Kal and Nicole's right with General Zhao behind him.

"Welcome back, General Norman and Colonel Bergeron," Ancient Wang said with a broad smile.

General Zhao remained silent but flashed a quick smile and gave them a nod.

"So what did you find out on the mission?" Samaha asked.

"The Nasi have massed their ships into a single fleet," Kal said. "They're hoping we'll attack them and then will crush us in one blow. We're uploading their location to you now."

"So they're hunting us?" Wang asked.

"It's a risky strategy to leave everything else unprotected," Zhao said.

"Not if you're confident that your enemy won't exploit the weakness," Samaha replied. "What do they have to lose? Sure, we can grab a few planets, but we lose that many ships again and we're done. The Nasi will hunt us down with impunity."

Wang's mouth twisted at the corner. "The question is how do we fight their superior force? They outnumber us, and I fear even our Jadid ships aren't an even match yet." He turned to look at Zhao. "What about the weapons? Are they ready?"

"Uncertain, sir. We've had some successful tests, but you saw the last time we tried them in battle."

"Let's save this for a private conversation," Samaha said. She turned to Kal and Nicole. "Sorry, this isn't something we can discuss with you around."

As members of the Skulls, Kal and Nicole couldn't be privy to the fleet's deepest secrets. The risk of their capture was too great. Kal knew that they'd been working on a new weapons program from what Chief Kanumba had told them but knew little beyond that.

"We'll let you know—"

"Wait. One more thing," Nicole said, interrupting the general. She'd become more confident in speaking her mind in these meetings. It was a change Kal appreciated. "With the changes in the Nasi, there may be an opportunity for negotiation. Is there a chance to end this in some peaceful way?"

From the reaction of the other three officers, Kal would've assumed Nicole had just suggested they kill one of their children. He appreciated she thought in different ways than the other officers. However, he didn't see how they could reach a victory through any method but militarily, and frankly, he didn't want to. The Nasi had done too much.

"What would you have us do?" asked Zhao. "Ignore the

billions they've killed and let them hold onto our planets? Let bygones be bygones?"

"I don't think we even have that as an option if we wanted," Samaha said. "We could stop fighting, but every single species would try to hunt them down to the ends of the galaxy."

Kal wasn't so sure about that. He'd seen plenty of people who were fine with the Nasi ruling their planet.

"I agree. We're beyond that," Ancient Wang said, his face impassive except for a slight narrowing of the eyes. "Esma is a blight that needs to be eliminated. Neither your universe nor mine will know peace until we've won."

Zhao looked to his side with a thoughtful expression, studying something that was off camera. "But what about intelligence and espionage? There may be opportunities to bring some of them to our side."

"Not a bad idea," Samaha said. "Send the information to the intel cell and see if they have any ideas."

"We—" Nicole started.

"Thank you," Samaha interrupted. "We'll need to plan. Get some rest while you can. We'll be leaving soon. With the intel you've gathered at least we'll attack with both eyes open."

# Chapter Twenty-Seven

It'd only been a little over a week since they left for Mariga, but being back onboard the *Ofira* felt strange to Nicole. Every time she rejoined the fleet after a mission, it took her a day or so to adjust. The close confines, routine, and uniforms were alien compared to the chaotic pace of their missions. It was jarring.

After their meeting with the commanders, Kal lay in their bed and watched old holos on his tablet. After hours of trying to get him out of the room, she gave up and went to the training area.

As she stepped off the lift, she was surprised to see Sergeant Kimathi outside a room setting up a training program on the large viewscreen next to the door.

"Getting in some extra training as well?" Nicole asked as she walked up next to him. He was paging through the various scenarios. The rooms could emulate almost any battlefield environment from a sniper attack to a force-on-force encounter. The only things limiting you were your skill and the number of people you had with you.

"Yes, ma'am," Kimathi said. "Figure I might as well get some training in while the brass figures out what to do next."

"Where's the squad?"

"I gave them some time off. They've earned it. I'll get 'em back to training in a few hours." He sounded defensive as if she was questioning him for not having the squad training at all times.

"They *have* earned it. You have too."

"Gotta keep training. I'm not a born soldier like Sergeant

Jones was. I've still got a lot to learn."

Nicole could sense the pressure the young man was putting on himself. He'd been a kid a year ago and had stepped into a legend's shoes. It was a heavy weight to bear. If she was being honest, Kal didn't help either. He was too hard on Ekon—maybe because of their past—and didn't seem to give him the benefit of the doubt.

Nicole smiled. "Feel like going a round?"

The training rooms had player versus player scenarios that were mainly used for fun or to let off steam. During an actual operation, a single soldier going up against another almost never occurred. Soldiers worked in teams.

"Sure." The sergeant smiled and started the scenario.

They both grabbed a simsuit from the rack next to the door, pulled themselves into the formfitting attire, grabbed a simrifle, and went to opposite sides of the room. Obstacles had been strategically placed about in order to create places to take cover and eliminate clear lines of sight.

*You ready, ma'am?* Kimathi asked.

*Ready!*

Holo projectors on the ceiling sprang to life, transforming the room. Nicole was now in a Wudexingqiu swamp, and she could hear waves lapping against the shore nearby. A thin moss covered the ground illuminated by the soft glow of the panoply of stars overhead.

They went through several rounds, changing the scenario's location each time. Nicole was surprised to find she won most of the contests. The holo projector transformed the room to snow-covered Marigan landscapes, dark tunnels, even a station. Every time, Kimathi was overaggressive, always defaulting to the attack. The sergeant grew more and more frustrated until he finally threw his weapon across the room with a curse.

"Ready for a break?" Nicole asked, wiping the sweat from her brow with a sleeve.

"Sure." The sergeant walked across the room and picked up his weapon, his shoulders slumped.

As they were putting their gear back, Kimathi slammed his simrifle into the rack, knocking several rifles to the floor. He swore and bent down to pick them up.

"You're lucky, ma'am," he said as he put the simrifles back in the rack.

"Why?" She wouldn't consider any of them lucky.

"You don't have all the pressure. You get to come here and mess around but don't have the weight on your shoulders during the real thing."

Nicole held her breath for a second before responding. "That's how you see it?"

"Yeah, I mean no disrespect, but I've got to lead the squad during our missions and face the enemy head on."

"I've got my own concerns as well."

He nodded. "I guess. Like dealing with all those officers and the planning meetings. I've attended a few of them myself." He smiled thinly. "I mean, kill me now."

Nicole laughed. "Yeah, it's not what I'd want to do with my free time. But they're important."

He grunted.

"Remember, Ekon, it's not all on you. We're a team and all

387

have a part to play. You're not solely responsible."

He sighed. "This squad, these kids"—Nicole was pretty sure Bhatt was several years older than Kimathi but let it slide—"they depend on me."

"They do," Nicole agreed. "But that doesn't mean you're responsible for *everything*. Just do your best. I know you care about them. They know it too."

"Whatever. I'll do my best until the Nasi or someone else kills me." He walked through the open door back into the hallway. "Wanna grab something to drink, ma'am?"

"Sure," Nicole said, following him out the door. "I've got a few hours until the briefing."

"I thought you'd be with the general," Kimathi said.

"He's...tired." Nicole said. "Things are wearing on him."

"Happens to the best," Kimathi said. "Or so I hear. He'll snap out of it." Nicole got the impression he said that more to reassure himself than her.

"Thank you all for coming," General Samaha said from a viewscreen.

Nicole sat in the pilot's briefing room of the *Ofira*. Kal and Colonel Petrov sat on either side of her, drinks in hand. They'd advised her to prep for the long haul; these briefings took hours and hours. The ship's various operations teams filled the room, waiting to hear the fleet's strategy for destroying the Nasi. Behind a holo of General Zhou, viewscreens displayed command teams from every ship in the fleet.

"We've received intelligence that the Nasi have massed their fleets near the J'Kalnik system. They have approximately three ships orbiting the system's habitable planet, Ffromar, as bait. In its entirety, the Nasi fleet has slightly less than fifty capital ships, compared to our thirty-seven. It means we're at a disadvantage, and that's not including their superior technology."

The officers around the room were shifting uneasily in their seats. They didn't need reminding that they were outgunned.

"The Nasi expect us to attack their ships at Ffromar, at which point they will fold in to surround and destroy us." A large three-dimensional map appeared in the middle of the room. "Instead, we will attack their main fleet in deep space and bypass the planet." A cluster of fifty dots in the shape of a sphere appeared in the center of the map. "We'll split our fleet in two and fold in on either side of their position. The goal is to crush their forces between ours." Two smaller clusters of green dots appeared on either side of the Nasi. "Our fighters will launch immediately and harry the enemy ships while we focus fire on the battleships and dreadnaughts. Once we've eliminated their big guns we'll focus on the carriers. The end goal is the complete destruction of the Nasi fleet." The red dots disappeared from the map, leaving the full contingent of green ones. An optimistic outcome if Nicole had ever seen one.

Samaha paused. "This battle will also mark the first time we'll be using an experimental weapon that our science team developed. Thanks to the combined efforts of all our scientists and engineers—including the Jadid—we've developed a new missile. The skip missile. They have both traditional thrusters and a fold engine built into them, which means they can fold through the enemy's point defense systems and detonate inside their ships."

A murmur ran through the attendees. *So that was what Taisha was working on,* thought Nicole. *This could mean the end of the war.* It could eliminate the Nasi technical advantage. Why did it seem so anti-climactic to her? The largest battle the galaxy had ever known, and she somehow felt let down.

Samaha handed the meeting over to General Zhao. He went into the plan's specifics then had each staff section provide detailed information on their area and answer questions. The general's time with the Jadid was already paying dividends. They were much more active in the briefing, asking questions and bringing up several good points. Zhao almost seemed like he was a part of the Jadid already. Nicole could understand why. Although Zhao was an easygoing person, as an officer, he was strict and by the book. The perfect Human complement to the Jadid.

After several hours, they finished. Bottom line for Nicole was that the Skulls wouldn't play much of a part in the battle since they'd just returned from a mission and were assigned to *Annie*. The ship wouldn't be able to do much in a battle like this one. With a chorus of cheers in various languages, the meeting ended, the viewscreens flickered off, and Nicole stood up. Her legs had fallen asleep, and she had to hold onto her chair to stop herself from falling.

"Seems too easy," Colonel Petrov said with a frown.

"Why does everyone say that after every briefing?" Nicole asked.

"Because it's usually true," said Kal.

"Here's to the last night before we save the galaxy," Nicole said, raising her wineglass.

Kal met her eyes and returned the smile. She could see the lie behind it in the lines on his face. The man was still haunted. He hadn't had a genuine smile in days. She'd struggled to get him out of bed and into the lounge for drinks.

"You ready to sit back and relax a bit?" Nicole asked.

"That *would* be nice."

The *Ofira*'s lounge was bursting at the seams. Soldiers occupied every table, stood along the viewscreens, and even sat in open spots on the floor. Although the *Ofira* was still damaged from the battle at Tamulk, they would fold with the fleet and their fighters would still engage the Nasi. The carrier itself would try to stay away from the battle as much as possible. Though they knew that ultimately they didn't have complete control over that; the enemy always had a say.

"I talked with Ekon yesterday." That got Kal's attention. "We went head-to-head in one of the battle simulators." She couldn't resist. "I won."

Kal chuckled dryly. "I have no doubt."

"He's got a lot on his shoulders."

Kal's eyes flashed. "He's no different from the rest of us."

Nicole raised her glass and took a slow sip, thinking about what to say. She wasn't a professional soldier like Kal. She hadn't gone through EDF bootcamp or officer training. But she knew he wasn't seeing things clearly. The two men were very similar in some ways, both caught up in their own personal struggles and unable to see the broader picture. Finally, she set her class down with a small clink.

"He's a kid, Kal. He's a few years out of school. Where were you at that age? What responsibilities did you have?"

"I was at the academy." He took a sip of the water in front of him. "It doesn't matter though; we have to fly the ship we can afford."

"It matters because he's trying his best. Sergeant Jones trusted him and so did you. You can't give up on him now. Just—"

"Colonel Bergeron! General Norman!"

Nicole stopped talking and turned around to see Chief Taisha Kanumba walking toward them with a bright smile. It was still odd to see her in the blue Samsara Fleet uniform instead of the merchant clothes of the Skulls.

Nicole set down her glass, stood, and gave her friend a hug. "Taisha, it's good to see you."

Kal gave a strained smile. "Chief Kanumba. How are you? I thought you'd be especially busy right now."

"I *have* been busy. They gave us a few hours off before the mission. All the work's done now. We're just on standby in case something happens."

"When you told us about what you were working on, you weren't lying. These missiles could mean the end of the war," Nicole said in a hushed tone. Although the senior officers knew about the skip missiles, it was still considered a fleet secret.

Kanumba idly touched the scar that ran across her otherwise sweet face. "I think of all we went through on our missions. What I did sitting in a chair on the *Ofira* may end up making the biggest difference in the end."

"Some of us don't have your smarts, Chief," Kal said, pointing at his head.

Kanumba looked away. "I don't know about that, sir. I'm just glad that I could—"

*Colonel Bergeron and General Norman,* said Colonel Petrov through the neural net. *Please come to my briefing room immediately. We've got an issue.*

Kanumba could see that they'd just received a message. "Everything okay?" she asked.

"Not sure," said Kal, standing up. "But it sounds important. We've gotta run."

Kanumba surprised Nicole with a hug as she stood up. "Be careful out there. I can't be with you right now, but I am thinking of you all, of the entire team."

"I promise we'll be okay," Nicole said, returning the hug. "You take care of yourself."

Nicole rushed out of the lounge with Kal, soldiers laughing around them, wondering what could go wrong. There were always issues and problems in war. To have one pop up right before they'd started the battle was not a good sign.

❖

Nicole and Kal rushed to Petrov's briefing room near the bridge. As they entered, Nicole could hear General Samaha's voice coming from a viewscreen.

"—could you let this happen?" General Samaha's face was twisted in an expression of rage.

"Ma'am, there's nothing that Ancient Wang or his staff could have done to prevent this." General Zhao stood next to Ancient Bao Wang on another viewscreen.

"General Samaha, please calm down," Ancient Wang said, his voice even, face placid. "This doesn't affect our plans."

"Doesn't affect our plans?" Samaha seemed genuinely at a loss for words.

"What's happened?" asked Kal as he sat at the room's conference table. Petrov shot a relieved look at Kal and Nicole.

"One of the Jadid's assault ships left their fleet and folded away an hour ago," Samsara said.

"We don't know why," General Zhao added. "But most likely, the two Jadid aboard were Nasi sympathizers and went to warn them."

Kal groaned, and Nicole felt the air leave her body. Their only advantage—gone. It was beyond a disaster. It was their entire mission on Mariga, thrown away for nothing.

"We don't know for sure that they went to the Nasi,"

Wang said.

Samaha scoffed. "Perhaps they went to New America for the casinos?"

"There's no need for that," Wang said as a flicker of annoyance splashed across his face. "We have to be logical about this. My question is, how does this change anything?"

Nicole thought about the question as the others continued to argue. They had to assume that the Nasi would be ready for them. But the Nasi also were looking for a decisive battle; she doubted they would leave their position. They'd set a trap, but Samsara Fleet would be ready for it. The mole had leveled the playing field, but they hadn't tilted it in favor of the Nasi.

"Colonel Bergeron. General Norman. You've been quiet," said Samaha. "I asked you here as you've fought the Nasi more than anyone else in our two fleets. You know how they think and you're the team that gave us their location. What do you think?"

Nicole paused, waiting to see if Kal would speak. He still seemed deep in thought. "I have to say I agree with Ancient Wang," Nicole said. "I think this shouldn't change our course of action. The Nasi know we're coming, but we still have the skip missiles. We still can end this war now."

Bao smiled. "Exactly! We can—"

"Most likely they'll move their forces and then wait," Kal said, scratching his hair thoughtfully. "When we fold in, they'll fold in around us and try to wipe us out. We'll need to adjust to it. But to Colonel Bergeron's point, if we wait, then we'll only delay a battle that is fated to occur. The Nasi have the advantage of time; they just need to wait. We need to end this *now* to stop any more supplies getting to their shipyards."

"Ma'am, the fundamentals of this battle remain the same," said General Zhao.

"Aamina," Bao's voice was silky smooth. "You know we have to continue with our attack. We've got no option. The risk of doing nothing is too high."

Samaha sighed slowly. "Seems like I'm outvoted here." She rubbed her hand along the back of her neck. "Fine. General Zhou, adjust our plans as necessary. We'll continue with the attack."

# Chapter Twenty-Eight

Kal looked around the *Salamis'* cockpit. It felt cutting-edge after flying his old ship for a week. The state-of-the-art viewscreens, equipment, and military finishes were at least a decade ahead of *Annie*.

After the change in the mission, Samaha had ordered that the Skulls be reassigned to the *Salamis*. Now that they were going to be in an active status for the battle, the fleet's medical staff had rushed Sergeant Bhatt's prosthesis. She had a cybernetic right arm, indistinguishable from the one she'd had before. The sergeant had been rather stoic about the new limb and had immediately set out learning to use it. Normally it took days, but it only took Bhatt a few hours to be somewhat proficient. Since they were back on the *Salamis*, Corporal Santo's team had rejoined the Tac-I squad and they were once again at full strength, seven soldiers.

"How are we looking?" Kal asked.

"We're set," Ramos said. "Just waiting for the fleet to jump."

Since the Nasi were expecting them, the two fleets would jump to one location and take on the Nasi in a single wave. They would press the attack and try to take out as many of the enemy as possible before the Nasi launched their ambush. Because the enemy fleet was in deep space rather than orbiting a planet, there was no way to scout them out. Any fold signature would immediately give away their presence.

"You good?" Nicole asked.

Kal nodded. She didn't need to worry. If there was one thing he was good at, it was compartmentalizing. He had a mission to do now.

"Sergeant Kimathi," Kal called over the ship's intercom, "your soldiers suited up?"

"Roger, sir."

"Ship's all set," Sergeant Chedjou reported.

Samsara Fleet was less than a light-month away from their target coordinates. They'd been folding for the past several days and then had stopped immediately before making contact to prep for the battle. Now was the final stage; they were a fold away from the target. The fleet had completed its precombat checks and all ships reported ready. The next hour would decide the fate of Humanity and the galaxy. No pressure.

There wasn't anything for the Skulls to do but wait. They'd piped the fleet's command net into the cockpit, and Kal listened to the back and forth of the various capital ships as they reported ready to fold. He knew every single soldier in the fleet was at their position. All the fighters and assault ships had their engines spun up and were ready to exit the landing bays as soon as the final fold completed.

"Attention, Samsara Fleet," General Samaha's voice cut through the quiet hiss of the command net. "We will be folding in five seconds. Remember, all the galaxy is counting on you. There is no option except victory."

The *Salamis'* viewscreens were tied to the *Ofira's* external cameras, allowing them to see what was happening outside the landing bay they were in. Seconds after Samsara's announcement, the stars outside the ship shifted—they were at the Nasi fleet's location.

Fighters immediately lifted off the bay floor and darted through the energy shield and into the space outside. As a scout ship, the *Salamis* would be one of the last ships out.

"Where are they?" Ramos asked, confused. "There's nothing out there."

Sure enough, the tacmap was empty. Not a ship in sight.

"Something just folded out of the area," Chedjou said.

"Get ready for them to fold in around us," General Zhou said over the fleet's command net. "Shield up, weapons armed, and get those fighters deployed." The general was on Wang's flagship, the *Galaxy's Edge*.

One by one, rows of fighters swept out of the landing bay. Finally the *Salamis* received word they could depart. They lifted from the bay floor and shot through the azure-tinted energy shield that kept the atmosphere in the bay. Despite the fleet of ships and tremendous firepower around them, the surrounding space looked empty except for the *Ofira* looming behind them.

"Get some distance from the fleet," Kal ordered. "We're not a fighter. We need to stay away from the other ships and be ready for instructions."

Chedjou nodded and continued to fly away from the *Ofira* and the rest of the fleet. Several alarms blared and red icons filled the tacmap in front of Kal. The Nasi fleet had entered the area—including two dreadnaughts.

"There they are," Chedjou said humorlessly.

"Stay away from the Nasi," Kal ordered. "We need to remain unengaged." If needed, they would be an assault team tasked to conduct a close-range attack. With their advanced defensive and cloaking systems, they were one of the few ships that had a chance of getting through the Nasi point defense. If things really went sideways, they'd be there to infiltrate a Nasi ship—an almost suicidal mission.

The Jadid and Samsara Fleets were now surrounded on three sides by the Nasi fleet which had just appeared, allowing the Nasi to triangulate their fire. The Nasi immediately launched salvos of missiles at the Samsara and Liberation fleets, who returned fire missile for missile and plasma round for plasma round. Lines of red dots streamed between the blue and red clouds of ships on Kal's console. Squadrons of fighters moved between the two fleets, creating a blanket to intercept incoming missiles. As the swarms of fighters met, icons dimmed on his screen, and he saw small flashes of ships being destroyed.

"Fire the first round of the skip missiles," Samaha ordered over the net. The plan was to fire an initial volley of five to test that they worked in combat.

On the tacmap, the five purple dots of the skip missiles streaked at the Nasi. They periodically disappeared and reappeared on the tacmap as they folded toward the enemy fleet. All five icons disappeared and Kal saw small pinpricks of light near where they had been on his console.

"What happened?" Kal asked.

"I'm not sure, sir," Ramos replied. "They're just gone."

Kal's heart sank. Their one remaining edge had disappeared. As if to emphasize the point, a brilliant explosion blossomed from the front of their formation.

"The *Starsweep*'s gone," Ramos said. It had been a Jadid

battleship.

Kal couldn't concentrate on the battle. He continued to study the space where the missile had disappeared.

"General Samaha, there's something strange coming from the Nasi fleet." The voice talking on the net belonged to General Pham, the fleet's intelligence officer. "It's like a...gravitational net that's coming from the center of their fleet. A zone of intensely strong gravity that's been placed around their fleet."

The Nasi knew. Of course they knew. Somehow they'd developed a defense against the skip missiles. Fold drives were notoriously finicky, and gravity disrupted the folding process. The Nasi had figured out a way to create a gravitational shield to defend against the missiles. A weapon Samsara Fleet had spent months developing had been neutralized in less than a day.

*Bo, get up here now,* Kal called out through his implant. The Jadid was one of the foremost experts in fold drives. The Liberation and Samsara fleets were getting battered by the Nasi onslaught, their status shifting from green to yellow on the fleet status screen on Kal's console. If they couldn't figure out a way to get the skip missiles to work quickly, they'd have to retreat—if possible.

*On my way.*

The Jadid rushed into the cockpit seconds later.

"Bo, you following what's going on?" Kal asked.

The Jadid nodded. "Yes. It's an interesting defense, crude but effective."

"Do you know what they're doing?" Kal asked.

"I think so. They've modified the artificial gravity on at least one of their ships to project its gravitational field outside the ship. I must admit, it's pretty impressive. This is something that isn't possible in our universe, but I'd theorized that—"

"Is there anything we can do about it?" Nicole asked.

"Sure, if you can destroy the ship or ships creating it," Bo screwed up his mouth thoughtfully. "There probably are other ways to get around or through it, but we'd need to conduct more research. I mean, if you can project gravity, then there may be a way to—"

Kal held up a hand, cutting off the scientist, and hailed General Samaha and Ancient Wang over the command net for a private talk. Less than a minute later, he heard her voice over the line.

"General Norman, what is it?" Samaha asked.

"We talked with Bo about the gravitational net," Kal said. "The Nasi have adjusted the artificial gravity on some of their ships to generate it."

"We've also been talking with the team that developed the weapon," General Zhao said. "They believe that it could only have come from one or two of their ships. Something about conflicting fields."

Bo hummed thoughtfully. "That does make sense. Additional gravitational generators would inevitably interfere with other. No single ship could generate a field that strong though. We have to presume that they only began development—"

"How do we know which ships are generating it?" Ancient Wang asked.

"The dreadnaughts," Kal said. It made sense. They were by far the largest ships in the Nasi fleet. "If they can only use a couple of ships to create the shield, then it would be them."

Silence greeted his pronouncement. Bo spoke over his shoulder. "That's true, sir. I can't think of any flaw in your logic. It would be good if we could validate this though I am not sure we have any time. There should be some ability to trace the flows of gravity—"

"Yeah, time's not exactly something we have a lot of," Wang interjected.

"The dreadnaughts are in the center of the Nasi formation," Samaha said. "There's no way our fleet can destroy them."

"We can—"

A wave of static drowned out Zhao's words. Kal looked out the viewscreen to see another Jadid ship explode, sending a spray of debris through space.

"That was the *Victory that* was just destroyed," Chedjou reported.

Kal looked at the fleet's status on his console. At least a third of the fleet had already sustained some damage and hundreds of fighters were destroyed. The Nasi had yet to lose a single capital ship. Samsara Fleet was running out of time.

"We'll need to infiltrate the dreadnaughts," Kal said. He nodded at Chedjou who was listening. "If we can make it on board, we can disable the net."

"You won't be able to make it near the ship," Samaha replied.

"Send as many fighters as you can spare with us," Kal

said. "If we activate our cloak, we may make it through their point defense." What he didn't say was that his plan would consign hundreds of fighters to certain death. The point defense system would lock onto the uncloaked fighters, and the *Salamis* would sneak through the overwhelmed system.

"May?" asked Ancient Wang. "That's not a good basis for a plan."

"Sometimes it's the only basis," Kal said.

"It won't work," General Zhao said. "I agree with Ancient Wang. We should retreat and cut our losses. Let's take the lessons from this battle and prepare for the next."

Kal involuntarily snorted. "Sorry, Frederick, there is no next battle if we retreat." This was their chance. If they waited, the Nasi would devise some other way to defend against the missiles. They'd built their gravitational shield in hours. Given days or weeks, who knew what they could build.

"We can't—"

"We'll send as many fighters with you as we can spare," Samaha said. "I'm going to send our other assault teams to infiltrate the other dreadnaught."

"Ma'am—"

"Kal's right," Samaha interrupted. "This is it. Good luck, General Norman."

Sergeant Chedjou activated the ship's optical screen concealing them and flew directly at the center of the Nasi formation. She pursed her lips together as she concentrated on weaving the ship and avoiding Nasi fighters or ships so as not to blow their cover. Chief Ramos hunched over her console, monitoring their optical cloak and scanning the net for any signs that the Nasi had discovered them. She'd been quiet so far, which was good.

Kal remained focused on the broader tacmap, looking to see how the fleet was faring. Samaha had sent around half their fighters with the *Salamis*. The rest continued to screen the Nasi missiles and fighters. They were slowly wilting under the Nasi bombardment, their icons fading from the map.

An explosion blossomed behind them, a bright white sun existing for only a moment.

"We got one!" shouted someone over the command net. At least they weren't going down without a fight.

"How long until we reach the dreadnaughts?" Kal asked.

"About five minutes, sir," Ramos responded. "We can't go full speed. We'll outpace the fighters."

Ancient Wang and General Zhao were right; their plan was heavily relying on luck. The Nasi point defense system would destroy any enemy ship or missile that came close. Their only hope was to overwhelm it with numbers so that the *Salamis* could sneak through and board the ship. It was a classic strength-in-numbers play that relied on the sacrifice of hundreds of brave pilots.

"Damn!" Ramos swore. "The Nasi reserve is heading directly at us."

Kal could see the mass of red icons sweeping toward them. There were at least four hundred fighters swarming through the capital ships in their direction. They didn't have time to meet the attack head-on; they needed to destroy the gravitational shield before the Nasi wiped the fleet out.

"Slow down," Kal said. "We won't engage. Let our fighters handle them. Our only goal is to remain unnoticed and get to that ship as fast as possible."

"Roger." They slowed until they were in the center of the hundreds of fighters that were covering them.

Two squadrons of fighters, around a hundred each, peeled off from the formation and engaged the Nasi. Pinpricks of light flashed in the distance as missiles and plasma bolts crashed into shields and bulkheads. Kal zoomed in on the skirmish in time to see the brilliant flash of a doomed fighter. After the light had dissipated, the only thing that remained was a small cloud of debris floating through space and the afterimage in Kal's eyes.

Kal felt a knot of worry tighten in his chest as they grew closer to the Nasi dreadnaught. He pictured fighting through the alien corridors in his battle suit, watching friends and enemies die painfully.

The Nasi fighters flew past the wave of Samsara responders and strafed the rest of the formation with plasma and missile fire. Small streaks of green and tiny white explosions dotted the space around them. On the tacmap the clouds of red and green merged, creating a blotch of yellow. Chedjou remained focused and continued toward the dreadnaught, sweeping left and right to avoid the enemy.

"We've got two Nasi fighters on our tail," Ramos shouted as the ship's targeting computer rang out, signaling the enemy lock on.

"I see them," Chedjou said between clenched teeth. Ramos released countermeasure drones that emitted signals and a holographic image. As they scattered behind them, Chedjou spun the yoke sharply to the left, causing their lateral thrusters to fire and turning them ninety degrees in a sweeping arc.

The missiles exploded behind them, fooled by the drones. They were close enough that Kal could hear metallic pings on the hull as the shrapnel hit the *Salamis*.

"Sir, I've got to engage," Chedjou said as she turned the ship again. "They're continuing to pursue, and I can't lose them."

Kal hit his fist on the arm of his chair in frustration. Engaging with the fighters would take up time they didn't have. Every second the Nasi gravitational shield was up, their comrades were dying. He didn't need to look at the fleet status screen to know that time was a luxury they didn't have.

Chedjou had continued to turn and reversed the *Salamis*. They were barreling at the two Nasi fighters that had been on their tail.

"What's the plan, Sergeant?" asked Chief Ramos in an uneasy tone.

"They're not very accurate head-on," Chedjou said. Her voice held a confidence, a cockiness that Kal hadn't heard before. "I have experience in this, so it shouldn't be a problem to take them out."

"I thought you had only flown atmospheric before," Kal said.

"Well, yeah." Her voice faltered for a moment. "But it's

pretty much the same thing. My brothers are excellent pilots."

"Wait, you're talking about mock dogfights against your brothers?" Ramos asked incredulously.

"Yes. Now let me concentrate and be ready to launch a full battery of our missiles on my mark."

*We're gonna die*, thought Kal. He desperately wanted to grab the controls away from the overeager sergeant, but he wasn't going to interfere with her as she was engaging the enemy. He'd made her a pilot, and now he'd have to live—hopefully—with that decision.

Kal could hear the incessant beeps from the computer that signaled a partial lock on their ship. Chedjou was right about one thing; it was much more difficult to target an enemy approaching you head-on.

The distance between the *Salamis* and the two Nasi fighters quickly closed. Kal waited for the incessant beeping of the soft lock to change into the hard tone of a weapons lock—but it never came. As they grew close, the Nasi fired plasma rounds, their weapons automatically adjusting the targeting to account for the ships' relative velocities. Chedjou fired back while erratically changing their direction. The Nasi's plasma bolts streaked around the ship. Several hit the front shields, dropping their energy level critically low.

"You do that again, and we're dead," Ramos said as she diverted energy to the shields.

"Only need to do it once, Chief." As they were about to pass the oncoming Nasi, Chedjou activated the reverse thrusters. The ship's inertial dampener absorbed some of the change of momentum, but Kal still slammed against his

408

restraints and heard the metal bulkhead groan under the strain.

Chedjou spun the yoke, turning the ship along its central axis until they were facing the sides of two Nasi fighters streaming past. Almost immediately, the targeting computer chirped as it locked onto both ships then emitted a flat tone indicating a full lock.

"Fire!"

Ramos launched missiles from all tubes. They sped away from the *Salamis* and swept toward the two fighters. Seconds later, two small bursts of light stood out against the darkness of space.

"Nice flying," Nicole said in an unsteady voice.

"Yes," agreed Kal. "Never do it again."

Chedjou reoriented them toward the two Nasi dreadnaughts in the distance and increased the throttle. Their fighter cover had almost completely passed them by, but they caught up quickly and took their position near the center of the formation. Nasi fighters continued to harass them, firing missiles and plasma bolts at the ships with increasing intensity as they got closer to the dreadnaughts. About half the fighters with them continued to engage the Nasi while the rest continued on course. The knot in Kal's chest continued to grow larger as he watched the Nasi pick off fighters in their escort.

The plasma cannons on the dreadnaughts in front of them fired, sending enormous rounds at the mass of fighters. The bolts streamed through the formation, engulfing several ships in flames—some of them Nasi. They were firing indiscriminately, trying to thin out their attackers as much as possible.

"How long until we're in the point defense range?" Kal asked, as another bolt streamed past the ship.

"Thirty seconds, maybe," Ramos replied. "We can't go too fast; otherwise, we'll lose our fighter cover."

"Sergeant Kimathi, your team ready?" Kal asked over the intercom.

"Roger, sir," Kimathi replied. "Are you and Colonel Bergeron joining us?"

Kal didn't want to. The tightness in his chest and sweat dripping down his face told him that, but he had to be with his soldiers. "Roger, we'll be down as soon as we're through the point defense."

The Nasi dreadnaught loomed in front of them. At first, it was a small discoloration of gray. But as they got closer, Kal could make out the menacing irregular shape of the ship. It was easily the largest he'd ever seen. The bulging, twisted hull, dotted with nacelles, grew in the viewscreen, blotting out the stars.

"We've got a fighter on our tail again," Ramos called out.

"Keep going," Kal said. "We can't engage."

"Divert all the power to the aft shields," Chedjou said as she began weaving the ship back and forth to prevent the enemy from locking on to them.

A Z'Ta fighter in front of them exploded in a flash.

"There's the point defense system," Ramos observed.

The surrounding fighters launched their missiles and fired their plasma cannons at the Nasi dreadnaught, hoping to overwhelm the tracking computers. The energy shield easily absorbed the plasma rounds, while the point defense system detonated the missiles before they were close enough to cause damage.

Explosions blossomed around them as the point defense system performed its task. Kal felt his nausea build as he looked around. Already, half the fighters that had joined them had been destroyed and the other half were rapidly dwindling.

"Yes!" Ramos said. "At least one missile got through." She pointed to a small hole in the ship's side, large enough for a single person to get through.

A jolt shook the *Salamis* and the status indicators on the pilot's console flashed red.

"What was that?" asked Nicole.

"The point defense hit a power nacelle," Ramos said. "Since we're still alive, it must have just grazed it."

"What's the damage?" Kal asked.

"Still checking." The chief's fingers flew over her console screen. "Not good. Looks like we lost our shields."

"So one hit and we're gone?" asked Nicole.

"Pretty much," Ramos replied.

Kal could see the Nasi ship behind them getting closer on the tacmap. At least they didn't have to worry about their missiles. Point defenses couldn't differentiate between friendly and enemy missiles and would target both.

"Route all energy to the thrusters," Kal ordered. "Speed's the only thing we got left." Ramos nodded and Kal flight a slight pressure as their acceleration increased.

The Nasi ship behind them began firing its cannons. The bolts flew past them and splashed harmlessly against the dreadnaught's energy shield. There were no stars in the viewscreen in front of them anymore; the massive capital ship was now occupying the entire screen. Kal could see tiny details on the hull—twisted antennae, nacelles, and faint glowing areas on the hull.

"That ship's getting too close for comfort," Chedjou said. "I won't be able to drop off the infiltration squad." They had to be moving relatively slowly to release the Tac-I squad. Otherwise, they'd send them hurtling through space or slamming them into the dreadnaught.

"Delta Squadron," Kal called over the net, "can you get the fighter off our tail?"

"Roger," replied the squadron commander. "Hang tight."

Several fighters turned and flew at the Nasi ship trailing them. It continued to fire a constant stream of plasma rounds which were getting way too close for Kal's comfort at the *Salamis*. Explosions continued to sparkle around them as the dreadnaught's point defense took out one fighter after another. They were close enough Kal could make out the small seams between the weaves on the bulkhead. If they didn't slow soon, they'd crash into the side of the capital ship.

Nicole's hands gripped her arm rests, her knuckles white. She muttered "come on" over and over as she watched her console. Only one of the Delta Squadron fighters was still engaging the Nasi fighter. Its shots were erratic, missing the Nasi fighter by a wide margin.

"They won't hit it," Kal said.

"Sir, I've got an idea," Chedjou said. "But it—"

"Anything that gets us on that ship alive is fine by me," Kal said. The Nasi dreadnaught was dangerously close, and the fighter was creeping closer. Sergeant Chedjou was on the controls, and they didn't have time for him to second-guess her.

She nodded and began furiously tapping on her console. The engine status creeped into the red as Chedjou funneled almost every last ounce of power into them. She turned the yoke slightly, aiming them at a tiny hole in the hull of the Nasi dreadnaught.

"Hang on and prepare for crash landing," Chedjou called over the intercom as plasma fire continued to rain around them.

As they were about to hit the dreadnaught's hull, Chedjou channeled all power to the reverse thrusters and began firing their plasma cannons. As Kal smashed into his restraints again, his vision grew dim as the sudden change in momentum overloaded the ship's inertial dampeners. Metal groaned and small clangs sounded behind them as anything that wasn't restrained in the ship slammed forward.

He turned and looked at Nicole, who was looking back at him. If he was going to die, he wanted it to be with her. Kal tried to reach out his arm to hers, their fingertips only a centimeter apart. As they touched, a screech of metal tore through the ship as the *Salamis* squeezed through a jagged tear in the dreadnaught's exterior. A one-in-a-million shot.

The lights and viewscreens went out, plunging the cockpit into darkness. Kal felt like he was being beaten as the ship tumbled and spun through the dreadnaught's interior. He heard snapping metal and could smell burning electronics. As he lost consciousness, all Kal could feel was pain and fear.

# Chapter Twenty-Nine

The stench of burnt electronics and plastics was almost overwhelming. It took a moment for Nicole to realize where she was. The last thing she remembered was looking into Kal's eyes then darkness and the screeching of metal as they slammed into the dreadnaught.

The cabin was pitch black. Nicole could hear the occasional pings of metal, small unidentified thumps of the ship settling, and a slight hiss of atmosphere slowly leaving the ship. She reached into her cargo pocket, almost crying out in pain as a lance stabbed into her shoulder.

*There it is.* Nicole pulled her small personal light from her cargo pocket and turned it on. She waved it around the cockpit expecting to see shattered screens and wires hanging from the ceiling. Instead, it looked the same as before except for some tablets floating in the zero gravity.

Kal lay slumped in his chair, blood floating out from a large gash on his forehead.

"Kal! Kal!"

His eyes opened with a small flutter, and he jerked slightly as he regained consciousness.

"Wha—" Kal squinted as he looked around the cockpit. "Chedjou! Ramos!" Kal called out to the two pilots.

Nicole couldn't see them from her chair. She unfastened her restraints and pushed herself up, gritting her teeth as waves of pain rolled through her body. She floated forward to examine the two women. Both were unconscious, but alive.

"Hey! You guys okay?" The voice came from the cargo bay.

"We're still alive!" Nicole shouted back as she roughly prodded the two women. "Just trying to recover."

Chedjou opened her eyes and looked around, coughing slightly from the small cloud of smoke drifting in the air. "Another perfect landing," she said, resting her head back against the headrest.

Ramos groaned. Nicole aimed her light at the chief. She was leaning forward, bracing her hands against the console in front of her, her face twisted in pain.

"We've got to get out of here," Kal said.

They released their restraints and exited the cockpit, each groaning or grimacing in pain as they floated through the *Salamis'* lifeless hull. The Tac-1 squad was in the bay, already fully suited up. Bo floated next to them, small droplets of blood hovering in the air around a wound in his arm.

"Glad you all made it alive," said Kimathi through his suit's speaker.

The crash had thrown the two remaining suits—intended for Nicole and Kal—out of their docks, and the squad had moved them into a corner of the bay. Nicole pushed herself to the suit and climbed in while Private Chadha held it. She activated it with her implant and the back zipped closed. The suit quickly went through its warmup sequence, and she could feel a cool wave flow across her body as it detected injuries and injected pain medication.

"I pulled out the diveculum and the other key components for the fold drive," Bo said as he held onto a small handhold on the bulkhead and held up the small component. "We should still destroy the ship though." Since the *Salamis* was

416

one of the few skip ships in existence, they couldn't let the Nasi get their hands on any of the technology.

"We've already got charges placed," Sergeant Kimathi said.

"So where are we going?" Nicole asked. The dreadnaught was enormous and filled with Nasi. They couldn't just wander around looking for the artificial gravity generators.

Bo held up a small device. "This is a gravimeter. It's normally used for fold drive maintenance. But it can also point us in the general direction of the generators on this ship. Although they are pushing—for lack of a better term—the gravity out, there is still a trace here."

"It'll be somewhere near the center of the ship," said Chief Ramos. "At least on a Human ship it would be."

Kal motioned at a corner of the bay with his metal arm. "Bo, Chedjou, and Ramos. Grab emergency suits from the utility chest over there. Also, there should be some life packs as well. There won't be any atmosphere when we exit the *Salamis*."

The two women pulled themselves to the corner of the bay and quickly put on the suits and life packs, strapped their weapons across their backs, and then gave a thumbs-up. Bo managed to fit his elongated frame in the bulky outfit, put on a life pack, strap on his comeca, and grab his weapons before finally giving a thumbs-up as well.

"Let's get out of here," Kimathi said as he pulled the cargo doors manual release.

The ramp sprang open, revealing an uneven floor made of Nasi weaves and letting the atmosphere out of their ship in a rush. The area was dark, the only light coming from the weaves making up the floor, walls, and ceiling. It was hard to say exactly where they were. The *Salamis* had crashed through the ship's bulkheads and turned several small compartments into a single debris-covered, misshapen cavity.

Their scout ship was a wreck. The crash had ripped away several plates and dented and scarred the rest. Behind the ship was a path of destruction that led to a gaping hole in the hull that opened to the stars outside. The space outside looked serene. There wasn't sign of the battle that raged around them, not even a flash of light to show that the fate of Humanity was being decided.

Bo pointed his arm at a small portal in front of the *Salamis*. Nicole followed the others and jetted forward until she was floating near it. The Jadid had a small device in his hand which he touched to the outside panel of the door. The Tac-I squad had taken positions outside the door, their weapons raised, as he continued to hack the security controls.

Finally the door opened, and a sudden torrent of atmosphere pushed them away from the opening. They used their thrusters to make their way through the door. Once everyone was through, Bo closed the portal, cutting off the rush of air. Nicole still had her thrusters activated and launched herself into the wall of the corridor with a thunk. As she recovered, she was glad to see she wasn't the only one who had made that mistake.

"Damn, another ship gone," Kimathi said as he activated the explosive charges on the *Salamis,* causing the hallways to tremble slightly and a low rumble to emanate from the wall.

"She was a *great* ship," Chief Ramos said, shaking her head sadly.

"I think we get the next one free," Chedjou said. The other two frowned at the joke.

"The generator's about fifteen decks above us that way," Bo said, pointing at the center of the ship.

"Great," Kimathi said. "Any idea on how to get there?"

"No."

"We need to find a lift," Nicole said.

"This way," Kimathi said, pointing to their right. "Corporal Sato, your team takes lead. Bhatt, you're on rear guard."

They flew down the twisting hallway, elliptical doors bracketing them on either side. It seemed like the Nasi had cleared out the area, perhaps because of the missile strike, though Nicole assumed there was a Nasi strike team heading their way.

"Where are all the Nasi?" Nicole asked Bo.

"Not sure, ma'am," he replied. "Perhaps they don't realize we're here. The missile probably wiped out all the sensors—"

A plasma bolt sizzled down the hallway and splashed against Private Chadha's suit's energy shield. Everyone activated their lateral thrusters, slamming themselves against the brownish walls.

Bo turned to Nicole, his back to the wall. "Disregard. They know we're here, ma'am."

Sato's team immediately returned fire, sending kinetic rounds—which worked better against the Nasi—down the hallway toward their attackers.

*Did any of you get eyes on them?* Kimathi asked. Now

that they were discovered, there was no point in avoiding using their direct neural net.

A chorus of negatives came across the net.

*Alpha Team*—Sato's team at the front of their formation—*continue to fire and keep the enemy's heads down. Bravo Team, move up and take them out.*

The three members of Alpha Team laid down a steady stream of suppressive fire, alternating their shots so at least one of them was firing. Nicole couldn't see where the Nasi were in front of them but heard their firing taper off.

Bravo Team shot toward the enemy, their weapons trained at the end of the hallway. Once they had passed Alpha Team, three antipersonnel rockets shot from their suits and exploded near the enemy's position. They followed behind the rockets at full thrust, firing their kinetic rifles at full automatic.

*Alpha Team, move up.* Kimathi ordered. Nicole, along with Kal, Bo, and the two pilots, followed the squad leader as he trailed behind Sato's squad.

By the time they reached Bravo Team's location, the battle was over. Two battle-suit clad Nasi floated in the intersection. Large droplets of blood floated through gashes in their battle suits and drifted in the air.

*Best thing I've seen all day*, Sato said over the net as he hovered next to the bodies. Despite everything, Nicole felt a wave of disgust at the comment. She didn't think she could ever take pleasure in any creature's death, even a Nasi's.

Nicole looked at Bo, but the Jadid's face didn't change. She wondered what he thought of the young corporal's statement.

*Bo, see anything that could be a lift?* Kimathi asked.

*No,* the Jadid replied, *but I'd guess it would be this way.* He pointed to the left. *Most likely, they are deeper inside the ship.*

They continued speeding through the hallways. In the corner of Nicole's mind was the knowledge that a battle was being fought outside the ship and their entire fleet was counting on them. They needed to get to the gravitational generators quickly. Although they were flying as fast as their suits could take them, Nicole felt it wasn't fast enough.

*There!* Bo called over the net, pointing at an irregular oval door that looked the same as every other one they'd gone past to Nicole's untrained eyes. As she studied it, she noticed a small black outline surrounding the door.

*Can you call the lift?* Kimathi asked.

*Wait,* Kal said. *If we take a lift, we're dead. They'll see us in there and just lock it down. Bo, is there some way to get through that door without calling the lift?*

*Sir, normally I can open doors with my comeca, but to open a lift door, I'll need to override the controls,* Bo replied. *I don't have the equipment to do that.*

*It'll take almost every explosive we've got to get through that door,* Kimathi said.

*I've got a better idea,* Bhatt said. She glided to the door, activated her suit's railgun, and fired several rounds at it. All of them ricocheted off, except for one, which pierced through the weave, leaving a small hole. A meter-long serrated blade sprung from the gauntlet of her battle suit. She drove it through the hole and began sawing through the Jadid weave.

*It's fabric, right? Fabric can be cut.*

Less than a minute later, the sergeant had cut through the door, revealing the smooth shaft of the lift.

Nicole heard her shield activating, and an alert flashed on the heads-up display in her visor. A plasma bolt had hit her shields and drained half their energy. She jetted backward while twisting to face her attackers, her suit's railgun already raised. The others had already started to return fire, and she joined in, sending high-velocity railgun rounds down the hallway.

*Can they see where they're firing?* Nicole wondered. She couldn't. Their attackers must have taken cover behind a bend in the twisting hallway. She continued to fire blindly, hoping that her shots would at least keep the enemy's heads down and prevent them from firing back.

*All unarmored personnel get in the lift,* Kimathi ordered.

Bo and the two pilots flew through the flap Bhatt had carved. Just as they were through, a missile shot from the Nasi's position and detonated against the wall next to Bravo Squad. The deafening sound of the explosion overloaded Nicole's suit's microphone, causing the interior of her suit to momentarily become deathly quiet, and rocked her backward against the bulkhead. She quickly checked her readouts; there was no serious damage to her battle suit.

Private Ramirez's icon was red. The explosion had hit behind him and sent him flying down the hallway toward their attackers. Nicole's first instinct was to activate her thrusters and recover the young soldier. She stopped herself. Ramirez was dead. If the red icon in Nicole's suit hadn't told her, then the motionless suit with large globules of blood leaking out of it did.

*I didn't even know him,* she thought to herself. *He just died in front of me, and I don't even know what planet he's from.*

A plasma bolt splashed against the wall in front of her with a sizzle, breaking her out of her momentary shock. The bolt had come from the opposite direction the missile had. The Nasi had them surrounded. Nicole fired at the source of the plasma bolt while keeping her back to the wall. At least they couldn't sneak up behind her.

*Everyone, get in,* Kimathi ordered as he launched a rocket at one of the groups of Nasi. One by one, the remaining Skulls jetted through the flap and into the shaft while he continued to fire, alternating between the two groups on either side.

*Head up,* Kimathi said. *I'll catch up.* He was already setting a cluster of proximity mines by the hole in the lift door.

Nicole followed the rest of the squad, shooting up through the shaft. It curved and branched as they flew through the Nasi ship. Although smooth, the walls were made from the same weaves as the hallways and emitted a dim glow to light their way. A Tac-I soldier would occasionally stop, set a mine, and then rejoin the formation as they climbed.

Nicole looked back as an explosion sounded in the tunnel behind them. She couldn't see a thing other than the smooth curving sides of the tunnel.

*One of the mines went off,* Kimathi said. *They're following us.*

More explosions sounded behind them at regular intervals. The distant sound of plasma fire rang through the tunnels. Nicole thought the fire was somehow directed at them before she realized the Nasi must be firing at the walls in front of them to destroy the mines that the Skulls had set.

*Lift incoming!* Bo called out.

Nicole could see the rounded bottom of a lift hurtling down the shaft at them. Thankfully another tunnel branched off halfway between them and the speeding car. She pressed her thrusters to their max—as did the others—and raced the lift to the tunnel opening. Looking back, she realized that Bo and the others using life packs wouldn't make it.

*Grab a hold,* Nicole shouted through the net as she reduced her thrust and fell back with them.

Once they grabbed ahold of her, she gradually increased her thrust, speeding toward the other tunnel. It'd be close. Her suit's display flashed red as she put every bit of energy into the thrusters, almost overloading them. She could only hope all of them were still hanging on. The Nasi lift was getting dangerously close and overwhelming her vision.

Nicole shot into the side tunnel as the lift hurtled down behind her. She turned around, afraid at what she would see. Thankfully the three others were still there, holding onto her leg and looking at her with wide eyes. Chief Ramos gave a weak thumbs-up.

*Still here, ma'am. Thank you,* Chedjou said over a private connection. *I'm pretty sure I ruined the suit though.*

*Bo, where to next?* Kimathi asked.

*We're close by, sir. One more level up, then we should be almost next to it.*

The group returned to the main shaft and rose until they reached the next door. As the others hovered around it, Bhatt shot another few rounds through the door and sawed it open. On the other side was another narrow twisting hallway, seemingly identical to the one they had entered the shaft from.

Bo waved the small gravimeter around before pointing to his left. *The generators are this way.*

Nicole kept her weapon at the ready and shot down the hallway with the others. She could feel small pangs of tension and nervousness course through her body. Each time they crossed through an intersection she felt another pang in her chest. They didn't have time to clear anything. If they were ambushed, they wouldn't stand a chance. Time was too short.

Bo stopped short in front of a door, holding the gravimeter in front of his face. He turned to look back at the group.

*It's in here.*

He tapped several buttons on his comeca, and the door dilated open in front of him. As it opened, a rocket shot through the opening, detonating against the far wall and hurtling Bo through the doorway. The blast sent Kal and Kimathi forward, crashing against the walls next to the opening.

Nicole felt her heart stop for a moment until she saw Kal's icon, still green, on her display. Sergeant Kimathi's was as well. She feared the worst for Bo. The emergency suit the

425

Jadid was wearing wouldn't be any protection against an explosion. Still, the Nasi was tough, much tougher than a Human.

*Alpha Team,* Kimathi said as pushed away from the wall next to the doorway. *Get ready to follow me through that doorway and break left. Bravo Team, I want you to follow us and break right.*

The sergeant began blindly hurling grenades through the doorway, throwing everything he had. As they detonated, he thrust through the doorway, launching rockets in front of him and extending his arms, spewing streams of plasma and kinetic rounds.

Alpha and Bravo Teams rushed through after him and Nicole saw the sergeant's icon flip to yellow. He'd been hit, though she couldn't tell how badly.

*We've got incoming,* Kal said.

Nicole turned to see several Nasi jetting down the hallway toward them, their datons raised. Streams of plasma shot from the weapons at Nicole and the others. She moved in front of the two unarmored pilots as they flew through the doorway. Her shields registered multiple hits before finally failing.

*My shields are out,* Nicole called out.

*Get inside,* Kal instructed, already taking aim with his railgun. He floated centimeters above the floor, his arm raised in front of him as plasma rounds coated the surrounding walls. There was a high-pitched whine and one of the approaching Nasi flew backward, their helmet dissolving in a cloud of gore as a round ripped through it.

Nicole entered the doorway and quickly dove to the left.

A cloud of gray smoke filled the room, obscuring the other side. As the Nasi and Skulls traded fire, their rounds created swirling eddies in their path as they crossed the room. Small bits of shrapnel and pieces of equipment floated through the air, bouncing off the floors and walls.

Nicole took cover behind a large console fastened to the floor. Bhatt, Sampson, and Fischer were to her left. They had taken cover behind a piece of equipment that looked like a large cylinder turned on its side. Identical cylinders ran down the length of the room in pairs. Large consoles, identical to the one in front of Nicole, were spaced every few meters between the cylinders.

*Sergeant Kimathi?* Bhatt called out over the net.

After a moment, there was a response. *I'm here. Took a round in the arm but otherwise okay.* There was a pause. *Bravo Team, provide cover fire and send everything you've got toward the other end of the room. Alpha Squad, bound forward and take out the Nasi.*

*We've still got Nasi in the hallways behind us,* Kal said.

*Can you hold them off, sir?* Kimathi asked.

*I'll need someone else.*

*Bergeron, can you assist?* Kimathi asked.

*Roger.* She'd like nothing more.

Bravo Team immediately launched everything they had toward the other end of the large room. Missiles streaked through the thickening smoke, their explosions partially obscured by the smoke. Nicole couldn't help wondering about Bo. Was there any chance he was alive in all of this?

She turned back and oriented herself, facing the door they

had just come through. It was still completely open, revealing the wall of weaves in the hallway outside. Nicole trained her plasma rifle at the opening, ready to fire as soon as she saw anything. Kal was across from her, his railgun trained at the door as well.

*Get ready for a grenade*, Kal warned.

Nicole could hear the gunfire behind them and desperately wanted to turn to see what was happening. She'd have to trust in the rest of the team though. Her responsibility was in front of her.

Nicole pressed the trigger stud of her weapon by reflex as a canister was thrown into the room. The plasma bolt missed by meters, and the canister bounced off the wall before exploding near Kal. Seconds later, two Nasi flew into the room, firing their datons and breaking in opposite directions as soon as they made it through the doorway.

Instinct took over. Instead of moving away from the enemy in front of her, Nicole jetted at them, flying up and then crashing down, using her plasma rifle like a club. She swung with every bit of force she could, and the weapon shattered across the Nasi's helmet, the end careening into a far corner of the room.

Nicole wasn't thinking anymore, at least not beyond the next second. She swung with her left hand, pounding into the Nasi's helmet and breaking the front plate off. Behind it, she saw eyes. They were yellow and wide with fear. The Nasi couldn't see her face, but Nicole felt like she—she could tell it was female—was staring right into her eyes. She faltered for a moment, her right arm frozen behind her shoulder, ready to smash into the Nasi's head.

The yellow eyes narrowed, and Nicole felt pain tear across her leg. Astonished, she looked down. The Nasi woman had fired the small plasma pistol holstered to her leg. The shot had grazed along the surface of Nicole's armor, melting a gash along her thigh.

Nicole's hand came down and slammed through the opening in the Nasi's helmet with a guttural cry. She sat with her legs straddling her opponent's suit, thrusters still firing downward to keep her on the floor. What did she feel? Nothing in the end. Perhaps some anger, pain, and fear, but not what she would have expected.

*We've found Bo,* Private Sampson called out. *He's responsive. Looks like he's got a lot of shrapnel wounds, but he's moving.*

*Keep him down,* Kimathi ordered. *We'll take care of him later.*

*Wait, bring him back here,* Kal said. *He can close the door.*

*I...I can do that,* Bo said. *I'll...be right there.* It was hard to tell his condition over the net. Although Bo didn't have an implant, he did have an earpiece that functioned in much the same way. Which meant that much of his tone and emphasis didn't make it through the transmission.

*Nicole. How badly are you hurt?* Kal asked Nicole through a direct connection. Her icon must have turned yellow on his display.

*I'm fine,* she replied. *Leg's hurt but the pain relievers are already kicking in.* She'd feel like hell in a few hours though.

Bo slammed into the wall next to Nicole. Several globules of blood floated around him, pumping out from the shrapnel wounds that covered every part of his body.

"I can close and lock the door," Bo said, his breath ragged. "We have to move fast. It will take a bit for them to override, but they will eventually."

He didn't wait for a response, his hand flying across his comeca screen, which had a large crack running along its face. Moments later, the door constricted shut in a sudden motion.

*We've secured the room*, Kimathi said. *Now what the hell do we do?*

# Chapter Thirty

Kal didn't want to look at the Nasi he'd killed. It had been too easy. The soldier had tried to rush Kal, expecting him to freeze or retreat. Instead, Kal had taken steady aim and placed a railgun round straight through the Nasi's helmet. The headless suit continued moving forward, running into Kal and knocking him backwards into one of the cylindrical pieces of equipment dotting the room. By the time Kal had pushed the corpse off him and recovered, Nicole's icon had turned yellow.

He couldn't remember a sweeter feeling than hearing she was okay.

Kimathi called out that the room was secure. Bo was looking over the large control panel in the center of the room while Kimathi had ordered the two teams to conduct a sweep of the room to look for intel and, more importantly, a way out. Kal hovered next to Bo, looking around.

Smoke and debris filled the room but was slowly being pulled out of the air by the ship's filters. Five Nasi bodies floated at one end and two at the other, their limbs contorted in strange positions. Although still in their battle suits, blood and gore leaked from their bodies and floated in the air like demonic clouds.

Bo looked up from the console. Many of the wounds that covered his body had already stopped bleeding. However, blood continued to seep from a deep wound in his leg. "What they've done here is impressive," the scientist said. "They've actually managed to direct the gravitational output of the ship's generator outside of the frame. It's the biggest leap in gravitational theory since we moved from using centrifugal force."

"That's really great, Bo. Good for them. Yay!" Sergeant Kimathi raised his arms in a sarcastic cheer. "What's it mean?"

"How do we stop it?" Kal asked.

"There's two ways. One, we put every single explosive we have in this room and blow it up. Most likely taking us and the ship with it."

"Not the biggest fan of that one," said Chedjou.

"*Or* we can overload the antimatter containment in the system," Bo said as he waved his arms at the cylinders surrounding them. "If we concentrate it all into a single cylinder, the system will go critical, imploding this ship, creating a gravity well, and most likely destroying anything around it."

"I *like* it," Kimathi said.

"How long will that give us to get out?" Nicole asked.

"I'm not sure. Maybe five minutes," Bo replied. "But the margin of error is pretty high. It's not something that I've ever seen done. I've only heard about it in theory."

"Can the Nasi reverse it?" Kal asked.

Bo shook his head. "No, it's a one-way process. There's no way to reverse it."

"Do it," Kal instructed. They didn't have a way out, but they were going to accomplish the mission. Surviving it would be a pleasant bonus.

"Roger." Bo turned back to the console and began manipulating the controls.

"We may have something over here," Bhatt called from

across the room. She was floating near a large conduit that emerged from the floor and turned ninety degrees before heading into the wall. It might *barely* be big enough for them to fit in.

"Bo, do you know what that is?" Kal asked.

"Guessing, sir? The coolant transfer," Bo replied, barely looking away from what he was doing.

"Could we go through the pipe?" He was sure there'd be at least twenty Nasi waiting for them on the other side of the door they'd entered. Exiting the same way would be suicide.

"Those in battle suits could," Bo replied. "For the rest of us, myself included, it would be...problematic. It's filled with a corrosive gas. There's a good chance it will eat away our emergency suits. I will"—he motioned to the gashes on his arms and legs—"certainly have a negative reaction."

An explosion rumbled outside the door. The Nasi were working their way in.

"I'm sorry, Bo." Kal really was. "But I think it's our only way out."

"Then we should do it, sir." He said it without hesitation.

Kal couldn't waste any more time looking for another exit which he was pretty sure didn't exist. "Bhatt, cut a hole in that duct," Kal ordered. He turned to Sergeant Kimathi. "You know what to do?"

"Yes, sir," the sergeant replied confidently.

The duct was metal rather than made of the weaves that comprised most of the ship. After several concentrated plasma blasts from Bhatt's pistol, it had turned red hot. She plunged her blade through the metal and sheared off a section. A gust of gas billowed through the opening and mixed with the smoke in the air.

Another blast sounded from outside the room. The Nasi weren't going to give up anytime soon.

"I've...configured the system," Bo said, pausing for a moment with a grimace of pain. He pulled his plasma rifle off his back and shot the console in front of him. The screen warped and then shattered under the heat of the blasts.

"Let's go," Kimathi shouted as he flew across the room to the open pipe. "Alpha Team, you're in the lead."

The pounding outside the room grew more insistent as Bhatt climbed through the hole, followed by Sampson and Fischer.

"You're up," Kimathi said, pointing at the two pilots and Bo.

They carefully climbed through the opening. Kal could hear a small wince of pain from Bo as the gas hit his exposed wounds. Kal maneuvered in after the Jadid. The duct was incredibly tight leaving no room for him to move his arms from in front of his face. For a moment, he felt a sense of panic. What if they got stuck? Surprisingly, the fact that they would die only minutes later was reassuring. The quick death of the ship imploding somehow was more palatable than being trapped in the cooling system for days.

*Let's go!* Kimathi ordered.

As soon as the words came over the net, an explosion sounded in the room with the gravitational generators. The conduit creaked from the force of the blast.

*Go! Go!* Kal inferred the urgency in the synthetic words of

Sergeant Kimathi.

At first, nothing happened. A thick white mist filled the pipe in front of Kal, giving the impression of floating in a cloud, and almost completely obscuring his vision. All he could see in front of him were Bo's feet. Kal tried to be patient. He knew the Skulls were stacked in the pipe, and each person had to wait for the soldier in front of them to move before they could.

Finally Bo's thrusters activated, and he shot through the pipe in front of Kal. Kal followed, keeping some distance in case the Jadid suddenly stopped. There was nothing in front of him except the white mist, the faint shape of Bo's feet, and the glow of his life pack's exhaust.

*Where are we going?* Bhatt asked.

*We're...heading down...we should...wait until we are...at the level of the landing bays.* Bo's response came out staggered as if he was having trouble breathing or was in deep pain—perhaps both.

*Where the hell is that?* asked Bhatt.

Samsara Fleet knew little about the dreadnaughts other than they were large, powerful, and could destroy systems. Kal knew that the fleet's intel cell believed the ship's landing bays were near the bottom, but trapped in the conduit as they were, there was no way to tell exactly how far to travel. At least their implants would tell them how far they'd gone.

*Keep going until I tell you to stop,* Kimathi said. *We'll have to guess.*

The group made their way down the pipe. Kal pictured a timer counting down in his head. Bo'd said they would have around five minutes—two had already passed. Time stretched in strange ways. For a moment, he could have sworn they'd been traveling through the conduit for an hour—then it was seconds.

*Stop*, Kimathi said. *Bhatt, cut a hole and get us out of here.*

Kal heard the faint sound of a plasma pistol being discharged in front of him. The light from the blasts reflected off the smooth surface of the pipe in front of him and glowed in the coolant's mist.

*Bingo*, Bhatt called over the net. *We're in a landing area.*

The mist ahead of Kal cleared as it trailed out of the hole Bhatt had created. Kal waited for Bo to move in front of him. The Jadid's feet remained motionless, floating just centimeters away from his face.

*Bo, let's go. Bhatt called.*

Kal gently pushed the Jadid forward by his life pack. His arms and legs floated lifelessly as he slid through the tube.

*Grab him*, Kal said. *Bo's out. The gas got him.*

A pair of battle-suit gauntlets reached through the opening above them and pulled the Jadid out of a jagged hole in the pipe. The material of his emergency suit melted and smeared wherever the gauntlets touched it, pulling apart as if made of liquid.

Kal pulled himself out of the conduit after Bo had been removed. It took him a moment to reorient himself. He realized he was floating upside down near the ceiling of a large landing bay. It was almost completely empty—there weren't any Nasi about and only a handful of ships remained on the pads. He turned and adjusted himself so that as the others came out of the conduit, coolant streaming around them, they looked to be descending into the room rather than climbing out of the floor.

"How is he?" Kal asked, looking at the inert Jadid body.

"I've got no idea, sir," Bhatt said. "All I know is we need him awake. Unless you know how to start one of these things." She pointed at the Nasi ships beneath them.

Kal gently grabbed the Nasi and roughly shook him. The thin material of the emergency suit seemed smeared off onto his gloves. Bo's normally vibrant purple skin was pale and faded. His chest rose and fell underneath his suit, so at least he was alive. But he didn't appear to be waking at all. Even if he did wake up, Kal doubted he'd be much help. He felt a moment of worry for his friend. Bo had given up so much for them and he wasn't even Human.

"I might be able to fly it," Kal said. He'd flown the *Park*, the experimental Nasi skip ship they'd stolen from a facility on Patagonia. He was hoping the controls would be relatively similar.

The hiss of a rocket and an explosion only meters from their position caused the group to scatter across the top of the bay.

"There's an open ship over there," Kal called out, pointing at a small ship with its rear door already open. Their attackers were somewhere on the opposite end of the bay, judging by the missile's trail. The Skulls began shooting down from ceiling and across the bay toward the ship. There wasn't time to engage. They fired their plasma rifles wildly in their attacker's direction while hurtling to the bay floor.

Kal landed a meter from the aft of the globular ship, the return fire from the Nasi flying over his head, and ran inside. The others ran in close behind and Kal slammed the small lever near the ramp, causing it to lift off the bay floor.

He immediately exited his suit and rushed to the cockpit, fast on the heels of Chedjou and Ramos, who were peeling off their emergency suits as they ran to the front of the small ship. They came off in sodden pieces, ripping along the seams as the women tore them off with faint grunts of pain.

"This looks confusing," Chedjou said as she looked over the controls. The small Nasi craft had significantly more analog controls—buttons and levers—than a Human one which relied on the touchscreens. After a moment, she pressed a large red button next to the yoke. The engine spun up with a low hum, gently rocking the ship.

Kal sat down next to her, trying to remember everything he had learned piloting the *Park*. The assault ship had at least twice the numbers of controls, making it difficult to map them to what he remembered. After several seconds, Kal had a theory of what several of the buttons and knobs in front of him should do.

"Strap in," Kal said as a rocket hit the ship with a loud thump. He pushed the lever that should turn on the maneuvering jets and heard them activate with a low rumble. But the ship remained on the pad. He looked at the readouts on the control panel, confused. Kal slapped his head. They were maglocked onto the landing bay floor.

"See any release button?" Kal asked. "We're locked onto

the landing pad."

Another blast rocked the ship. Kal wasn't sure how much fire it could take, nor did he want to find out. According to his implant, it had been five minutes since Bo had hot-wired the gravity generators. Time was running short.

"Just increase the thrust," Chedjou said.

"We can't do that. As soon as we overload the magnetic clamps, we'll shoot into the ceiling." Kal continued to scan the array of controls before him. Finally, a small yellow button caught his eye. He pressed it and they immediately launched off the pad and crashed against the ceiling. Thankfully, from what Kal could tell, there hadn't been any damage to the ship though he heard several curses from the cargo bay behind him.

Kal shot a look at Chedjou as he pressed the throttle forward, and they shot out of the landing bay. There was a clatter of suits and more curses as the small ship's artificial gravity took control and their acceleration overloaded the inertial dampeners, pushing everything in the ship against the aft bulkhead.

It took a moment for Kal to get used to the strange icons and colors of the Nasi tacmap. Once he did, he realized that the two dreadnaughts were closer than they had been when the Skulls had first infiltrated the ship. He guessed they'd closed ranks to protect each other against what they thought was a bombing run. Normally it was a sound tactic, but to Kal's delight, it probably meant the second Nasi ship would be pulled into the gravity well.

"Don't head back to the *Ofira*," Kal said. "Stay between

the two fleets."

"Sir," Chedjou turned to look at him, "we'll be without support."

"They don't know we're friendly," Kal said. "If we head toward Samsara or Liberation Fleet, they'll destroy us faster than the Nasi."

Chedjou grunted and changed course, heading toward a gap in the Nasi ships, parallel to a battle line with Samsara Fleet.

Kal stared at the Nasi dreadnaught on the small personal viewscreen in front of him, unable to look away. How much time did they have until the ship imploded and started pulling in everything around it? Minutes or seconds?

"How far away do we have to be to not get sucked in when that ship goes critical?" Chedjou asked.

Kal wasn't sure if she'd directed the question at him. Either way, he didn't have any idea, so he kept quiet. Finally Chief Ramos spoke up from the jump seat in the back of the cockpit. "The only person who might know that is Bo, and I doubt he does. We've just got to put as much distance between us and that dreadnaught as possible."

"We've got incoming," Ramos said seconds later. "Two Tounous fighters are on us."

Kal's mind raced. Tounous fighters were more lethal than the Human ones, but who knew what a Nasi ship like this could do. What were they willing to do? He wouldn't kill their allies to save his own skin. To accomplish the mission, sure. But the mission was complete. They were just trying to get the hell out of there.

"Do what you can to evade them. We've done what we can." Out of nowhere, he felt the depression return—a black cloud that seemed to have a mind of its own. He could feel it covering him and pulling him down. The cloud was something that had always been a part of him. For most of his life, he'd kept it at bay until the loss of his family had caused it to overwhelm everything else. Only recently he'd thought he'd defeated it when he'd met Nicole and felt a sense of purpose again. Despite everything going on around him, Kal had been—happy wasn't the right word—content. But the cloud had returned, and he could feel it trying to take control.

"There's a Nasi ship over there." Ramos leaned to point at the tacmap in front of Chedjou. "Can you fly around it?"

"Yeah." The sergeant angled them at the Nasi battleship to their right. The two triangular fighters turned and continued to give chase. Thankfully, the small Nasi ship they were in was fast and the Tounous couldn't close the distance.

"Sir, any idea if there are any countermeasures on this ship? Any shields or defenses?"

Kal shook his head. "No."

A loud clanging reverberated through the cockpit. Kal could see two small dots streaking at them on the tacmap. They'd launched missiles.

"Sir, any idea at all?" Ramos' voice was barely suppressed panic.

"Head toward that ship." Kal pointed to a Nasi battleship in front of them. "Its point defense will take care of the missiles. Anything I do is just as liable to kill us as to save us."

He turned and looked at the tacmap again. He was a lot

less confident than he acted. It would be close, very close. The Nasi battleship was almost impossible to see through the viewscreen, just a small gray smudge among the infinite white stars in front of them. The dot grew, slowly transforming into the large misshapen hull of a Nasi battleship.

Kal glanced down at his console. The missiles were getting dangerously close, and they wouldn't reach the Nasi battleship in time. A sense of calm descended over him, wiping away the depression. He'd done his best. He'd done some good things and some bad, but at least he'd tried. It was out of his control now. He closed his eyes and waited for something to happen.

A blast rocked the ship, slamming Kal against his restraints and bashing his head against the bulkhead. He heard the others in the back cargo bay cry out and the sharp pings of metal striking against the outside of the ship.

"That was close." Kal opened his eyes at Chedjou's words. They were still in one piece.

The Nasi battleship loomed in front of them. Somehow they'd made it into the ship's point defense range. The two Tounous fighters had veered off, unwilling to approach any further.

Kal closed his eyes and turned his head away from the viewscreen as a searing white light overwhelmed everything on the screen. A second later, the light faded, leaving an afterimage.

"Damn," Ramos shouted.

Kal adjusted the small console screen to focus on the Nasi dreadnaught and zoomed in. All that remained was a small spot of black that stood out even in the darkness of space. The light from the surrounding stars bent slightly, looking almost smeared around the black dot. Kal heard small whoops of happiness erupt from the cargo bay behind them.

"The battleship is getting pulled toward the Nasi ship," Chedjou said. Kal looked at the tacmap. She was right. All the Nasi ships near the imploded dreadnaught were being pulled toward the black hole created by the overloaded gravity generators. Smaller ships, like the one they were in, were able to resist the pull, but the large capital ships were helpless.

Chedjou pulled on the yoke as the battleship turned, trying to orient its engines to pull away from the former dreadnaught. They bounced off the battleship's side and careened away. Kal jolted against his restraint and heard the sickening crunch of metal bending and failing.

"I never did this with my brother," Chedjou muttered under her breath.

Ramos tapped Kal on the shoulder. "Sir, we really need to reach the fleet."

Kal looked around the panel in front of him. The *Park's* radio had been a simple affair, nothing like what he saw in front of him. The labels on the controls weren't helpful either. As he studied his console, Chedjou continued to dodge the turning battleship while reorienting them to point away from the small black hole that the dreadnaught had created.

The reflection of another brilliant explosion reflected off the ships in front of them as the black hole pulled in the other Nasi dreadnaught. Several other Nasi ships were coming perilously close to the event horizon, turning through space as they attempted to escape their doom.

"Gotta say it's a pretty picture." Ramos placed her hand on Kal's shoulder. "Eh, sir?"

Kal couldn't muster up the pleasure in the Nasi's destruction that the chief had. Instead, he simply grunted in acknowledgement.

Chedjou oriented them away from the gravity well of the imploded Nasi ship, and the engines overwhelmed every other sound in the cockpit as the pilot increased their thrust to maximum. They were slowly pulling away from the well, passing by the large battleship which was still turning.

Occasional flashes appeared behind them as the black hole pulled in more Nasi capital ships.

"The fleet has launched the skip missiles!" Ramos shouted.

Kal adjusted his console to examine the portion of the Nasi fleet closest to Samsara and Liberation Fleets. Samsara Fleet had launched several volleys of the experimental missiles, and they were already wreaking havoc on the Nasi. They skipped across the space between the fleets and opened enormous holes in the Nasi hulls. One of the Nasi ships exploded in an enormous ball of white light as a skip missile bypassed the ship's point defense and hull, exploding inside.

"Execute battle plan bravo," a Nasi voice commanded over the speakers in the cockpit.

"They're retreating!" Chedjou said.

She was right. The Nasi ships were turning away from the Samsara and Liberation Fleets. Their fighters maneuvered to cover the escape. The Nasi ships remained faster than either the Jadid or Samsara Fleets' and were able to put distance between themselves and their enemies. Their front line was decimated, but the ones between the frontline and the gravity well remained unharmed and began folding out of the system.

Kal watched as one by one, the Nasi ships left the area. He estimated the black hole had destroyed at least ten of their capital ships, including two dreadnaughts. The skip missiles had taken care of another twenty. It was amazing. In one battle, they'd wiped out over half the Nasi force.

The realization spread through Kal's mind like fire. A decisive and complete victory. Despite everything, their mission to liberate the colonies had worked. For a moment, the cloud dissipated.

Another blaring alarm broke Kal's short reverie.

"Crap, we've got Qudoru fighters on us," Ramos said.

"There's nowhere to go," Kal said. "Time to press buttons and hope for the best."

Kal began to methodically manipulate the controls in front of him, flicking switches and pressing buttons hoping that he didn't blow them up, and continually repeating, "Don't fire. This is General Norman of Samsara Fleet."

Finally, a Qudoru voice came from the cockpit speakers. "General Norman, we're pleased to see that you're alive. Your Eternal must believe you still have a use in this life."

"I second that." General Samaha's voice came over the net a second later. "Head back to the *Ofira* and I'll meet you there. I can still use you for sure."

# Chapter Thirty-One

"Thank god you're alive," Chief Kanumba said, her arms wide as the ramp lowered.

Nicole stepped down the ramp and into her friend's embrace. She felt a small amount of the weight lift from her shoulders. With the mission complete, Kal had retreated into the depths of his depression, casting a pall over what should have been a moment for celebration.

Nicole also felt a small measure of redemption for everything that she'd done prior to the Nasi invasion. Surely her actions were some sort of atonement for her crimes. It seemed so long ago, and she'd been so naïve and bitter. It wasn't an excuse, but it was a reason for her actions. The glimmer of hope that she'd been holding onto had turned into a sun with the defeat of the Nasi. Surely her actions had played a significant part.

Pilots, crews, and maintenance teams filled the landing bay. A sizeable crowd surrounded the Nasi ship the Skulls had commandeered, while the rest of the people were already repairing and retrofitting the ships. Some pilots stood unmoving by their ships, staring out into the dark stars beyond the open landing bay door as they reflected on the battle. Although they'd won, thousands had been lost. It was a heavy price to pay.

"Your missiles worked." Nicole stepped back from her friend.

Kanumba smiled and looked down, clearly embarrassed. It was always amazing to Nicole that this quiet, bashful woman was the same one who could jump in the gunner's seat and lay down support fire while under enemy attack.

"It's not *my* project. There's a lot of us working on it—practically the entire R&D staff in the fleet." Her eyes widened. "What happened to him?"

Nicole turned around. Bo was being lifted from the back of the Nasi ship on a medical stretcher bot. He was still unconscious, his face locked in an expression of pain and fists clenched against his sides. Kal walked next to him, his face emotionless. As the bot reached the end of the ramp, it hovered in place. Bo was to wait there for the medical team the Jadid had sent.

"It's hard to explain…he was poisoned when we had to escape the ship."

Kanumba raised an eyebrow. "I wasn't talking about Bo. What happened to General Norman?"

Nicole could feel a sense of despair at the words. She was losing Kal; she could feel it. She could sense it in his hunched shoulders and downcast eyes. He'd told her about his life after losing his family, and she could see that man returning.

"Hey." Kanumba grabbed Nicole by the shoulder. "He'll be okay. He's got you, right? He's got all of us." She waved her arm around the bay.

"Colonel Bergeron," General Samaha said as she approached them. "Welcome back. You're a hero. Once again."

"You sound disappointed, ma'am," Chief Kanumba said.

"Only disappointed in myself, Chief. We shouldn't have to rely on the same group of people to save us every time."

"The entire fleet is full of heroes, General," Nicole replied.

"I'm just doing whatever I can. Like everyone else."

"I've been reading the mission reports that you and General Norman filed. I think it's time to use your skills more fully."

Nicole didn't like the sound of that but decided not to ask questions now. The general seemed happy to leave it at that, and she wasn't ready for answers she didn't want to hear. Instead, she simply nodded.

"I was a lieutenant colonel like you when I fought in the Torgham War. But I didn't see a tenth of the combat that you've been through, and you're basically a civilian. You missed your calling when you become a diplomat. Glad to see that you ended up here with us in the end." Samaha gave her shoulder a tight squeeze.

Nicole couldn't say that she agreed. People like Samaha, Jones, and even Kal were soldiers through and through. They acted without doubt in what they were doing. That was not something she'd mastered. She continued to wonder about the lives lost on both sides of the war and hoped for another way out, no matter how naïve and unrealistic that might be.

A small Jadid tender floated through the bay's energy shield and landed nearby. The cargo ramp opened, and Ancient Bao Wang walked down the ramp with an enormous smile. Four Jadid trailed behind him, leading several pallet lifters filled with equipment.

"General Samaha! Colonel Bergeron!" Bao said heartily. "What a battle. We've sent those bastards back to hell where they belong."

The man's language shocked Nicole. *Weren't those the*

*same Nasi that he referred to as his children?* The war had changed all of them, and the Ancient was no different from anyone else.

"It was a great victory." Samaha sighed as she said the words. "But it's not done yet, Ancient Wang. I'll save my celebration for when we liberate the Human colonies."

"Ancient Wang." Having safely handed Bo off to the Jadid medical staff, Kal stepped forward with a nod of his head.

"Kal, you've saved the day once again." Bao wrapped an arm around the man's hunched shoulders. "I would love for you to come and teach some of my scout teams how you're able to do it."

"Not yet, Ancient Wang," Samaha said. "We've still don't know where those Nasi ships went. I still need General Norman and his team."

"I could really use some time to rest," Kal said. The statement was so uncharacteristic that no one responded immediately.

"You can rest, Kal," Samaha said with a slight frown. "You've earned it."

"So they're splitting us up?" Sergeant Kimathi asked indignantly.

"Yeah," Nicole replied. "What's better than one elite scout team? Two. I guess."

"But we've been successful together," Private Sampson said. "They split us up and...well who knows what'll happen?"

The middle-aged private had just come into his own. He'd been a fine pilot, but according to Sergeant Kimathi, he might be an even better Tac-I soldier.

"We'll be fine," Sergeant Bhatt said. "Besides, Colonel Bergeron is too damn good not to have her own team."

The Skulls were having a celebratory drink in the *Ofira's* lounge. Their mission infiltrating the Nasi dreadnaught had only added to their unit's mystique. When they entered, conversations stopped and people stared as they walked to their customary table. Somehow it was always open.

General Samaha had told Nicole she was splitting the Skulls into two teams with Nicole leading one and Kal the other. Honestly, it made sense to her though she didn't like it. Despite everything they'd seen, the Skulls had become a family of sorts, and she hated to see them split apart. There was no use protesting even if she'd wanted. The mission always came first.

The Jadid medical staff had treated Bowen's wounds, and he'd pulled through. It still wasn't clear what the long-term effects of the coolant poisoning would be. He continued to be continually fatigued. Despite that, he'd left the medical center—against doctor's orders—to join them in the lounge.

"How will they split up the team?" asked Corporal Sato.

"Yeah, who gets the kids in the divorce?" Kimathi added.

Kal gave a small, genuine chuckle. He'd picked up somewhat since they'd returned to the *Ofira*. "We haven't decided who'll get stuck with you yet, Sergeant. We'll figure it out in the next few days."

For now, the Skulls were out of action. The losses they'd

suffered, both physical and mental, took time to heal. There wasn't much for them to do now anyway. Samsara Fleet had their scouts out looking for the Nasi. So far, there'd been no evidence of where they'd gone to.

Kimathi raised a glass. The beer swirled over the edge, drenching his forearm. "To the Skulls."

They each stood and raised a glass, clinking them against each other. Nicole smiled and looked around the table. They'd done the impossible. Even Kal smiled as he met her eyes.

The lounge's viewscreens flickered and the images of General Samaha and Ancient Wang replaced a placid mountain stream.

"Attention soldiers of Samsara and Liberation Fleets," Samaha said. The lounge instantly grew quiet. The members of the Skulls placed their glasses back on the table and sat down. Half the table turned in their chairs to face the nearest wall. "A few days ago, we won the largest battle that has ever been fought in this or any other universe. Your dedication, skill, and sacrifice overcame an enemy that has wiped out billions. I wanted to let you know our campaign has been a success. Our scouts have conclusively reported that the Nasi have abandoned all colonies and returned to Human space. I would like to be the first to say congratulations to my friends—the Kurz, Qudoru, Tounous, and Z'Ta. You have liberated your planets and your people are free once more."

A cheer broke out in the lounge. Although the room was mainly filled with Humans, there were a few of their allies there. Each one instantly became the center of attention, with groups of people hugging them and affectionately slapping their backs.

"Although we are exceptionally pleased at your well-earned freedom, we ask that you remember the pact that we have all made," continued Ancient Wang. "We must not rest until the last Nasi is defeated. We've cornered them on the Human planets, and they will be desperate. If we rest or relent, they will take advantage and return. For us soldiers who are dedicated to freeing this entire galaxy from the Nasi, there is no stopping."

Nicole knew that Samaha and Wang were worried the other species would leave the fleet now that their citizens were liberated. Nicole had more faith in them than that.

"But there is a period for rest," Samaha smoothly added. "For now, we will recover and remember those who we lost. I've instructed my staff to enforce only minimal manning and operations. In a few days, we will return to Human space and crush the Nasi, wiping them from this universe."

The general paused for a moment, her face solemn, eyes fixed directly on the camera. Nicole felt like the general was looking directly at her. "Each of you has suffered loss, whether it's your family and friends in the initial attack or your comrades during this war. Take a moment to remember them and why we fight. Your sacrifices matter. Your struggle matters. And I thank you personally for everything that you've done to realize this victory."

The screens flickered, and the mountain stream returned. The lounge was quiet as everyone seemed dazed and lost in their own thoughts, a sharp difference from the hum of conversation before the announcement.

Kal stood back up and raised his glass to the table. "To everyone we've lost." His voice was subdued.

The other Skulls raised their glasses and looked at each other. Nicole could see the pain etched into each one of their faces as they silently held their glasses aloft. She looked into Kal's eyes and saw a single tear streak down his cheek. She couldn't bear to see the pain so plainly visible in the face of the person she loved.

"To the future," Nicole said quietly as she turned to look at Chief Kanumba, who was starting to show. "To those that we are fighting for who are yet to come."

Sergeant Kimathi smiled. "That's right, ma'am. We got a future Numbskull to protect."

## Epilogue

Ancient Esma Baykara screamed as she threw her tablet across the room. White-hot rage filled her veins, pushing out every other emotion. She needed this moment, needed the release. Damn Bao. Damn his betrayal and machinations. He was a snake, waiting in the grass and striking when you least expected it.

She didn't know how her fellow Ancient had managed it, but he'd somehow defeated her fleet. Now she had to return to the Human colonies, unable to stand against the Jadid fleet with their ragtag group of remnants from this universe.

"Grand Ancient?" Her personal aide stood by the doorway, his face as placid as a lake. The man had seen enough of her "releases" to be unfazed at this point.

"Give me a moment." Esma sat back in her chair, struggling to keep her voice even. "I'll let you know when I need you."

The aide opened the door with his comeca—she didn't understand how the Humans were okay with having chips implanted in their heads—and smoothly stepped backward through it.

Esma turned and looked at the stars in the viewscreen behind her. It had taken a while to get used to this universe after spending hundreds of years on Altterra. The bright white stars and the constant pull of the gravity all felt strange to her.

She plucked an errant white hair from her scalp and held it in front of her. She'd been getting more and more of them. Being back in this universe had somehow restarted her aging process. It was something that she'd thought was likely to happen, but it was still interesting to see it occur. She didn't fear death; she'd lived too long for that. No, she feared not achieving what she'd set out to do, make them pay for what they'd done.

Esma's family had been destitute. They'd had nothing growing up on the streets of Istanbul. Then her father had sold her—sold her—to become a test subject. Even now, hundreds of years later, the thought was bitter in her head.

She'd just returned home when the two men came to take her, policemen in full tactical gear. As they dragged her screaming out of the small room she shared with her parents and two sisters, her father had done nothing. He'd just watched and said, "Esma, don't resist. You'll be back soon enough."

He was long dead, of course, along with the rest of her family. She wondered how much the government had paid him for his oldest daughter. Had it made a difference in her family's life? She doubted it. Humans were all the same. Take for themselves and keep everyone else in poverty and need. Bao was that spirit personified.

It'd taken a while for her to realize that fact. At first, she'd been like the rest, focused on survival and trying to rebuild everything they'd lost. Then she'd realized that the Humans had given them a gift. The ability to start over and create a better society. Esma no longer thought of herself as Human. How could she? She'd lived for centuries and done more than any Human. She'd built her Nasi to return and reshape Humanity, to make them better than they were.

Earth had been a necessary sacrifice. You can't build a

new house on old foundations. Burn the whole thing to the ground. She'd held onto an irrational affection for her old home world, so it had been a hard decision at first. But once she'd made it, she'd felt freed.

Esma had always known Bao was a conniving weasel but hadn't realized how much the man lusted after power. How little he cared for anyone or anything other than himself. He'd been an ally at first. But when he'd been given the chance, the man had immediately began plotting her downfall. However, even he couldn't strike the Human worlds. Her plasma cannons made sure of that.

Esma had lost the battle, but she wasn't defeated. She'd been laying out her plans for over a hundred years. A single battle couldn't change the course of the war. No, a single battle couldn't change the force of nature that was Esma Baykara.

She smiled. The rage had subsided, and she realized what she needed to do. Ancient Bao Wang was going to find out that he'd made a fatal mistake in betraying her.

She called for her aide. They had work to do.

## Author's Note

First of all, I'd like to say a few words of thanks. The first is to you, the reader. Without you, none of this means anything. If just one person reads my book, I feel like it has been a success. Second, to my wife and family. I am grateful for your support and words of encouragement. Another big words of thanks to Lisa and Sal who edited and proofread this novel. Any mistakes that are in here are my own, and you've done a wonderful job in turning raw thoughts and concepts into an actual story.

This is my fourth novel. With each, I feel like I learn a little bit more about writing, the process of publishing, and about my characters themselves. Taking the threads of my characters and ideas and weaving them into a tapestry that entertains is a marathon. It's finding whatever small patches of time you can to write and working with editors and collaborators across the world. It's reading your own words for the umpteenth time, trying to craft the words into something that sounds *just right*. But in the end, it's worth it. It's worth it because you are taking the time to read it.

I will continue to tell the story of Kal and Nicole and the rest of Samsara Fleet. I hope that you stay around for it. If you are willing, a review on Amazon is always appreciated and you can follow me on Facebook or through my website (https://www.rileycollins.info) where you can subscribe to my mailing list. Also, I am always on the lookout for beta readers, so if you would like an advance copy of future books and are willing to provide honest and open feedback, please contact me at r.collins.author@gmail.com.

Thank you,

*Riley*